THE EDGE

Chris Simms

First published in Great Britain in 2009 by Orion Books,
an imprint of The Orion Publishing Group Ltd
Orion House, 5 Upper Saint Martin's Lane
London WC2H 9EA

An Hachette UK Company

1 3 5 7 9 10 8 6 4 2

A CIP catalogue record for this book is
available from the British Library.

ISBN (Hardback) 978 1 4091 1105 4
ISBN (Trade Paperback) 978 1 4091 1106 1

Typeset by Deltatype Ltd, Birkenhead, Merseyside

Printed in Great Britain by Clays Ltd, St Ives plc

The Orion Publishing Group's policy is to use papers that are natural,
renewable and recyclable products and made from wood grown in sustainable
forests. The logging and manufacturing processes are expected to
conform to the environmental regulations of the country of origin.

www.orionbooks.co.uk

To Mark and Paul, who made writing this novel
a surprisingly enjoyable experience.

When thou seest an eagle, thou seest a portion of genius;
lift up thy head!

William Blake, 1757-1827

One

Jon Spicer felt himself slowly emerging from the depths. He kept his eyes shut and let the urge to stretch take him. Cool sheets brushed against his knuckles as his arms straightened out.

The sound of giggling froze his movement – the noise was too far away for his daughter to be in her room. It was only a few weeks ago that Holly had progressed to a junior bed and the freedom it gave her meant she frequently rose early to explore the house with no adult watching over her. His wife laughed back and he realised they were both downstairs. He patted the other side of the bed to confirm it was empty.

Hand lingering where Alice usually lay, he registered the smell of coffee and opened his eyes to a room bathed in a warm glow. Turning to the curtains, he saw cracks of sunlight forcing their way in, refusing to be denied their spell of dominance over the dark. His mind turned to the previous night. Thank God, he thought, no nightmares disturbed me. That must be getting on for two months now. Maybe, he hoped, time has finally worn the memories down so they are no longer able to sour my sleep.

He blinked, savouring the sense of relief. Sunday morning and not back on duty for three days. The thought released a burst of energy into his limbs and he climbed swiftly out of bed to draw the curtains. The sun had just cleared the tops of the houses opposite and the street was totally quiet. Come on, the day seemed to beckon. You've missed part of me already.

Alice was sitting at the kitchen table, Holly in her high seat opposite. His wife's lips were pressed against the top of an egg, and as her cheeks puffed out, a long drool of slime began to emerge from a hole in its base.

I

'Morning.' He smiled, tying the waistband of a frayed bath-robe as he entered the room.

'Daddy!' Holly cried, waving her plastic spoon with delight. A clump of soggy cereal flew off and Punch, the family dog, snaffled it up the instant it made contact with the floor. The Boxer raised his head, stump of a tail wagging, brown eyes glued to his master.

Jon looked back at Alice. 'What are you doing?'

She lifted her face from the egg and a burst of air shot out from her collapsing cheeks. 'Blowing it, of course.' He raised an eyebrow suggestively and she batted a hand in his direction. 'Not unless you do a heck of a lot more housework.'

He grinned. 'And why are you doing that?'

'Because you can't decorate an egg while it's still full of yolk, anyone knows that.'

Of course, Jon thought, suddenly remembering their arrange-ments. It was Easter Sunday and they were heading over to Lyme Park, the enormous National Trust estate south of Manchester. Apart from an egg-painting competition, there was an egg hunt and an egg-rolling competition down a slope in the landscaped grounds. After that, it was over to his mum and dad's for a Sunday roast.

She pushed a cup of coffee towards him. 'I was about to bring it up to you.'

He regarded his family, wishing his arms were long enough to stretch around everyone at once. Instead, he placed a hand on Punch's head, tickling behind the dog's ears as he stooped to kiss his daughter's cheek. He stepped behind her and crouched before his wife, lifting a strand of blonde hair from her face before letting his fingers trail down her arm and on to her stomach. 'How's you and the sprout?'

'We're fine.' She smiled, cupping a hand over his. 'Both of us slept well.'

He pressed his palm lightly against her stomach. Three months pregnant and Alice thought she could just feel the flutter of their next child's kicks within her. He kept his hand there, feeling the usual sense of wonder and delight. Centimetres from his palm were the beginnings of another little person. Not much as yet, but in around six months' time, a fully formed baby would emerge. There isn't much else in the world, he thought, that genuinely deserves to be called a miracle.

'Good,' he replied, straightening up to look at the saucepan on the hob. 'Boiled eggs for breakfast?'

'No,' Alice said, lifting Holly out of her seat. 'They're for the egg-rolling competition.'

As he watched the spherical objects bumping around in the boiling water, his mobile phone started to ring. Holly ran across the room, plucked it from the shelf above the radiator and flipped it open. 'Hello? Hello? Me Holly. Who you? Who you?'

Grinning, Jon reached down and coaxed it from her grip. Some number on the screen with a weird area code: 01297. Where the hell was that? 'Jon here.'

'Hello, who is this please?'

'DI Spicer,' he replied, his voice lowering as he sensed the call was work related.

'DI? You're a policeman?' A note of relief was in the stranger's voice.

'I am.' A faint feeling of unease caused him to turn away from his daughter's upturned face. 'Who am I speaking to?' From the edge of his vision he could see Alice was motionless, eyes on him, too.

'This is Superintendent Mallin, Derbyshire police. And you're with?'

'Greater Manchester Police. Major Incident Team. What's this about?'

There was a pause. 'We've just recovered a phone. I don't want to alarm you but ... erm ... this is very awkward.'

Jon felt a pang of irritation. His Sunday off and here was some uniform from Derbyshire being all vague with him. 'I'm not following you here. You've recovered a phone and it had this number in it?'

'That's correct. You are down in the address book as Big Bro.'

Trepidation welled up. Our kid. What the hell has he done

now? 'I have a younger brother called Dave. Sounds like you've got his phone. Where are you calling from?'

'Haverdale.'

Haverdale. One of the towns in the Peak District National Park. Jon remembered driving out to play their rugby team a few years back. Big meaty farmers who kept it in the pack, trying to maul their way slowly up the pitch. What was Dave up to out there? 'You say you've recovered the phone. What do you mean?'

The other officer coughed needlessly. A delaying tactic to precede bad news. Jon looked down at the eggs jostling among the bubbles. The shell of one had cracked and a nodule of white bulged out.

'As I said, there's been an incident. I think we may need you to come out here.'

'What sort of an incident?'

'We've recovered a body.'

Oh Jesus. The sound of boiling water seemed to be getting louder. 'Description?'

'An adult male. Thirty or thereabouts. Of thin build, signs of intravenous drug use, but not recent.'

Following repeated clashes with their dad, Dave had been thrown out of the family home in his late teens. He'd ended up living in squats, sliding into a life of petty crime and drug use. The last time Jon had seen him, he suspected his brother may have started dealing. 'Long hair?'

'No. Shaved very short. Dark brown.'

The crack in the egg had widened, releasing a white strand that flicked around like a tendril of some aquatic plant untouched by any sun. He turned the gas ring off and the water suddenly became calm. As the eggs settled onto the base of the pan he heard the clicks through the water. 'How tall?'

'That's hard to say.'

'Sorry?'

'We can't ... we can't quite tell at this stage. We're waiting for the patholog—'

Jon cut in. 'Superintentent, just take a guess.'

That cough again. 'I think it would be better if you came out here.'

Jon turned his back to the room. 'Will you stop pissing me about here?' he hissed. 'How tall is the man you've found?'

'We can't tell. I'm sorry to say this, but the body has been dismembered.'

He felt a tug on his bathrobe belt and looked down to see Holly peeping round the curve of his leg. She looked frightened. Jon forced himself to smile and, in an absurdly casual voice said, 'OK, I'll be on my way.'

Two

After miles of deserted countryside, Jon saw the Haven Inn at the side of the road and knew Haverdale must be close. He took the next turn, crossed a small bridge and then a set of railway tracks. Seconds later he was on the high street, eyes roving for any sign with a large red H. A right turn led him down a quieter side road, bed and breakfast notices in the front windows of many of the houses that lined the street. Another minute and the hospital came into view.

As he drew closer, he felt like an actor in a performance. Here's the main entrance, he thought, pulling into it. Now I slow up and check the sign for where the mortuary is. Probably they've placed it near the bottom, so I have to read through a load of other departments first. Orthopaedics. Cardiology. Children's Unit. Maternity. An image of Alice flashed in his mind. Wasn't it their thirteen-week scan day after tomorrow? Pharmacy. Mortuary. Turn right.

He glanced at the main building as he did so. Like most of the town, the hospital looked like it had been constructed during the Georgian period. Heavy blocks of sand-coloured stone whose upper edges were now tinged with black. He took in the regimented rows of windows and square lines before his eyes were drawn to the large glass dome that curved above the main building's roof. He guessed it was some kind of place for recuperating, a light-filled space to coax a previous era's sick and infirm back to health. No doubt with the assistance of the town's famous spring water.

His car glided round the corner and a second, smaller sign directed him off to the left. This side road was narrower, more private. It led to the rear of an annex, dayglo markings of a police car contrasting with the building's sombre stone. Two uniformed officers waited for him at the entrance. He manoeuvred his car into a space, the feeling of detachment still there. Turning the engine off, he flexed his fingers. Pins and needles surged up his forearms. A sharp intake of breath sent them scurrying back the other way, right to the ends of his fingers. Come on, Jon, let's get this done. He climbed out of the car and the tarmac seemed slightly mushy under foot. Walking towards the waiting officers, he hoped they didn't notice the unsteadiness of his step.

'DI Spicer?' the one on the left asked, a slightly nervous-looking man in his mid-twenties.

Jon felt his lips peel apart and he realised his mouth was dry. 'Yes.'

'The Super told us to look out for a big bloke; he'd seen your photo after that case with the church arsonist a while back.'

'My fame spreads before me.' Jon tried to smile.

'They feed you on some kind of protein mix in Manchester?'

Jon appreciated his attempt at lightening the tone of their meeting. At six foot four and just over fifteen stone, he was used to his size dominating most people's first impression of him. 'Got to keep up with our steroid-abusing criminals.'

The officer's grin widened. 'I'm Constable Spiers. And this is my colleague, Constable Batyra.'

Jon held out a hand. 'Have you got first names?'

He relaxed slightly. 'Chris.'

'I'm Jon.' He shook, then turned to the female colleague.

'Shazia,' she announced. An Asian woman of a similar age to Chris, black hair tied back, a slightly pudgy face that normally would have looked kind. Now Jon saw only concern in her brown eyes. They shook, her grip light but firm. 'The Super sends his apologies for not being here in person. With the way things stand ...'

'Of course,' Jon replied. 'He's got a murder investigation to run. I understand.'

She pointed weakly towards the heavy wooden doors, then turned back to Jon. 'Are you absolutely sure, sir? About doing

7

this? We've got photos back at the station. You could make an ID from them.'

Jon flicked his eyes at the building. A narrow window high up in the wall, cardboard boxes pressed against the other side of the frosted glass. 'Don't you worry, I've been in one or two mortuaries before.' The comment had popped out and he realised it must have sounded patronising. 'If it's Dave, I'd prefer to see him in person.'

She glanced uncertainly at her colleague. 'What was the code again?'

'Three three eight four.'

The panel was directly below the door handle. Curved little buttons that clicked as she pressed each one. She turned the handle and pushed the door open. 'After you, sir.'

Jon stepped into a familiar smell of antiseptic. Behind him he heard Spiers mumble, 'Just need to check something out with Mallin. I'll be through in a minute.'

The door swung shut and he and the female constable were now alone in a small, silent room. It had an austere, functional feel – bare walls and a few formal notices. One was entitled: 'Moving and handling of the deceased.' Below were four dense paragraphs of instructions. Across the room was a double set of doors.

'They're expecting us, the Super rang ahead,' Batyra sighed. She moved to the doors and rapped on a glass panel, half opening it as she did so. 'Hello? Constable Batyra here.'

Jon heard a male voice from further inside. 'Come on in.'

Shazia beckoned and he followed her into the next room. This was just as drab, a row of tall grey lockers lining one side. Lurking in a corner was a heavy-looking metal gurney. Like much of the hospital, it looked like a relic from an earlier age. A padded layer of red leather covered the top, straps with thick buckles lying across it. Directly ahead was a single door, a notice screwed squarely into its middle: 'Please put on yellow overshoes before crossing the red line.'

A white metal cabinet was positioned to its side and Shazia opened a drawer to fish out two pairs from inside.

'Thanks,' said Jon, taking his and slipping them over his shoes, one palm against the cold concrete wall to steady him.

The inner door was swung open, revealing a red line across the floor. A member of the mortuary staff was standing there, head to toe in white overalls. The smell of cleaning fluids picked up in strength.

'Is Dr Henderley here? We rang about an hour ago,' Shazia asked.

The man's head shook. 'He had to nip home.'

Jon caught her look of irritation. 'We're here to view the body brought in earlier.' She turned towards Jon. 'This is ...'

'DI Spicer. Major Incident Team, Manchester Police.'

The man nodded. 'He's here.'

Jon took a quick breath, then stepped across the red line and into the mortuary itself. Christ, this can't have changed in over a century, either, he thought. The end wall housed a double row of square metallic doors, brass handles giving them the appearance of opening hatches from a submarine. A high ceiling and, low over the three autopsy tables, strips of light hanging by chains that must have been over twelve feet long. One table was empty, one held a shrouded body and one was being used for what appeared to be the mortician's equipment bag. To his side, water dripped from the nozzle of a hose mounted at waist height on the tiled wall.

Jon's eyes went back to the middle table. Oh God, don't let it be him. It's only his phone they've recovered. It could have been stolen off him by one of the scrotes he got caught up with. Maybe he sold the thing for a bit of cash. To buy what? Drugs? He pushed the thought aside. Oh God, it's going to be him.

The mortician moved towards the table and Jon shadowed him, plastic overshoes scraping on the damp stone floor.

But the mortician reached for the green case, unzipping it and throwing the lid back in one swift motion. Dave's decapitated head was still in the perspex bag used to prevent any forensic evidence from being lost. Jon could see his face through the layer of clear plastic, mouth half open, eyes rolled up in his head. For a moment it looked like he was suffocating and Jon wanted to reach out and tear the bag open. My brother. My, my ...

Time lurched to a sickening halt as memories flashed by like an out-of-control slide show. His mother's yelp as a three-year-old Dave ran in from the garden, a live worm dangling from his mouth. The beach on some holiday, hours spent constructing a knee-high fortress, then watching the creeping waves take it. Hiding in the bushes at the local park, lighting up a cigar they'd stolen from their father's pocket and coughing until they retched.

'The rest's in the freezer if you want to see it.'

Jon strained his eyes, but he couldn't look away. Fragments of mud were caught in the stubble covering his brother's head, caked blood darkened his chin.

'I'd say it was a saw from the serrations to the bones. We haven't pieced him together yet. Dr Henderley's the fan of jigsaws.'

Slowly Jon's eyes began creeping down towards the ragged neck itself.

Batyra's voice from far away: 'It's his brother! For God's sake, it's his brother!'

The mortician's movement broke the spell and Jon lifted his eyes, registering the man's look of horror. 'You said you were police ...' He was fumbling for the nylon lid, trying to fold it back over.

Jon turned away, feeling the floor starting to tilt.

Shazia's eyes were wide, a hand half raised. 'I'm so sorry.'

'It's Dave.' He felt himself moving towards the door, the voices continuing as he stumbled into the locker room.

'He said he was with Manchester Police. No one told me—'

'He'd come to ID the body, for Christ's sake.'

'If I knew that I'd have prepared the viewing area ...'

The doors shut behind him and he continued across the foyer, shouldering open the outermost door and sucking in clean air. Christ, oh Jesus fucking Christ. That was Dave. That was Dave's head in that ... He wrenched his eyes to the side, trying to prevent the image from taking hold.

Spiers was half sitting on the bonnet of the police car, one foot extended as he hurriedly ground out a cigarette.

Suck it back, Jon. Suck it back. He used every trick he'd ever learned on the rugby pitch for hiding pain; for squashing it down and appearing unaffected. Punches, stamps, head-butts, hands grabbing his bollocks and twisting hard. Nothing, he insisted to himself. You cannot feel a fucking thing. He drew in breath. 'Can I have one?'

'Course, mate, help yourself.' He held the pack of B&H out, lighter pinned to the top by his thumb.

Jon lit up, leaned against the wall and dragged heavily.

'It's him then,' Spiers murmured.

Jon tilted his chin. 'Yup.' He released a pale cloud at the blueness above.

The outer door opened and Shazia appeared. 'DI Spicer, I can't say how angry I am. We rang ahead and clearly explained the visit – its circumstances. That man should have been—'

'Breakdown in communication.' Jon took another drag. 'It happens.' He looked at her. 'Not much they could have done to make him presentable, let's face it.'

Her look of acute embarrassment didn't alter. 'There's no excuse. The whole thing ...' She paused. 'Are you OK?'

He sucked again, noticing half the cigarette had vanished. 'Better for this.' He looked at the thing in his hand, cursing yet loving it. 'To be honest, we'd lost contact long ago. I've barely spoken to him in years.' The ball of sickness in his stomach wouldn't budge. 'First time I've seen a mortician mortified.'

She didn't smile at his attempt at a joke.

'Come on,' Jon said, pushing himself from the wall and flicking the butt at a nearby drain. It bounced once and vanished between the bars. 'Tell me what you know.'

'What, here?' Shazia glanced around.

'Good a place as any.'

'Shall we at least get a cup of tea? There's a canteen in the main building.'

Jon shrugged, beginning to feel like he was regaining control, managing a front of normality. 'OK, let's get a brew.'

He'd started walking nonchalantly across the car park when he heard Shazia speak behind him. 'DI Spicer, you've still got your overshoes on.'

Three

Brightly coloured paintings by local school children lent the canteen a cheerful air.

'What are you having?' Jon asked, pulling a five pound note from his pocket.

Shazia glanced at Spiers, whose hands remained in his pockets. 'Let me get them,' she said, unbuttoning the side pocket of her tunic.

'Don't be silly,' Jon answered, turning to the lady behind the counter. 'A coffee for me. Black, no sugar. And whatever these two would like.'

Once he'd paid for the drinks they took a corner table, far away from the few other customers. 'So, how long have you been in the job?' Jon asked, pressing the pads of his fingers against the hot mug, using the pain to keep his focus.

'Four years,' Spiers replied.

'Same,' added Shazia.

'What about you?' Spiers lifted a cup of tea to his lips.

'Almost eleven.'

'What's it like in the MIT?'

Jon recognised the note in the younger man's voice. The Major Incident Team was Manchester Police's modern-day equivalent of the Flying Squad. The ones who got all the big robberies, along with murders, rapes and any other serious crime. Some officers aspired to it, some despised them as glory boys who swooped in to snatch all the really interesting stuff from the city's divisions. Spiers, he suspected, dreamed of getting in one day. 'It's full on.'

The younger officer nodded. 'I bet.'

Jon looked to the side. 'Well, you've got yourselves a big case here. When was he found?'

Spiers leaned forward, licking his lips in preparation.

Shazia cut in first, sympathy showing through her matter-of-fact tone. 'It was a horse rider, out at first light. She was riding over Highshaw Hill when she spotted three bin liners. Once home, she rang the park rangers' office to let them know.'

Jon frowned but kept silent.

'Two rangers drove up there once they'd got the phone message – their office doesn't open until eight. They drove the bin liners over to the fox-hound kennels for incineration.'

'I don't follow you,' Jon interrupted. 'Is this some sort of arrangement?'

'Sorry, I should have explained,' Shazia replied. 'It's a sort of informal agreement.'

'Involving who?'

'The poachers and the rangers.'

'Poachers?'

'They kill the deer. The animals are very destructive, you see. Stripping saplings, damaging older trees, eating moorland plants. Officially, it's the park rangers' job to keep their numbers in check. Unofficially, poachers do the job for them. They go on to the moors at night, on foot, and pick a few off.'

'With rifles?'

'Crossbows, I believe. Quieter. The deer are butchered where they fall and the best cuts of meat removed. So long as what's left is neatly bagged up for the rangers to dispose of, everyone's happy.'

'That's what the rangers thought was in the bags,' Spiers added. 'The remains of a deer or two.'

My God, Jon thought, trying not to picture the clumps of meat filling the bin-liners. Sections of my brother's arms, legs ... he pressed the knuckles of his fingers against the mug, searing the image from his mind. 'And they take the bags to an incinerator?'

'Yes,' Shazia replied. 'At the High Peak Hunt's kennels. Their incinerator is used for disposing of all the animals the hunt catches.'

'Or caught before that idiot of a Prime Minister banned it,'

Spiers added, sitting back, arms crossed. 'The rangers threw in one bag and were just about to throw in a second when a mobile phone went off inside. So they opened it up and found ...'

'That's when they called us,' Shazia concluded. 'The phone was in the leg pocket of a pair of cargo trousers.'

The comment conjured more unwelcome images in Jon's mind. A shudder took him and he picked up his coffee to mask it. Lowering his head to take a sip, he used the movement to momentarily close his eyes. Fucking hell, I can't handle this. He swallowed, then sniffed.

Shazia's eyebrows had tilted and she looked like she was about to reach across and squeeze his hand. 'I'm really sorry, but I don't know how to make telling you any easier.'

Jon was feeling queasy again. Breathing deeply, he said, 'Just give me the details straight, I'll deal with it.'

'You're sure?'

He nodded.

'Well,' she continued. 'The rangers had the presence of mind to turn the incinerator off. The pathologist was able to recover, you know, most of what was inside.'

'You mean parts of my brother's body?'

Her eyes dropped towards her drink. 'The bag had obviously melted, there were the remains of a sweatshirt and some of the smaller ... the smaller pieces were badly damaged.'

Jon slid his cup aside. This was too much. 'Look,' he worked his lips. 'I'd better get going. There's a lot of stuff to sort out. Has a doctor signed a medical certificate? I'll need to register the death and start arranging for the funeral. Christ, I don't even know if he had a will.' He glanced at the two officers as if they might know. 'He probably didn't. God knows. Is there a medical certificate?'

'DI Spicer,' Shazia said in a whisper. 'We've only just in-formed the coroner. There'll have to be a post-mortem and after that, an inquest. He won't be able to issue a certificate for the time being.'

'Of course, of course.' Jon blinked. That's basic bloody stuff.

Jesus, get a grip. He coughed with embarrassment. 'But my family need to know. I should be off.'

Shazia glanced at Spiers, then turned back to Jon. 'Could you pop back to the station with us? There's the identification form to complete and we really could do with asking you a few—'

'I'll call you later, if that's all right.' The urge to be in his car and driving far away from this place was overwhelming. He stood.

Shazia was shifting in her seat, about to get up. 'Are you sure you're OK? Can we drive you back to Manchester?'

He moved away from the table, gesturing for her to stay sitting down. 'I'm fine. Seriously. You finish your drinks. I'll speak to you later.'

He was on the road back to Manchester before he registered where he was. Autopilot had got him out of the hospital grounds and along Haverdale's high street. His younger sister, Ellie, would be at Mum and Dad's by now, Sunday lunch in the oven. Oh shit, Holly can't be there when I break the news. He pulled into a lay-by, staring over jagged hills as he readied himself to call Alice and ask that she stay away.

The reception for Key 103 was almost non-existent, so he hit the retune button on the car's radio. It settled on 'Waterloo' by Abba. Dave, skipping round the front room, maybe seven years old? Breathlessly announcing that he was going to write to *Jim'll Fix It*, asking to meet the band in Sweden and get their autographs. Jon remembered the pang of jealous fear as he ridiculed his brother's idea. What if the letter worked and Dave got on the telly? What if the blonde-haired one they both adored kissed him in front of the camera?

The song played on and Jon stared out of the windscreen. Oh Dave, you stupid bastard. What the bloody hell happened? He breathed deeply, remembering his younger brother leaving home, his dad's shouted dismissal as the door slammed shut. His mum had been sobbing and Ellie was silent as Dave walked down the garden path and headed off up the street. Jon squeezed his eyes shut. I should have been there for you during your years on the streets, living in squats, slipping further and further from us all.

Part of his mind started up its usual refrain: You can sort it out soon. Make the effort to find him when things are a bit less hectic in your own life. He stopped the train of thought in its tracks. He's dead, you fool. There's never going to be a chance to sort things out.

A terrible sense of being too late bore down on him. I've missed him, he thought. So much that I wanted to say. The man who abused you, who sent you spinning off into oblivion. I found him, Dave. I found the bastard for you. I found him and then I killed him.

He straightened his fingers, then curled them back around the steering wheel, repeating the action rhythmically, encouraging the waves of tears to come. But his eyes stayed dry and when he studied his face in the rear-view mirror, it looked like he'd been drugged.

Four

The front door to his parents' house was unlocked and he let himself into the front hall. The smell of roast lamb was all around him as he looked fearfully at the framed photos that covered the walls. The three of them in school uniforms, Jon's hair a frizzy mop on his head, Ellie with gaps for front teeth, Dave looking off to the side. Later ones of Jon newly qualified in his policeman's uniform. Ellie on her graduation day, black gown draped over her shoulders. None of Dave as an adult, nothing past his teenage years.

Jon looked towards the archway into the lounge, the ball of sickness swelling in his stomach. He'd rung ahead to announce that Alice and Holly couldn't make it. Ellie's voice was audible in the background as he'd told his dad he'd be there in twenty minutes.

'It's me,' he called out, removing his jacket and hanging it on the banister.

'Hello, Jon.' His mum's voice, full of cheer. Sunday lunch and all her family around her.

He stepped into the front room, noticing the dining table was already laid. Alan was in his armchair to the side of the patio doors, the sports section of the *Observer* in his hands. 'All right, Dad?' Jon asked, catching the questioning look on his father's face.

Something clanged in the kitchen and his mum spoke through the open door. 'What were you saying on the phone? Holly's ill?'

'Just a bit of sickness, Mum. We thought it best she stayed at home.'

'That's a shame. Maybe you could take a plate of food back for Alice.'

He broke away from his dad's stare, moving so he could see into the kitchen. Ellie was draining a saucepan of potatoes at the sink, steam ballooning around her. It rose up and then vanished to leave the window coated in a foggy layer. His mum had just placed a ceramic tray on the work surface. Inside was a roast leg of lamb, the severed bone jutting off to the side. Jon's eyes shied away. Anything but the sight of a hunk of butchered meat. His mum removed her oven gloves. 'And where were you ringing from? Haverdale? What were you doing out there?'

'I've got some news, Mum. News for you all.'

A flicker of wariness in her sideways glance. She smoothed her apron, cheerfulness now sounding slightly forced. 'Why don't I serve up first? You can tell us when we're all sitting down.'

Ellie stepped round her, holding a corkscrew and bottle of red towards him. 'You can open this, too.'

He took the wine, wanting to puke. 'Look, ah ... just sit down at the table, will you?' The bottle was dragging his arm down and he placed it on the dining table. 'It's about Dave.'

He saw their expressions change. Real concern now on his mother's and sister's faces. Behind him, the newspaper rustled and he knew his dad had lowered it. Not taking her eyes off Jon, Mary stepped out of the kitchen. She took a seat, Ellie next to her.

Jon pulled a chair out for himself, angling it so he could also see his father. His mind had frozen. How many times, he asked himself, have I broken this news to other people? Be simple and direct, don't make them suffer by beating about the bush. 'It's bad news.' He registered his mum's slack-jawed look of dismay and cut his eyes up to the ceiling. 'Dave's no longer ... he's no longer with us.'

Silence.

He looked back down. Mary was raising a palm towards her mouth, leaving Ellie scrabbling for where her mother's hand had just been. He saw it in their eyes. Doubt, confusion, fear. Shit, they don't know for certain what I mean. 'He ... Dave's been ... he's dead. Mum, Dave's dead.'

She spoke from behind her hand, eyes beginning to shimmer. 'No.'

'What do you mean?' Ellie asked, voice rising upwards and starting to break as she latched on to Mary's forearm.

Jon fought back the tears. 'Ellie, he's been killed.'

'Who's told you that?'

'The police called me earlier this morning.'

'Well, they could have made a mistake.'

I wish. I so bloody wish. He shook his head once. 'I've just identified his body.'

In the corner of his vision, he saw his dad raise the paper back up. The pages started to tremble. Mary leaned towards her daughter and Ellie wrapped an arm around her. 'How?'

The air shuddered in his throat as he tried to breathe in. 'He was found on top of a hill just outside the town. The local police are involved. It looks like someone killed him.'

A moan. He looked towards his mum and sister, unsure at first who'd made the noise. Mary was trying to gulp. 'No, no, no, no.'

Jon reached across the table and took her hand. No words would come.

'And you're sure?' Ellie's face was white. 'You're certain . . .'

He looked into her eyes and the rest of her sentence dried up. She tilted her head to the side, resting a cheek on top of her mother's head. A tear fell from her eye. He looked at it, a glistening bead that slowly melted into his mother's silvery hair. The paper crumpled as his father suddenly stood. He removed his pack of Hamlets from the uppermost shelf of the Welsh dresser then moved stiffly to the patio doors, fumbling at the handles for a few seconds before sliding them open.

'You!'

The sudden shriek made Jon jump. He looked round at his mum. Both hands were clutching Ellie and her mouth was open, jaw jutting out, lower teeth exposed.

'This is your fault,' she snarled at her husband's back.

The room seemed to shrink as Jon turned back to Alan. His father stood there for a second, then stepped silently outside. Mary's head dropped and the moaning started again.

Jon ducked his head slightly to catch Ellie's eye. We've got to tell them, his look said. We've got to let them know what happened to you and Dave when you were both younger. She stared back at him and slowly shook her head. Keeping his eyes on Ellie, he spoke. 'Mum, I'll take care of everything. We'll get him back and give him a proper burial. Ellie's going to stay with you.'

Her moaning subsided into silence.

'Stay with her,' Jon whispered to his sister, then crossed the room and stepped out onto the patio. His dad was trying to light one of the small cigars. Shoulders hunched, neck craned forward. Suddenly Jon saw him for the sixty-three-year-old man he was. He'd never noticed his frailty before.

'Can't light the bloody thing.'

Shock, Jon thought. Robs you of your coordination. He slid the pack and lighter from his father's fingers and extracted a cigar for himself. After lighting both up, he handed the slim box back. His father cradled it as he stared across the small garden, legs apart as if bracing himself for the roll of a ship.

Jon took a drag, circling his tongue inside his mouth, lips open to let in air. He inhaled and his throat and chest briefly burned.

Alan's voice was flat. 'What happened?'

Jon glanced to the side, but his father's eyes were still fixed on the garden. I can't tell him. I just can't. 'Not sure. The police are investigating.'

'He was killed. Someone killed him?'

'Yes.'

'Drugs?'

Jon shrugged. 'I don't know.'

'How did he die?'

Jon shut his eyes. I can't tell you what they did to him. 'Stabbed maybe. They'll find out.'

A long hissing sound. He turned his head. Tiny plumes of smoke were emerging from between Alan's clenched teeth. 'Stabbed. It was drugs, I know it.'

Anger flashed like a neon sign in Jon's head. Maybe a fucked-up life because you threw the poor bastard out while he was still just a teenager. Years spent trying to cope with that rejection. Endless replays of you telling him to never come back. Maybe, you heartless bastard, that played a bigger part in his death.

'She's right, your mother. It's my fault.'

Jon didn't dare look at his face. 'We're all to blame, Dad. Even Dave.'

'No. I slung him out on the streets, no one else. Thing is? I've regretted what I did for bloody years. I forgave him ages ago, but could never bring myself to tell him. He never made the effort to call, so neither did I. Pride. Stupid bloody pride.'

Jon heard a wet sniff and froze. Fuck, he's crying. My dad's crying. He maintained his silence, looking straight ahead as Alan rubbed at his face. When his father spoke there was a crack in his voice. 'I'm the reason he's dead.' He pulled on his cigar then held it before his face to study the glowing tip. 'It's my fault.'

Actually, Jon wanted to say, it's not. It was a paedophile who screwed him up. But because of who that man was – and what he represented to your wife – I can't tell you. 'It's not, Dad. Dave was out of control. If anyone had a chance to talk him round it was me, and I was too busy with my life to make the effort.'

Alan shook his head. 'I should never have disowned him. There should have been a door open for him at this house. I slammed it shut.'

'Dad, he was leaving anyway. He'd packed a bag. He'd made his choice. If you'd tried to call him back that day, he would have laughed in your face and carried on.'

His father didn't reply. Jon knew he'd be raking over the events that led up to the final confrontation. Dave had never been a well-balanced kid and in the years following the abuse, he'd started dabbling in drink and soft drugs. After being arrested for stealing a car, Alan had slapped him round the house, slowly, methodically, choosing the blows for maximum effect as Mary shrieked at him to stop. The pain obviously had no effect be-cause Dave was arrested again within weeks. There followed a hostile silence between father and son. Jon had guessed the reason for Alan's lack of action: no one had ever acted like this with him before. Not on any rugby pitch in the north-west, not in any pub he drank in after a day working on the docks. Jon knew of his dad's reputation around Salford as a younger man, a man who had knocked down men far bigger than himself in numerous pub fights. And he knew Alan simply didn't know how to handle someone who defied him with absolutely no concern for the consequences. After Dave was arrested for stealing cars a third time, Alan threw him out.

'I don't know where I went wrong.' His father directed the end of his cigar towards Jon. 'Look at you. You've come out fine.'

Jon blinked. His dad had never given him such an open compliment before.

'Ellie's fine, too. Where did I go wrong with the lad?'

Jon felt his throat seizing up. 'He just had something loose in his head, Dad. You couldn't fix it, none of us could.'

Alan sighed. 'Someone did though, didn't they?' Anger had steadied his voice. 'Some bastard fixed him for ever.'

'The police out there will find whoever did it,' Jon replied, an image of the two young constables in his head. He drew in breath as questions started popping up. Who had rung Dave's mobile that morning? How did the killer know about the arrangement between poachers and park rangers? Why would Dave have gone out to some hill top in the middle of the night? Shit, I didn't even think to ask.

'Police?' Scorn curdled his father's voice. 'Twenty years ago, I'd have dealt with this myself. Too old now, though.' He regarded his hand, the loose skin on the back of it dotted with liver spots. Jon could see the little scars among the myriad wrinkles. The result of a lifetime of rugby, the scratches, the cuts, the skin torn by stamping boots. His own hands were dotted with similar injuries, too.

'Find them, son. Find whoever killed our kid and hit them hard. Give it them back in spades before you bring them in. Make them regret what they did to Dave.'

Christ, Dad, Jon thought. This isn't a half-time talk. You're not dealing with an opposition rugby team here. These people hacked Dave up. They fucking sawed his body into pieces.

'Will you do it, son? Twenty, no ten, years ago, I'd have done it myself. You know that.' He jutted his chin up, challenging Jon to dispute the fact.

'Yeah, Dad, I know you would have.'

He stepped sideways, now squaring up to his son, fire in his eyes. That's more like it, Jon thought. You were never so comfortable as when imposing your will on other men. 'So will you do it? Will you find them?'

He felt himself nod. 'I'll go back, start asking questions.' He dropped the cigar butt into the plant pot behind him, glad to retreat from his father's bristling stare. Taking out his phone, he selected his DCI's home number and called it. Buchanon answered after a couple of rings, the sound of chatting and laughter in the background. A nice Sunday lunch with the family, Jon thought.

'Hello.'

'Boss, it's DI Spicer here. Sorry to call you at home like this.'

'I'm sure you've got good reason.'

Jon nodded. Yeah, I've got good reason all right. 'Family bereavement, sir.' He hesitated, a part of him unwilling to state what happened, fearing how it would seal the event as an indisputable fact. 'My younger brother.'

'Christ. Take all the time off you need. Can I ask what happened?'

'I'd prefer to let you know in person.'

'Of course. What else can I do?'

'Nothing, thanks. I'm not due in for three days, so hopefully I'll only need a day or two of compassionate leave.'

'Take the week – just call if you need more.'

'Cheers, boss.' He hung up and glanced at his father. Alan stared back, face like a block of stone. Looking away, Jon rang his home number. 'Alice, it's me.'

'How is it? You've told them?"

'Yeah.'

'And?'

'Not too good.'

'Oh, Jon. Think I should come round to be with your mum?'

He had to pause and gulp in some air. Here I go, he thought bitterly. Lying to her again. He pictured Alice at the other end of the phone, the concern on her face. And here you are, about to deceive the one person who's been there for you more than any other. A rotten taste filled his mouth; like he'd bitten into some bread, then realised the underside of the sandwich in his hand was furred with green mould. 'Listen, can you pack me a bag? Couple of pairs of trousers, T-shirts. Enough for a few days. My hiking boots and windproof as well.'

'Hiking boots? What's going on?'

'I'm going back to Haverdale to help out.'

'Haverdale? They've asked you to help? But you're his brother, how can they ask that?'

Knowing it was the only way Alice would allow him to go, he steeled himself for the lie. 'They need someone with a good knowledge of murder investigations.'

'Jon, slow down. This is ridiculous. What about your work? Buchanon?'

His eyes strayed to his dad. 'He's signed me off. Compassionate leave.'

'Jon, hang on. You haven't thought this through—'

'Just pack the bag, will you? I'll be home in half an hour.' He snapped the phone shut and his dad nodded his approval. 'What will you do with Mum?'

His father shrugged. 'We'll muddle through.'

'She needs your support.'

He grimaced. 'She gets all the support she needs from that bloody church. Your mum and I share a house, son. That's pretty much all we've done for years now.'

Jon looked out across the garden. Primroses had begun to appear in the rockery. He reflected on his parents. Have I misinterpreted their relationship? Are their frequent silences not the comfortable periods of quiet between two life-long companions, but the simple lack of words between a couple who have drifted apart? No, it's not that bad, surely. But now the issue of why Dave left home has reared its ugly head ... I have to sort this mess out, Jon concluded. Finding Dave's killer isn't just something I owe my younger brother. It's the only way to stop Mum and Dad from tearing their marriage apart.

As Jon climbed out of his car, Alice opened their front door. He could see his bag in the hallway behind her. She looked at him, uncertainty all over her face. 'Thanks for packing that for me,' he announced.

'Are you at least coming inside?'

Jon half turned his head. Sounds of a kiddy's programme on the TV. Holly would be there, face lit up by the glow from the screen. He looked at his wife, afraid she would sense his lies. 'Yes.' He stepped into the hallway, saw the door to the front room was shut and wrapped his arms around her.

'Oh, Jon. I'm so sorry. How are you feeling?'

'Surreal, to be honest,' he replied in a low voice so Holly wouldn't hear him. 'Like this isn't quite happening, you know – for real.'

'That's a natural part of the grieving process.'

'Yeah?' A few months ago Alice had volunteered to help in a Manchester-based charity that offered support to traumatised asylum-seekers. Every week she came home with a horrific story. Trafficked women, torture victims from the Middle East, shell-shocked African teenagers who'd seen their parents hacked to death. She'd embarked on a counselling course as soon as she could. 'Thanks for packing my bag,' he repeated.

He saw her eyebrows dip a fraction.

'Alice, I don't need to start feeling sorry for myself. I can't afford to.'

She shrugged. 'It's not about feeling sorry for yourself. It's about addressing your emotions. And you can't do that if you bury yourself in this investigation.'

He sat down on the bottom stair and hung his head in his hands. You've started lying, now you can't stop. 'I haven't got any choice. I saw what they did to him, Ali. I saw it. I have to help find whoever killed him. Even if they didn't want my services, I think I'd still have to go out there.' He looked up at her. 'Can you understand that?'

She crouched down, pressed a finger against his lips and then touched her forehead against his. They stayed like that for a few seconds, then she searched out his hands and straightened up, pulling his arms as she did so. 'Come into the kitchen, sit down for a minute.'

She led the way and as Jon followed, he looked at her blonde hair tied back in a loose ponytail. What, he thought, would I do without you? 'I'm sorry for being a bit sharp with you. I didn't mean to be.'

As her arm swung back, she flicked a wrist.

They sat down at the table, holding hands across it. Jon spotted a couple of chocolate Easter eggs on the shelf above the radiator, still in their wrappings. Next to them was a painted egg. He could make out the faint pencil lines where Alice had drawn circles and diamonds on the shell. Filling the shapes were crudely applied blobs of paint. Propped against it was a certificate entitled, 'Lyme Park's Easter Egg Painting Competition.' His daughter's name had been handwritten beneath the words. 'She won?' Jon asked proudly.

Alice gave him a look. 'Every kid wins a certificate at those types of events. She's a toddler, Jon.'

He smiled. Another minor event in my daughter's life that I've missed.

'It's not your fault what happened to Dave.'

The smile fell from his face. 'But it is in a way, isn't it? Where was I for him? What did I do to actually help him – even after Ellie told me the truth about what happened to the pair of them.'

'You mean the man who—'

'Yeah, him,' Jon cut her off. The man you don't realise I murdered.

'Maybe you and Ellie should think about telling Mary and Alan the truth.'

'What? That a fellow member of the church she lives for,

27

preyed on her trust to sexually abuse her son and mentally abuse her daughter? Ellie swore me to secrecy about the whole thing, and I can see why. It would destroy Mum.' He rubbed at the back of his neck. 'They've fallen out over this already, you realise? Mum said to Dad it was his fault. Dad's that gutted, he admitted as much to me out on the patio.'

'But not to your mum?'

'Not yet. If I can help clear things up in Haverdale, it will give them the opportunity to patch things up, I'm sure. Until then, they're stuck, resentment festering between them.'

'Was it him?'

'How do you mean?'

'Was it Alan who encouraged you to offer your services?'

Jon avoided her eyes. 'He's keen to know who killed him, same as me.'

'Christ, Jon. What sort of a hold has that man got over you?'

'He's my dad, Alice. You never had one, so it's hard for you to understand.'

Alice looked away.

'I'm sorry, that wasn't meant to sound harsh. But he walked out when you were tiny. It's hard to explain, but yes, I want him to be pleased with me. Doesn't everyone seek that kind of approval?'

'I want my mum to be proud of me, but I know she just wants me to be happy.'

Happy? Jon wanted to laugh. Is that why, he thought to himself, she only ever turns up here when there's been a disaster in her life? Like being dumped by the latest boyfriend.

Alice sighed. 'Your dad. He says jump and you say, How high? I don't get it.

Neither do I, thought Jon. Neither do I.

She squeezed his fingers. 'Jon, this whole thing? We'll go through it together. Remember that.'

He returned the pressure, wanting to blurt out that he had no official role in the investigation. Toes curling in his shoes, he fought the urge back, knowing Alice would never allow him to leave the house if she was aware of the truth. 'Listen, I'd better go. I'll just look in on Holly.'

His daughter was lying on the floor, head propped on the stomach of their sleeping dog. 'Hi there.'

'Daddy!'

She sat up, Punch scrabbling to his feet, too. Jon knelt, one hand going behind his dog's ears, the other going under his daughter's chin. 'I saw the egg you painted.'

'Me painted,' she smiled. 'Egg!'

'Yes, you clever girl. It's beautiful.'

'Beut-ful!'

He wanted to kiss her face. 'And you won a certificate.'

'Yes!' she beamed, though he could tell she now had absolutely no idea what he was talking about. You, he thought, are so damned gorgeous. 'Daddy's got to go, now. I'll see you soon.'

'See you soon.'

He bent down and kissed her smooth cheek, gave Punch a last tickle, then climbed back to his feet.

Alice was standing in the hall, a faint smile on her face. 'Call me later, OK? I don't like the idea of you out there all on your own.'

'I'll be fine,' he replied, picking up the hold-all and then kissing her lips. 'I love you.'

'Love you, too.'

Five

Jon reached the turn-off for the hospital, but continued up Haverdale's high street. He passed a couple of outdoor shops selling hiking and camping gear, a tearoom, estate agent's, a couple of pubs, a restaurant, small art gallery, an old-fashioned ironmonger's and another estate agent's. All the while he scanned for anything that would indicate the location of the police station itself.

The row of shops on the left was broken by a large hotel, grandiose portico entrance shrouded in ivy. Large gold letters spelled out 'The Imperial'. A throwback to Haverdale's brief heyday as a wealthy spa town. Now the practice of taking the waters, as it was known, had passed. With Buxton and Harrogate not far away, reinventing itself as a conference venue wasn't an option. Jon could see the town was struggling to find a new role.

A short distance later he spotted three patrol cars in the car park of a building set back off the road. Here we go, he thought, eyes snagging on the signage of the mini-supermarket next to it. Beers, wines, spirits. I'll be paying you a visit later.

He climbed the station's steps, passing beneath the quaint blue lamp above the front entrance. The foyer was unmanned, just an intercom buzzer to the side of a secure door. An elderly couple were seated in one corner, several sheets of paper draped across the woman's knees. He heard them discussing the circumstances of a burglary, going over ground they'd doubtlessly covered several times before.

'The side door was locked. It's always locked.'

'How can that representative assert that it wasn't?'

'Don't fret, Margaret, the police officer will verify it – he saw how the back gate had been forced.'

'You're sure you've got the incident number? He'll need it to check his notes.'

Insurance companies, Jon thought. Do they ever change? A young man sat in the far corner, arms crossed, the corner of a driving licence peeping out from beneath one armpit. Breaking the speed limit, Jon concluded, moving across the room and pressing the intercom. Nothing for thirty seconds. He buzzed again.

'They'll keep you waiting. Been here twenty minutes, the cunts.'

Jon glanced over his shoulder, catching the conspiratorial look on the bloke's face. We're in this together, it said. Pretty much partners in crime. Jon pressed the buzzer again, this time holding it down.

The intercom eventually crackled. 'Take your finger off the button.'

'DI Spicer, Greater Manchester Police. Here to see Constables Spiers and Batyra.'

'Hang on.'

Jon turned around, seeing that a wary look had now crept over the younger man's face. From the way the old couple were regarding him, he could tell they were thinking about pleading their case with him. To discourage any approach, Jon picked up a copy of the *Haverdale Herald* and sat down. It was a day old but he didn't mind.

'Nighthawks swoop again,' read the front headline. He scanned the lead paragraphs.

Yet more evidence of people illegally digging for archaeological artefacts has been discovered on the edge of town, this time on Round Knoll. Like the other incidents over the last few weeks, an excavation had been hurriedly made during the hours of darkness. Stacey Morris, Head Librarian and Chair of the Haverdale Archaeological Society, shed light on the mystery.

'The fact that each dig has taken place on a hill top proves, in my mind, the culprits are searching for a barrow, probably an iron-age site. Though it's indisputable any such find would be worth many thousands of pounds to unscrupulous collectors, what these people are hoping to find here is beyond me, since all the barrows in this area have been excavated long ago.'

Jon's eyes strayed to a photo in the top right-hand corner. It was of very poor quality, little more than a prickly blob of brown topped by a curved greyish form. The two-tone split behind it suggested land and sky, divided. Superimposed over the corner of the image was a small graphic device depicting a swooping bird of prey with the words, 'Osprey Watch'. He looked to the copy for further explanation.

Mum's the word – has our female osprey laid her clutch? Captured here, proudly sitting atop the nest she and her mate have recently constructed in a pine tree overlooking a nearby reservoir, Diva looks every inch the expectant mother. Keep an eye on 'Osprey Watch' to find out if she and her magnificent mate, Alto – the first ospreys to nest in the Peak District in living memory – are to become parents. Photo kindly supplied by the Park Rangers' Office.

He heard the inner door open and glanced up to see Shazia Batyra beckoning. 'Afternoon.'

'Hello.' Jon dropped the paper on the next seat and stood up.

'Anyone going to check my licence?' the young man demanded, holding it up.

'Someone will be down soon.'

'Is Constable Taylor in?' The elderly lady from the couple asked. 'Someone said they were checking. It's Mr and Mrs Gower.'

'I'll have a look around for him,' Shazia replied, stepping back to allow Jon through, then closing the door with a sigh of relief.

'Not the best way of maintaining community relations,' Jon stated matter-of-factly as they set off down the corridor.

She glanced back at him. 'Easter Sunday. They could have picked a day when there are more of us in.' She paused. 'I didn't expect you back so soon. Did you go home?'

'Yeah. The family know.'

Her eyes searched his again. 'I'm really sorry about what happened at the hospital.'

'Not your fault, don't worry about it.'

'The identification forms are upstairs. If we could take a statement and get some details about your brother too, it would really help.'

'No problem.'

They climbed the stairs and headed down another corridor, the walls of which were dotted with various photos of the station's officers lined up like members of a sports club. By the time they'd got to the far end, the photos were black and white and most officers had large moustaches or beards. In the room beyond was a general-purpose office, desks spread out in groups of four. He counted seven people.

'Les,' Shazia announced. 'That couple downstairs is waiting to see you. The Gowers.'

An overweight officer somewhere in his forties looked up from the Sunday papers spread out on his desk. 'Shit. Forgot about them.'

'Their insurance company's trying to reject their claim,' Jon said. 'You'll need your notes that verified the lock to their side door had been picked. There's also a boy-racer who's brought his driving licence in.' He thought about how the lad had sworn in front of the old couple. 'No harm in letting him wait, though.'

The officer turned to Shazia for an explanation.

She waved a hand in introduction. 'DI Spicer, Greater Manchester Police.'

Jon watched the other officer as his face changed. 'Sorry for your loss.'

'Thank you.' He looked round again: four other uniformed officers, including Spiers. Two civilians, admin assistants by the look of them. He met all of their eyes, registering the guarded looks on their faces.

'We're in the corner.' Shazia pointed towards her colleague.

'No dedicated incident room?' Jon asked as they made their way across.

'No space for one. Those other doors we passed are offices for the senior ranks.'

Nightmare, Jon thought, realising the investigation into Dave's murder would be sharing a space with any other incidents that came in. He knew the distractions that would occur, not to mention the potential for paperwork to be placed in the wrong tray, moved to another, misfiled and finally lost.

'This is Rachel Scott,' Shazia announced. 'She'll be helping us, entering reports into HOLMES and the like.'

One indexer, Jon thought, trying not to shake his head. 'Who else is on the case?'

'Constable Spiers and myself. Then there are Sergeant Brooks and Constable Conway who are due in tomorrow.'

'What about the guy who called me – Mallin?'

'Yes, Superintendent Ray Mallin is Senior Investigating Officer. He's in his office making a few calls, I think.'

So, not a lot going on then, Jon thought, making sure his irritation didn't show.

Shazia was removing the identification forms from a file on her desk. He looked at the evidence bags on the adjoining table. 'These Dave's things?'

She looked momentarily alarmed. 'Er ...'

There's not much that can be more distressing than seeing my brother's head in a bag, Jon nearly said, stepping round the desk. 'All this was removed from the hill where he was found?'

'No, his hotel room.'

Jon looked across the table at her. 'Dave was staying in a hotel?'

'The Haven Inn.'

'The one on the edge of town?' He remembered passing it on his journey in.

She nodded.

Cheap and anonymous. Sounds like Dave's style. 'How did you know he was there?'

She looked uneasy. 'Haverdale's a pretty small place.'

Jon thought about the number of B&B places on the residential road leading to the hospital. 'Small, but it's got a fair few places to stay.'

She shrugged. 'You know … word gets around. People not from here get noticed.'

There's more to it than that, Jon wanted to say. He let it pass, focusing on the bags instead. The first contained several train tickets. Manchester Piccadilly to Haverdale.

'He was using them as bookmarks,' Shazia said.

Jon examined the next bag. It contained an Ordnance Survey map for the Haverdale area, beneath that was another bag with a slim booklet inside: *Walks of Note Around Haverdale*. Jon felt himself frown, unable to picture his younger brother developing an interest in hiking. Other bags contained clothes, toiletries, a pair of binoculars, a crumpled white towel.

'And there was this, of course.' Constable Spiers was holding up a smaller bag which contained a mobile phone. Dried blood covered it, clogging up the keys and obscuring the lower part of the screen. Jon leaned forward. Above the rust-coloured smear, the top half of the screensaver was visible. It was an image of a young woman, black hair tied back, delicate cheek bones. Her mouth was open in mid-laughter, revealing a pair of sharp incisors that weren't aligned with the rest of her teeth. Jon looked at her eyes. Despite their happiness, there was something about them. Jon hoped she was just tired, but he'd seen that same sunken appearance on countless women he'd booked in for illegal use of drugs.

'You've noted down the contents of the address book?' he asked.

Spiers replaced the phone and swivelled a piece of paper round. 'What there was in it.'

Jon picked it up. Seven entries: Big Bro. Doug. Jock. L.A. Marco. Stew. Zoe.

'You were the first and most obvious choice to ring.'

'The others have all been called?'

'That's right. The Super did it.'

Jon looked at him, eyebrows half-hitched.

Spiers hunched a shoulder. 'I'm not sure. A couple of answer-phones, one number no longer in use. You'll have to ask him.'

'What about the last ten calls made and received?'

'The Super's noted them down. He's been on it in his office.'

'And the person who called this morning. Did it ring off, go through to answerphone, what?'

Spiers nodded. 'Answerphone.'

Jon gave him a second but nothing more was forthcoming. 'Got a transcript?'

'The Super has.'

The Super, Jon thought. You're not going to tell me another thing without his say-so. 'What about these park rangers? The ones who recovered the bin bags from the top of the hill. I'd like to hear what they have to say.'

Shazia spoke up. 'I took their statements. I'm sure you'd be welcome to have a look.' She opened a file and extracted two forms. Jon started to read the mechanical language, eyes quickly beginning to skim the lines before moving to the bottom. 'It would be far more useful to speak with them in person. Where might ...'

Batyra and Spiers were now looking over his shoulder. He turned round to see a thick-set man in his fifties, greying hair just long enough to be curling out at the sides. Jon's eyes flicked to the epaulettes of his uniform. Superintendent. So this is Mallin.

'What's going on here?' he demanded, bushy eyebrows lowering into a frown.

By pushing her heels outwards, Zoe Croxton could feel tiny ripples in the concrete through the carpet. Bumps and nodules where some workmen hadn't been arsed to do a proper job. And now the bastard things would torment her for fuck knows how long. Leaning on the arm of the sofa, she groaned with frustration.

The woman at the housing association place had said she was

lucky – this was the first flat from a batch they were refurbishing that year. She looked at the carpet, it was the colour of dead leaves and not much thicker either. Eleven floors up was no place to be stuck with a baby, she thought. Christ, he's already into every cupboard and drawer. What about when he's able to climb? Every bloody window will have to be nailed shut.

Once again, she turned the mobile phone over in her hand, studying the beads of water trapped behind the screen. She glanced at her son who was sitting on the other side of the room, happily playing with several brightly-coloured action figures. 'You little monkey. Of all the things you could have done, you had to do the worst. Dropping my phone down the bloody toilet. Jesus.' Her eyes carried on across the floor, stopping at the small circular socket just above the skirting board. What she'd do for a landline now.

Hearing her, he lifted his head. For a moment it was Dave looking at her and she felt herself flinch. Their eyes were just the same. Oh Christ, Dave, where are you?

He was holding up an empty beaker, a questioning look on his face.

She glanced into the minuscule kitchen, knowing there was less than a litre of milk left. 'Not now, kidder.'

As he lowered it again, the people who lived on the ceiling began moving about. A door closed, sounding almost like it was in her own flat. A few seconds later she heard a toilet flush and the wall whispered as liquid cascaded down the pipes.

Lighting a cigarette, she stood up and stared out the window. Just below her a seagull, strayed in from the coast, wheeled and circled. It slid off the edge of a current, dropping away to another and then rising smoothly back up. Enviously, she watched it, remembering how she could drift and float for hours, lying on the floor with an empty syringe at her side. Just to ride that feeling again, if only for a few minutes. She thought about the gang who ran the tower block. They had plenty of the stuff; they'd sold it to her often enough in the past. And if it hadn't been for Dave, she'd still be pressing it into her arms now. She clutched her sides and looked down.

Way below, cars were moving along Trinity Way, two opposing streams of traffic destined never to touch. A person was crossing the footbridge, a stick-like leg momentarily emerging from below his head and shoulders. The torso tilted forward again, and just as the man looked like he would topple over, the other leg appeared in the nick of time.

She lifted her eyes, clearing the straggly edge of Manchester, scooting over the suburbs and sweeping miles of countryside in an instant. At the far right-hand edge of her view were shadowy hills. That's where he is, she thought. Somewhere out there. Why aren't you back, yet? Christ, Dave, I miss you. She pictured his face, the light that danced in those bright, blue eyes. Even when things were at their most shit, even when they'd had no money and nowhere to sleep, the sparkle refused to fade. He'd sit, never silent for more than a few minutes, before glancing up at her with a grin. 'We'll work something out, Zoe,' he'd say. She felt herself smile.

'You'll be back,' she whispered, turning away from the distant slopes. And if this bloke you've been on about is all that you reckon he is, we won't be stuck in this shitty rabbit hutch for much longer.

Stubbing her cigarette out in the ashtray on top of the telly, she turned to her son. 'Where's your Daddy, then?'

His eyes immediately turned to the door leading in from the corridor. 'Dada?'

'No.' She smiled, lifting him up and sitting back on the sofa with him perched on her knees. 'He's not here, Jake. He's out there, somewhere.' She jutted her chin towards the window. 'With Redino, isn't he?'

She punctuated the question with a bounce of her knees and the little boy giggled.

'Going to make us lots of cash, isn't he?'

Another bounce, followed by laughter.

'Going to take us away from this bloody place, isn't he?'

With this bounce, his laughter gave way to a series of little coughs. Zoe's knees remained still and she held an ear to his mouth, just able to hear a faint crackling sound each time he drew in breath. She looked at the milky mucus emerging from his nostrils, suddenly aware of how his ribs were corrugating beneath her palms.

Oh no, it's not coming back again, she thought. That's the last thing I fucking need. Especially without Dave here to help. She slid her fingers round to his sternum, and by holding them there, could actually feel a tiny rattling inside. Shit, shit, shit.

She tried to remember the details of Jake's last attack. How long before his lungs were hardly working and the fever set in? Two, or was it three days? All she could recall was Jake's temperature suddenly rocketing. She and Dave had wheeled him down to Dr Griffiths' surgery and the doctor had immediately rushed their son to the nearest A & E.

The flap of her letter box lifted, filling the flat with a creaking sound.

'Zoe.' The man held the end of her name, like a kid calling another one out to play.

Immediately, she clamped a hand over her son's mouth, eyes wide with fear. Jake stared back, knowing not to move.

'He's not there, is he? Your useless tosser of a boyfriend has done one. Just you now. And if I can't get the money off of him, I'll get it off of you.'

She said nothing, palm pressed against Jake's lips.

'Zoe!' The sing-song tone was gone. 'You know how you're going to pay me, because it's the only fucking way you know how to earn money. It's your choice. Come out of there and start looking for business or I'll bring the punters up. Think about it, girl. I'm not going anywhere and neither are you.'

The letter box creaked shut, leaving her with the sound of Jake's wheezing breath.

Six

Jon turned and held out a hand. 'DI Jon Spicer.'

The hostile challenge in Mallin's eyes almost disappeared. 'Superintendent Ray Mallin. You have my condolences.'

'Thank you.'

The Super's stare shifted to his officers and Jon saw his eyebrows lift a fraction.

'DI Spicer is completing the ID form,' Shazia explained. 'And he's agreed to answer a few questions about his brother.'

'Good. Thanks for your assistance, Detective.' Mallin turned to go.

'These possessions of Dave's ...' Jon let his brother's name hang in the air. 'They were recovered from a hotel room, I understand.'

Mallin did a stiff turn about. 'Correct.'

'How did you know which hotel to call at?'

Mallin's eyes connected with Jon's, neither man speaking. Come on, Jon thought, let's hear what's making you all act like my brother's the fucking criminal here.

The Super's posture didn't soften. 'Your brother had come to our attention before this morning.'

Jon kept his silence.

Mallin pursed his lips, the breath coming out through his nose. 'Listen, there are drugs in this town. A lot of them. First it was a trickle, now it's becoming a flood. We've got all the attendant problems starting to show themselves. Burglaries are up. Car thefts, shoplifting, kids getting mugged for their mobile phones. We've got absenteeism from work and domestic breakdown. Last week three children from the same family were finally taken into care.'

Jon frowned. This sounded a lot more serious than weekend use of cocaine. 'What sort of drugs are we talking about here?'

'The most destructive.'

'What, crack?'

Mallin shook his head. 'I believe it's known as crystal meth.'

Jon couldn't believe his ears. Methamphetamine, a wickedly strong derivative of speed, was already wreaking havoc in towns and cities across the States. He'd attended a seminar given by a sheriff visiting from Washington State last year. The man had explained how the drug was relatively easy to manufacture – little more was needed than a few kitchen utensils, coffee filters, over-the-counter cold remedies, rock salt and ammonia. Recently, the drug had started appearing in Britain's larger cities, but mainly on the club circuit. He'd heard stories of people not eating or sleeping for days while their supplies of 'ice' lasted.

'You've got that here?"

'We have,' Mallin replied. 'And its corrosive effects are even more marked in a rural community like this.'

From his expression, Jon knew he was fishing for some kind of agreement. Until you've said what you have to say about my brother, he thought, you're getting nothing from me.

Mallin continued. 'We're not sure where the narcotics are coming from, but you know as well as I do, dealers from our inner cities are looking for new markets. A small town like Haverdale is ideal. Jump on a train from Manchester and you're here in half an hour.'

So there we have it. Jon wanted to laugh. My brother's been travelling here from Manchester, therefore he's dealing drugs. 'What are you saying exactly?'

Mallin kept his hands at his sides. 'Trevor Curtis, the landlord of the Spread Eagle, a pub used by the town's younger residents, had voiced his concerns. He suspected your brother was dealing on the premises.'

Jon nodded. 'Did he produce any evidence to back up this accusation?'

Mallin shifted slightly. 'No. As I said, he merely voiced his concerns.'

41

'And if Dave was Haverdale's chief dealer—'

'I didn't say chief dealer, DI Spicer.'

'Sorry. Don't know how I picked up that impression. If Dave was a dealer, where's his equipment? Surely you're not suggesting he was cooking up crystal meth in his hotel room? I've seen a presentation on how the stuff is produced – do you realise the stink that's involved in making it?'

'No.'

Jon shrugged. 'Believe me, that entire hotel would have known about it.'

'I imagine he would have been bringing the drugs here ready-made.'

Would have, Jon thought. A statement of fact. He gestured to the evidence bags. 'So where's the paraphernalia a drug dealer uses? The rolls of cling film, tinfoil, razor blades, electronic scales. Where are the actual drugs?'

'We're unsure, as yet.'

You've already decided, Jon thought. Dave was the disease making this town sick and you're certainly not going to bust a gut finding whoever killed him. 'I'm sorry, but I think you've judged my brother prematurely, to say the least. I noticed the front page of the local paper. There was a story about night-hawks. People searching for buried treasure. The only things my brother seemed to have in his room were walking books and maps. Did it occur to you he was here on some hare-brained scheme like that?'

A flush was now creeping up from Mallin's collar. Jon softened his voice, realising his anger wasn't helping his case. 'What about the phone call this morning? Who rang my brother's number?'

'A female called Zoe.'

'The same Zoe from the address book in Dave's phone?'

'We can't say. That was a mobile number. It transpires this morning's call was from a public payphone on Cateaton Street, near Deansgate – which, I gather, is in Manchester's city centre.'

Right next to the cathedral, Jon thought. His mind went back to the last time he'd seen his brother alive. Jon had been trying to trace a suspected arsonist known to frequent the Booth Centre, the cathedral's facility for homeless people. While checking the place out, he'd come across Dave negotiating some sort of deal that involved a mountain bike. The skeletal man selling it had accepted a ridiculous price in return for what Dave could get him.

'What did this girl say?'

Mallin tapped a forefinger against the seam of his trousers before coming to a decision. 'The transcript is in my office. Follow me.'

Jon could feel everyone watching as he crossed the silent room. Mallin's office was two doors down the corridor, a spacious room lined with cabinets along one wall. The couple of spider plants and framed photos on top of them partially succeeded in adding a less formal feel. As Mallin closed the door and walked round to his desk, Jon studied the photos: the Superintendent, thigh deep in a river, waders up to his chest, fly-fishing rod angled over his head. Another of him with a near identical man, both crouched before a spread of salmon laid out on the grass. Your brother, thought Jon. No doubt still alive and enjoying life. Your next fishing trip with him is probably booked already.

'How long have you been in the job?'

Jon turned round. Mallin was sitting behind his desk, waiting for an answer, fingers interlaced across his stomach.

'I joined in 1995.'

The Super inclined his head. 'And you got into the Major Incident Team four years ago.'

Jon met the other man's eyes, surprised the other man would know a detail like that. 'Correct.'

Mallin waved a hand in explanation. 'You were involved in an investigation year before last. The spate of attacks on churches round Manchester.'

Jon nodded cautiously and Mallin spread his hands, gesturing to the chair opposite. 'I have an interest in ecclesiastical architecture, the case was one I kept tabs on. You faced some challenge there.'

Jon eased himself into the seat. That's one way of putting it,

43

he thought. Though you wouldn't describe it like that if you knew what the bastard had done to my brother and sister.

'It was a shame the culprit perished in the final fire.' Mallin's voice rose slightly at the end of the sentence, fishing for more explanation.

Culprit? Jon reflected on the word. That's one way of describing the piece of shit.

'I gather you sustained some pretty serious burns, too.'

Jon didn't look at the slightly puckered patches of skin on his hands. Only in the dead of night when everyone else was asleep, did he run his fingers over the scars. Any time other than that, he acted like they weren't there, terrified that if he allowed the memory a foothold in his mind, the knowledge that he killed a man would come to dominate his daytime thoughts.

Outside, a siren suddenly began to wail. An engine revved and the noise began to lose strength as the vehicle shot off down the high street. Mallin waited a moment longer before saying, 'OK, I understand. You'd prefer to keep your counsel.'

Jon raised his eyes. 'I've just lost my brother. Sorry if I'm not in the mood for this kind of chat.'

Mallin stared at him. Oh dear, Jon thought. You and me are never going to be friends.

The Superintendent reached for a piece of paper. 'The message from Zoe.'

Jon took it, eyes searching out the small paragraph at the bottom.

'Dave, it's me, Zoe. You all right? How's it all going? Has Redino come through for you, yet? Struck gold and all that? I'm missing you. It's you know ... not easy. Money.' Her voice was beginning to waver. 'Come back, Dave. I've got Salvio on my back. Him and his bloody gang, kicking the door at all hours. He wants paying and you know what he does to people who – ah, the frigging pips. I've got no more coins. Got no money, full stop. I need you here, Dave. All this with Salvio, it's doing my head in. When are—'

Jon flipped the sheet over, as though more might be on the other side. 'She sounds pretty scared of Salvio, whoever he is.'

'Indeed.' Mallin shrugged. 'I think we can assume Dave and

44

Zoe were a couple.' He slid another piece of paper across. The last ten calls made and received on Dave's phone were listed. All were to Zoe and from Zoe. Jon thought of the face on the screensaver.

'This answerphone message. Was it left by a female who sounded fairly young?'

'She seemed to be.'

'Manchester accent?'

'Yes.'

'And you've tried the number for Zoe that's in the mobile's phonebook?'

'It goes straight through to an out-of-service message. I've put in a request to see if the number is registered with anyone. My guess is it will be a pay as you go, leaving us none the wiser.'

Jon was racking his brain. Dave and Zoe speak on a regular basis, using their mobiles. Suddenly she switches to a payphone and her mobile number is dead. She said she's short of money, perhaps unable to top up her credit. Maybe she's been cut off by the phone company itself. But why not use a landline rather than walk to a call box? 'What about the other phone book entries? Who are they again: Marco, Stew, Jock?'

The Super took in a breath. 'None prepared to help. Either they're not returning messages or they hang up when we identify ourselves. Jock – a Scottish gentleman – wanted to know where Haverdale was, then roared with laughter when I told him.'

Scottish, Jon thought. That last time at the Booth Centre, a Scottish guy was trying to warn Dave off buying the mountain bike. The man's rasping comment rang in Jon's head. It's a death trap man, a fucking death trap.

'I realise this is hard for you, DI Spicer, but why do you think your brother was staying here in a hotel? Especially if his partner was short of cash.'

Jon looked away, searching the diamond pattern on the carpet. 'How long had he been booked in for?'

'Three nights. And he'd been here on another three occasions over the last few weeks. Three nights, away for a night, back for another three. Shuttling to and from Manchester ...'

'Picking up fresh supplies of drugs.'

Mallin blinked.

'Just thought I'd finish your sentence off for you.' Jon's voice was cold.

Mallin tilted his head slightly to the side. You said it, not me.

Jon put the piece of paper back on the desk and crossed his arms. 'How many digs have been discovered lately?'

'Four.'

'Do they coincide with my brother's stays in that Haven Inn?'

'I'm not sure. I don't think all the digs were discovered immediately, but I could probably check. However, no spades, nothing of that nature was left on the hill where your brother was found.'

'Can I see this hill?'

'We need to know more about him, DI Spicer. Where did your brother live? Who did he work for? What sort of company did he keep? You know the routine for a murder investigation.' He removed a print-out from his file. 'I have his record here. Juvenile offences involving cars: Taking Without Owner's Consent. Then the odd arrest for possessing drugs. Breaking and entering a residence by Lake Windermere. Another fine for possession of Class B drugs.'

I know my brother's bloody record, Jon thought. 'I'll tell you what I know. Do you want it before or after I visit the crime scene?'

Mallin's eyes flashed again. 'DI Spicer, this is a Derbyshire Police Authority investigation. You're not involved in any professional capacity. Not even an advisory one, understood?'

'Fine. I just want to see where my brother died, that's all.'

'Tell me what you know and I'll have Constables Batyra and Spiers drive you out there.'

Jon leaned back in his seat. 'Thank you. My brother was thrown out of the family home a bit before his eighteenth birthday, following his third TWOC. He went to live with friends in a central Manchester squat. Over the past decade I've come across him maybe six times. Not a lot was said. Family news, that sort of thing.'

Mallin was frowning. 'Here you are, a detective inspector. What set your brother off on such a contrasting route?'

A face flashed into Jon's head before he could stop it. The monster who'd got to Dave when he was just a young kid. Jon felt his fingers flex, the memory of his fist slamming into the side of the man's head so strong. The way he'd toppled into the long grass, flames engulfing his unconscious body. 'Boozing. A taste for trouble. He had a wild side and I suppose it took over.'

Mallin's eyes were narrowed. An interview-room stare. 'How did your brother support himself all those years?'

'Unemployment benefit. Cash-in-hand jobs. He'd pick fruit on farms, stuff like that. He spent one summer in the Lake District. No rent to pay when you're squatting in someone's holiday home near Lake Windermere.'

Mallin's eyes touched on Dave's record. 'But the links to drugs are there. Possession at least.'

'Possession and nothing else. No convictions for dealing. He was a dosser, a bit of a rogue.' Once again, the memory of Dave outside the cathedral returned. His brother riding off on a perfectly good mountain bike, exchanged for ... what? Jon leaned forward. 'OK. My brother had a trivial involvement in drugs. Perhaps that involvement stretched to selling the odd bit here and there, who knows? But what you're describing in Haverdale is dealing on a professional scale. The people behind it will be making huge amounts of cash – and they don't give a shit about the damage they're doing. My brother rejected a conventional life, but he still had morals.'

Mallin pushed his bottom lip out.

Fuck you, Jon nearly snarled. 'What about the phone message? This Redino or whatever his name is? Zoe's talking about striking gold. That could be a reference to an archaeological find.'

Mallin sighed. 'I'm going to contact the drug squads in Sheffield and Manchester to see if Redino is a known name. I think you'd better face the likelihood your brother wasn't in

Haverdale searching for buried treasure. Striking gold is, in my opinion, a reference to sealing a drug deal.'

'And the maps? The walking book? The recent digs?'

'Your brother had to stash his drugs somewhere.'

Jon shook his head. 'No. This isn't adding up. Can I see the crime scene now?'

'For ten minutes in the outer cordon. I have forensics up there and they don't need any interruptions.'

'No problem. I just need to use the toilet before we go.'

The Superintendent pointed to his side. 'End door on the left. I'll give Batyra and Spiers a shout.'

Jon let himself into the toilet area. A row of sinks, four urinals and two cubicles; both empty. He turned round, closed the door leading back into the corridor, took his mobile phone out and quickly selected the number of his partner in the MIT. 'Rick, it's Jon.'

'OK, mate. Why the whisper?'

'I haven't got long. I need a favour.'

'Work? Christ, Jon, it's a Sunday. In fact it's Easter bloody Sunday. Do you ever stop?'

'Did I ever mention my younger brother, Dave?'

'Yeah, once. Moved out of Manchester, lost touch with your family.'

'He's dead.'

Two second's silence. 'What happened?'

'I'll tell you later. Listen, I wasn't straight with you. He didn't ever leave Manchester, not completely.'

'It was him, wasn't it? That time we were making enquiries at the Booth Centre summer before last. He was with the homeless lot.'

Jon turned away from the door, glimpsing himself in the mirror above the sinks. Hunched, furtive, sneaky. 'How did you know?'

'The way you kept me at arm's length. You used his name and I asked Alice, just to make sure.'

Jon lifted his chin, the weight of the secret suddenly gone. 'Yeah, that was him.' Emotion suddenly welled up and his throat muscles clamped about his voice box, choking the words before they could reach his mouth. He coughed twice, but when he spoke, there was still a tremor in his voice. 'He's gone, Rick. All those times I meant to find him and sort things out between us. I kept putting it off and now I'm too fucking late.' His words petered out and he found himself staring down at the urinal's gutter. That's where I left you, he thought. Sloshing around with the dregs. You bastard, Jon. You total bastard.

'Don't beat yourself up, mate. I saw him too that time, remember? It was him pushing you away.'

'I know. But he was in the mess, not me. I shouldn't have let him fob me off like that. It was all he was ever going to do. I should have tried harder.'

'Things aren't that easy. Not if the person doesn't want to be helped.'

Noises in the corridor. Batyra, Spiers and the jangle of keys. Jon raised his chin. 'Listen. Dave didn't just die, he was murdered.'

Shock distorted Rick's voice. 'How?'

'I'm trying to find out. All I've got at the moment is some kind of a link to poaching. Whoever killed him appears to have some local knowledge of it. I'm going to try looking into that, but I could do with you checking something with the homeless crowd.'

'OK.'

'I need to find a girl called Zoe. She could well knock around with that lot.'

'Any description?'

'She's pretty, but thin. Catwalk kind of look. Black hair, canine teeth, overly pointed, like on a vampire.'

'Got it. What's the connection?'

'I think she's Dave's other half. There's a message from her on his phone and she mentions a name. Redino. It's only guess-work at this stage, but I reckon he may well have played a part in Dave's murder.'

'Where are you?'

'Out in Haverdale. I'll be taking this week off. Compassionate leave. There was also a Scottish guy with that Booth Centre lot, may well be known as Jock. If he's there, start with him. Know anyone in the drug squad?'

'A couple.'

'Can you get this Redino name checked on the quiet?'

'Spelling?'

'God knows. Got to go.'

The connection cut and Rick lowered his hand to look at the receiver while he tried to gather his thoughts. 'Sorry,' he eventually said, carefully replacing the handset and glancing at the two women sitting in silence on his leather sofa. 'Work call, as you probably gathered.'

'No problem,' said the older one on the left with a smile. The black rectangular frames of her glasses lent her a slightly officious air, further reinforced by the harsh lines of her dark bob. 'It must be such an interesting thing to be in, the police.'

Rick's smile only touched one half of his mouth. 'Interesting? That's one way of putting it.'

'Aside from the hours, of course,' she hastily replied with a glance to the phone.

Rick wiped the air with one hand. 'I'm not complaining, really. I love it, to be honest. It's just that my partner can be ...' He stopped short of anything negative, aware of how Jon had loyally backed him against hostile colleagues and violent criminals alike. He thought about the time three drunken lads had targeted him in a dimly lit street on the edge of Manchester's Gay Village. Jon had stepped in without a moment's hesitation, blocking the first punch and then almost crushing the leader's windpipe with his other hand. 'Anyway, where were we?'

'Yes.' The younger one with the wavy blonde hair looked down at the piece of paper on her lap. 'We were wondering if you have much of an interest in sport? From the perspective of playing it.'

'Well,' Rick replied. 'Not as much as I'd have liked since graduating. I keep fit, mostly by visiting the gym downstairs; all residents are free to use it.'

'From where did you graduate, by the way?'

Rick's gaze moved to the one with the bob, slightly wrong-footed by her change of tack. 'Exeter. History and Law.'

'And,' she added, 'you're on the fast-track graduate scheme within the Major Incident Team, is that right?'

Christ, Rick thought, Sheila really has briefed them thoroughly. 'I am.'

'So you must have got a good class of degree?'

'A two one.'

She nodded approvingly. 'Firsts are too much work, no play. Makes Jack a dull boy.'

Rick tried to smile. Somehow the comment made him feel that he was little more than a specimen in the woman's eyes. 'True. To get back to your earlier question,' his eyes returned to the younger woman. 'I played hockey and tennis for my hall's team. And I joined the university rowing team in my first year, but that was a kind of hangover from my school days. I'd dropped it by my second year. Too many early-morning starts.'

'Where did you go to school, if you don't mind us asking?' Her pale eyebrows were raised encouragingly.

Is that really relevant? Rick thought, leaning forward and reaching for the stainless steel art deco teapot on the table between them. 'A little place down in Surrey. Charterfield?' The name drew a blank. 'There were only a thousand or so of us there. More tea?'

Their heads shook in unison.

'Boarding school, I take it?' the older one asked.

'Yes.' He examined their features for any of the usual reaction provoked by revealing he'd been schooled privately. Their faces remained neutral.

'So,' the blonde one continued cheerfully, 'after Charterfield you—'

'Sorry, Isabelle,' the older one cut in, looking at Rick. 'Which A levels did you take?'

Rick pointed to the computer in the corner. 'I could print you a copy of my CV, if you like,' he joked. 'I'm sure I'll have an earlier one knocking about that lists my GCSEs too.'

'Good idea,' the older one immediately replied. 'Would you mind?'

Rick got up, relieved to move away from them. This was all getting a bit much.

'It's a lovely place you've got here. Isn't it, Cathy?' Isabelle remarked.

'Yes,' the older woman replied. 'Very nice.'

He glanced round his apartment. Bare brick walls, polished wooden floors, exposed girders spanning the ceiling. 'It was a fruit warehouse in its day. Bananas, I think. The apartments on the floor below still have the mechanisms they used for winching the crates up.'

'Such great views of the city,' Cathy stated.

'Yup.' He didn't need to look out of the floor-to-ceiling windows before him to know that, on a clear day like this, you could see across the city, right to the faint smudge of Welsh hills on the western horizon.

He joggled the mouse to bring his screen to life, opened a folder, selected a version of his CV dating from the nineties and pressed print. The machine below his work station whirred before a single sheet of A4 slid out. Stepping back towards the sofa, he glanced over it. GCSEs in subjects that included Maths, English, History, Geography, Chemistry, Latin, Drama and Art. All A or B grades. Weird, he thought, how passing those things was the most important thing in my life at the time. They now seemed so trivial. 'There you go.'

'Thank you.' Isabelle smiled.

To Rick's relief, she didn't start poring over it there and then, but slid it into her plastic folder instead. Filed for later inspection.

'OK,' Isabelle said, now looking slightly hesitant. 'Could we run through a few questions relating to your health?'

Rick opened his palms as he retook his seat. 'Fire away.'

'Is there any history of major illness in your family? Cancer, heart disease, strokes, that kind of thing?'

'None that I'm aware of. Mum and Dad are both fit and well.'

She nodded, ticking a box on her sheet of paper. 'Mental illness?' she asked, head still bowed.

Shocked at the question, Rick looked to the older woman, but her eyes were glued to the form, too.

'No,' he replied.

'Great. And you're generally in good health?' Isabelle glanced up. 'You certainly look it to me.' Another smile.

'Yes, I'm fine. Obviously, with work, my fitness levels are monitored.'

The older woman cleared her throat. 'Could I ask if you take AIDS tests on a regular basis?'

Regular basis? Rick felt his face flush. This wasn't what he expected. Not at all.

'I'm sorry,' Isabelle interjected. 'It's a perfectly routine question with this sort of thing.'

'This sort of thing?' Rick repeated. 'Tell me, were you happy a few years ago when insurance companies could turn applicants down purely on the basis of them being gay?'

'No.' Embarrassed, the younger woman looked to the older one for support.

Adjusting her glasses, Cathy sat forwards, hand draped across her knee, fingers flicking to emphasise her speech. 'As Isabelle mentioned, it's routine. If you walked into any fertility clinic, it would be obliged to screen and quarantine any sperm you donate. It's a regulatory requirement to protect against sexually transmitted diseases and genetic disorders.'

Rick sat back. 'OK, fair enough. My partner and I both underwent an AIDS test when we started seeing each other year before last. And, before you ask, I haven't slept with any other men since.'

The younger one ticked a final box, laid the pen down on the sheet of paper, then placed her hand over the other woman's. 'Thanks for agreeing to see us. It's been a real struggle for us to get this far. I hope you can appreciate that?'

He nodded. 'I can. Sorry if I got a bit defensive just then.'

'No! Absolutely not. You're quite right; it's intrusive. But can you see things from our point of view?'

'Yes, I can.'

'Well,' Cathy clapped her palms on her thighs in readiness to get up. 'We should be going. Leave you to enjoy the rest of your Sunday.'

'It's certainly a nice day.' Rick stood and walked them over to the door. 'Sheila mentioned you're keen to get on with things.' He opened the door, not sure if he actually wanted to be part of the process any longer.

'That's right.' Cathy nodded eagerly. 'We're seeing one other person this afternoon and we'll make a decision in the next forty-eight hours.'

Rick blinked.

She caught his look of surprise. 'Didn't Sheila mention?'

'No, she didn't.'

'Sorry. Yes, another,' she raised her hands and double-dinked her fore and middle fingers, 'friend of a friend asked to be considered, too.'

Asked to be considered? Rick smarted at her choice of words. Who's doing who the favour, here?

'Don't worry,' she continued. 'We'll ask him exactly the same questions we did you!'

'OK.' Rick hoped his smile didn't appear as forced as it felt. 'Well, I look forward to hearing from you.'

They stepped out onto the landing and Isabelle held up a hand. 'Thanks, we'll be in contact soon.'

'Thanks!' Rick closed the door with a sense of relief. He turned round, not really seeing the room before him. Another bloke. He shook his head. Thirty seconds ago, I was ready to back out of this whole thing. But now they've mentioned someone else is in the running ... he rubbed at his chin, surprised at the competitive urge suddenly coursing through him.

Seven

Shazia paused at the station's rear doors and raised a despairing eyebrow at Spiers. 'Three o'clock on a bloody Sunday.'

She pulled the doors open, revealing the source of commotion beyond them. Jon recognised two of the uniformed officers from upstairs. They had hold of a youth, mid-teens at the most. A long fringe had flopped over his face and the buttons on his shirt were missing. As they marched him up to the doors, he writhed and struggled, kicking out at the walls to try and impede their progress.

'Get off me! Get the fuck off me!' Spit flew from his lips.

Shazia stepped out of the way. 'Sunday roast and then a few pills for pudding?'

Fighting to keep hold of an arm, one of the arresting officers replied through gritted teeth. 'So it would appear.'

The youngster looked up, eyes bright and glassy. 'Fuck you, Paki!'

Shazia shook her head. 'I'll pretend not to have heard that.'

The officers bent the youth almost double and forced him toward the cells.

Jon watched with a sense of disbelief. It wasn't the sleepy Peak District town he'd imagined it to be.

They walked over to a patrol car and Spiers pipped the locks. But once inside, rather than turn right down the high street, Spiers spun the wheel to the left.

Jon leaned across the back seat for a better view out the side window. 'I thought we'd be heading for the A6187.'

'No,' Shazia replied. 'We're going north towards the Manchester to Sheffield road. There's a turning off which leads us to Highshaw Hill, where your brother was found.'

The narrow road led out into the countryside, kinking and twisting as it negotiated the sharply rippled land. After about two miles they reached the A6013, a far busier road that led south towards Derby. Spiers waited for a couple of lorries to trundle past, then turned left and continued north.

Jon looked at the undulating fields bordering the far side of the road. Criss-crossing drystone walls divided them up, cows silently grazing in the nearest, sheep in the ones that were further away. Jon let his eyes follow the walls as they clung to the ever harsher terrain, eventually taking his gaze to the tops of the nearest hills with their crests of exposed rock. To their left, the land also rose upwards, coppices of pine trees separating swathes of moor.

The silence in the car had now lasted a good five minutes and Jon guessed the two constables weren't about to break it soon. There was no way he could squeeze them for more information if things remained as they were. He tried a little small talk. 'Is this all national park?'

Shazia nodded. 'Mostly. Some of that land on our left is privately owned.'

'Who by – the Royal Family?'

'Close. The Beaumonts. Back in the eighteen hundreds, Samuel Beaumont turned Haverdale from a cluster of shepherds' houses into what it is today. He built the watermill that powered the town's two cotton factories, paid for the school, library and original part of the hospital, too. He also built the Imperial when staying in spa towns was all the fashion, even extending the hospital into a sanatorium for wealthy, but sick, Londoners.'

Jon thought about the glass atrium he'd seen when looking for the mortuary. It had seemed too extravagant a feature for a town hospital. 'Where's the family pile, then?'

'To the west of the town, massive old place called Grinstay House. You see the gatehouse first, the driveway's about five hundred metres long. Big gardens, pool, stables, the lot. Not that they're around to enjoy it much.'

'How come?'

'They've got other places in Scotland and Devon. Plus a castle-type thing in Italy.'

'Old money then,' Jon replied.

'Proper aristocracy,' Spiers agreed. 'They come back each August for the grouse season and that's about it.'

'Apart from the son,' Shazia cut in. 'What's his name?'

'William.'

Jon caught Spiers' sneering tone. 'Trouble, is he?'

'Just a Hooray Henry. Too thick to get into university, so they paid for a place at an agricultural college near Sheffield. He comes back some weekends with a few mates, driving around in his Aston Martin, playing Lord of the Manor.'

'He drives an Aston Martin?' Jon asked. 'That's serious money.'

Shazia turned in her seat. 'The parents are lovely, but he's a little so-and-so. They don't let him stay in the main house after he held a party that got out of hand. We were called out in the early hours. They were chugging back wine from the cellar that apparently cost over four hundred quid a bottle. Now he's got the keys to the gatehouse and that's it.'

'How awful, making him rough it in there,' Jon murmured.

Spiers indicated left and started to slow. At the head of a small side lane was a uniformed officer, his car parked on the grass verge. Spiers turned into the lane and lowered a window. 'All right, Steve? We're heading up to the crime scene.'

'Right you are.'

The lane led into a pine wood, ending at a gate some two hundred metres later. Yellow crime-scene tape sectioned off the last ten metres, stretching up each side of the gravel track beyond. Parked under the trees to their right was a white van. Scene of Crime Unit, Jon concluded as they climbed out. He breathed in the fresh woodland scent, listening to the twitter of unseen birds. The tops of the pine trees combed the gentle breeze, creating a low and constant sigh. It should have been a pleasant place to pause and take in.

Jon frowned at the ground beyond the yellow tape. Thick tyre tracks had gouged the soft mud immediately before the gate. Beyond the barrier were just two sets of tracks. 'That's where the rangers drove up on their quad bikes?' asked Jon.

'Yes,' Spiers replied, approaching the stile at its side. 'We cross here, the Common Approach Path is to the side of the track proper.'

As Jon climbed over he noticed the 'Right to Roam' emblem tacked to the gate post. 'So we're in the national park now?'

'Yup. The Beaumonts' land borders the edge of this conifer plantation.'

They continued in single file, walking to the side of the track with its faint tyre marks. Every ten metres or so, a waist-high plastic pole had been driven into the ground and yellow crime-scene tape twisted through the loop at the top. The ground started rising more sharply and Jon could see the end of the wood ahead.

A minute later they reached the tree line and the cordon of tape finished. Jon studied the rough moorland beyond. First the track led through a carpet of dead bracken, then, after around thirty metres, it reached shaggy grass that was dotted with the odd patch of heather. By the crest of the hill, the track had narrowed to a thin path.

'Where's the Common Approach Path now?' Jon asked.

'Here,' Spiers replied, stepping onto the track itself. 'We've been over it from this point to the summit. Nothing but tyre tracks from the rangers' quad bikes and an empty crisp packet.'

Slack, Jon thought. Very slack. Crime-scene protocol dictated officers took the approach least likely to have been used by the offender. They continued up, Jon's eyes fixed on the heels of Spiers' shoes, keeping in time with the other man's step.

A burst of motion to their left and two grouse erupted from the heather, stubby wings beating furiously as they cut low across the moor, emitting metallic cries of alarm as they went. Jon was beginning to breathe a little more heavily when Spiers stepped to the side. 'Almost there.'

Jon looked around. The crest they were standing on levelled off slightly before rising to another. When they reached that, Jon glanced to each side. Another band of level ground appeared to circle the summit. 'This looks like it could be man-made,' Jon observed.

'That's because it is,' Shazia replied behind him. 'You're standing on the upper defences of a bronze-age hill fort. Three thousand or so years ago, this would have been a walled ditch.'

Jon raised his eyebrows. 'So it's an archaeological site, then?'

'Yes,' she answered. 'But one that's been thoroughly excavated during Victorian times. The only thing you might find nowadays is the odd microlith – flint objects like scrapers.'

Jon looked up, realising the top of a white hood was visible above the long grass ahead. They climbed the final section of path and the rest of the forensics officer was slowly revealed. To his side a colleague was on all fours, collecting samples from the muddy patch that topped the hill. They were working inside a ring of yellow tape that fluttered in the light breeze. A uniformed officer stood watching at the side.

Jon studied the scene in silence, eyes on the exposed soil. 'I thought it was all peat round these parts.'

'Not quite,' Shazia answered, brushing a strand of black hair that had caught on her lower lip. 'We're at the edge of a horseshoe-shaped band of millstone grit, but below us it's actually limestone. A few hundred metres west and south are some pretty impressive cliffs, and stretching beyond them are the peat bogs and acid grasslands you're thinking of.'

'You all geology experts out here?' he asked, adding a half-smile to show the question wasn't serious.

One hand swept dramatically outward. 'You have to understand the rock, otherwise it's like listening to poetry in an unknown language. You hear the beauty, but you miss the meaning.'

'Did you just make that up?'

'I wish.' She smiled.

Jon's grin fell away as he turned back to the crime scene itself. He stared at the clotted stain at its centre. Dave's blood, pints of it. A close-up image of an arm wielding a saw. He lifted his eyes, regarding the land as it stretched away in a series of similar hills, the tops of more pine trees visible behind the nearest. Away to his right, the A6013 followed a shallow curve along the lower part of the moor. A motorbike was speeding along it, gaining quickly on a slow-moving lorry. The bike hovered a moment at the vehicle's rear bumper, then jinked out to swiftly overtake. A second later the sound of its throttle opening up reached Jon's ears.

So, he asked himself, what actually are you trying to achieve here? You're going to find your brother's killer – and then what? After all, you found the man who abused Dave and you killed him. What will you do when you find the person who sawed him into little pieces?

Silencing the voice in his head, he turned back to the crime scene, making an effort to study it as he would any other. To the left of the forensics officer on all fours were signs of recent digging. 'That wasn't you, I take it?'

The one standing up turned his head. 'Sorry?'

'The digging.' Jon nodded at it, taking out his ID. 'Detective Inspector Jon Spicer, Greater Manchester Police.'

'It was his brother – the person found up here,' Shazia hurriedly added. 'DI Spicer is helping us with some questions about him.'

The forensics officer trudged closer, white overshoes forcing him to step higher in the grass. A spaceman, Jon thought, trekking across the surface of another planet.

'Your brother was the murder victim?'

'He was.'

'I'm really sorry.' He looked back over his shoulder. 'No, we haven't touched that spot.'

Jon narrowed his eyes. The quad bikes' tracks ended where the grass died away. Dotting the soil was a variety of impressions – shoe prints, the clove-shaped dents left by sheep, semicircular depressions left by a horse's shoes. 'Are all those tracks recent?' Jon asked no one in particular.

Spiers spoke up at his side. 'Last heavy rain was lunchtime yesterday. We reckon it's fair to assume they are.'

Jon's eyes roved the edge of the clearing. 'No sign of the implement used for the digging?'

'No,' Spiers responded. 'Or the weapon used to ... used by the killer.'

Jon glanced at him. 'Apart from the body, clothing and mobile phone, what else was in the bin bags?'

'Well, as we mentioned, the first one was partially burned. The remains of a sweatshirt were recovered from the incinerator, along with the actual ... you know ...'

I do, Jon thought. 'And the other two bin bags?'

'One had the trousers with the mobile phone inside, the other was just ... there was no clothing in that one.'

'No footwear?'

'No.'

'Though that stands to reason, doesn't it?' stated Shazia. Jon looked at her. 'If you're making it look like the remains of a deer,' she continued, 'you're not going to put shoes in.'

'You're right,' Jon replied, eyes back on the ground that surrounded the crime scene tape. Heather and mats of bilberry bushes clung in every dip. 'So, whoever did this left the scene carrying Dave's shoes, a spade and a saw at the very least. How far is it to Haverdale from here?'

'Three, three and a half miles,' Spiers replied.

'So, we're assuming the killer – or killers – didn't walk back. In which case they drove out here with Dave, parked at the gate at the bottom and walked up.'

'Yes, the tyre tracks suggest that. Certainly no vehicle except the park rangers' quad bikes went further than the gate.' Shazia nodded.

'Who else has used that lane in the last twenty-four hours?'

'Along with the forensics' van, just us when we came to seal off the area. As far as we know.'

'And you parked right in front of the gate?'

'Yes.'

Obliterating any earlier tyre tracks, Jon thought. Idiots. 'This horse rider. Where did she come from?'

Shazia pointed to the next hill on their left. 'Round Knoll. There's a bridle path to it from the village. It leads over to here and then on into the national park.'

Jon followed the direction of her finger as it pointed to the undulating land that stretched away before them.

'And these digs, the ones mentioned in the local paper. Wasn't one on Round Knoll?'

'Yes, the most recent.'

'Where were the others?'

Shazia looked at Spiers. 'I'm sure the first was Rebellion Hill, wasn't it?'

He nodded. 'Yeah.'

'That hill overlooks Haverdale itself. Just a quick walk up from the town centre.' She looked at her colleague again. 'Then was it Sharston Edge?'

'Yes, and after that Toot Hill beside it.'

'Where are they?' Jon asked.

Spiers gestured behind them. 'Other side of Haverdale.'

'Also walkable from the town centre?'

'Easily.'

'Have you plotted these digs on a map?'

Shazia shook her head. 'It's hardly been a priority. Not with the recent stuff kicking off in town.'

Maybe not to you, Jon thought. He started walking round the crime-scene's perimeter, examining the ground for any signs of disturbance. Sheep droppings peppered the wiry grass that shifted in the breeze. He'd nearly got back to where he'd started from when he spotted the horse's hoof marks in the aisle between two patches of heather. They led to what was little more than a sheep trail which dropped down the hill towards the wood they'd emerged from earlier. 'Did the horse rider return to Haverdale this way?'

Shazia followed him along. 'I'm not sure. I can check when we get back to the station. I have her number there.'

'Where does this path lead?'

'Back to the Haverdale road, by the looks of it.'

Jon thought about the numerous bends they'd negotiated to get here. 'Not the safest route back if you're on a horse. Are you sure?'

'Chris! Where do you reckon this trail leads? Back to the road?'

Spiers ambled over, hands in his pockets. 'Don't know.'

Jon followed the semicircular impressions for about five metres, then stopped. A tyre track was clearly visible in the soft soil. He crouched down, eyes on the fan-shaped curve where a motorbike had been parked up, its front wheel turned to the side. Just behind it was a sharp gouge. The point where the bike's stand had been lowered. Is this how you got up here, Dave? he thought. On the back of someone's bike? If it was I'm looking for just one man. The person who drove this machine. 'Can you get forensics over?'

As Spiers walked quickly back up the path, Jon leaned forward on his knuckles. Moisture rose up through the grass by the side of the thin path, probing at the creases of his curled fingers. The rear tyre had left a good imprint, a section of the diamond-shaped tread clearly visible.

'What have you got?'

He turned to see the forensics officer standing behind him. 'A tyre mark. Motorbike, at a guess. Can you take a cast?'

The man looked uneasy. 'It's been a while ...'

'Your colleague, then?'

'I'm training her, afraid not.'

Jon stood. 'There's a crime-scene manager I've worked with many times.' His mind went back to the Butcher of Belle Vue case, when Nikki Kingston had captured a perfect cast of the killer's footprint. 'I can give her a call. She could be here in no time; and do the main crime scene for you as well.'

The forensics officer hesitated. 'I'm not really sure about that. It would raise complicated budgeting issues.' He looked at Spiers.

The constable registered the glance. 'Yeah. We'd need to clear it with the Super first.'

Jon shook his head, taking his mobile out. 'There'll be no charge. I'll see to that.'

'Even so ...' the forensics officer blustered.

'Listen, mate,' Jon said, turning to face him. 'This won't affect your chain of command. She'll take the casts, give them to you and go back to her own work, OK?'

Without waiting for a reply, he brought Nikki's number

up and pressed green. As the phone started to ring he glanced at Spiers. 'We'll need to know where this path goes as well. Reckon the park rangers might know?'

Rick followed the narrow flagstone alley down the side of Sinclair's Oyster Bar, emerging into the relatively spacious surroundings of Manchester Cathedral. The squat brown building lay on the other side of a lawned area, tower made stubby through the absence of a spire. He turned away from the dark lattice-work windows lining its side and walked towards the cathedral's front end.

A shallow flight of stone steps led down to a pair of wooden doors. The notice at their side announced he was at the entrance to the Booth Centre. Voices could be heard within, someone asking impatiently for 'the bastard sugar'.

He pushed the right-hand door open and looked inside. A couple of rows of formica tables, serving hatch to the kitchen, an IT suite off to the side, computers lining its walls. Looking back at the formica tables, Rick glanced over the people sitting round them. Only two women, both well past their twenties. He looked at the assortment of men. Some were bowed over their brews, methodically working their way through plates of biscuits, others were constructing roll-up cigarettes. One was simply staring at his upturned palms, as if reflecting on the whereabouts of some possession that had slipped from his grasp. Yeah, Rick thought, your life. You poor bastard.

He caught the enquiring look of a woman, apron tied around her middle, pot of tea in her hand. Giving a little smile, Rick approached, knowing his well-cut suit and tidy hair had already created a favourable impression. Once up close, he spoke quietly. 'Hi there, I wonder if you'd mind me asking one or two questions of your visitors?'

She cocked her head, eyes still on him. Reading the question in her eyes, Rick mouthed, 'I'm a policeman.'

With a glance towards the serving hatch, she said. 'Best you check with Norman. He's in charge.'

'Thanks.' Rick poked his head through into the kitchen area.

The man he remembered from when they were searching for the arsonist was standing at a central table arranging sandwiches on several plates.

Rick slid his warrant card out. 'Mr Green, isn't it? We met briefly, though it was well over a year ago. I don't know if you remember.'

The man looked up, then his eyes moved to the side, searching what he could see of the room beyond the hatch. 'Where's your big brute of a partner?'

Rick winced at the memory. After chasing the suspected arsonist round the cathedral, they'd trapped him in a side porch. Jon had been less than subtle with his method of arrest. 'He's not here.'

'And so what brings you back?'

'Same sort of thing, I'm afraid. Trying to track down someone who's giving us cause for concern.'

Green harrumphed at the choice of words. 'I trust, if you find your man, you won't express that concern again by frog-marching him out of here?'

Rick slipped his warrant card back into his jacket. 'Not my style. And it's a woman, not a man. She's called Zoe, late twenties, straight black hair?'

'Zoe?' The man narrowed his eyes. 'There was a Zoe who popped in here for a bit. She was a heavy user. But that was months back.'

Rick held a hand above his forearm and lowered an imaginary plunger into it.

Green nodded. 'Pretty much standard with much of this lot, I'm afraid. Heroin, crack, they're exposed to everything that's washing through the streets. Here,' he handed a plate of sand-wiches over, 'make yourself useful while you're asking about.'

'No problem.' Rick took them and surveyed the main room. In the far corner a man was sitting on his own, a green and white striped ski hat on his head. Celtic? Rick wondered. There was no beard on the bloke, but that didn't mean it wasn't Jock. He wandered across, offering the plate to people as he passed. One picked a sandwich off the pile, peeled it open to reveal the fish paste inside and then tossed it into the centre of the table.

Rick reached the guy in the corner. He appeared to be somewhere in his twenties, but the deep grooves channelling down from his eyes made it hard to say for sure. 'Sandwich?'

His glance fell off the side of the plate. 'Nah.'

Definitely a Scottish accent, Rick thought. He made a show of looking round the room. 'Have you seen Zoe?'

The man's head stayed down. 'No.'

The answer was out almost before Rick had asked the question. He tried again. 'Zoe, black hair and the pointy teeth. Like a vampire's.'

'How should I know?'

The answer left Rick stumped. 'How should you know if you've seen her?'

'You what?'

Shit, this wasn't going well. The bloke was already getting agitated. Rick sat down. 'She used to come here. Zoe, you remember her, don't you?'

The man leaned forward, placed his elbows on his knees and worked a thumb into his palm, digging down at the flesh. 'I don't know any Zoe.'

'I just thought, you know, because she popped in all the time.'

The man's arms had stiffened. One more question, Rick thought, and he's going to erupt. Rick stood up and stepped away, ears cocked for any other Scottish accents. None. He gave a cough. 'Anyone seen Zoe in here recently?'

Conversations paused and a few people looked in his direction. Heads went back down and murmurs resumed. Rick placed the plate on the nearest table. Finding this woman, he thought as he walked back out the door, is going to be a total nightmare.

Eight

As they followed the road back to Haverdale, Jon studied the summits of the nearest hills with new interest. 'Are there many archaeological sites like that hill fort around here, then?'

Shazia spoke over her shoulder. 'Dozens.'

'Like what?'

'There's another hill fort, called Mam Tor, about seven miles north-west of here. But the whole region's been inhabited since prehistoric times. Chambered cairns, stone circles, burial grounds. It's riddled with them.'

'But they've all been excavated?'

'The Victorians were really into it. Like in India, they'd just rip into a site with spades. Anything of value got taken away years ago.' She gave an impish grin. 'My dad's spent dozens of Sundays trying to get some pay-back by going over these parts with a metal detector. He's never found a thing.'

Somehow, Jon couldn't see her father also being in the force. Asian police officers were still a relatively new phenomenon. 'What does your dad do for a living?'

'He's retired, now. Used to run a dental practice in town. It always confused me when his patients called him doctor. But there's a joke around these parts that goes like this: what do you call a dark-skinned man if he's not serving you a Big Mac?' She paused for a beat. 'Doctor. You have to laugh.' She grinned over her shoulder.

Jon thought back to the abuse which had been directed at her as they'd left the station. He shrugged. 'Or you could just arrest them.'

'I could.'

He sat back, impressed at her ability to handle people's racist attitudes so well. He wasn't sure he could keep that kind of control. His thoughts turned back to Dave. *I could just imagine you out here on some pea-brained plan, digging for buried treasure. You bloody idiot.* He stared out of the window, noticing the clusters of spiky reeds that thrived in the slight hollows of the surrounding fields. They looked like colonies of sea urchins on an ocean floor. 'So, we're going to make it back to the visitor centre in time?'

Spiers rotated a wrist to glance at his watch. 'Just. They lock up at five.'

Jon thought about Nikki, working her magic on the hill top in the fading afternoon light. A track cut a corridor into the pine woods on his right. 'That looks like a path we just passed.'

Spiers' eyes went to the side mirror. 'That? Fire break. They criss-cross the plantation, but they're not public rights of way.'

Like you'd care about that if you're trying to leave a murder scene undetected, Jon thought. 'This poaching arrangement you described to me before. Assuming our bike-rider is a suspect, he's got knowledge of the trails around here. He also knows all about the poaching arrangement, seeing as he was trying to use it as a way to dispose of my brother's body.'

He watched the backs of the constables' heads turn slightly as they exchanged a glance.

'Mallin showed me the transcript of the woman's call to Dave's mobile. She was asking about a Redino. Familiar?'

Spiers let out a sigh. 'We're not supposed to be discussing any details with you. We shouldn't even be taking you to see the rangers.'

Mallin, Jon thought. *Guarding the case like it's a toy he doesn't want to share.* 'It's my brother, for Christ's sake.' He waited, letting the silence get uncomfortable.

Eventually Shazia half turned her head. 'We've never heard the name before.'

By now they were entering Haverdale itself. They passed the police station, and continued down the high street. Jon looked at a couple chatting happily at the counter of a takeaway pizzeria. It seemed hard to believe this rural community was beginning to struggle with an influx of hard drugs. The place seemed so nice. But then, he realised, he was looking at it from a visitor's perspective. The mindset of a holidaymaker, here for a leisurely break away from it all.

It must be different for the people who live here on a permanent basis, watching the numbers of visitors to the town rise and fall with the holiday seasons. The long, quiet months of autumn and winter, hotels barely full, fruit machines blinking across empty pubs. The mind-numbing wait for the next flurry of tourists or gaggle of businessmen.

They took the second turning on the left towards the library. The National Park visitor centre was opposite, a single-storey building with low sloping roof sections that, instead of tiles, were covered in a living layer of moss and grass. Wooden signs in the car park pointed to a camping area to the side of the building. A few dome tents were huddled in one corner. Two men in walking gear were dismantling one, packing up as their weekend of hiking drew to a close.

The visitor centre doors opened on a large, open-plan room. In the middle of the floor was a waist-high platform topped by a three dimensional map of the region. Jon glanced at the place names dotting the ridges and bumps: Glossop, Buxton, Chapel-en-le-Frith, Castleton, Bamford, Bakewell. Displays lined the walls, many with colour photos of the flora and fauna that lived in the unspoilt terrain. Jon saw images of grouse, white hares, barn owls, peregrine falcons, water voles and adders. In the corner was a separate display entitled 'Osprey Watch'. A small monitor stood on a table, the screen frozen on what appeared to be the top of a pine tree.

Spiers spoke at his side. 'Robert, hi there. Could I introduce you to someone?'

Jon turned to his right. Behind several stands displaying maps, walking guides and postcards, was a wiry man in his fifties. He wore hiking boots with red flashes at the side, dark brown trousers and a red fleece. On its left breast were the words: Park Ranger.

The man moved with a lightness of step and, as they shook

hands, Jon was impressed with the firmness of his grip. Probably a fell runner, he thought. 'DI Jon Spicer, Greater Manchester Police.' He waited for Shazia to qualify the introduction.

'It was Jon's younger brother who was killed,' she stated quietly behind him.

The man's eyes were bright and clear in his weathered face. 'Your brother? I'm very sorry to hear that.'

'Thank you. I gather you and a colleague collected the bin bags?'

'Yes.' He turned to the partially open rear doors. 'Michael! Have you got a second?'

A moment later, a younger man stepped through them, wiping his hands clean on an oily rag. As he approached, Jon saw he was wearing an identical uniform to his older colleague. This man was in his early twenties by the look of him, taller and heavier, brown hair in a neat side-parting. The tilt of his eyebrows lent him a slightly apprehensive air as he nodded curtly at Shazia and Spiers, directed his eyes at Jon and did the same.

'You OK, Michael?' Shazia asked, a note of concern in her voice.

'Yes.' He glanced at his colleague. 'She's running perfectly again, now. Buggered if I know what's up with her.'

The older one shrugged. 'Quad bikes for you.'

'I know you were about to lock up,' Shazia interjected, 'so we won't keep you long. It's been a long day for the both of you.' She flicked a glance at Jon.

'Yes,' Jon added. 'A few questions, that's all.'

The two rangers had the look of competitors entering the last stage of an endurance test. Just one more hurdle, Jon thought, and you're home. 'We spotted a trail leading down off Highshaw Hill. It wasn't the main path leading up from the A6013, but it seemed to be heading down towards the road.'

The older ranger looked at his colleague, a frown on his face. 'That'll be the plantation track, won't it? Crossing the Beaumonts' land.'

'Sounds like it.'

The older ranger stepped over to the relief map in the middle of the room. 'Here's the A6013 and Highshaw Hill. This path dropped down in a southerly direction?'

Spiers bent forward. 'Yes, to the side of Round Knoll.'

'Plantation track,' Robert nodded. 'It merges with an old holloway. A path worn by the trains of pack horses that carried down lead and stone from medieval times.'

'Where does it go?' Jon asked.

Robert traced a finger round the edge of the dark green patch that indicated the plantation of conifers. He tapped a blunt fingernail at a point just to the side of the high street as it left the village. 'Here, not a hundred metres from the police station.'

'Could you get a motorbike along it?'

The rangers looked at one another.

'I reckon so,' replied Michael, the younger one. 'The main gate is locked, but the smaller side one isn't. I know horse riders coming down off the tops pass through it.'

'How Mrs Phillips, who spotted the bin bags in the first place, could have returned?' Shazia asked.

Both rangers gave agreeing nods.

'Great, thanks,' Jon said, eyes returning to the map. 'What are the black dots on the hills?'

'Potholes,' the older ranger replied. 'Do you know much about the geology of the area?'

'I'm learning. Limestone, isn't it?'

'Correct. Carboniferous limestone. One hundred and fifty metres of crushed coral and seashells, riddled with potholes, caves and old mine shafts. I was saying to Michael earlier, a far better place to get rid of a body.'

His younger colleague coughed awkwardly. 'He's right. You know – sorry to say.'

Jon waved the comment aside. 'Don't worry.'

'Many don't feature on any map, you see,' Robert continued. 'Not even the Ordnance Surveys. Mine shafts from God-knows-when, bunged up centuries ago with rock. Sometimes the plug falls in and you've got another hole.'

Jon crossed his arms. 'Interesting. I was assuming the killer had local knowledge, seeing as this arrangement you have with

71

the poachers was being used by him to dispose of the body
...' He paused, aware that Robert's eyes kept cutting across to
Michael, who was shifting from foot to foot like a schoolboy
needing the toilet.

'Sorry, Detective. Could Michael get going?'

'It's my mum,' the younger man blurted. 'Sundays is her bridge
night, in the community centre. I need to drive her there.'

Jon swivelled round. 'Sorry, mate, I said only a few questions.
You get going, and thanks for your help.'

He hurried over to the counter and unhooked a red jacket
from the row of pegs on the wall. 'Be seeing you,' he called
out, quickly slipping through the rear doors and into the dusk
beyond.

Robert waited for the doors to swing shut. 'Poor lad. This
business really shook him up. Never known anything like it.'
His eyes skittered across Jon's face. 'With all due respect.'

Jon found himself waving another comment away. 'Of course.
So, these poachers – where does the venison they butcher end
up?'

'All round the place. Pubs, restaurants, hotels. Anywhere with
game on the menu. Ask and the general answer is it's legally
sourced from the managed herd on the Lyme Park estate at
Disley. But that meat comes at a premium, poached stuff is half
the price.'

Jon drummed his fingers on the edge of the giant map. 'How
can you tell the difference?'

'Once it's cooked, you can't. You need to see it in the fridges.
Lyme Park stuff comes in shrink-wrapped packages, properly
labelled. Poached meat will be in ugly great lumps, wrapped in
greaseproof paper, freezer bags or something similar.'

'And who are these poachers?'

The ranger rubbed his chin. 'Chris, Shazia? Who do you
reckon they are?'

Spiers pursed his lips. 'There hasn't been a prosecution for
poaching in years. It'll be local people who're short of money,
needing a few quid to see them through. I doubt many are at it
on a regular basis.'

'No, I imagine they're not,' Robert agreed. 'We collect the bin bags once, twice a month at most. Can't see it being a main source of income for anyone, that's for sure.'

'And this morning,' Jon asked. 'There was nothing to suggest anything was out of the ordinary?'

'No. The bags were on the top of the hill. We took the quad bikes up and just slung them ...' He swallowed. 'Put them on the carry platforms at the rear. A couple of ties to secure them and we were at the kennels half an hour later.'

'Where the incinerator is?'

'That's right. We've used it for years. Fox, deer, mink, crows. The odd hound, too, when they sicken and die.'

Jon pictured a squat construction fashioned from sooty bricks with a blackened grate. A burning place for vermin and dogs. He clenched his teeth, waiting for the surge of anger to pass. Looking back at the ranger, he caught him glancing at the clock on the wall. Suddenly the details of his brother's death sickened him and he didn't want to be there, either. 'Well, thanks for your help, Robert, it's really appreciated.'

The man bowed his head. 'Glad if it's been any use. And sorry to meet you in these circumstances.'

'Me, too,' Jon answered, turning for the exit. Out in the cark park, Shazia's phone began to ring.

'Hello, Sarge. Where are we? Outside the visitor centre. Just following up a couple of things with Robert Wood and Michael Lumm. They are? OK, we'll be there in a minute.' She closed her phone and looked at Jon. 'Forensics have just turned up at the station. Your colleague's taken a whole pile of casts, much to Mallin's annoyance, I gather.'

Nine

They entered the main room at Haverdale police station and Jon saw everyone was gathered round a table in its middle. He watched the petite form of Nikki as she laid out her evidence bags on the wooden surface. Each one contained the lumpy white form of a plaster cast.

Thank God she's back to her old self, he thought. He reflected on how involving her too closely in a previous investigation had led to their nightmare experience on Saddleworth moor: racing back to his car with something dark and malevolent in pursuit. She'd been signed off with stress for almost half a year and it was that long again before her confidence had fully returned.

There was a note of scepticism in Mallin's voice as he prodded at the bag nearest to him. 'So, what did you use to make these things again?'

'Denstone KD,' Nikki replied a little too curtly.

'Oh,' Mallin shot a pleased glance at his crime-scene manager. 'Isn't Crownstone the best stuff to use?'

Nikki sighed. 'Some prefer Crownstone. I go for Denstone KD.'

I wonder, thought Jon, if they've been putting you through this bullshit all afternoon?

With the dozen or so casts now in a row, she pushed straggles of black hair away from her forehead. The thick locks shortened in length away from her face, ending at a bob at the back of her neck. The style gave her a boyish look which contrasted sharply with the authority in her voice. 'Now, it's a hard one to call. Definitely three sets of footprints. These partials, to me, indicate one more.'

'So a total of four people at the crime?' Mallin asked his CSM, turning away from Nikki.

The man rubbed the knuckle of a finger across his lips. 'I'd say those partials are two different sets of prints.'

'So five, not four, people,' Mallin stated.

Nikki shook her head, eyes still on the table. 'No, four. The markings around the heel area look pretty much identical to me. And see that V-shaped bump on the inner edge? That suggests a nick in the sole of the boot. It occurs on most of the partials we've got.'

'Well,' responded the CSM, 'we'll have to agree to disagree on that.'

'Are two sets of the prints made by the same type of sole?' Jon asked across the room. All eyes turned to him and he saw Nikki puff out her cheeks. Exasperation and relief in one gesture.

'Yes,' she said, fighting back the beginnings of a smile. Support had arrived. 'These two. Maybe a size eleven and a size nine.'

'I think you'll find those belong to the park rangers,' Jon replied, approaching the table. 'The uniform includes the same type of hiking boot.'

'Ah.' Nikki divided off four of the casts and looked at the remainder. 'So that leaves these.'

'Did you get an impression of the tyre track?' Jon's eyes searched the bags for a long thin strip of plaster. Each cast was marked with that day's date and the initials NK.

'For what it's worth.' She gestured at the end of the row. There was no more than thirty centimetres of white cast inside the bag.

'But you got one,' Jon said. 'So, modes of transport at the crime scene appear to be the rangers' quad bikes, and an un-known motorbike. A ranger on each bike ...' He let his voice trail off, not bothering to state that motorbikes were good for a maximum of two, not three people. Therefore Nikki's estima-tion of four people being at the crime scene would be correct. From the expression on Mallin's face, it was obvious he'd done the maths too.

He turned to his constables. 'Did the horse rider, Mrs Phillips, dismount at the scene?'

Shazia shook her head. 'No.'

Give up, Jon thought. Your CSM was wrong, and you know it.

Mallin pondered the table for a few more moments. 'Thank you for your assistance, Miss Kingsley.'

'Kingston,' she corrected.

'Kingston.' The smile barely lifted his lips before it vanished. 'We'll get this over to our lab in Sheffield. I'm sure the specialists there can provide us with some definitive answers in due course.' He gestured towards the CSM, who reached out both arms and began sweeping the bags towards him like a winning poker player.

'Careful.' Nikki's hands fluttered protectively. 'They won't be properly set for another twenty hours.'

The man lightened his touch as he began to place them in stacks and Mallin rubbed his hands together. He seemed to suddenly discover the presence of a watch on his wrist. 'Well, I'd expect you two will want to start making the trek back to Manchester. It's been a pleasure.' He briefly shook with Nikki, then turned to Jon. 'DI Spicer.'

Jon held the superintendent's hand in his grip. 'How did your enquiries go this afternoon? Anything more on this Redino character?'

Mallin shrugged. 'Nothing so far, in Sheffield or Manchester. Nothing on the database either, general search or narcotics offences.' He pulled gently, trying to extricate his fingers.

That, Jon thought, is because this isn't about drugs, you fool. He relaxed his grip, letting Mallin's hand escape. 'And the phone records for Zoe?'

Mallin was stepping away, one arm held towards the doors. 'Maybe Tuesday. Most people don't work on Sundays, DI Spicer and it's a bank holiday tomorrow. Now, if you'll excuse us, we have a lot of work to get through before then ourselves.'

Twat, Jon thought, reluctantly letting himself be herded

76

towards the exit. 'OK. Would you keep me updated on any developments?'

'Of course, we maintain regular contact with the family in cases like this.' That smile again, genuine as an alligator's grin.

Jon waited as Nikki grabbed her carry case. They walked the length of the corridor in silence and were halfway down the stairs before she spoke. 'I felt about as welcome as a fart in a lift.'

'Yeah, sorry. I didn't have time to explain the politics.'

'What, Brian Salt being a total waste of space?'

'Was that his name, the crime-scene manager?'

'Yup. He did a stint with Greater Manchester Police. Lasted less than two years. I knew he'd applied for a more rural posting. Surprised he didn't work the scene in his pipe and slippers. Lazy bastard then, lazy bastard now.'

'Bloody great,' Jon said, holding up a hand with his thumb and forefinger barely apart. 'So, paired with Mallin, prospects for an effective investigation are about this big.'

'Are you helping out?'

He snorted. 'You heard him back there. It's thank you and good night for the pair of us.'

They reached the bottom of the stairs and as he held the door open for her, she paused and placed a hand on his arm. Memories instantly flared. The kiss they'd shared in the Bull's Head when she'd cracked the forensics on the Butcher of Belle Vue case. Their bodies colliding as they'd clambered over a ditch while investigating the Monster of the Moor. The way she's clung to him before he finally broke away. For God's sake, Jon. You're using this woman. Playing on the fact she fancies you to get her help.

'I didn't really have the chance to say earlier. I'm so sorry about your brother. I can't imagine how you feel.'

He nodded at the empty corridor. 'Cheers.'

She let her hand slide down towards his elbow. A gentle squeeze and contact was gone. 'You never mentioned him.' She set off in front.

'No. We weren't the best of mates. Sadly.'

They walked on into the reception which was now empty of people, opened the door to the street and stepped outside. Night-time proper, streetlights casting their orange glow. A bus trundled past, empty except for the driver. 'Where are you parked?' he asked.

'Next to yours.'

They walked to the left-hand side of the car park. The back seat of her BMW Mini was folded down and Jon could see her cases inside. He thought about Salt's gloating expression as he gathered in the plaster casts. 'Did you get back-ups?'

'Of course,' she replied matter-of-factly, pipping the lock.

'Including the motorbike tyre?'

'That's what you asked for.' She lifted the rear hatch. 'But as I said in there, it's hardly worth shit. Thirty centimetres max, less than a fifteen per cent revolution of the wheel.' She glanced at him. 'Oh, don't give me your hang-dog look.'

'Surely there's a chance something will stand out?'

'The tread print is good, I'll give you that.' She placed her carry case in the car. 'But on first glance, I didn't spot anything else.'

'So you should be able to identify the brand of tyre?'

'Yes, but without any mould characteristics, not the actual batch.'

'What about those other things you look for ... incidentals?'

'Accidentals. Wear and tear marks on the tyre itself. I'll try. But again, don't hold your breath.' She closed the boot. 'The footwear casts are good, though. I doubt Salt will get round to it, so I'll put them on SICAR first thing tomorrow.'

'That being?'

'Shoeprint Image Capture and Retrieval. Get me the footwear of your suspect and I'll tell you if he was at the crime scene that night.'

'Great, Nikki. Thanks for coming out here on your weekend and all that. I really appreciate it.'

'Something tells me we're not driving back to Manchester in tandem.'

He turned towards the town's modest centre, studying the

huddled rows of houses, trails of smoke rising from the odd chimney. 'I'm staying here.'

'Who with?'

'Hotel,' Jon answered, an image of the Haven Inn his brother used in his mind's eye.

He could see the information sinking in and was careful not to make eye contact. When she spoke, there was a cautionary note in her voice. 'You think that's a good idea? The welcome here was hardly the warmest I've ever had.'

Jon thought about Mallin's blinkered and defensive attitude, Spiers' and Batyra's caginess and Salt's lacklustre skills. This is my brother they're writing off as some worthless drug dealer. My little brother. His glance bounced off the lit windows on the station's first floor. 'Fuck them. There's a shed–load of questions I want answering before I leave this dismal little shithole.'

'Here you go.' She tightened the cap on the stubby bottle, then bent down and handed it to him.

His little face beamed, eyes sparkling in their sunken holes as he raised it to his lips. After a few gulps, he had to release the teat to take a quick succession of breaths. The crackling in his chest had grown stronger and, for a crazy moment, she pictured a nest of spiders, weaving an ever-thickening web inside his lungs.

To her relief, he began drinking again, and when he paused for air, his breathing didn't sound quite as laboured. Maybe I'm being paranoid, she thought, pointing towards the front room. '*Teletubbies*?'

Slowly, he crawled off in the direction of the telly, bottle gripped in one hand. With a sigh, she held the milk carton up. Half a litre. That would barely see them through the morning. She opened a cupboard, searching for an alternative to cereals. Something that didn't need to be mixed with milk.

A packet of Cup-a-Soups, a tin of tuna, some pasta. A can of spaghetti. Half a bag of sugar. Bottles of ketchup and brown sauce. Dave's brown sauce. Her shoulders sagged. Shit, where are you? The next cupboard held a box of honey nut loops and

79

a tin of tomatoes. Beside them was a sachet of instant custard powder. She took it out, wondering if Jake would be happy with a watered down version of that on his cereal. Christ, this was ridiculous.

Footsteps across the ceiling and some music came on. Country stuff – a woman with a twang to her voice. *Did they have a phone up there? I've got to speak to Dave, get him to come back right now. They must have a phone.*

Jake was on his cushion, eyes fixed to the TV screen as Po raced between psychedelic flowers on her scooter. She tiptoed through to the hallway, stopping at the front door.

No noises outside. Slowly, she undid the bolts, then turned the Yale lock back. With some effort, she began to pull the door open, the steel panels Dave had reinforced it with considerably adding to its weight. The crack opened, revealing the concrete walkway and balcony outside. A pigeon was perched on the handrail, head bobbing up and down, a beady eye turned in her direction. She opened the door fully and it hopped back into the void, wings slapping together. It struggled to gain height before disappearing in the direction of the tower block roof.

She poked her head out, looking quickly in both directions. As usual, her floor was deserted – the front door to every other flat covered by thick metal mesh. *Refurbishments later that year.* She wanted to laugh. *And in the meantime I'm stuck up here alone, Billy bloody no mates.*

She could hear an engine revving in the courtyard far below. Lads were laughing and an empty can clattered off a wall. They'd be there, hanging about, doing a bit of business. A wrap of speed here, a bag of powder there. The muscles in her stomach clenched with desire and she edged across the walkway to peer down.

They were grouped in the toddlers' play area, some perched on the backs of the benches, feet dirtying the area for sitting on. Another two were on the see-saw, taking it in turns to thrust up with both feet and return to the ground with as big a bump as possible. Off to the side a miniature football match was underway, a battered drinks can the target of their kicks.

Her eyes settled on the only grown man among them: Salvio, surrounded by the rest of the estate's gang. Memories of Siobhain came back. Sweet, lovely Siobhain, with her deliciously soft way of speaking. Salvio had found her hanging around outside the Burger King in Piccadilly Gardens, joking later that she was so fresh from the Emerald Isle, he could smell the clover on her. Luck of the Irish, he'd told the girl, setting her up in his own flat, booze and everything else on offer.

But when Siobhain realised what the payback involved doing, she had screamed and fought. Said she would go to the police. Zoe remembered the day in the terraced house Salvio had moved the poor girl out to. She remembered sitting in the corner, too scared to move as Salvio had ordered Siobhain to be pinned down, someone holding her head in position while he boiled the kettle. Siobhain's shrieks when water was splashed on her forearm. A whisper, Salvio had hissed, holding the steaming spout inches from her face, so much as a whisper and you'll get this whole thing poured down your throat.

But Siobhain had never really given in. Always finding ways to kick against him, however bad the beatings got. Someone said he'd eventually shipped her on to some men in Gorton. That or sent her across to Nottingham. Whatever it was, one day she simply vanished.

She often wondered what became of Siobhain. Did she ever make it back to that village in Ireland she'd come from? Somewhere near a city called Cork. There was something about her, something Zoe could tell was good. We could have been best mates, she thought bitterly.

The engine of the car they were looking at revved again, noise building to a whine before the driver released the clutch. The wheels span furiously before gripping the tarmac and the vehicle flew forward, leaving a cloud of blackness hanging in the air.

Salvio threw his head back, but his roar of laughter abruptly stopped. Shit! She ducked back below the level of the barrier, realising the door to her flat was ajar. Light spilled out from the naked bulb hanging in the hall.

On all fours, she reached across and tried to pull it shut. A loud whistle echoed up from below. Salvio's voice. 'Yo! Riggers – Dave's bitch is out. Three decks above you!'

She cocked her head towards the stairwell and listened. Seconds later she heard the sound of footsteps rapidly approaching. She scrambled to her feet and shouldered the door open. It banged against something and Jake flew back, bottle of milk landing beyond his head. A moment of open mouthed silence before the screaming started.

'Oh, kidder.' She stepped inside, scooped him up, then turned round, pushed it shut and started sliding the bolts across. 'I'm sorry, baby, I'm sorry.' The footsteps came to a stop outside and there followed a series of bangs as they started kicking her door. Jake screamed louder and she pressed him to her chest. 'It's OK, it's OK, Mummy's got you.'

She ran down the corridor and into the front room, pushing the door shut behind her. 'Shush now, kidder. We're safe, we're safe, we're safe.' Eventually his crying petered out, replaced by rattling little sobs. She rested her palm across his back, listening to the wheeze of his congested lungs. Oh God, he's getting worse. He is definitely getting worse.

Suddenly she thought of the bathroom. Maybe there was a bit of the stuff left that Dr Griffiths had given them. She pictured the little canister, how pressing on it had released a fine mist into the cone Dave would hold in place over Jake's nose and mouth. Christ, Dave, I need you here. I can't look after him on my own. Never bloody could.

The kicking outside had stopped, and with him clinging to her neck like a drowning monkey, she tiptoed down the corridor and into the bathroom. Rummaging with one hand among empty bottles and discarded blister packs of pills, she eventually found a little canister in the cabinet's top drawer.

She picked it up and shook it. A bit of the stuff was still inside. After wiping the dust off, she peered at Dr Griffiths' label: 'Verasone. Use every three or four hours. Once seal is broken, discard after two weeks.' She looked at the date on the label. Bollocks, it was over four months old.

Ten

The car park of the Haven Inn held a smattering of cars. Some drivers had chosen to park their vehicles as close to the wing of rooms as possible, others had crowded the area directly before the front entrance, seeking safety there. Jon parked away from them all at the outer edge.

Adjoining the motel was the obligatory pub restaurant, mock traditional decor on the outside and a menu of ready-made meals that could be microwaved in seconds. As he walked across the smooth asphalt, he examined the motel. Windows glowed on both floors. A token effort had been made to clad it in stone that was sympathetic to its surroundings, but the chunky blocks were too uniform, their sandy-coloured shade almost without variation. Aggregate, Jon guessed, pressed together in some grotesque industrial unit.

The front doors slid apart and the receptionist looked up. 'Good evening.'

'Hi there,' Jon smiled, placing his holdall down and fishing his ID from his jacket. 'DI Jon Spicer, Greater Manchester Police. I'm here to help with the murder investigation.'

Her eyes yo-yoed between his photocard and face. Young girl, probably earning money to fund her studies. He glanced at her name badge. Suzy.

'The one they found stuffed in the bin bags?' she asked.

Jon maintained his friendly expression. The one they found stuffed in the bin bags. Whoever earned my brother that epithet is going to fucking well regret it. Why? A voice in his head, immediately replied. Exactly what will you do to make him reg—

Jon cleared his throat to drown out the question. 'That's the one.'

'Do they know his real name, yet? The local paper called in earlier and everything. I mean, he was signed in as Dave Smith, but they reckon that was made up.'

'No, still unidentified. Now, the officers at your police station inform me he'd been staying here.'

Her eyes moved towards the doors leading to the inner part of the motel. 'That's right.'

'And the room he was in for his last visit was ...'

She completed the sentence for him. 'Number eight.'

'That's it, number eight. Superintendent Mallin rang earlier about me borrowing the service key?'

Her forehead wrinkled and she looked below the counter. 'I've only just come on shift. Dianne hasn't left anything.'

'You work nights, then?'

'Yes. Well, three times a week.'

'Studying for something?'

'I am.' A hand went to the horse-shaped pendant about her neck. 'Equestrian Studies, with the Open University.'

Remembering one of the first chats he'd ever had with Rick, Jon raised a forefinger. 'Wise move. Less to pay for the course and tuition fees, right?'

'Right.'

He allowed a slight frown. 'It was about mid-afternoon when he rang. The room key recovered from the crime scene has gone for fingerprint analysis. The lady he spoke to said there is a service key I could borrow.'

'Yes.' She stood up, went over to the pigeon holes mounted on the rear wall and removed a key card from the end compartment. 'This will work.'

'Thanks. Oh, and I'll need to check in myself. Murder investigations are notoriously slow.'

'Here? You want to stay here?'

He grinned. 'Police expenses don't stretch to much. Though, to be honest, I prefer this kind of place. Quieter than the town centre.'

She reached for the computer keyboard, adopting her work

mode. After entering his details and swiping his card, she looked up. 'Would you prefer a ground or first-floor room?'

'Ground please. Anything left next to number eight?'

'To the side or opposite?'

'Opposite please.'

'OK, so that's room seven.' She handed him another key. 'Through the doors and to your left.'

'Cheers.' He slid the service key into the breast pocket of his jacket, picked up his bag and headed for the corridor. He immediately spotted Dave's room because a blue sticker covered the lock mechanism. White words announced: 'Police – Do Not Enter'.

He clicked his own door, slung his bag inside then turned back to Dave's. Muffled TV commentary from further down the corridor. A crowd burst into laughter. He peeled back the blue sticker just enough to allow the card into the slot. Down, hold, up. The light changed to green and he lowered the door handle with the tip of a knuckle. Light from the corridor illuminated the row of switches just inside the door. No haze of aluminium dust sprayed out by the zephyr brush. Batyra and Spiers must have bagged whatever they thought relevant, leaving Salt to dust for prints at a later date. Using the tip of a biro, Jon flicked on the lights.

God, the anonymity of these places. A watercolour print of flowers in a field, pastel shades beneath a weak blue sky. All the substance of a marshmallow. The TV on the side unit with an A card on the top, no doubt tipping off visiting businessmen about the pay-to-view porn channels.

He looked at the kettle and tea-making tray. Ripped sachets of sugar, empty miniature cartons of UHT milk, crumpled tea bags with edges that had dried a lighter shade of brown. One cup used, residue of Dave's last brew clinging to the bottom. The bed was unmade, duvet peeled halfway back, the mattress wrinkled only on the left-hand side. Sticking to protocol, Dave? At home, did Zoe prefer the right?

Memories of him, Dave and Ellie staying at their grandparents' house popped up. Dave and him getting to share the double bed in the spare room. One time they'd sneaked a torch and some comics along in their bag and created a den by piling up their pillows under the covers. Waking up hot and sweaty at some unknown hour, the torch batteries long dead and crumpled copies of *2000 AD* beneath them.

Jon saw the bedside table's drawer was fully open, just a bible lying inside. Down on all fours, he peered beneath the bed. Nothing.

He stood up, turned to the wardrobe and hooked the biro under the curved handle. The door swung open to reveal a vertical row of empty shelves. He bent down, spotting fragments of soil at the bottom. What happened to your shoes, mate? What has the bastard who killed you done with them?

He stepped into the bathroom. Apart from a spare towel still folded on the corner shelf, absolutely nothing. He crouched to examine the screws on the base panel of the bath. Pristine, with no damage to the surrounding paintwork. Back in the main room, he placed a chair beneath the air conditioning vent high up on the wall. A fine layer of dust clung to it and he could tell no one had tampered with it in months. He looked for telltale signs of powder on the corner table. A few strands of tobacco and that was it. No way, no bloody way, was Dave using this hotel as a base for dealing.

Back in the corridor, he smoothed the sticker back over the lock, stepped across to his room and let himself in. It was like entering into a reflection of Dave's. The same insipid print, the same model TV on the side unit, identical type of cover on the duvet.

The shower head pressed out multiple streams of hissing water and Jon ducked his head under the cascade, nodding slowly from side to side, relishing the bombardment on his skull. Back in the main part of the room, he paused, eyes on the mirror that stretched the length of the bathroom door. A row of welts stretched round his ribs, almost touching the towel at his waist. He swivelled his arm, spotting long-forgotten evidence of other ancient gouges and stamps. The nicks in the skin of his fingers and the puckered burn marks also stood out. The fluorescent bulb in the bathroom plinked and he realised it was that causing his rugby scars to glow. Looking up, he saw that the line running through his left eyebrow was also in sharp relief. Spicer, he shook his head, you look like one ugly great plank.

Unzipping his holdall, he pulled out a pair of jeans and ribbed black sweater. Alice? His wife's face appeared in his mind. What did you pack that for? He almost tossed it to the side, aware of how tight the top felt across his chest, shoulders and arms. Then he paused, thinking about the evening ahead. Physical intimidation would almost certainly feature at some point.

The receptionist glanced to her side as he came back through the doors.

'Thanks for your help, Suzy.' Jon handed the service key back. 'I forgot to ask Superintendent Mallin about the room's phone records. Is there a log of calls I could look at?'

'I don't know, I've never been asked that before.'

'It's easy. Just bring up his room bill, it'll probably show them there.'

'Of course,' she said, fingers on the keyboard once again. 'He owed us for three nights.'

'How did he pay on his previous visits?'

'Cash.' Her eyes moved down the screen. 'No. Just a meal on room service, ordered last night.'

'From that place next door?' He craned his neck.

'Yes.' She turned the screen so he could see. 'Chicken korma, rice and naan. Eight pounds ninety-five.'

Jon could see the entry. 'Right. No calls, just like you said. Thanks.'

The walk into Haverdale took him back over the small bridge. He looked down, unable to see the water in the inky shadows below. Somewhere behind him an owl hooted, urgently repeating its call before receiving a distant reply.

Up ahead, the lights of the railway station provided a row of beacons in the night and soon he was striding over the level crossing, a deserted platform on his right, silent track stretching off to his left.

The high street opened up before him, dark shop windows on either side. Two cars were parked at the top of a side street, and spotting the beads of glass scattered across the pavement, Jon paused for a closer look. The side windows of both had been smashed in and wires hung from gaping holes in the dashboards. Two people's days would get off to a shitty start tomorrow, he thought.

The fourth shop he passed was a butcher's and he looked at the empty display stand at the front. Spotless steel trays dully reflected the street lights behind him. His attention turned to the row of stickers in the window's bottom corner.

'*Rick Bestwick Ltd, Chesterfield. Wild and natural rabbit.*'

'*Genuine agent for Macsween Haggis.*'

'*High Peak Lamb. From the farmer, to the butcher, to you.*'

'*Lyme Park venison.*'

Jon examined the logo: a pair of antlers that curled round the National Trust's oak leaf emblem. Further up the high street was the first restaurant, Grumble Tum's. He let himself in and a table of four watched him in silence as he approached the small bar at the far end.

'Good evening,' the elderly man behind it announced, placing the glass he was polishing to the side. 'A table for one?'

'Could I have a quick look at your menu first?'

'Of course.' He retrieved one from next to the till.

Jon flicked it open and scanned the contents. Bangers and mash, fish and chips, a few pasta dishes and some steak. 'I was hoping to try some of the Lyme Park venison I've heard so much about.'

'Ah.' The man gestured to his left. 'The Tor, or before that, Hugo's.' He leaned forward and winked. 'Hugo's is the better bet, by all accounts.'

'Many thanks.'

Jon stepped back out onto the street. More dark shop fronts separated him from a lit sign. Hugo's. The lettering was in loose and stylised brushstrokes, as if casually daubed by a painter. Almost opposite was a pub, the door lintel topped by a green sign, bold letters hovering above an undulating skyline. The Tor.

As Jon approached Hugo's, he noticed an Aston Martin parked outside. William Beaumont, Jon thought. And no one seems to be breaking into your car. The dimly lit restaurant was quiet, except for a braying group in the corner. Jon spotted a couple of champagne buckets and several wine bottles on the table. Well, the young aristocrat had to blow his week's allowance somehow.

Jon took a seat on the leather sofa, plucked a menu from the coffee table and started scanning. This was more like it.

Grilled fillet of local trout, crushed potatoes and braised leeks.
Roast breast of Goosnargh duck, mulled red wine and pear and celeriac.
Cumbrian salt-marsh lamb with caper sauce, carrot and turnips.
Fillet of Lyme Park venison with wild mushrooms and mozzarella.

An elegant-looking lady in a long apron bearing the Hugo's signature approached. She was in her late twenties, too old to be a student waiting on tables for a bit of spare cash. 'Hello there, sir. Would you care for a drink while you decide?'

'Actually, I'm interested in the venison. Is it freshly prepared?'

'Absolutely. Simon, our chef, drives to the estate every week to personally select his cuts. I can check which he has, if you wish?'

Jon stood, sliding his warrant card out from his back pocket as he did so. He kept it by his side, using the waitress to screen it from the rest of the restaurant. 'DI Spicer, Greater Manchester Police. I'd prefer a quick word with him in person, if I may.'

She stepped back, having to tilt her head to maintain eye contact. 'Erm, you want to speak with him now?'

'If I could.' He stepped into the main part of the room. 'Let's be quick and avoid a fuss.'

She smoothed her apron, a touch of irritation in the gesture. 'Please follow me.'

Jon trailed her to the rear of the restaurant, round the corner of the bar, through a pair of swing doors and into the kitchen area beyond. The glare of stainless steel hit him. Massive extractor fans, a couple of large hobs, wall units and work surfaces – everything seemed to shine.

'Simon, I have someone from the police.' She glanced back. 'Sorry, what did you say your name was?'

'DI Spicer,' he replied, stepping round her, warrant card raised once again.

The chef was leaning over an island unit, playing a small blow torch across a row of ramekins. He glanced to the side. 'How can I help?'

'Just a quick enquiry, sir. You serve venison from Lyme Park?'

The chef turned a wheel on the blow torch and the flame vanished. 'They're good to go.'

The waitress moved round to the island, lifted the tray and made her way back to the double doors.

'I do,' he replied, adjusting a headband that held a mass of black curls in check. 'Is this a health and safety thing?'

'Hopefully not, sir. Could I see a sample of the venison you have?'

He wiped his fingers on a tea towel hitched into the belt loop of his blue trousers. 'OK. Am I the only place you're checking?'

'No, it's part of a wider enquiry.'

The man walked to a large fridge and pulled its door open. The upper shelves contained assorted clumps of vegetables, the middle ones a variety of tubs and pots. The chef squatted, pulled out a lower compartment and rummaged among the vacuum packed contents within. 'Here you go, Lyme Park venison. Sold on Friday, fifteenth April. Is this what you're looking for?'

Jon took the compressed lumps of dark brown meat. The label bore the same logo as at the butcher's, complete with the printed date. 'That's fine. Sorry to have bothered you.'

The chef looked bemused. 'Can I ask what this is about?'

My younger brother, Jon thought. Whoever killed him knows exactly how the poaching arrangement in this town works. So I intend to find the poacher. 'Sorry, sir. You'll probably hear in due course.'

Somewhere nearby, a burglar alarm was ringing out, two notes repeating over and over again. A single car was making its way down the deserted high street, music thudding away inside. Two young men were in the front and Jon watched the vehicle pass before crossing over. The Tor was first and foremost a pub, but one obviously trying to increase business by offering 'Traditional English Fayre', according to the blackboard by the door. He slipped inside and looked about. A few drinkers were perched on their stools at the bar. A large table in the corner was taken by a group of adults. Jon noticed their fleeces and outdoor trousers as they talked about enjoying the views from Kinder Scout earlier that day. Football played on a silent screen at the far end of the bar. Jon sauntered over to the middle-aged woman standing behind the row of beer pumps.

'What can I get you, love?'

He scanned the blackboard at the end of the bar. Steak and ale pie, fish and chips, gammon and pineapple, roast chicken. Towards the end of the list he spotted venison pie. Turning to the beer pumps, he saw she had Black Sheep in. 'Half of that, please,' he said, nodding at it.

As she worked the pump, he glanced around once again. 'This your pub, then?'

'Yes. For the last two years, anyway.'

He picked up a menu. 'Still serving food?'

'We are. Let me know what you'd like.'

'The venison pie looks interesting. Do you make it your-self?'

She placed his half pint on the beer mat and his hand was on it immediately. 'We do, in a lovely rich gravy. Delicious it is.'

He felt the creamy foam press against his top lip before the cool beer broke through from beneath, flooding his mouth with a bitter-sweet taste. He savoured it for a moment before gulping. 'Cheers.' The drink was placed back on the beer mat, first two inches now gone. 'Venison? I've never tried it before.' The beer had tasted so good, he didn't want to leave it now. The glass rose again and he took two more good pulls, feeling a slight lift as the first wisps of alcohol entered his blood stream. Jesus, he thought, that was fast. He realised he had forgotten to eat since breakfast.

She gave a tired smile. 'Is that your order? Venison pie, with chips or mash?'

Another gulp, another surge in his blood. He couldn't put the question off any longer. 'Actually, I'm making enquiries into the supply of venison round here.' He slid his open warrant card across the polished wooden surface. 'DI Spicer, Greater Manchester Police. Could I have a word with your chef?'

'Tony? He's not done anything.'

Too defensive, Jon thought. 'He orders in your meat, I take it.'

'Yes.'

'So could I have a word, then? Two minutes, that's all.'

'About the venison?' Her mouth was set tight.

'About the venison.'

'Hang on then.' She turned away and started reaching for the till.

Ringing in my drink first, Jon thought, lifting his drink and knocking the last of it back. He kept the glass tipped up, watching the blob of foam at the bottom detach itself and slowly slide towards his open mouth. He looked over the rim of the glass. She'd picked up the receiver of a little wall-mounted phone by the side of the till and was speaking rapidly into it. Sneaky cow! Jon was off his stool and round the bar. A door at the end read, Kitchen. Private.

She was waddling towards him, arms outstretched. 'You're not allowed round here.'

'Oh yeah?' Jon yanked it open and nearly fell up the stairs immediately beyond. Taking them two at a time, he raced up. First floor kitchen, cramped and stuffy. A skinny man was on his knees in the far corner, scooping paper-wrapped lumps from the base of a fridge and dropping them into a plastic crate. Strands of brown hair failed miserably to mask a bald spot that had taken over the top of his head.

'Ingredients for your special pie?' Jon announced, feeling his heart pumping in his chest.

The man's head half turned and his shoulders slumped.

The landlady called up from the bottom of the stairs. 'Tony?'

'We're having a chat.' Jon shut the upper door behind him. 'Where did you get that meat?'

The chef struggled to his feet, a package still in his hand. Now upright, Jon could see the bloke sported a large beer belly. Solid and round, it looked stuck onto his thin frame. 'A local butcher's.'

'My arse.' Jon stepped over and took it from his hands. Greaseproof paper, roughly folded over. He opened up a flap. The lumps of dark meat had been hacked up, some marbled with fat and gristle. 'This has been poached. Where did you get it?'

'Poached? No way.'

The whites of the man's watery eyes were tinged with yellow and the end of his bulbous nose was an angry purple. Alcoholic, Jon thought. 'Right, Tony. You're coming with me back to Manchester. A night in the cells in Longsight. There's no booze there, my friend.'

The other man's face lit up with alarm.

'This place.' Jon waved a forefinger. 'Looks filthy to me.' He pointed to the corner where the fridge met the wall. Brown stains ran down it and scraps of something long dried out dotted the lino floor. 'I'll be putting in a call to environmental health. Or you can tell me where this meat came from and I'll stop ruining your life.'

The man sighed. 'It's a guy who lives here in Haverdale.'

'Name?'

'Flynn.'

'That's it?'

'Ian Flynn.'

'Where can I find him?'

He gave a weak shrug. 'The Spread Eagle?'

The Spread Eagle, Jon thought. Mallin mentioned the landlord there had suspected Dave was dealing from his pub. 'Where's that?'

'Back across the high street. First left is Bent's Lane and it's fifty metres up. It's a locals' pub.'

So I'll stick out then, Jon thought. 'What does this Flynn look like?'

'Around your height. Probably an inch shorter and a couple of stone lighter.'

'Age?'

'I don't know. Late twenties?'

'Hair?'

He shook his head. 'Shaved.'

'Anything else?'

'An earring.' He touched his left lobe.

'Does he flog this meat to other places in the town?'

'Yeah. At least he always has a load more in his bag when he pops in.'

'OK, we'll play it like this. I don't mention this visit to anyone and you don't either. Especially to this Flynn. When I talk to him – maybe tomorrow, maybe the day after – no one makes a connection to you. Understood?'

The chef licked his lips. 'Can you leave it a week or so?'

Jon paused. The guy was nervous. 'Anything else I should know about him, Tony?'

He scratched at an ear. 'He's got a reputation for having a bit of a temper. I don't know what he does for a living – but he always seems to have something for sale.'

Jon picked up on his choice of words. 'What sort of something?'

'You know – this and that.'

'No, I don't.'

The chef squirmed. 'Illegal stuff.'

'What? Knocked-off phones? Pirate videos? Is that what you mean?'

'That too, but ... other stuff as well.'

Jon went through the options. 'You're talking about drugs?'

'He's only mentioned it. I've never actually seen anything.'

'What sort of drugs?'

'I have no idea. What would I want with that nonsense? He said once he could get me anything. Pills, whatever that means.'

Poaching and now dealing, Jon thought. I can't wait to meet this guy.

'I don't want any trouble from him.'

Jon laughed. 'You mean he's Haverdale's bad boy?'

'I suppose so.'

Good, Jon thought, tossing the package of venison back. If he tries something with me, I can rip his bastard arms off.

Eleven

The street lighting didn't extend up Bent's Lane and Jon picked his way carefully along the dark and narrow street, eyes sweeping the cramped terraces on either side. The road curved to the right and a glow spilled out across the pavement ahead. The Spread Eagle. Above the doorway hung a small sign depicting a bird of prey with vast, outstretched wings.

Pausing on the front step, Jon listened to the muffled sound of music and laughter inside. Coats were piled on the row of pegs in the porch area. Battered waxed jackets, moth-eaten overcoats, a ski jacket spattered with flecks of different coloured paint. Locals' pub all right, Jon thought, pushing the inner door open.

The place was half full and several heads turned. He felt himself being looked over, conversations halting for a beat before resuming once again. Jon could guess their conclusions. Tourist, ventured off the beaten track. A quick pint and hopefully he'll bugger off back to the high street where he belongs.

A side room housed a wide screen TV. The same football match was playing as in The Tor, but this one was being watched by a group of lads. Jon made his way across the flagstone floor, careful to dip his head as he passed under a couple of low beams. As he reached the bar, a customer placed his empty pint glass on a beer mat. 'Cheers, Trevor. See you tomorrow.'

Trevor Curtis, Jon thought. So you're the man who tipped the police off that my brother was a dealer.

The bloke had a bushy mop of brown hair hanging down, a long nose, thick moustache and eyes that drooped. Overweight and slow in his movements, he made his way over. 'Evening.'

'Evening,' Jon answered, glancing at what was on. The Black

96

Sheep had left him with a slightly sticky mouth. 'Pint of Stella, thanks.'

He flicked the tap. 'Here on business?'

'Yeah. Well, Sheffield actually. I'm getting the train in.'

'Well, there's a fair few of them passing through,' he replied, failing to inject any interest into his voice. 'Two quid, please.'

Jon fished out a couple of pound coins, realising he'd never paid for his drink in the last pub. Serves her right for selling poached venison. The landlord took his money, dropped it in an open till and didn't come back. Jon looked around. There was a corner table tucked in by the fruit machine. That gives me the best view of the pub as a whole, he thought. As he sat down the final whistle sounded on the TV screen.

A couple of minutes later the lads started filing towards the door. Jon kept an ear cocked, eyes on the fruit machine's bank of flashing lights.

'Cheers, Trevor,' the chorus rang out.

'Night, lads,' the landlord replied, slowly making his way to the tables of empty glasses.

'No Flynn then.'

The comment was murmured between the two at the rear of the group.

'Yeah, he popped in earlier.'

'Owt on him?'

'Tomorrow, he said.'

They passed through the door and were gone. Tomorrow, Jon thought. Selling what? Youngsters like that were hardly in the market for a brace of poached grouse. Each sip of cold lager felt like it was bouncing off the bottom of his stomach and Jon glanced at his watch. Shit, almost ten and I still haven't eaten. With Flynn not in until tomorrow, there was no point in hanging around. He sank the rest of his drink, relishing the effect he knew it would soon have.

He stood, ready to nod his thanks at the landlord. The man studiously avoided his look. Cheers for making an out-of-towner feel so welcome, Trevor, Jon thought. I'll be back for the same friendly reception tomorrow.

Heading back down the road, he felt the booze powering his step. The pleasant numbness in his head built in strength and by the time he'd got to the high street, the desire for more alcohol had taken hold.

The convenience store next to the police station looked like it was still open and Jon hurried up to its doors. A member of staff was standing at the end of the aisles, arms crossed. Jon passed him with a nod, heading straight for the booze section. As he grabbed a bottle of Famous Grouse, he could see the staff member had moved to the top of his aisle. Jesus, he thought, how much stuff are you having nicked to warrant that kind of suspicion?

The man at the till eyed him warily. 'Anything else?'

'No, thanks.'

Back on the empty street, he listened to the sound of his footsteps and began to think about his younger brother. What were you up to, mate? Staying in a soulless little hotel room, escaping out for a pint in the evening. He looked down at the pavement, watching each foot as it swung out. Left, right, left, right. Did you walk back to the hotel on this side of the street? Did you tread on this exact slab? Suddenly he wanted Dave to be standing there before him. More than a desire to know what happened, it was a need to know how his brother had been feeling in his last few hours.

Jon raised his eyes to the dark sky. Why didn't I do more to try and find you? How was I too busy to look out for my little brother? And where did you end up as a result? In three fucking bin bags. 'I'm sorry. God, I am so sorry.'

Suzy's head was down as he stepped up to the doors. They parted and she looked up, eyes widening just a fraction as he stepped through with the bottle in his hand. 'Hello.'

'Hi there.' He felt light-headed and realised his face was prob-ably flushed. 'You know the restaurant place next door – they do room service, don't they?'

She glanced at her watch. 'If you order right now.'

'Great.' He pretended to think. 'The curry will do fine.'

'OK,' she said. 'It'll be about ten minutes.'

He went to his room, opened it up and grabbed the glass off the shelf above the bathroom sink. The seal on the Famous Grouse crackled as he sharply twisted the cap. Whisky sloshed into his glass. A mouthful, straight down. His throat burned, swiftly followed by his stomach. The thoughts were multiplying, quickly growing in strength. He dipped his head and rubbed the top of it with the heel of one hand. Ah shit, Dave. Why? Why did you have to come out to this place and get yourself fucking killed? Another gulp of whisky and the spotlight of his anger began to swing round. And what did you do, he asked himself. What did you do to help your little brother? Sod all, except berate him for being a loser. He screwed his eyes shut, remembering his heavy-handed tactics. Idiot, stupid bloody idiot.

Another glass was almost gone when the knock sounded at his door. 'Room service.'

He opened up and kept a hand on the door frame for balance. A lanky teenager stood there, tray held out before him. 'You ordered a curry?'

'Thanks.' Jon pulled out a ten pound note and they did an awkward swap. Waving the offer of change away, he shut the door with his foot, sat at the little corner table and hunched over the plate. Breathing in the pungent aroma, he shut his eyes and pretended to be his brother. Lifting the naan, he ripped off a chunk and tested its sponginess, imagining Dave doing the same. He placed it in his mouth, chewed as Dave would have chewed. You ate this meal, just across there. Thirty feet away. He took another bite of the soft bread. Then you went out. Did someone pick you up from here? Or did you walk to a rendezvous point?

He'd half finished the curry when his phone started to ring. Jon reached round and slid it from his jacket draped on the back of the chair. Alice. He felt a sense of relief. 'Hi, babe. I meant to call you. Sorry.'

'How are you?'

His throat clenched up and it took an effort to get the mouthful of bread down. 'OK, I think.'

'You don't sound it, Jon.'

'Well, you know, I've had better days.'

'What's happening out there? What have they got you doing?'

He rubbed above his eyebrows, glad she couldn't see his face. 'This and that, working out the last twenty-four hours. Finding out who he associated with in Haverdale. Routine stuff.'

'Jon, you're going to have to tell your parents the truth.'

His finger stopped moving. Does she know I'm not really helping with the investigation? 'What do you mean?'

'About your brother, how he died. What was done to him. I only got back from your parents' an hour or so ago. Mary's a wreck, Jon. But she wants to know what happened.'

'And Dad?'

'He's not saying much. Just sitting in the corner behind his paper. They need the truth, Jon. You can't hide it from them.'

He thought about the hotel receptionist telling him how the local paper had been sniffing about. Bollocks, as usual Alice was right. As soon as he signed the identification forms, his brother's name would make the papers. Thank God he hadn't completed them earlier at the station. 'I can't tell them, Ali. I just can't.'

'Someone's got to.'

'I'll speak to the people here. They've got family liaison officers who are trained for that sort of thing.' He pushed the plate away, the smell suddenly cloying and unwelcome. 'Alice, I'm sat across the corridor from where Dave stayed.'

'Sorry?'

'I'm sat across the corridor from where Dave stayed.'

'Oh God, you've booked yourself into the same hotel?'

'Yes.'

'Why?'

'I'm trying to eat what he ate. His very last meal and all it's making me feel is fucking well sick.'

'Are you drinking?'

'Yeah, I'm drinking.' He shoved his feet out and took a breath in. 'You know what, Ali? I don't feel sad. I just feel so pissed off. But who can I be pissed off with?' He glanced round the room. 'There's no one else here.'

'Jon, you're grieving. You're literally in grief. Come home.'

'I'll come home soon, Ali. But there's some more things I need to know.'

She sighed. 'Let's talk tomorrow then.'

'OK. But I need to know more, Ali. People are lying to me out here. Left, right and fucking centre, they're lying.' Anger surged and he poured another glug into his glass.

'It's the scan on Tuesday, Jon.'

'The scan?' Oh shit, at the hospital. First glimpse of their unborn child, little more than a yolk inside Alice. 'The scan, yeah.'

'At one o'clock.'

'Yes, I remember.'

No reply. It's your decision Jon, the silence said. I won't force you to come, but think very carefully before you decide.

'Let me work some stuff out, Ali. I'll speak to a few people. You know, see if there's any way I can—'

'Jon?'

'Yeah?'

'Stop drinking, please? Try to get some sleep.'

'OK. I love you, Alice. You know that?'

'I love you, too. Night.'

'Night.'

The line died and he stared at his mobile for a few seconds, then placed it next to the whisky. Sleep. She was right. Lifting the tray, he staggered slightly as he rose to his feet. The fork slid off one side and bounced on the carpet. Holding the tray with one hand, he bent his knees and scooped the piece of cutlery up. The plate of food started edging to the side of the tray and he managed to right it just in time. In slow motion, he straightened up and walked over to the door. Careful to not look at Dave's old room, he left the remains of the meal out in the corridor. Shutting the door behind him, he unplugged the kettle and filled it up at the bathroom sink. He stared at the little sachets of coffee. Bollocks, I can't be arsed making a drink now. The kettle's lid refused to close properly and he put it down, fell back on the bed and closed his eyes.

Dave's voice, coming from far away. The words were muffled, but Jon could tell he was happy. He was talking fast, explaining something. Jon's mind struggled to come awake. Dave? He tried to say his brother's name, but sleep had turned his tongue into a slug in his mouth. Frustrated, he redoubled his efforts to wake up. Dave, is that really you? I can hear you! Just hang on.

The voice was getting fainter, words becoming more foggy. Jon felt his head beginning to turn. Greyness was around him. Where am I? He didn't know if his eyes were open or not. Dave was sitting in a chair at the end of the bed. It was really him. This whole thing was a mistake, a grotesque misunderstanding. Again, he tried to speak and this time felt his tongue begin to stir. He heard himself groan and another layer of sleep slipped away. Dave's words began to coalesce, forming into actual syllables.

'So I said to him, if that's your idea of efficient time management, you've got another thing coming. Exactly. What else could he say? I had the spreadsheets right there. OK, yes, OK, I'll see you just after nine.'

It wasn't Dave's voice any longer, but someone outside the room. The doors at the end of the corridor banged shut and the voice was gone. I'm in a hotel, Jon thought. In Haverdale. But Dave was there, sitting right there. His eyes opened fully and he found himself looking again towards the end of the bed. His jacket was draped on the back of the chair, and above it, the last vestiges of his brother's face faded into the feeble morning light filling the room.

Jon sat up, temples pounding. An aching filled his gut, making him wonder if he was about to puke. The sensation passed, immediately replaced by a raging thirst. He stepped over to the kettle, raised it to his face and started gulping, water spilling over each cheek, running down his top and soaking the waistband of his trousers.

Twelve

The morning had a brittleness about it – the air was cold and the damp tarmac shone under the bright morning sun. As Jon trudged across the car park, he squinted against the glare reflecting up at him. He felt like a fissure was opening up behind his eyes, as if his brain was slowly tearing free from the membrane mooring it in place, allowing it to bump painfully against his skull with every step. Pushing the door to the restaurant open, he stepped into the dim interior and breathed a sigh of relief.

'Morning, sir. Table for one?'

Jon blinked at the young man standing behind the waist-high wooden lectern. It was the same bloke who'd brought his curry over last night. 'Hey.' The word came out as more of a growl and Jon had to clear his throat before carrying on. 'Cramming in the shifts, aren't you?'

'Sundays and bank holidays. Overtime's great.'

'I bet.' He vaguely remembered tipping the bloke the night before. Good move, he thought, knowing it would now bring him more favourable treatment. 'Can I have somewhere away from the windows?'

'Follow me.' He turned on his heel and led Jon to a table lit only by a soft wall light above it. 'This OK?'

'Perfect. And can I have a jug of water?' Jon slid into the seat and reached for the laminated menu.

'No problem.'

'And a pot of coffee, cheers.'

He stared at the menu for a while, trying to gauge the state of his stomach. The smell of bacon registered and he realised he was famished. That accounts for the stabbing viciousness of this hangover, he thought.

The young man returned with a small tray in his hands. 'Water.'

Ice clinked in the jug as he placed it on the table. You beauty, Jon thought, picking up a glass.

'Coffee and a copy of this morning's paper.' He placed it all on the table and took a step back. 'Anything to eat?'

'Yeah. Full English with extra toast, sausage, black pudding and bacon.'

'OK.'

Jon sank a glass of water in one and an icy feeling wormed its way into him. His stomach felt like a sponge, greedily sucking up the liquid to ship it out to his parched system. Life looked up a fraction. He finished off another glass then spooned two sugars into a cup and poured himself a coffee. The *Haverdale Herald* caught his attention and he unfolded it to reveal the front page.

GRUESOME FIND SHOCKS RANGERS

Park rangers made a gory discovery yesterday when disposing of bin liners containing, what they first assumed, were the remains of poached deer. On examining the contents more closely, they were horrified to realise the contents were actually human.

Police were immediately called in and Superintendent Mallin, heading up the investigation, stated, 'I can confirm that bin liners recovered by park rangers yesterday morning from Highshaw Hill, three miles north of Haverdale, contained the remains of an adult male, aged around thirty. I'm unable to elaborate at this time, but there is no reason to believe residents of Haverdale should worry for their safety and, until a formal identification of the body has been made, I cannot comment further.'

Speculation is rife as to how and why the man was killed. One source close to the investigation suggested that identification has been delayed due to extensive mutilations to the body – a theory backed up by the fact the remains were in not one, but three separate bin liners.

Jon shut his eyes. That was it – the last sentence alone would have attracted the attention of Reuters and Associated Press. Their news release would have already gone out on the wire and the larger papers would be aware of the story. Shit. He looked at the copy once again. One source close to the investigation. Which bastard was that? Spiers, Mallin, the fat twat reading the Sunday papers in the incident room? It could have been any number of police officers, the guy at the mortuary, even the park rangers themselves. He found himself hoping that some other major incident might have occurred to keep his brother's story out of the national press.

'Here you go, sir.'

Jon looked up to see the waiter lowering a plate towards the table. It was almost overflowing with fried eggs, sausages, bacon, grilled tomatoes, mushrooms, black pudding and baked beans. He placed a rack of toast to the side. 'Enjoy your meal.' He pointed to the paper. 'Though I'd skip that story – might put you off.'

'Yeah, thanks.' He waited for the waiter to walk away before hurriedly folding a piece of toast around a sausage and shoving the entire thing in his mouth. Sorry, Dave, he thought, but I'm fucking starving here. His eyes moved back to the story.

Other questions cry out for answers. Why was the man killed? Our source hinted that drugs may well have been in-volved, raising the possibility this was a gang-land execution linked to the recent influx of narcotics plaguing the town.

Jon speared a rasher of bacon, shovelled beans into its folds and popped it in with the half-chewed sausage and toast. His jaw abruptly stopped moving. Oh Christ. Mum and Dad. They can't find out from some breathless announcement on the local news. How far had the story already spread? Flicking his phone open, he selected the number for Carmel Todd, senior crime reporter at the *Manchester Evening Chronicle*. As the phone rang, he knew his name would be displayed on her screen.

'DI Spicer, to what do I owe this pleasure so early on a bright bank holiday morning?'

Bank holiday, thank God for that, Jon thought. There was a chance the story hadn't been picked up by the few staff that would be in the paper's Deansgate offices. 'Hi, Carmel, what are you working on today?'

'The Cheetham Hill shootings, of course. Three dead and the killer a kid on a mountain bike – or was it a moped?'

Yeah, yeah, Jon thought. Typical Carmel to try and wheedle out a bit of information like that. 'No idea, I'm on holiday. When was it?'

'Last night, just before midnight. If you're on holiday, why the call?'

'I can't get through to Rick. Nothing else on a regional basis? There was something on the radio just now, but I didn't quite catch it.'

'On the radio? A murder?'

A glimmer of hope. She didn't seem to know. 'Yeah, I think so.'

'Whereabouts?'

'Not sure, I was stepping out of the shower.'

'Are you at home?'

'No.'

'Well, where are you? If you were listening to local radio, that would give me a clue as to where the incident took place.'

Bollocks, he thought. She's closing in on me here. 'Hang on – that's room service. I'll call you back, it was probably nothing.'

He cut her off, knowing her antennae would now be up. Still, it seemed like all attention was on the Cheetham Hill thing. For the moment. He continued to demolish his breakfast but, as his thoughts turned to his parents, his appetite seemed to shrivel. I'll have to tell them. They've got to hear it from me. He chewed on a piece of toast, the sight of grease-laden mushrooms having now lost their allure. Putting the plate on an adjacent table, he poured himself another coffee and sat back. Oh God, how will I do it? What will I say? Dread felt like a snake curling around his waist, squeezing his stomach tight.

By the time he got to the outskirts of Manchester, his heart was racing and his face kept flushing hot and cold. I can't do this, he thought. I can't look my mum and dad in the eye and tell them what really happened to Dave. He lowered the windows, then pulled off the M60, taking a few breaths as he did so.

The slip road led up to a large roundabout, ugly industrial buildings surrounding it. He took the first turn-off and found a quiet layby to park up in. Nervously, he turned his mobile over in his hand. It's probably best, he concluded, that I break the news from somewhere else. That way, they've got time to take it in without having to worry about how they react in front of me.

Feeling like a complete coward, he lifted his phone and selected their number. The line began to buzz. Please, let Dad answer. Or Ellie, if she's still there. Anyone but Mum.

On the other side of the spiked fence was a tree. There were no leaves on it whatsoever, just partially open blossoms perched on the tip of each bare branch. Looking at the large white petals curling upwards, he had the sudden impression they were a plague of insects, descended on the tree to strip it before being frozen in the act of taking off.

'Hello?'

'Mum, it's me. Jon.'

She gave a slight cough, but the quiver in her voice remained. 'Jon, are you all right?'

'I'm OK, Mum. And you?'

'Yes.' Her voice sounded distant. 'Where are you? Are you coming home?'

He reached for the gearstick and picked at the leather trim, avoiding eye contact with someone who wasn't even there. 'I'm wrapped up with the investigation, Mum. They need all the help they can get. It's not a big place, Haverdale.'

'Yes.'

'How are things with Dad?'

'You know ... we're all finding things hard at the moment.'

'He isn't to blame, Mum. We all are, to an extent. It's not fair to put all this on him.'

'When will they let me have my boy back?'

'Soon, Mum.' He ran his tongue around his mouth, the urge to retch growing. 'Mum? There are some more details about Dave you should know. The paper out here is twisting things. They're trying to find a link between Dave and drug dealing. It's all lies, Mum, they're just trying to stir up a story. There's not a single piece of evidence, OK? Despite what you might read.'

'I believe you.'

'And there's more information about how he died. Is Dad there?'

'Yes, he's sat in his chair across from me.'

Good, that meant she was on the sofa. 'Mum, you know how I said Dave had been killed?'

'Yes.' Her voice had dropped.

He glanced to the side and spotted three men at the rear loading bay of the nearest industrial unit. They were kicking around a football, watched by another two men with cigarettes in their hands. He could hear their laughter as a lump rose in his throat. 'They're not sure how he died yet. But afterwards, whoever did it had to dispose of the remains.'

'What happened?' she whispered.

He raised a hand to his forehead and pressed a thumb and forefinger against his temples. 'Mum, he was dead, remember?' He thought about her religion, her love for the Catholic faith. 'He's with God now, Mum. It's just his body that was left behind. You agree with that, don't you?'

She was crying now, though not enough to totally distort her voice. 'What did they do to my boy?'

'They put him in bin bags. Parts of his body in bin bags – trying to dispose of it that way.'

'Oh no, oh no.'

He heard the sound of the telephone receiver brushing against something. Mary's sobs and then his father's voice, muffled in the background. More movement and Alan came on the line. 'Jon?'

'Yes, Dad.'

'What's going on? What did you just say to Mary?'

He sucked in air. I cannot go through this again. 'I was saying—'

His Dad was almost shouting. 'What's happening out there? Are you any closer to finding who did it?'

'I'm working as fast as I can, Dad. There's—'

Mary's voice came back on, words spilling out between chokes. 'Bring him back, Jon. Just bring my baby back home.'

He felt the tears running down his cheeks. 'I will, Mum. I promise you I will.'

Thirteen

When he got to the cafe just before the main entrance to Piccadilly station, Rick was already waiting for him, knees together, hands on his lap under the table. Jon held an imaginary cup to his face and mouthed the word, 'Coffee.'

Rick gave a grimace in return.

Once he'd paid for a mug of tea, Jon joined him at the table. 'No sign of Nikki yet, then?'

Rick shook his head. 'You certainly pick your bloody meeting places.'

Jon couldn't help but grin as he glanced towards the menu on the wall. In its centre was a photo of the small circular loaf known in Manchester as a barm. He read the listing:

Barm with cheese.
Barm with bacon.
Barm with chips.
Barm with kebab meat.
Barm with sausage.
Chef's special: Barm with sausage and onion.

The kebab in the corner rotated slowly round on its pole, the lump of miserable-looking meat weeping fat into the tray below. 'It's the only place I could think of near here that serves a decent cup of tea.'

Rick leaned forward, careful to not let his jacket touch the pockmarked plastic table. 'Let me enlighten you. There's a Starbucks in the station.'

Jon took a sip of his dark brew. 'As I said, it's the only place I could think of near here that serves a decent cup of tea.'

Rick flashed him a sarcastic smile before his face turned more serious. 'I'm really sorry about your brother.'

Jon licked his lips. 'Yeah, well. I'd been fearing that phone call for a long time. I always thought it would be an overdose or something, though. Not this.'

'What actually happened?'

Jon put his mug on the table. 'Someone killed him, chopped him up and stuffed him into three bin bags.'

Rick's face didn't move and Jon saw the cartilage in his windpipe raise, then lower. 'Fuck.'

'Yeah. And now some yokel prick by the name of Mallin is heading up the investigation. Forensics is being handled by an imbecile called Salt and a couple of constables are bumbling about searching for clues. It's a disaster scene of the highest fucking order.'

'So you've brought in Nikki. Just to help out.'

Jon heard the tone in his partner's voice and didn't need to actually look at him to see the disapproving expression. Rick was fully aware of the fact Nikki had a major soft spot for him; and his partner was also aware of how close he'd come to being tempted. 'I couldn't stand there and let that man fuck up the crime scene.'

'Tread carefully, mate.'

He glared at his partner. 'You honestly think I'm going to use my kid brother's death as an opportunity to get laid?'

Rick flinched. 'No. But she'll be seeing someone who's hurt, who's vulnerable.' He sat back. 'You know she's bad news.'

'Give her some credit, Rick. You make her sound like one of those women who lured sailors to that island ...'

'Sirens.'

'There you go,' he smiled. 'Your posh education's come in useful again.'

Rick smiled briefly, checked the surface was free of spillages, placed his elbows on it and pressed his lips against his interlinked fingers. 'Jesus Christ. I wish I had something for you on this Zoe.'

Jon's chin went up. 'You went to the Booth Centre?'

Rick nodded. 'The guy who runs it, Norman Green,

remembers her. Hasn't seen her in months though. Who is she by the way?'

'Dave's girlfriend, wife or whatever. Seems that way from his recent phone calls.'

'It's likely she's a user, Jon. Green indicated as much.'

'I'd guessed. The photo of her on Dave's phone said it all. Skull pretty much showing through her skin. What about the hostels with beds for females?'

'Checked them. Nothing.'

'Soup kitchens?'

He shook his head.

'Custody, maybe?'

'I checked the system. Two Zoes, but neither matched the description.'

'Bloody hell, she can't have just vanished. Styal prison? There's plenty of female addicts locked up in that place.'

'I'll give it a go – but I'll have to fit it in around this shooting in Cheetham Hill. Buchanon texted to say that's what I'm on while you're taking compassionate leave.'

'Fine. What about this Redino character? Anything from your contact in the Drug Squad?'

'He's never heard the name. But he's back in the office to-morrow, so he'll check then.'

'Nice one. Get him to check if it's an alias of Ian Flynn.' Jon spelled the surname. 'I've got a good feeling on this one.'

The door opened and both men glanced towards it. Nikki Kingston was shouldering her way inside, a large attaché hanging from her shoulder.

Jon immediately stood. 'Drink, Nikki?'

She nodded. 'Tea, cheers.'

'Rick?' He grinned provocatively. 'I'm sure they could try whipping you up one of your frothy coffees.'

He pretended to think. 'You know what? I'll pass.'

Jon headed up to the counter with his empty mug. 'Two more, please.'

While the lady poured them out from a massive silver pot, Jon glanced at the mirrored wall. Nikki had taken the seat opposite Rick and, though neither looked that pleased to see the other, they were conferring across the table in whispers. Good, he thought. You two get the grisly details over with. As he approached the table, the muted conversation came to a halt and they both looked up.

'How are you doing, Jon?' Nikki's eyebrows were raised. 'You look tired.'

'I'll survive.' He put the drinks down and eased himself back into his seat. 'So. Any luck with the casts?'

'Not a lot.' She released the catches of her case and removed several printed sheets. 'I went on SICAR first thing this morning. The size nine and the size elevens are Merrill.' She slid a piece of paper over. 'Any of these look familiar?'

He scanned the panel of thumbnail photos. The hiking boots the park rangers had been wearing were on the second row down. 'Those ones.'

'Well, that's something.' She placed a tick next to the image. 'Now, our other two sets. One I didn't need to go on the computer to work out. Looking at the cast itself, I spotted a familiar logo halfway down.' She flipped a piece of paper over. 'Recognise it?'

As Jon stared at the graphic representation of a tree, Rick clicked his fingers. 'Timberland, isn't it?'

'Ten out of ten,' Nikki replied. 'See the circular stamp next to it? The letters inside are BSFP. I went on their website and it's some sort of efficiency system they've trademarked. It's on all their mass-market hiking boots. Probably tens of thousands of them out there.'

Jon crossed his arms and sat back. 'And the fourth set?'

'These are the ones I've not had any luck with. They're size ten and the nearest match SICAR could produce was a pair of Norwegian army boots.'

'They'll have been Dave's,' Jon answered immediately. 'He used to buy all his clothes from army surplus stores, like that one on Oldham Street. Camouflage coats, combat trousers, army boots. You know the look. He probably bought a dog-on-a-rope from there, too.'

'Well, they're very distinctive,' Nikki replied without a smile.

Jon nodded, realising it wasn't the time to be cracking feeble jokes. 'How so?'

'Loads of wear and tear to the soles.'

Jon's eyes shifted to the other sheets in her pile. 'And the tyre treads?'

'Christ, Jon. I was in at half seven this morning running the shoe prints. Give me a bloody chance.'

'Sorry. Do you know when you might be able to ...'

'Probably tomorrow. There's bloody loads on at the minute.'

'OK, cheers. I appreciate it.' He sipped at his team, mind running over the scraps of information. Shit, there was so little to go on. Just finding Zoe in Manchester and Flynn in Haverdale. 'Listen, this Mallin – the SIO – is working on the basis Dave was out in Haverdale to deal drugs. And we're talking Class A stuff, including crystal meth.'

Rick suddenly seemed fascinated by the surface of the table.

'Now, I know my brother's lifestyle wasn't exactly run-of-the-mill. Maybe he sold a bit of cannabis here and there. But I will not accept he was a full-time dealer pushing the worst sorts of shit on a sleepy little Peak District town. He just wouldn't. So I need your help, mate.'

Rick looked up and their eyes met. 'Go on.'

'I need to find this Zoe, because I reckon she can tell us what Dave was really up to – and who this Redino is. And Nikki, if I get anything more from Haverdale – be it a walking book or a whole bloody motorbike – can I bring it to you?'

'Of course.'

'Jon.' Rick stirred uneasily in his seat. 'I've got to ask you this. What do you think your brother was doing out there?'

Jon pursed his lips. 'Searching for something, an archaeological find of some sort.' He looked at them and their carefully maintained expressions of neutrality said it all. 'I know it sounds stupid, but someone's been digging on the tops of the hills around the town over these last few weeks. The local paper reckon it's the work of nighthawks, people searching for buried artefacts. Unearth a fortune for minimum effort; it's just the sort of plan I could see Dave hatching.'

Nikki gave a sad smile. 'Not a lot worse than buying tickets for the National Lottery.'

Glad of her support, Jon nodded. 'Only he stumbled across something that got him killed.' He turned his eyes to Rick.

His partner shrugged. 'So what are you actually planning?'

'I've got this poaching avenue to follow up in Haverdale. Looks like the guy called Ian Flynn is into all sorts of other stuff – dealing included. The papers will be sniffing around very soon, so it's only a matter of time before my brother gets portrayed as drug-peddling scum and I can't have my mum and dad living with that. Their marriage is close enough to collapsing as it is.' He pushed aside the last of his tea.

'Are you driving out there now?' Rick asked.

'Yup.'

'Have you called in on Alice, yet?'

Jon saw Nikki's gaze suddenly skitter off to the side. Warily, he looked at his partner's face. 'No.'

'You should do. She'll be worried.'

In the periphery of his vision, he saw Nikki give a single nod. 'OK. But one thing, Rick. Alice doesn't realise I'm not officially on the investigation. Things need to stay that way.'

'Jesus Christ, Jon.'

'There was no other way round it.'

'You've told her Derbyshire Police requested your assistance?'

'Basically.'

Rick shook his head. 'While really you – sorry, we – are going behind everyone's backs. Including your wife's.'

Jon kept his silence.

'Shit,' Rick cursed. 'You can be such a bloody fool. I'm seeing her later on. Now I'll have to lie to her as well.'

'You're going over to mine?'

Movement as Nikki got up. 'I'd better be off.' Awkwardly, she brushed a straggly black hair from her forehead. 'There's loads on back at the lab.'

'Cheers, Nikki,' Jon said, one hand held partially out. 'I really appreciate this.'

Their eyes stayed together for an instant longer and Rick crossed his arms.

'I'll call as soon as I have anything.' She shouldered her bag and headed for the door.

Jon examined his mug, feeling Rick's hostile stare. 'I didn't know you were popping over.'

'It was meant to be the three of us. She's making a Thai curry, remember?'

'Bloody hell.' Guiltily, he ran a finger along the edge of the table.

'So you're not turning up for your own wife's meal?'

'I can't,' Jon muttered. 'Flynn is likely to be in a certain pub at some point tonight. When you see Alice, you can just gloss over my role in Haverdale, yeah?'

Rick blew out his cheeks. 'Yeah. I just hope you know what you're getting yourself into here.'

As he opened his front door, the sound of nursery rhymes hit him. A piano, accompanied by a lady with a clipped English accent warbling about Incey Wincey Spider.

Keep it together, he told himself. Keep it together, Jon. 'It's me!'

Punch appeared in the kitchen doorway, and his head bucked with joy as he bounded down the corridor. Jon heard Holly's shout of delight as she tottered into view. God, he thought, I can't believe I was going to avoid all this. He bent forward to grab his dog's jowls, its tongue lapping against his cheek as Holly shouted again. He opened his eyes to see her running towards him, knees picking up too high, arms jerking as if her movements were being controlled by a puppeteer yet to learn his craft.

'My princess,' he announced, wrapping her in a hug and getting to his feet.

Alice hovered behind, a questioning smile on her face.

'I should have rung, I know.' He shifted Holly into the crook of one arm. 'It's good to see you, Ali. Is everything OK?'

'Yeah, we're fine. Have you spoken to Mary and Alan?'

Jon felt nausea wash around his stomach. 'This morning.'

'How did it sound between them?'

'Not good. Mum avoided the question.'

Her face showed both sympathy and admiration. 'That took a big heart, Jon.'

He felt Holly's legs begin to flex against his stomach and he put her down, allowing her to totter back into the telly room.

As soon as she was out of sight, he turned to his wife. He opened his mouth to speak, but raw emotion surged up instead. He squeezed his eyes shut and pressed a hand against the wall.

'Jon?'

He shook his head, eyes still closed.

'Oh, Jon.'

He felt her palms on his cheeks as she pulled his face towards her. 'Come on, let it out, Jon.'

Both arms went round her and he rested his face on her shoulder, wanting to whisper the truth into her hair. 'I couldn't do it, Ali. Not face to face. So I pulled into a layby and called them from there.'

'You told them what had been done to Dave's body over the phone?'

He kept his silence, waiting to be admonished.

'Well,' she shrugged, 'you've done it now, that's the main thing.'

Taking a deep breath, he pulled back to look at her. 'I feel so shit. Mum was so upset.'

'What did you say?' she murmured.

'The only thing I could think of was her religion. So I told her Dave had gone to a better place – and that all we're talking about here are his remains. It's weird, for the first time in my life, I want to believe that stuff, too.'

'And Mary? How did she take it?'

He looked down at Punch, finding comfort in the absence of judgement in the animal's stare. 'She just wants him back.' He glanced back at his wife and she slid her arms round his neck.

Silently, they embraced. 'I've missed you, Ali.' The urge to just stay in his house began to overwhelm him and he had to lift his face from her hair. 'What a bloody nightmare this all is.'

Alice leaned back, her eyes searching his face. 'You shouldn't be out there on your own.'

He couldn't meet her stare. 'It's keeping me busy. That's what they say, don't they? Don't sit around and dwell.'

'Yes, as long as you're not avoiding the fact he's gone. It's natural to feel disbelief or to be numb or depressed. Even angry. People don't realise that fury is a common response to losing a loved one.'

Fury, Jon thought. Oh, I feel that all right. But I'll wait for the right person to release that particular emotion on. 'It's not helped by the fact the team investigating this whole thing don't know their arses from their elbows.'

'Be tactful, Jon. Don't start throwing your weight around and getting their backs up.'

Too late for that, he thought. 'What are you up to with Holly this afternoon?'

Her hands dropped from his neck. 'You mean you're not staying here?'

'I can't, Alice. There's so much needs doing out there.'

'But Rick's coming over later. I invited him for dinner, remember?'

'Yeah – Thai curry. He's coming anyway, I told him I can't make it. You two will have a good catch-up without me.'

'But you'll pop back tomorrow, won't you? For the scan.'

'Of course. I might have to meet you at the hospital, but I'll call before I set off from Haverdale.'

She nodded, then looked towards the doorway of the telly room. 'I don't know what we'll do this afternoon. I suppose see if Mary needs a hand.'

He thought about how the call to his mum had ended and a lump rose in his throat. 'Probably a good idea.' He stepped around her and into the kitchen. One of the Easter eggs on the shelf above the radiator was now partially eaten. Next to that was a row of books, mostly ones on cookery. He walked his fingers past them, then plucked the Ordnance Survey map from the end. Flipping it over in his hand, he looked at the front: *Explorer OL1. The Peak District.*

They'd bought it for Sunday afternoon walks round Edale and Ladybower reservoir. Knowing he'd be using it to try and plot his brother's last movements, he couldn't imagine plotting leisurely strolls with it ever again.

Fourteen

As he left the relatively flat countryside that surrounded Manchester and entered the undulating landscape of the Peak District, he studied it with fresh interest. At its outer edges, patches of oak interspersed with pine trees thrived by the side of the road. But, as the low, green hills began to buckle and rear more dramatically, the trees were increasingly confined to grooves and ruts in the land.

The exposed slopes became wilder in appearance, their covering of coarse grass broken only by the endless drystone walls and occasional gnarled bush that bristled with spikes.

By the time he was approaching the turn-off for Haverdale, his eyes were flicking continuously to the hills on his right. A small car park came into view and he pulled into it, glancing at the wooden sign at the entrance: 'Footpath to Sharston Edge'.

That was where one of the digs had occurred, he remembered, climbing out of the car. The wide gravel track led him across some steep fields, the occasional rock or boulder making progress tricky. The land levelled off at the summit and he paused, hands on hips, as he got his breath. A light breeze caressed his ears and in front of him a line of stone formations rose up out of the exposed rock. They had the appearance of dollops of ice cream that had been left out of the freezer too long – curved edges bulging out. He recalled more dramatic examples on the cliffs that overlooked Edale: millstone grit, worn smooth by millennia of sleet, snow, hail and wind.

Glancing about, he could see no evidence of where the nocturnal dig had taken place, so he stepped nearer to the melting towers of rock for the view beyond. Fields and hills stretched away below and he craned his neck to see how big the drop was. Lying at the base of the cliff some forty feet down, he was shocked to see the twisted remains of a dead sheep, its tattered fleece contrasting sharply with the sombre grey boulders around it.

Suddenly aware of his own vulnerability to an unexpected gust of wind, he stepped back, hand searching out a grip on the rough pillar of stone at his side. A blurred spot in the sky caused him to blink, and for a moment, he didn't know if the object was rushing at him, or away. He felt the muscles behind his eyes contract as his brain tried to fix it in his view.

Then he realised it was doing neither, the thing was a bird of prey – a kestrel – wings rapidly moving, tail feathers splayed against the buffeting swirls of air. He guessed it was hovering a couple of hundred metres off, close enough for him to see the hunching of its shoulders as the bird's head tilted down. Both wings stopped and suddenly the life could have gone out of it; a dead thing, dropping from the sky. The horizon swallowed it and Jon concentrated on the fields themselves, scanning for movement of any kind.

Seconds later it flashed across a lighter patch of grass, keeping low and banking sharply towards a copse of trees. He couldn't see if anything was in its talons.

He turned to the stones around him. So, had this spot really once been used as a burial place for men not long out of caves? Perhaps the sentinel-like formations acted as a kind of tombstone, intended to mark for ever the resting place of family and friends. And if true, had Dave really been out here, trying to plunder their graves?

Before his car had even come to a halt, he could see the library was shut. Damn, bank holiday. He cursed, reaching for the glove compartment and searching for a piece of paper inside.

Using the road map as a rest, he scrawled out a note, folded it over and then got out of his car. The letter box was located at the base of the library's front door and through the criss-cross of wire in the glass panel above it, he could see a couple of books on the doormat.

He pressed his note against the window and wrote, 'FAO The Head Librarian', then slotted it through. Open again tomorrow, he thought. I'll call back for some answers then.

He swung the car round, rejoined the high street and proceeded to the police station. This time the waiting room was deserted as he pressed the buzzer.

A minute later, the speaker crackled. 'Can I help?'

'DI Spicer, Greater Manchester Police. Are Constables Spiers or Batyra about?'

'Hang on.'

Another minute before the speaker came back to life. 'What's it about, please?'

Jon had stepped back, his hand on the door handle in readiness to be buzzed in. 'Sorry?'

'What is the nature of your call, sir?'

The nature of my call? The back of his neck tingled. The bastards won't let me in. He paused, just about to let rip. 'Formal identification of my brother. I forgot to sign the papers.'

This time a gap of seconds before he recognised Constable Batyra's voice. 'I'll meet you on the stairs.'

The lock finally buzzed and Jon yanked the door open so hard it banged against the wall, knocking a flake of plaster to the floor. Fuck them.

Halfway up, Constable Batyra spoke out from the flight of stairs above. 'DI Spicer, thanks for popping back. I was thinking a drive over to Manchester was coming my way.'

Jon glanced up to see her face peering over the railing. 'No problem.' He made himself smile.

When he reached the top, she was holding the door to the corridor open. 'Can I get you a tea or coffee?'

'Coffee would be good.'

'Black, no sugar, wasn't it?' she said with a backward glance, leading him down the corridor.

'Yes, thanks. How are enquiries going?'

'Fairly well. Full support will be in tomorrow. Superintendent Mallin is briefing everyone first thing.'

They entered the main room and Jon's eyes swept about.

Six people this time. All round one desk. No sign of Spiers and the corner put aside for Dave's investigation was deserted. He looked questioningly at Batyra and her hand flapped awkwardly in the direction of her colleagues. 'There was a fatal RTA on the Snake Pass late last night. One car's turned out to be stolen and its driver fled the scene. The dead person is the daughter of one of the town's councillors. Everyone's kind of tied up on that.'

'And the investigation into my brother's murder?'

Shazia looked towards the doors. 'The Super mentioned about putting a request in for some extra manpower from Sheffield.'

Jon nodded, keeping himself calm. 'I see. Are the papers at your desk?'

'Yes.' She set off.

As Jon followed, he examined the pile of evidence bags across the room. Nothing looked like it had been moved since the day before.

Batyra retrieved the forms from her top drawer. 'OK, I've typed up your statement. If you could check it over and sign, we're all done.'

'Of course.' He made a show of clearing his throat. 'Any chance of that coffee?'

'Sorry, yes. I'll be right back.'

He bent over the forms, watching in the periphery of his vision until she'd left the room. As soon as the door swung shut, he stood up and stepped over to the evidence bags. Picking one up, he saw it contained the booklet entitled, *Walks of Note Around Haverdale*. The bag was narrow, only allowing him to get the pages partly open. Searching the contents pags, he saw a tick by walk number three. Haverdale – Sharston Edge – Wimble reservoir – Round Knoll – Haverdale. 6 miles, medium difficulty.

He strained the plastic of the bag, trying to see to which page he should turn. Short of breaking the seal on the bag and taking it out, it was useless. Putting it aside, he picked up the Ordnance Survey map. *Explorer OL1*, same as the one he had in his car. It only just squeezed inside the bag and there was no way he could unfold it to see what markings Dave might have made on the part that covered Haverdale.

The mobile phone caught his eye. Swapping bags, he studied the handset. The screen was blank and he pressed the power button, hoping the battery still had some life. To his relief, it lit up, moving through the registration stage before settling on the screensaver.

Jon studied the woman's face, just visible above the dried blood that covered most of the screen. There was something familiar about her. Not the actual person, more her expression, or perhaps posture. The way one shoulder was slightly raised? Through the plastic, Jon tried to scratch at the mobile's screen, working his nail back and forth in an attempt to remove his brother's blood.

'Spicer! What the bloody hell are you doing in my station?'

He turned to see Mallin standing in the doorway, face red with anger.

Constable Batyra appeared at his side, a cup in each hand. 'Sir, I let him in. He's signing the ID papers.'

Mallin's head jerked in her direction. 'I said that man was not to be allowed past reception, did I not?'

Jon watched the exchange, phone half raised towards them. 'Superintendent—'

'Did I not say that?' Mallin bellowed. 'I don't even want him in this town!'

'Sorry, sir. It's just that he came to formally—'

'He came to meddle in my investigation again. That's what he's come to do, Constable Batyra.' He pointed a finger at Jon. 'Put that evidence bag back, Spicer. Now!'

Jon tried again. 'This Zoe—'

'Now! Or, by God, I'll have you thrown out of here.'

Jon held the other man's eyes. I'd like to see you try. Turning round, he pressed the phone's off button and placed the bag with the others.

'What the hell are you playing at, Spicer?' Mallin was now striding towards him.

'Meaning?'

'I received a complaint from the owner of Hugo's. You barged into his kitchen, demanding to see what sort of venison was in his fridge.'

Shit, Jon thought. I should have realised word would travel fast in a dump like this.

'And I know an incident also occurred in The Tor, though the landlady is reluctant to elaborate beyond stating that you failed to pay for your drink.'

Jon glanced towards the window, envying a little bird as it flitted past. 'There's a link between poached venison and my brother's murder.'

'So you presumed to conduct your own investigation, in my town? Your arrogance astounds me.'

Jon caught the other man's eye. No, he wanted to say, the only astounding thing here is your incompetence.

'Then I receive a call from the manager at the Haven Inn. You actually entered the room your brother stayed in, claiming I authorised it?'

Jon wanted to step back, but didn't. 'Of course I didn't go in.' He swallowed, hoping that Brian Salt was as useless at gathering forensic evidence as Nikki had made out. 'I just opened the door to see the last place he'd stayed.'

Mallin narrowed his eyes. 'And eat the last food he'd eaten? There's something morbid in your brain, DI Spicer. Get some help.'

Jon gestured at the table. 'Just let me see that map and walking book. Dave was here trying to find something, I know it.'

Mallin shook his head. 'You've done enough damage already – to this investigation and your career. Count yourself lucky that, rather than having you arrested, I elected to phone Manchester instead. I've spoken to a DCI Buchanon. Expect a call.'

Jon seriously considered grabbing the evidence bags and making a run for it. 'Can you not ...'

'DI Spicer, you have three minutes to get out of this building. No, you've got thirty minutes to be out of Haverdale altogether.' He turned to the watching officers. 'Sergeant Brooks and Constable Conway will escort you downstairs and back to the Haven Inn. Once you're there, you'll pack your bags and bugger off back to Manchester.'

Jon dragged his gaze from the evidence bags and took a step towards the door. 'You need to find Redino, can you not see that?'

There was a rustle of paper behind him. 'And put your name on this before you go.'

Mallin was holding up the ID form. Jon looked at it, knowing that if he did, his brother's name would be in the next morning's papers. 'And give you a green light to brief the press that Dave was dealing drugs to this town?'

Mallin half lowered his eyes and let out a sigh. 'DI Spicer, either you sign or I ask your parents out here to make another identification.'

Jon took a step back towards Mallin and he saw a flicker of fear in the other man's eyes. 'Don't you dare try talking to them.'

Mallin edged back an inch. 'Well, don't force my hand.'

Jon snatched the sheet from the other man's grip. 'Where's a fucking pen?'

The patrol car followed him down the high street, all the way back to the Haven Inn. He parked by the front entrance and walked in. The man behind the counter started fiddling with his name badge.

'You the manager?' Jon demanded.

'Yes.'

'Give yourself a gold star for that poxy badge of yours. And I need to check out.' He carried on through to the corridor and strode up to his door. His room looked a mess as he snatched crumpled clothes and shoved them in his bag. The whisky bottle was still by the telly and he laid it across the top of his things, zipped up the bag and walked out.

Halfway down the corridor, his phone started to ring. Seeing Buchanon's name on the screen, he shoved it back in his pocket and let it ring out. After signing his bill, he walked outside and saw that the patrol car was still there.

Taking his time, he opened up his own vehicle, started it

up and pulled slowly out onto the road, eyes on his rear-view mirror. The police car followed him for a good three miles, before flashing its lights and pulling into a layby.

Jon continued on the road towards Manchester, passing through the villages of Hope and Castleton on the way. But when he reached the junction with the A624, he took the right-hand turn and followed the road up to the A57. He turned right again, driving back out into the National Park, along the side of Ladybower reservoir and finally to the turn off with the A6013. Forty-five minutes later, he'd completed his circle and was entering Haverdale from the north end of its high street.

The patrol car was back in the station car park as he drove past, turned into Bent's Lane and parked outside The Spread Eagle pub. His phone started ringing: Buchanon, again. He scrolled through the menu and diverted all calls straight to answerphone.

The cloying smell brought Zoe out of her reverie. Dragging her eyes from the distant hills, she looked at her son. 'Christ, Jake, have you shat again?'

He shook his head and turned back to the telly, nappy distended under his Babygro, an action figure grasped in each hand.

'For fuck's sake.' She ground her cigarette out, then lifted him up and carried him through to his bedroom. Inside was a cot and a set of drawers Dave had found advertised in a nearby news-agent's. The naked bulb hanging from the flex made the room too bright. She placed him on the changing mat and opened the top drawer. Nine nappies left. She ran a hand through her hair. This can't go on much longer. I can't go on much longer.

'Come on, then,' she sighed, undoing the poppers on his Babygro and pushing it up around his chest. Each breath seemed to suck at the skin between his ribs. The Velcro tabs on the nappy made a ripping sound as she peeled it open. Diarrhoea. Watery-brown paste was smeared almost all the way up to his belly button. The smell intensified.

He whined and tried to touch his behind.

'Don't!' She pushed his hand away and he started to whimper as she tugged wipes from the packet. 'Dirty. Don't touch.'

'Mama.'

'I know, kidder. Mummy make it better.' As she mopped his skin clean, revealing bright red patches on each buttock, Jake's hips began to writhe and his wheezes grew louder. Holding him still with one hand, she tried to position a clean nappy under him with the other. He managed to grab a corner and pull the thing to the side.

'Stop it!' she yelled, palm raised to slap him. His wheeze changed to a little gasp of terror and, for a moment, things teetered on the brink. Then she lowered her hand and lifted him up. 'I'm sorry, Jake. I'm sorry.'

She pressed him to her skinny chest, feeling his ribs heaving beneath her hand. After a few minutes, his cries subsided into sobs and then to shallow breaths. Just as she was wondering if he was asleep, he looked up and their eyes met. 'OK, now?'

He raised a finger to her lips and she kissed it before saying, 'Come on, then. Let's get you sorted.'

He didn't protest when she gently lowered him back down. Just as she was wrapping the clean nappy round him, the letter box creaked open.

'Mind the baby doesn't nick this.'

Salvio's voice. She stood still, waiting for anything else. But the letter box clanked shut, leaving her with the sound of Jake's labouring lungs. Placing him in his cot, she peeped out of the doorway. A small, silver square of foil was lying on the carpet. Keeping on tiptoes, she walked quickly over, picked it up with a finger and thumb and ducked back in to Jake's room.

He moaned, little fingers reaching over the bars towards her.

'Hang on,' she murmured, eyes on the little package. Knowing the way Salvio's mind worked, she could guess what would be inside. Slowly, she peeled back the diagonal folds. A teaspoon's worth of brown powder. The sneaky shit. Before she could stop it, her mind jumped to the kitchen. She had a cigarette lighter and there was a straw attached to one of Jake's drink cartons. She could be smoking this in no time. An ache in her stomach opened as she gazed at the tiny mound of granules. Oh, that soft, sweet feeling, she thought. It used to cradle me so beautifully.

'Mama?'

She glanced to her side, unable to look him in the eye. A few more toys and he'd be happy sitting there for a while. Besides, it was time for his sleep soon.

'Plenty more where that came from,' Salvio cooed from out-side her door. 'Come on, Zoe, open up.'

She stepped towards the corridor, foil cupped protectively in her palm. The muscles in her legs tensed as urges fought in her head. Memories of how good it felt, then vague recollections of the dark days when Dave weaned her off it for the first time. His presence at her side. Always at her side. She remembered surfacing from delirious bouts of sleep, the sticky sheet wrapping her like a shroud and Dave above her, a cool flannel in his hand.

His look of shock when he sussed that she was on it again, seven months' pregnant with Jake. It was the closest she'd seen him come to crying when she'd admitted to having been using again for weeks. Coming off it once more, this time confined to a hospital ward. But she'd done it and now Salvio was here posting the stuff through her door.

'Mama?'

'Shush now, Mummy's coming back.' Guiltily, she glanced back at her son then stepped from the room.

Fifteen

The Spread Eagle was pretty much deserted – a couple of old men were sitting in the bar area chatting to Trevor Curtis and Jon could hear they were discussing the murder, idly speculating on where the dead man might have come from and what he had done to deserve such a fate.

Next to the fireplace was a younger couple sharing a basket of chips. The large-screen TV in the side room was tuned to a sport channel, where a couple of pundits were in earnest discussion. Jon read the words running across the base of the screen: 'Live Rugby Union, Sale Sharks v Newcastle Falcons, kick-off 5 pm.'

A few minutes' time, Jon thought, casting a quick glance around the rest of the pub. No Ian Flynn. He rested his elbows on the bar. 'Afternoon, pint of Timothy Taylor, please.'

Curtis reached up for a glass, revealing a sweat patch under his arm. 'Finished work, then?'

Jon remembered that he'd mentioned getting the train into Sheffield for his job. 'Knocked off early. Not much you can sort out on a bank holiday.'

'What is it you do, then?'

Recalling his days in uniform when he'd chat with bouncers outside Manchester's night spots, Jon reverted to his customary story for when his real job needed to be kept secret. 'Helping to set up a nightclub opening in Sheffield. Security.'

'Oh? You mean on the doors?' He placed a full pint on the bar.

Jon straightened up, handing over a fiver. 'Everything – over-seeing the CCTV system, buying intercoms for the doormen, all that stuff.'

'Sounds like the Wild West in some of those city centre places nowadays.' Curtis rang the drink in and fished change out from the till's drawer.

A voice called out. 'Get in there! Billy fucking Whizz, my man! Trev, can you turn the sound up?'

Jon glanced towards the side room. The two teams were now running out onto the pitch and, tucked away in the corner with his eyes glued to the screen, was a man. Angular features, shaved head and the glint of metal in his ear.

'Right you are, Ian.' Trevor pointed a remote and the volume increased.

'Think I'll watch that, too.' Jon took his drink and stepped into the side room. If Flynn had noticed his entry, he didn't show it. Jon chose the table in the other corner and sat down. 'Should be a good match, this.'

Flynn's eyes didn't move from the television. 'Yeah.'

'Sale are in cracking form.'

'Play, do you?'

'Did.' He took a sip. 'Body can't take it now. You?'

Flynn's head shook, eyes yet to actually connect with Jon's. 'Just like watching it. You get good fights in rugby.'

'You're not wrong there.'

The match kicked off and they sat in silence, Jon biding his time, sizing the other man up. After a few minutes Flynn lit a cigarette, holding it where his fingers joined, so when he took a drag, his hand wrapped around his mouth like it was a gag.

The fly-half kicked deep into Sale's territory and Jason Robinson caught the ball.

Flynn jabbed his cigarette at the screen. 'Fucking go, Billy! Run at them.'

From his own try-line with less than ten minutes gone? Jon thought. Flynn obviously didn't have a bloody clue. Robinson cleared the ball out of his half and the two sets of forwards gathered for the line-out.

'Trev, another pint in here, mate.' Flynn waved his empty glass.

The landlord appeared a few moments later, placed a fresh pint on Flynn's table and took the empty one.

'Put it on the tab, cheers,' Flynn said, hardly looking at the man.

'Another for you?' Trevor nodded at Jon's glass.

He tilted his half-finished drink. 'Table service?'

'Only when it's quiet.'

'Go on, then. A Landlord, please.' Jon's phone beeped and Flynn's head cocked slightly to the side. 'Bloody work,' Jon apologised. 'I'll turn it off in a minute.' He glanced at the screen and saw it was a text from Rick: 'Buchanon's after you, big time. No luck with finding Zoe. Sorry.'

Jon cursed to himself. She had to be somewhere. Quickly he keyed in a reply.

'Please keep looking.'

'What do you do?' Flynn's eyes were on Jon for a split second before he turned away.

'Nightclub security.'

'Yeah? Whereabouts?'

'North-east, mainly. But my boss is opening a place in Sheffield, so I'm based down here for a bit.'

Flynn spoke from the side of his mouth, unwilling to miss any of the match. 'Staying in Haverdale?'

'When you're stuck in clubs all night, you appreciate open space.'

Curtis returned with Jon's drink. 'That's two thirty.'

Jon handed him thirty pence too much. 'And one for yourself.'

'Thank you.'

He was just taking another sip when Flynn spoke again. 'What's it like dealing with those Geordie nutters?'

Jon smiled. 'They're all right. Still settle things with their fists most of the time, up there.'

Light from the screen played on Flynn's face. 'Never been. Heard it's mayhem, though.'

'You're probably thinking of the Bigg Market on a weekend. That place can get interesting.'

The two teams locked together for a scrum on Newcastle's twenty-two. Jon saw the props grappling with each other's arms on the side away from the referee. Next instant the scrum collapsed and the referee blew for a reset.

'Bollocks,' Jon said quietly. 'That was a penalty to Sale.'

Flynn was frowning. 'What happened?'

Jon sat back. 'Roberts, the Sale prop, is turning his opposite man inside out. So the Newcastle player collapsed the scrum.'

Flynn took a proper glance over and Jon knew the other man would have noticed the scar running through his eyebrow and the lump where the bridge of his nose had been broken. 'That right?'

'Watch,' Jon replied. 'If he brings it down again, there might be some punching.'

Flynn sat forward as the two sets of forwards came together once more. Jon saw the Newcastle player trying to slip his binding again and next thing the two players' heads went up and fists started to fly.

'Fucking do him!' Flynn shouted delightedly, shadow-punching the air. The referee got between them, cheeks puffing on his whistle.

Flynn swivelled his chair towards Jon. 'Good call, mate, you were right.'

'It'll probably kick off again before full time.'

'Yeah? Better get another drink, then. You want one?'

Less than a quarter of Jon's pint was gone, but he wasn't going to miss this opportunity. 'Yeah, cheers.'

'Trev!' Flynn yelled. 'Two more over here, mate.'

By the second half of the match, they were chatting during any break in play, Flynn pumping Jon for stories about rugby fights. By the end of the match, Jon had moved over to join Flynn at his table and they were four pints up. The pub was now getting busier and, as Jon headed to the bar to get another round, the lads from the night before trooped in.

One peeled away from the group, ducked his head into the side bar and said something. Flynn gave a nod and the lad headed straight for the toilets. A few seconds later Flynn followed him through the door.

Jon returned to their table and sat down. After a minute, Flynn returned, rubbing his hands. He slid back into his chair beside Jon's. 'What's next?'

'Highlights of the other pool matches,' Jon replied, tapping his trousers for change. 'I need some smokes.' He stepped back into the main part of the bar, one eye on the doors to the toilets. The lad emerged, and as he approached his mates, raised a thumb at waist height.

Their shoulders relaxed and the group broke into grins. Jon fished the packet of cigarettes from the tray and rejoined Flynn. 'So, what do people do for a living in Haverdale?' he asked, ripping the cellophane off the cigarettes, cracking the lid and partially sliding two out. He held the packet towards Flynn.

'Cheers.' He took one and picked up his lighter. 'A bit of farming, tourist stuff. More and more incomers who catch the train into Sheffield or Manchester. Yuppy types.'

Yuppy, Jon thought. Last time I heard that word used in seriousness was back in the eighties. 'Farming's not an easy game nowadays.'

'Wouldn't know.' Flynn smiled, taking the hook Jon had dangled.

He feigned surprise. 'That's not what you do then?'

'Nah. Get up at the crack of dawn every day? Fuck that.'

Jon gave a knowing grin. 'Easier ways to make a living than that.'

Their eyes touched for a moment.

'So this security business.' Flynn lit their cigarettes. 'Who gives you the nod, for the doormen?'

Jon regarded Flynn for a second, letting his eyes narrow just a fraction. 'What do you mean, mate?'

Flynn leaned forward. 'Come on. In Manchester, no one gets employed without the say-so of the gangs. Longsight Crew, Pit Bull Crew, Salford Mob, that lot. The Noonan family, ever heard of them?'

Jon sat back. The guy had been watching too much bloody television. 'You know Newcastle, then?'

'No. But I know how things work. Is the city divided up between gangs, like Manchester?'

Jon shrugged. 'I don't know. When we employ door staff, we go through the proper channels. Everything's done by the book.'

'Yeah, right.' Flynn grinned, taking a drag. 'And that's how you're doing it in Sheffield, too?'

'So, how do you earn a crust?'

Flynn bobbed his chin from side to side. 'Bit of this, bit of that. Whatever comes my way.'

As Jon gave a knowing nod, Flynn's mobile started to ring. He pulled it from the side pocket of his combat trousers. 'Yeah?'

Jon sat back, pretending to be interested in the television.

Flynn turned away. 'The Spread. Where are you? Now? Yeah, could do.' He cut the call and stood.

'You're off?' Jon asked, glancing up at him.

Flynn shook his head. 'Night's only just getting started. I need to see someone out front.'

Once Ian Flynn had hurried from the room, Jon shifted his chair to the side and craned his neck to peer through the mullioned window set deep in the pub's thick wall. An Aston Martin pulled up on the road outside.

Flynn appeared, circled the car with his hands in his pockets and leaned down to the driver's window. After a few words there followed a quick exchange, Flynn ramming whatever he'd been given deep into the pocket of his trousers before straightening up. He lifted a hand to his brow and doffed an imaginary cap as the car pulled away.

Jon leaned back, eyes on the TV screen as he replayed what he'd just seen. An exchange had just taken place, but he couldn't say who was doing the buying and who the selling.

Sixteen

Alice opened the front door to see Rick outside, holding up a bottle of white wine. 'Hello, my darling.' She smiled, waving him inside. They embraced, planting a kiss on each other's cheek as they did so.

'You're looking great, Alice,' Rick said, pulling back. 'Started your kick-boxing classes again?'

'I don't think my doctor would recommend it in my state,' she sighed.

'Well, it looks like you've been doing something.'

She ran her hands down her slim waist. 'Wheeling Holly around in that buggy. She weighs a ton, that girl.'

Rick glanced up the stairs. 'All tucked up, is she?'

'Yeah. Look in on her, if you want. She's fast asleep.'

'Can I?' Rick beamed, handing over the bottle of wine and swiftly climbing the stairs.

Alice walked down the short corridor and into the kitchen. A plastic knocking sound was coming from the corner, where Punch was trying to remove every speck of food from his dog bowl. After popping some rice in the microwave, she checked the curry was simmering nicely, the aroma of galangal and lemon grass rising up as she peeked under the lid of the pan.

The wine was open and two glasses poured when Rick walked into the kitchen. 'She is so adorable. Does she always sleep on her stomach like that?'

'Bum in the air?'

'Yes.'

'Ever since she went into her junior bed. God knows why.'

'So sweet.'

Punch crossed the room, avoiding Rick's outstretched fingers and sloping off towards the front door.

'Suit yourself,' Rick shrugged.

'It's because you're a man,' Alice explained.

'It's because I'm not Jon,' Rick replied with an awkward smile. He glanced at the chair where Jon usually sat. 'God, I hope he's all right.'

Alice's eyes were on the empty chair, too. 'I know. I think he's still in a state of shock, to be honest. Though what is beginning to sink in is the guilt. That's what's driving him on. Feeling like he failed his little brother.'

Rick rubbed at an eyebrow. 'I can't believe it's well over a year since Jon and I saw him that time outside the cathedral.'

'Neither can Jon. He's kept a lookout since then, scanned the arrest logs – always meaning to make a proper effort to find him.'

'Dave didn't want to be found. That was the problem. He probably wasn't even in Manchester during that time.'

'I know, but try telling Jon that. So now, typically, he's thrown himself into the investigation. Can you believe they've asked him to help find his brother's killer?'

Rick reached for his glass and took a long sip. 'It does seem odd.'

'Odd? It's bloody out-of-order. Of course, Jon's leapt at the chance, but they should never have given him it in the first place.' She paused. 'What do you reckon Dave was up to out in Haverdale?'

Rick looked down at the table. 'I don't know.'

'Could it have been to do with drugs?'

He sighed. 'This doesn't ever get to Jon?'

'Of course not.'

'It doesn't look good. Loyal to the last, Jon's fighting his corner. But it doesn't look good.'

'That's pretty much what I thought,' she stated sadly. 'But once he decides on something, that's it. I just hope it's another officer – and not Jon – who finds Dave's killer.'

'Me, too. Isn't anger another early stage of grief?'

Their gazes touched, and Rick saw the unease in Alice's eyes. He thought back to the case with the church arsonist, doubt about Jon's explanation of how the man actually died still plaguing him.

Alice sat down. 'Come on then,' she patted the table. 'What do you know?'

Glad to shelve his suspicions, Rick hung his jacket on the back of his chair and sat down. 'Plenty. But first, how's things with you, Mrs Spicer? Another baby. How bloody exciting is that?'

'I know.' She placed a hand across her lower stomach. 'It's the first scan tomorrow.'

'You'll get a print-out?'

'Of course.'

'I can't wait to see it. Another little Spicer, God help us all. Still want it to be a boy?'

Alice reached for her wine glass, running a forefinger round its base. 'Yes,' she said slowly, 'it would be nice to have a boy. I think it would be good for Jon, too.'

'He couldn't dote on Holly any more.'

'Exactly. She's got him round her little finger. He'd be different with a boy, less of a lump of jelly.'

'He'll have the poor thing out on the rugby pitch before he can walk. I can see it now. In an England shirt, if they make them small enough.'

Alice laughed. 'Oh, believe me, they do. He's already checked the RFU website.' She took a sip of wine. 'How's things with you and Andy?'

Rick thought about his boyfriend. Andy was an events manager who seemed to have half the phone numbers for Manchester United's and Manchester City's football teams in his mobile phone. 'It's his fortieth this November. Can you believe it? Me hitched up with a forty-year-old.'

'He could pass for someone a lot younger than that, and you know it.'

'I'm not so sure. He's got a few grey hairs creeping in.' He brushed the tips of his fingers above an ear.

'Yes, but that body. Christ Almighty.'

He grinned, picturing Andy's torso. 'The body? I suppose it might take a few years off him.'

Alice whistled. 'And the bloody rest. It's like something from the cover of *Men's Health* magazine.' She gave him an impish glance. 'No wedding bells as yet?'

Rick waved a hand. 'No, thank you. Actually ...' He sat up and placed an elbow on the table. 'Remember I mentioned that couple? Team mates of Sheila who plays lacrosse?'

'The lesbian couple? Asking about sperm donors, weren't they?'

'I met them the other day.'

'No! You didn't?' Now Alice was leaning forwards. 'Go on, tell me.'

'It was weird, actually,' Rick replied with a frown. 'They came to my flat. Kind of interviewed me.'

'Your flat? Last time we spoke, you were only thinking about it.'

'I know. I reckoned it couldn't do any harm to meet up. Once I told Sheila, that was it: they were on to me straight away.'

'So what happened? They came to your flat ... and?'

'Yeah, to see where I live. They've read books, or a guide, or something. It was all, I don't know, a bit clinical, somehow.'

'How do you mean?'

'Like I was under the spotlight. Loads of questions about my health, education, degree course. I even joked at one point that they could have a copy of my CV. They were delighted.'

'That's outrageous! They wanted your CV?'

'Yes! I had to print one off, there and then. Straight into their file, it went.'

Alice took another sip of wine, looking thoughtful. 'I suppose you'd want to know as much about a donor as possible.'

'Yeah, I guess. But it started putting me off, to be honest. They were so intense. At least, the older one was. I got the impression she was the one pushing everything forward.'

'But you haven't agreed to anything. You haven't, you

know …' With a light-hearted grimace, she waved a finger in the direction of Rick's crotch. 'Produced anything?'

'No.' Rick crossed his legs, feigning indignation. 'I have not produced anything.'

'How will they do it? Just out of interest.'

'IVF. There's a clinic off Deansgate that's very sympathetic to lesbian couples. Isabelle – the younger one – has had a load of eggs harvested and put in storage. Now they just need to add some little wrigglers.'

Alice giggled. 'What are the couple like, then?'

Rick hunched a shoulder. 'Professionals. Own a house in Chorlton. Cathy's a lawyer, Isabelle is a manager for John Lewis.'

'Nice, were they? Apart from the interrogation.'

'Oh, they were just on edge. I could tell they were fine. They're both obviously intelligent and organised. You can just tell it's something they've really set their hearts on.'

'And which one will carry the baby? Doesn't one partner sometimes become pregnant with the other's egg?'

'Cathy, the lawyer, is nearly forty. Isabelle's early thirties. She plays in attack for the lacrosse team. Very athletic looking. Your sort of build, in fact.'

'Thanks.' Alice smoothed a hand over a slender thigh.

'Well, it's true. Anyway, she'll carry the baby.'

'Fair enough. If they're a stable, well-balanced couple, why not?'

'Exactly.' Rick's voice lacked conviction.

Alice studied him. 'But there's something else?'

He shifted a little. 'Yes. At first, I said I'd prefer just to donate the sperm, then have nothing more to do with it. But I've been thinking about things and now I'm not so sure.'

'Why?'

'Well … you know, a baby's going to be born. I'll see a photo of it and I know it won't be enough. I don't mean full involvement. The couple wouldn't agree to that, anyway. But the odd bit of contact as the kid grows up.' His hand flipped over, fingers stiff with agitation. 'Then there's school. What if he or she gets bullied for having two mums? If I'm at least a presence − if only in the background − it might make things easier.'

Alice closed a hand over Rick's, smoothing his fingers flat against the table. 'You would make such a great dad.'

He looked down, embarrassed.

'You would,' she insisted. 'Just the fact you're already concerned about things like that. And you're a natural with Holly.'

'One thing would be really funny if I had more involvement − Jon's reaction if I turned up here with a little baby and then told him it was mine. Could you imagine his reaction?'

Alice laughed. 'That would floor him more effectively than any rugby tackle. We'd have to bring him round with some brandy.'

'It would be something to see,' Rick agreed.

'What does Andy think about all this?'

There was a hint of regret in Rick's smile. 'He's not bothered. As long as I'm happy.'

'He's never mentioned kids, then?'

'Andy?' Rick looked shocked. 'God, no. He's not the slightest bit interested.' His voice lightened. 'It might get in the way of his sessions at the gym.'

'So, what's the score with this couple? About the dad's part.'

'They envisage him playing a minor role. But they seemed fine when I said I'd prefer no involvement.'

'Maybe you'd better let them know you're thinking along their lines now.'

'There's more.'

Alice raised her eyebrows, inviting him to continue.

'I'm not the only one they're talking to.'

'Sorry?'

'As they were leaving, they just dropped it in. There's some other guy who said he'd be prepared to help out.'

'Bloody hell, this gets more complicated by the minute.'

'I know. But you know what's strange? It really got my hackles up. Me, hardly your typical alpha male, really − and I mean really − wants to beat this bloke. I've never met him, seen him, spoken to him, but I so want to beat him.' A mock sternness entered his voice. 'My sperm will fertilise that egg. Not his. Mine!'

Alice burst out laughing. 'Fucking hell, Rick. You're going all Tarzan on me.'

He slid his hand out from under hers and beat his fists lightly against his chest. Alice cocked her head to the side. 'Rick? That's really not you.'

He lowered his hands. 'Couldn't agree more. But I tell you, it's really got to me. I mean, what if the other guy is some perfect physical specimen? With a doctorate from Cambridge? He probably runs marathons before breakfast, makes cordon bleu meals with one hand while trading stocks and shares over the internet with the other. He probably makes George Clooney look ugly.' He paused for breath. 'Come to think of it, I wouldn't mind shagging him.'

'Me, too,' Alice agreed. 'So what's the score, now?'

'They said they'd be in contact within forty-eight hours.' He glanced at his jacket. 'I can't stop checking my bloody phone for texts. It's ridiculous.'

The microwave pinged and Alice got to her feet. 'They'd be mad not to pick you. You'll get the call, I know it. Now, shall we eat?'

Seventeen

'Time, please! Come on, gents, sling your bloody hooks.'

Jon looked around, exhaling smoke as he did so. Glasses littered the table and the ashtray was sprouting a forest of butts. Shit, he thought, feeling the tightness in his chest. I'm not used to hammering it like this.

'Haven't you two got a home to go to?' Curtis began stacking their empties into a tower.

Jon pictured his car parked outside. A crappy few hours of sleep and then what? He couldn't prove to Mallin that any drugs being sold in The Spread Eagle were coming from Flynn.

The other man sank the last of his pint. 'Fancy carrying on? I've got plenty of stuff at mine.'

Jon sat up. The night wasn't over yet. 'Yeah? How far is it?'

'Two minutes. On the bike.'

'You've got a motorbike?' Jon glanced towards the window. 'Sounds like a plan to me.'

Flynn led the way out of the back door and they crossed a yard cramped with empty tables and plastic chairs. A security light came on, revealing a motorbike propped on its stand in the lane behind the building. Jon noticed the chunky diamond-shaped tread on the tyres. 'Off-roader?'

'Kawasaki KDX 250.'

'What about the Old Bill?'

Flynn laughed. 'Round here? They'll be sitting in their beds by now, sipping cocoa.' He removed a black helmet hanging from the handlebars, a skull and cross-bones curling across the shiny dome. 'Want this?'

'No, you have it.'

Flynn raised his eyebrows. 'Sure? I might be a shit driver.'

Jon landed a token punch on Flynn's arm. 'You're not going to fucking-well crash.'

He chuckled in agreement. 'You take the seat and hang on to my sides. I'll stand; it's not far.'

Jon climbed on, feet resting on the ground as Flynn kicked the engine into life. The machine moved forward and Jon raised his legs. There was nothing to rest his feet on, and as the flexor muscles in his hips began to ache, he remembered the same sensation from his childhood. Dave, straining to propel his Grifter forward, Jon sitting on the seat behind, yelling, 'Yee-har!' at the back of his brother's head.

Flynn whipped them round a succession of sharp bends, each abrupt burst of acceleration making the trial bike's engine bark. Jon was glad of the rush of air; it cooled the flush of alcohol in his blood, allowing him to think.

Whatever you find out tonight, he told himself, you will keep in control. And if it turned out this man killed Dave, you will not put your hands around his neck and crush the miserable fucking life out of him.

By now they were at the edge of town and the few houses at the side of the road were spaced well apart. Beyond, the blackness of the countryside sat heavy and silent. Flynn turned sharply to the right, gunned the engine up a short, steep driveway and came to a halt before a seventies-style bungalow.

The porch light was on and Jon climbed stiffly off the bike. 'That was beginning to wreck my legs.'

Flynn laughed over his shoulder as he rocked the bike back onto its stand. Making a show of massaging his thighs, Jon then bent his knees. Using the light from the porch, he examined the rear tyre of Flynn's bike. There, imprinted on the inner edge of the rubber were the words, Bridgestone. He tried to make out the four or so letters and numbers next to it. A 'T' and possibly an 'O'.

'You coming?' Flynn called over, shouldering his way into the porch.

Straightening up, Jon looked at Flynn's home. Antlers were mounted on the wall next to the front door. Once inside,

Flynn's bungalow was as messy as Jon expected. Old copies of tabloid papers and men's magazines were strewn about on a faded settee and two armchairs. A coffee table with a few empty cans and a half-full ashtray. Cheap framed prints dotted the walls. Muhammad Ali looking down on an opponent lying at his feet, one of his shoulders jerking upwards, mouth wide open in a victorious shout. Marilyn Monroe, wearing a puffy ball gown, leaning forward with a languid look in her eyes. Robert De Niro, straps of a shoulder holster digging into his bare flesh as he held a magnum .44 towards a mirror. Jon's eyes returned to Marilyn's cleavage for a moment. These were the types of posters students picked up in Athena over ten years ago.

'Take a pew.' Flynn gestured at the sofa. 'Vodka?'

'Nice one.' Jon piled up a few copies of *FHM*, *Loaded* and the *Sun* and placed them on the table before sitting down.

As soon as Flynn headed for the kitchen, Jon's eyes systematically began searching the room. A desk and set of drawers in one corner. Next to it a flimsy-looking cabinet of videos and DVDs. *Rocky. Predator. First Blood.* Claude Van Damme, Steven Seagal, even Chuck Norris films. The worst macho shit Jon could imagine.

He looked up at the lampshade. Jagged plastic panels of beige arranged around four candle-shaped light bulbs. Two weren't working. He guessed that, apart from the pictures on the walls, nothing had changed in here since Flynn inherited the place from his parents.

Somehow it didn't look like the pad of an organised pusher. No flashy sound system or widescreen TV. None of the usual touches to announce the owner had serious money. It was just too ... Jon searched for the right word. Sad, he concluded. Flynn was a criminal all right. But strictly small scale, nothing more.

'Right.' Flynn walked back in and placed a bottle of Smirnoff, a bottle of lemonade and two glasses on the low table. He took the armchair opposite, hunching forward to pour the drinks. 'Splash of lemonade?'

'Yeah, why not?'

They clinked glasses and Flynn took a long sip, then breathed out. 'Fucking hits the mark, that.'

Jon swallowed, suppressing the sour taste by not breathing out until the liquid was well down his throat. God, he thought, I can't stand vodka. 'Beautiful.'

'So.' Flynn sat back, knees apart and glass cradled on his crotch. 'How are you sorting things out in Sheffield? Things must have been arranged already.'

Jon made a show of weighing the other man up. 'My boss takes care of all that stuff. He's the one with the connections.'

'That right?'

Jon lit a cigarette, holding it in his hand as he bent his head forward to scratch behind an ear. 'He runs a good chunk of Newcastle.'

Flynn looked pleased at the admission. 'So, he's branching out, then? Looking for a slice of Sheffield?'

'I wouldn't say that. His – what do you call it? The brother of his wife.'

'Brother-in-law?'

'Yeah, brother-in-law.' Jon deliberately widened his eyes, then looked down at his glass. 'Fuck, the vodka's already getting to me.'

Flynn laughed, pouring another glug into both glasses. 'Brother-in-law, then?'

'Yup. He's from Sheffield – that's the connection. It's just a favour to him.'

Flynn helped himself to one of Jon's cigarettes. 'What's his name?'

The casual way he asked it set off an alarm bell in Jon's head. How much does Flynn know about the scene in Sheffield? Probably more than me. 'What is this? Twenty questions?'

'Nah, just interested, that's all.'

Jon shrugged. 'Mick. Don't ask me his surname, though.'

Flynn took a drag, eyes staying on Jon as he did so.

Jon looked at the CD player in the corner. 'Let's have some music.' He stood up, making sure he appeared to lose his balance slightly as he stepped over. The untidy stack of cases was made

up of rave stuff, techno, trance. All of them best-of compila-
tions. 'You got a nightclub in Haverdale?'

'One. Kelly's.'

'Any good?'

'Well, it shuts at four.'

Jon searched lower, looking for anything that he'd be able to
stand for more than one track. 'I'm getting old. Just listening
to this club stuff makes me feel out of breath.' He settled on
Leftfield's *Leftism*. That would be a blast from the past. He put it
on and listened as the space noises and chirpy notes slowly built.
From behind him he heard Flynn announce, 'Tune!'

Notes from something like an electronic flute floated in just
ahead of the guy's voice. He remembered nights with Alice,
well before they'd even considered kids, swaying and bouncing
in a packed club. The drum kicked in and he felt a surge inside.
'Is that what you do, then? Work in Kelly's?'

Flynn hunched a shoulder. 'I go there some nights.'

'Working on the doors?'

Smiling he reached down to the floor at the side of the armchair and produced a kitchen tray that was littered with torn
packets of Rizlas. 'Any work I do there is for myself. Smoke?'

Jon was looking at the paraphernalia. Christ, the last time I
had any of that stuff was probably in the club where this track
was playing. A joint, passed round on the corner balcony where
he'd been dancing. 'Great.' He took his seat, watching Flynn
arrange cigarette papers in a delicate mosaic. 'So, it gets pretty
busy in the place?'

'Can do. Not that I'm allowed in there any more.'

'Oh?'

'Disagreement with the management.' He examined the
knuckles of his right hand by way of an explanation.

Pretending to place his drink on the floor out of Flynn's
sight, Jon quickly tipped most of it out on the carpet. 'Another
shot?'

'Go for it.'

He poured the lemonade first, then added a dribble of vodka
to his glass. Flynn got three times the amount. 'Cheers.'

The other man glanced up from the tray, took the drink Jon was holding out, knocked half of it back and continued crumbling the contents of a cigarette into the overlapping papers.

Jon's mind raced. He knew that, once the joint was handed over, his ability to manipulate the conversation would be quickly lost. Flynn produced a plastic pouch stuffed with green clumps and began to add little bits to the line of tobacco. Grass, thought Jon. But how strong? He nodded at the joint as Flynn rolled it up and licked the gummed edge. 'That's what you meant by working in Kelly's?'

Flynn gave another smile. 'How about this club in Sheffield?' He lit up and took a long drag. 'You're all covered on that front?'

The pungent aroma hit Jon just as the song began to build speed again. Treble notes lifted it to a wavering level before the bass drum began to thump. Jon remembered being in the club, the ability to talk draining away as the cannabis had taken hold. It was now, or never. 'Not necessarily.'

Their eyes met and Flynn sat back. 'Not necessarily?'

Jon tipped his head to the side. 'My boss is talking to someone locally, but he's a businessman. Why don't you make me an offer?'

Flynn went very still. 'Serious?'

'Serious.'

The other man held the joint across the table and Jon took it. He sucked in smoke, releasing a cloud from his mouth while trying to inhale as little as possible.

Flynn watched in silence as he blew a stream out. 'Good shit, isn't it?'

Jon examined the glowing tip, feeling his scalp begin to tighten. The music thudded on, someone now singing in African over a robotic hum. He took another shallow drag before handing it back. 'Certainly is. Home-grown?'

'That is. But this,' he produced another little plastic bag, this one full of browner plant heads, 'is what I can get you, any amount you want.'

Fucking bingo! Jon sipped his drink, trying to clear his head with more alcohol. His arm felt jerky as he put the drink back on the table. 'What's the difference between the two types?'

'This stuff?' Flynn held the joint beneath his nose and savoured the trail of smoke rising up. 'I keep for special occasions only. I got it from a guy who passes through every now and again.'

Jon's head went up as an image of Dave appeared in his mind. 'How do you mean?'

'He shows up around here, on and off.'

Something inside him started to sink and Jon was overcome with the urge to prop his chin on the heel of his hand. He forced himself onto the edge of his seat. 'Travelling salesman?'

Flynn passed the joint back. 'Something like that.'

'And he sold you this gear?'

'Yup.'

Jon dragged again, unsure if it was the drug or conversation causing his feelings of nausea.

'I've got other stuff, too. E's, speed, coke, rocks.' He produced a plastic bag, no bigger than a credit card. 'Ice. Can get all you want of this: the kids love it.'

Jon tried to focus. The bag held several crystalline lumps. Crystal meth. He squeezed his eyes shut. Oh, Christ. 'What did this bloke look like?'

'Bit shorter than you, skinny. Why?'

'Hair cropped? Your sort of length?'

Flynn stared for a second. 'Could have been. You know him, or something?'

Jon placed the joint in the ashtray and took another sip of vodka, swishing it round in his mouth before swallowing. Do I really want to know the answer to what I'm about to ask? 'Was he called Dave?'

Flynn's head stopped nodding to the music. 'Now look at who's asking all the questions.'

Head bowed, Jon rubbed at his temples. 'What was his name?'

Flynn's voice had hardened. 'You seem to know already. Yeah, it was Dave. What's it to you?'

Jon felt his head droop lower and his breath flooded out

as if someone had punched him in the stomach. His younger brother's descent played out in his head. Smoking dope now and then, moving on to stronger stuff, then dealing to fund a rapidly growing habit. His life contracting inward until just one priority remained: feeding the addiction. And before he knew it, he's in an unsuspecting country town, corrupting the community with the most addictive drugs known to man. Dave, you stupid, stupid bastard.

Flynn's voice sounded above the music. 'I said, what's it to you?'

My brother was Flynn's source of drugs. I can't believe it. Jon forced his head up and saw the other man was now also hunched forward, elbows resting on his knees, the knuckles of one hand brushing rhythmically against the palm of his other.

'You what?' Jon frowned, trying to buy a second to think. 'It was in the paper. Police identified him.'

Flynn's eyebrows shot up. 'What was that?'

'They identified him. That body on the hill.'

The other man licked his lips, eyes still wide. 'Which paper? The local one?'

Jon's thoughts were sliding into each other and he had the sense that the room was about to start revolving round. 'I think so. I only glimpsed it on the counter in the newsagent's.'

Flynn slid a magazine off the coffee table and picked up the copy of that day's *Herald* that had been lying beneath. 'There's nothing here. Was it front page? There's nothing here.'

Jon was staring at the carpet. You fucking idiot, Dave. You were here pushing everything under the sun.

'You sure it was the *Herald*?'

A shudder rattled through him, causing his legs to shiver. That was it, then. He got to his feet and this time the floor did lurch. The singer chanted on, African words lilting. Was that a French accent he had?

'You need to piss?'

Jon felt the blood draining from his face. He needed oxygen, but the air was thick with fumes. 'I'm off.'

'You're going? We're just getting started.'

'I'm off.'

Flynn stepped round the table. 'Wait up, what about business?'

Jon raised a hand, ready to slam the other man back into his seat. He guided his hand to the side, turning the movement into a flimsy wave. 'Another time, OK? I need to go.'

Flynn stood his ground, confusion clouding his face.

Woodenly, Jon moved past him and made for the door. 'I'll see you.'

Eighteen

Unable to see a thing, Jon worked the heel of his shoe into the softness at his feet, slowly swivelling his foot to gouge the rut deeper. As he lifted the bottle of Famous Grouse, the slosh of whisky inside was the only sound to break the utter silence.

Knowing it would do nothing to counter the desolation that filled his chest, he sucked more of the fiery liquid down. His brother had come to Haverdale to peddle drugs. That was the simple truth. A solitary shooting star rifled down the night, like a missile loosed at the earth by some vengeful god.

He looked to his side, knowing that, in the darkness probably no more than ten feet away, was the spot where Dave had died. There had been no crime-scene tape to stumble into when he'd finally made the summit. Like a blind man, he'd felt around for a decent hummock of grass to sit on.

So, was it Flynn? Had he murdered Dave? Somewhere a bird cried out, the beseeching noise sounding more like the mewl of a kitten. Unable to decide, Jon replayed his conversation with Flynn yet again. He'd needed a reason for knowing Dave's identity, and unable to think of anything else, had blurted out the story about the newspaper. Had Flynn been genuinely surprised, or was it alarm that had flashed across his face? Once again, the image of the little bag of crystals broke Jon's train of thought. Flynn's voice echoed in his head. Ice. Can get all you want of this: the kids love it.

Jon shook his head. Flynn wasn't organised enough to be manufacturing crystal meth himself. Someone had to be supplying him with it. William Beaumont? He definitely handed something over to Flynn outside The Spread Eagle. Jon shook his head again. Clutching at straws, mate. Face it. Dave was supplying Flynn. They fell out over something and the bastard killed my brother. End of story.

The bottle swung like a pendulum between his knees. Oh, Dave, you stupid shit. He was suddenly aware of the phone in his jacket pocket. Christ, I'll have to call Mum and Dad and confirm that everything in the morning papers – the innuendo, the speculation, the conjecture that their youngest son was a drug dealer – is true. He bent over and spat. Dad will be demanding to know who did it, pursing his lips in that disapproving way when he realises no answer will be forthcoming. No answer for who killed his youngest son, or why.

Jon sighed. And then there's Alice. Letting her know I was mistaken; Dave did have it in him to join the very worst scum of society.

He dug and gouged at the earth with the heel of his shoe. Despite all the evidence, a part of his mind still refused to believe that's what Dave had been doing.

The bird cried again, its call answered this time. Jon lifted his head and, staring ahead, was just able to make out the faintest smear of grey in the blackness before him. As the minutes slid by, lighter hints joined it to reveal a fraction of dark horizon. He realised the few stars away to his right had lost their lustre and his eyes returned to the smudge, watching as a gossamer-like loop of yellow slowly stretched itself across a dip in the distant hills. The bright thread began to widen and sunlight started to flood in. Night had ended.

Soon, he could see mist clinging to the lower valleys, dry-stone walls emerging from the gloom. The birds cried again and now Jon was able to spot one of them. A hawk by the look of it, wheeling round and round the dim silhouette of pine trees peeping over the crest of the next hill.

Again its mournful cry was answered and Jon realised the mate must be in the trees. The ospreys that had featured on the front page of the *Herald*.

Voices drifted up from behind him and Jon turned to see a couple of dim shapes trudging up the path that led from the conifer plantation. They spotted him sitting there and their conversation stopped. He recognised the younger of the two as the park ranger Michael Lumm. Accompanying him was a thin man in his late forties, a powerful pair of binoculars hanging over his large green coat. A little warily, they approached.

'Morning,' Jon said over his shoulder, suddenly aware of how red and itchy his eyes felt.

'Morning,' the ranger replied. 'We wondered if anyone was up here. Your car's parked at the bottom.'

'Yeah, I'm …' He looked to his side and saw the crooked crucifix he'd tried to make in the night. Two twigs grabbed from the forest floor, lashed together with a stem of bracken. In the light of day it looked amateur and pathetic. He tipped the last inch of whisky out on the bare soil and got stiffly to his feet. Coldness made his very bones ache. 'I'll be on my way.' He turned to go, then paused. 'What are you two doing up here?'

Michael nodded towards the tips of the pine trees. 'Checking the osprey nest. We received a call.'

'They've been screeching away since before dawn broke. Do they always make so much noise?'

The two men exchanged a concerned glance as another succession of cries rang out.

'Distress calls,' announced the older man with the binoculars, raising them to his eyes. 'The female's on the nest. The male's circling. No, she's airborne too.'

Jon squinted towards the trees. Now two forms were in the air, they circled the trees one more time, then the pair started flying away. The man tracked them with his binoculars long after they'd vanished from Jon's sight. 'They've abandoned the nest,' he stated, lowering the binoculars, an anguished look on his face.

Jon turned to Michael. 'What's going on?'

The ranger began to speak, gaze still directed at the other hill. 'A member of the public called in to say the birds were acting strangely. We hoped it was the police activity on this hill that was unsettling them.'

'No. Some despicable … worthless bastard has been up there.'

The older man raised his face to the sky. 'Why? Why do they do it?'

Jon's eyes moved between the pair. After a couple of seconds, Michael gestured. 'Sorry, this is Bill Riley. He works for the Royal Society for the Protection of Birds.'

Riley looked at Jon, anger and suspicion all over his face. 'And what exactly are you doing up here?'

Michael cut in. 'He's a policeman, Bill. That crime I mentioned – it was his brother who died.'

Riley looked down at the crucifix, then back to Jon. 'I'm sorry.'

Jon shrugged. 'Someone's robbed the osprey's nest?'

Riley adjusted the straps of his backpack. 'We'll soon see.' He set off down the other side of the hill.

Michael glanced at Jon, then set off after the other man. Jon watched them for a second, then turned towards the path that would lead him to his car. The thought of driving back to Manchester made his legs go weak. How do I tell my family Dave was destroying this town with drugs? How can I show my face, only to drop that bombshell?

He looked back at the receding forms of the other two men. Anything was better than the long drive home to his parents. He slipped the empty bottle into his coat pocket and began to follow.

Halfway down, the sound of trickling water stopped him in his tracks. A stream of fat droplets was falling from the overhang of a moss-covered boulder. He crouched, angling his mouth, listening to the plopping sound as his cheek filled up. He gulped the icy liquid back, suddenly aware of how parched he was. Once he'd drunk enough, he held his head under the miniature cascade, letting the droplets land on the back of his neck, the water running across his cheeks to fall from his chin and nose. Standing up, he shook his head and blinked.

By the time he made the top of the other hill, Bill Riley was rummaging inside his bag. Examining the smooth pine trunks rearing up before them, Jon became aware of the sheen of water behind. 'Is that a lake down there?'

'Wimble reservoir,' Michael Lumm replied, hands crossed behind his back as his eyes searched the tops of the trees. 'Damage to the bark, Bill. On the lowermost branch.'

'I've seen it. Climbing rope, wouldn't you say?' After slipping waterproofs on over his trousers, he produced two metallic objects that were shaped like the soles of shoes. But in place of an upper part were just straps. Bill stepped into them and secured the buckles across the tops of his walking boots.

'Climbing irons,' Michael explained. 'So he can check the nest. You need a licence from English Nature to do this sort of thing – ospreys are a Schedule 1 species.'

Riley uncurled a leather strap and approached the tree. He passed the strap round the back of the trunk, lifted a foot and swung the heel inward. The large spike at the climbing iron's inner corner sank into the bark and he straightened his leg, shifting the strap higher. Then he swung his other foot against the tree. Repeating the sequence of actions, he quickly gained height.

'First ospreys to nest in the Peak District in living memory,' Michael murmured sadly.

Jon peered between the trees. 'Is that where they caught their fish?'

Michael nodded. 'There and Ladybower a bit further north. But if their eggs have been taken, they'll not be back. They'll return to where they came from, the Lake District or maybe Scotland.' He shook his head. 'Tragic.'

Jon looked up and saw that the lowermost branches of the tree had all been sawn off at the trunk. The first was a good fifteen metres up. Riley's waterproofs were now covered in a thick red substance. 'What's that covering his legs?'

'Tracer paint. The RSBP apply it to trees where rare birds like these are nesting. You can't ever fully get it off clothing – it helps in any prosecutions. But it looks like whoever's gone up this tree got round it by looping a climbing rope over that lowermost branch, then winching himself up.'

'Christ,' Jon said. 'That must have taken some doing.'

'I know,' Lumm murmured, tugging gently at his lower lip

before dropping his hand. 'There's only one egg collector I've ever heard of capable of something like this ...' His voice died away.

By now Riley was level with the highest branches, directly below the large platform of a nest. He reached a hand over and felt around inside. A second later, he placed something inside his jacket. He felt around again and retrieved another object, stopping to stare at it for several seconds.

'Anything in there?' Michael shouted up.

Riley shook his head and started climbing down. When eventually his feet touched the ground, Jon could see the man's face was white with rage. 'The clutch has gone.'

Michael let out a sigh. 'But something was in there?'

'Oh, yes. Something was left.' He kicked off the climbing irons, removed the sticky waterproofs then reached into his jacket and produced a canister. By tapping it gently against his palm, he dislodged the broken remains of a large cream-coloured egg, its blunt-end mottled with chestnut. 'He would have been mortified about that.'

'About what?' Jon asked.

'For it to count as a truly successful raid, eggers have to take the entire clutch,' Riley explained. 'It's a point of pride. Don't ask me to explain their twisted logic. He was clumsy on this occasion, though. Most unusual.'

Jon could see the dried remains of a yolk clinging to the inner shell. It looked like it had yet to totally harden. 'When did this happen?'

Riley breathed in. 'I was on the other hill at dusk on Saturday night. Nothing was wrong then.'

Saturday night, Jon thought. Dave was still alive then.

Michael spoke up. 'And the member of the public called yesterday to say he'd first noticed the birds were distressed on Sunday morning.'

'So he carried out the raid some time before dawn that night,' Riley said. 'If I ever get my hands on him, so help me God.'

Jon was frowning. 'You know who did it?'

Riley's voice was stone cold. 'He left his usual calling card.'

He placed the remains of the osprey shell on his backpack, then tipped the canister up again. This time a beige-coloured egg rolled out into his palm.

That's a chicken egg, Jon thought, spotting a word scrawled in what appeared to be lipstick on the side: 'Crag'.

'He's started again,' Lumm stated.

'Though he didn't need to leave this to let us know,' Riley spat, glancing back at the tree. 'Only he could execute a climb like that in pitch darkness.'

Jon's mind was swirling with questions. 'This person is a professional egg thief?'

'The country's most prolific. He and his brother, between them they've stripped the nests of peregrines, white-tailed eagles, marsh harriers, goshawks, golden eagles. You name it.'

Jon looked at the tree and realisation struck. Sweet fucking Christ. Hardly daring to let the thought take hold, he said, 'This guy raids nests at night?'

'Correct. He was a professional climber. Sponsorship, every-thing. Lost it all to his obsession for stealing eggs.'

Jon looked down at his feet, still not daring to hope that there might actually be a witness. Someone who could confirm if it was Flynn who killed his brother. The prospect of uncovering the truth about Dave's death made him feel dizzy. 'You think the nest was raided at some point on Saturday night?'

'It must have been – the birds were distressed from Sunday morning onwards.'

'How would he climb a tree like this in the dark?'

'He uses night-vision goggles – that's what he admitted in court. A pair was seized when police raided his house and arrested him last year.'

A tingling sensation was spreading across Jon's chest and he knew his heart had started beating faster. 'You said it was unusual – the fact he broke an egg.'

'Very unusual. I've never known him to do that before.'

Jon craned his head back, assessing the height of the nest. 'Tell me. When you were at the top of the tree, you could see across to the hill where my brother died?'

'Of course – that hill normally acts as our observation point, it was only because of . . .' He stopped speaking. 'You think Crag saw something? That's why he was so clumsy.'

Jon swallowed. 'Who is this Crag? What's his real name?'

'Craig Budd. Crag on account of how he loves to climb.'

Jon paced towards the tree, turned and addressed the RSPB officer. 'And how do I find him?'

Bill pursed his lips. 'That, I would love to know. He's been on the run for almost a year.'

'He was inside?'

'Yes. We successfully prosecuted him and his brother, Stuart. They were both sentenced to six months, the maximum amount under the Wildlife and Countryside Act.'

'What? Put in prison for nicking birds' eggs?' Jon was incredulous.

'You think it's a trivial matter?' Riley's face was flushed with anger. 'Fines, community orders? Nothing like that deterred them. Thank God they strengthened the Act – now we can lock the bastards up.' He smirked. 'You know, in prison, they're regarded as one up from paedophiles? Deviants. Regular criminals give them a really hard time. They can't understand why someone would risk a spell inside for stealing something with no monetary value.'

Jon took in the gleam of delight in the other man's eyes. You really hate them, don't you? 'So what's the score with the Budds?'

'After two months, they were both transferred to low-security prisons. Craig down to one in Sussex. Within a week of arriving, he'd assaulted a guard, climbed out a fourth-storey window, scaled the perimeter fence and vanished.'

'And the brother?'

'Stuart? He served a third month in his prison in Norfolk and was let out last September, I think.'

'Where is he now?'

'I don't know. Our Chief Investigations Officer, Greg Thurrock, might. But even if he does, I doubt Stuart will help you.'

That's where you're wrong, Jon thought. If Craig saw something, Stuart will help me find him, whether he wants to or not. 'I'll be the judge of that.'

Riley was shaking his head. 'You don't know the Budds. And you certainly don't know the bloody weird world of egg collectors.'

'Tell me about it.'

The other man gave a dry laugh. 'How long have you got?'

Jon spread his hands. 'I have to find this Crag character.'

'Then your best bet is with Greg Thurrock – he's the closest you can get to being an egg-thief without actually stealing the things. Knows all their habits and little cliques.'

'Where can I find him?'

Riley looked over at Michael Lumm. 'I'll take him down to my car – I can log this in at the cabin.'

Michael nodded. 'OK, I'll head back to Haverdale – the visitor centre needs opening up.' He turned to Jon. 'Good luck. If I can help in anyway, you know where to find me.'

'Thanks, I appreciate it.' Jon reached out and shook the younger man's hand.

With a last nod at Riley, Lumm turned round and started trudging back towards the hill where Dave had died.

'We rendezvoused in the car park at the side of the reservoir,' Riley said. 'I'm parked next to the National Trust cabin down there.' He put the chicken egg and remains of the osprey egg back in the canister, packed his other stuff away and slung the backpack over his shoulder. 'This way.'

Jon followed the other man along the rough path that led between the pine trees. Soon they reached an expanse of collapsed brown bracken that stretched right down to the edge of the reservoir itself.

Jon examined the shoreline. The level of water was low, exposing the blackness of the reservoir bed. Rocks dotted the dark soil. His eyes travelled to the opposite shore where a lone fly-fisherman was standing thigh-deep in the brown water. At that distance, the man's spindly rod was invisible. Methodically, he worked his right arm back and forth over his head, building up to the final cast with an exaggerated throw-down of his hand.

After a few seconds, he began the sequence of actions again. There was something about the repetitive nature of his movement that lent him an air of zealousness. An adherent of some archaic religion which believed that, by pleading and remonstrating with the impassive water, a revelation might be drawn from its inky depths.

Nineteen

Rick Saville paused in the foyer of his apartment building. Can I really be arsed checking yet another soup kitchen? Last one, he decided. No luck this time and I'm throwing in the towel. Zoe has either left the city or departed this world all together.

A panel of postboxes lined one wall and he unlocked the door for number one and looked inside. Nothing. Damn it! All night he'd been nursing the hope that Cathy and Isabelle might have written their decision down and popped it through the front door.

Trotting down the steps of the renovated warehouse, he could see the centre of Manchester was still relatively quiet. Whitworth Street carrying the first of the morning's commuters into the city. He tapped a foot against the pavement, trying to decide what to do. Wondering whether to just turn right, walk round the side of the building to the residents' car park and drive to work. He hesitated, car keys dangling from one finger.

Jon was now in serious shit. Buchanon's frustration had steadily mounted over the course of yesterday afternoon and the man, convinced Jon was deliberately avoiding his calls, had started leaning on Rick. Knowing Buchanon would be in the office already, Rick could also guess what his SIO's first demand of the morning would be: where the hell is Spicer?

Glancing at his watch, Rick sighed. He owed it to Jon and, besides, getting in ten minutes later was hardly going to make much difference. He turned on his heel and walked quickly up to the corner of Whitworth and Sackville Streets, then turned into the Gay Village.

Canal Street was silent, as if it were recovering from the night before. A couple of pigeons were harrying a chip tray, pecking at the polystyrene, trying to feed on the congealed gravy inside.

Rick crossed Portland Street, then cut up through Chinatown where the unloading of a lorry was the only sign of life. In the covered seating area to the side of the giant arch, a group of oriental men sat watching and smoking in silence. Immigrants, gathered there for a chance of a day's work.

Rick continued along the edge of the car park, reaching the small round pagoda in the opposite corner. Inside it, two drunks were chuckling at each other and from the number of cans littering the curving bench, Rick guessed they'd been there all night.

One of them cracked open another can, peered out of the circular structure and announced to Rick, 'We're just two lost souls swimming in a fish bowl, year after year.'

Rick held up a finger. 'Running over the same old ground?'

He heard them roaring with laughter as he hurried towards the back of the Piccadilly Plaza, quickly spotting the white van in the empty loading bay by the ramp that led up into the NCP car park.

On reaching the vehicle, he approached the side hatch. A bald man was pouring coffee into a tray of polystyrene cups. He looked down, a benign smile on his face.

'Morning,' Rick said. 'Do you know of a girl called Zoe by any chance? You may have served her drinks sometime recently.'

The man thought for a second and shook his head. 'Sorry, we don't get many females using this service.'

'No,' Rick replied. 'I didn't think so. Thanks, anyway.' Off to the side a huddle of men were chatting. Voices low and ragged. One burst into a bubbling cough of a laugh, prompting another to slap him on the back.

'Get it out, man.'

Rick caught the Scottish accent. Below the bloke's black ski hat there sprouted a huge beard. Rick looked at the cups lined up on the tray. 'Can I take these over?'

'Thank you, that's very kind.'

Casually, Rick wandered across and held the tray out towards

163

the group. None of them seemed interested. 'Brew, anyone?'

The bearded man looked up, laughter still causing his eyes to twinkle. The lines around them looked like they'd been gouged with a chisel. He nodded at the flat lid of a nearby wheelie bin. 'Just set them down, son.'

Rick did as he was asked, taking a drink for himself at the same time. 'Are you known as Jock, by any chance?'

The man's eyes had lost their friendly edge. 'Aye. And you, officer. What's your name?' He pushed up a sleeve to scratch at his forearm and Rick spotted the rash of tattoos under the layer of dark hair.

'Detective Sergeant Saville. Rick.' He lifted the polystyrene cup and sniffed it. It smelled like that weird chicory stuff. No wonder they're all leaving it well alone, he thought.

Jock's eyes bore into him. 'What do you want with me?'

'Nothing. I'm trying to track down a girl who knocked around on the streets. Zoe? Late twenties, dark hair. These two teeth,' his finger wagged like a metronome between his incisors, 'quite sharp-looking.'

'Because?'

'We're concerned for her safety. She left a phone message with someone and she sounded very distressed.'

'Zoe?' Jock looked at his two companions, but they were keeping their faces blank. 'With the bairn? Used it on the trams to get change?'

'I don't know. You're saying she had a baby?'

'Aye. Rode the trams, shoving it in people's faces. Made good money doing it.'

'She still at that now?'

He shook his head. 'Haven't seen Zoe in a long while.'

'What, months?'

A chuckle in return. 'Officer, I'm a piss-head, right? Most days I drink more than you'd believe. My memory has gone to shit.'

'Roughly, then. Half a year? More than that?'

Jock now scratched ruminatively at his beard. 'Easily.'

'A year, then?'

'Let me consult my Filofax.' He paused between each syllable as if the name were three separate words. 'What are we in now?'

Rick frowned. 'How do you mean?'

'What month is it?'

'April. It's the nineteenth of April. A Wednesday.'

'April? Right, spring is in the air and all that. Wasn't in the summer. Maybe a year, then.'

A year ago, Rick thought. So the baby would be crawling now, maybe more.

'She were near the cathedral the other day.'

Rick looked at the man opposite Jock. Do it yourself haircut and sunken eyes entirely ringed by purplish skin.

'She were there,' he repeated. 'After coins, for the payphone.'

'When do you mean?'

He screwed his eyes shut, the skin puckering to resemble that of a wrinkled prune. 'Don't know. Yesterday or something.'

Realising the bloke wasn't doing very well handling the attention, Rick spoke gently. 'She called someone, then?'

'The payphone on the corner. She used that.'

'Was this in the morning, or afternoon?'

He raised a hand to his lips and nibbled on a filthy fingernail. 'Morning.'

'Did she have the baby with her?'

He nodded. 'Little one. Didn't want to be in the buggy. Kicking and stuff.'

'And what did she do after the phone call?'

'Fucked off across Deansgate, Salford way.'

'She had a boyfriend,' Jock announced.

Rick turned back to him. 'Who was he?'

'Spindly lad, called Dave.'

'Yeah? And is he still around?'

'Aye, still around.' His eyes searched the empty street. 'Not now, though.'

'When did you last see him?'

Jock looked at his mates. 'What do you reckon? A week?'

The anxious one gave a nod.

'And what,' Rick said, feeling guilty for asking, 'did this Dave get up to?'

Jock scowled. 'Ask him.'

Rick bowed his head, knowing he'd now pushed a little too far. 'Last thing. Ever heard of a Redino?'

Quickly, he looked up, but none of them reacted to the name. Either they've never heard it or they've suddenly developed great potential for poker, Rick thought. 'Well, thanks for your help.' He placed his cup back on the tray and turned to go, but Jock raised a finger.

Rick paused. 'Yes?'

He pointed to the tray of drinks. 'Away with those and get us some teas.'

Twenty

Bill Riley strode across the asphalt of the car park, removing some keys from his pocket as he neared a wooden cabin. Next to a padlocked hatch in the wall was a notice board plastered with photos of ice creams.

Slipping the empty whisky bottle into the bin below it, Jon looked at the garish images, thinking how badly their colours clashed with the natural tones all around. 'So, is this some kind of visitor centre?'

'More of an information point we share with the National Trust. And it's got a shop bolted to the side,' Riley replied, unlocking the door and reaching in to turn on the lights. The inside held a faint aroma of pine and the wooden walls were lined with racks containing pamphlets and booklets. A sectioned-off kitchen area was in one corner, and on the inner side of the locked hatch was a counter with cardboard trays of flapjacks, health bars and chocolate snacks.

As Riley sat down at a desk on the opposite side of the room, Jon wandered over to the snacks. Jesus, I am so hungry. He picked up a few flapjack bars and placed sufficient change by the till. Behind him, Riley began to speak.

'Morning, Greg, it's Bill Riley here. I hope I haven't called too early? Good. No, it's bad news, I'm afraid. The osprey nest overlooking Wimble reservoir. Yes, the entire clutch. Well, one egg was left broken at the scene, along with a chicken's egg.' He nodded. 'Yes, it was Craig Budd. He managed to get a rope over the lowermost branch, then winched himself up. Sometime on Saturday night.'

As he bit off chunks of flapjack, Jon's eyes wandered over the desk. Next to a phone and a computer monitor, there was a stack of National Trust membership application forms. He reached down and picked up the framed photo beside them. A woman in her thirties, seated on a park bench. Balanced on her lap was a smiling baby. Jon's gaze went back to the woman. There was something about how her arms formed a barrier across the baby's torso to prevent it toppling forward.

Riley continued talking. 'He'd have used night-vision goggles. There's no other way he could have done it. I know, it makes you want to spit.' He glanced at Jon. 'Actually, Greg, I've got someone here. He's a policeman. He happened to be at the scene when the park ranger and I walked up there this morning. No, a different matter. I'll let him tell you. He wants to find Craig. There's a chance he witnessed a very serious incident. Look, shall I just put him on? OK, here he is.'

Jon took the receiver. 'Hello, this is DI Spicer, Greater Manchester Police.'

'Morning, Detective Inspector. Which division are you with?'

Jon paused. The man obviously knew more about the police than most. 'The Major Incident Team.'

'Ah. After my time, that.'

Jon tried to gauge the man's age from his voice. Late forties? 'You were in the job, then?'

'For nearly fifteen years. Stockport, mainly. What brings you out into Derbyshire, then?'

'A murder. Timing-wise, there's a possibility Craig Budd saw something from his position in the tree. At present it's about the best lead I've got.'

'Sounds like you're desperate, then.'

'You could say that.'

'Did Bill give you the background on Crag?'

'Craig Budd. Official Sad Person. Sentenced to six months for raiding rare birds' nests.'

'Sad?'

'Well, it's a bit of an anorak's activity, isn't it?'

'DI Spicer, Craig Budd is no anorak. The older brother, Dyson, maybe. But not Craig.'

'Dyson?'

'Stuart Budd is known as Dyson in egging circles. Due to his habit of vacuuming up everything he can. Four years ago he made it onto an outcrop of low rock just off the Orkney Isles and cleaned out an entire colony of terns' eggs.'

'So what makes Craig different?'

The other man paused. 'He was a pro climber, did you know?'

'Yes.'

'The guy has that weird attraction people like him seem to exert. People who seem to embrace the prospect of dying, like it's the only way they can feel alive. Most eggers are sad, lonely and fixated. Craig? I always suspected he collected eggs as much for the thrill of the climb.'

Jon replaced the photo on the table. 'What does he look like?'

'Stereotypical climber. Straggly hair. Muscly, but lean with it. Face matches the nickname: sort of chiselled. A certain way of moving. His was the only egg-collector's trial I've attended where female journalists outnumbered the males.'

'So, it became a bit more than a hobby to these brothers.'

Mirthless laughter came down the line. 'It came to take over their entire lives. It does to all of them, in the end. We're talking about an obsession that drives a man to get up at two in the morning, travel to Scotland, trudge across miles of wilderness in the dark, then risk his life climbing a cliff to clean out a nest he'd scouted the previous year. I've known eggers swim freezing lakes, burrow into riverbanks, anything to get the trophies.'

'That's some effort.'

'Oh, it doesn't end there. They can't risk being caught with them, so what they do is then bury them, drive home and resume their lives. Months later, once the breeding season is over and we're no longer patrolling, they drive all the way back, recover the eggs and add them to their collection.'

'And it's not even about money?'

'Absolutely not; it's about the challenge. They spend their

lives building up a collection they never actually display. They don't dare risk it.'

People never cease to amaze me, Jon thought. 'How common are eggers?'

'Less and less so. Oology – that's the study of eggs – is a peculiarly British impulse. A hangover from the Victorian age when people would bring back specimens from across the Empire.'

'So how do I find Crag? Is there some sort of forum, internet site? How do they communicate?'

'DI Spicer, eggers are more paranoid and suspicious than any type of criminal I ever came across as a policeman. It will take you years to break into the circle.'

'I don't have years.'

'Sorry. I'm at a loss as to how I can help. They use chat rooms, but if you can find one, guess the necessary password first time so the whole thing doesn't just vanish, then successfully pose as an egger, please tell me how you did it. I've yet to manage it and I know the scene better than anyone.'

Jon turned so he could perch on the edge of the desk. 'There has to be some way to find this man. How did you finally nail him and his brother?'

'Stuart Budd's wife. That's often how it goes – tip-offs. Disgruntled wives or girlfriends, sick of playing second fiddle to their partner's obsession. Sometimes through a feud. One egger might believe another is holding out on the location of a new nest. Or one from a successful raid sneaks back before the agreed time and digs the eggs up for himself.'

'So Stuart Budd did his time. What about his wife?'

'Believe it or not, they're still together. They now work for the Cumbria Falconry Centre as a husband and wife team, doing displays.'

'And do you think he's really put his collecting days behind him?'

'Yes, I do. When we raided his house, we couldn't find the actual eggs. Note books, photos, maps, but no eggs. Nichola Budd thought they were hidden in a compartment behind the wardrobe in their bedroom. Then Stuart breaks down. He actually took my hand and thanked me for putting a stop to it. It had totally ruined his life by then – probably had done for years. Every spring the urge to go out and collect took hold of him like a fever. He led us to the garage. The bloke didn't even trust his wife. Two days before we crashed down his front door, he thought she was acting strangely, so he transferred the entire collection into his garage roof. Over eleven hundred eggs. He asked – no he begged – that I take them away.'

Jon raised his chin, sensing the brother was his only chance. 'Where's this Falconry Centre based?'

'Hawkshead, of course. You know it? Between Coniston and Windermere in the Lake District. But I don't think he'll be able to help you, even if he wanted to.'

'Why?'

'The collection was his brother's too. Craig might have done it as a way of climbing, but those eggs meant just as much to him as they did to Stuart. When Stuart handed the collection in, he broke a bond. In the court cells, Craig attacked Stuart and it took three guards to drag him off. Stuart gave evidence with rake marks all over his face. Craig tried to gouge his eyes out.'

'Nice.' Jon's mind flicked back to childhood incidents with Dave. Encouraging his brother to jump up and down on a lump of earth at the end of the garden. The wasps had surged out of the underground nest and stung Dave dozens of times. A few days later, Dave threw a dart, somehow missing the board and landing it in the back of Jon's head. His fingers searched out the little pockmark. Brotherly love. 'Maybe when I explain the danger Craig's in. The people we're looking for sawed their victim to pieces, and I think Craig's a witness to the crime.'

'Jesus. Who was the bloke that died?'

'My younger brother.'

Ian Flynn placed the Mars Bar and pint of banana milkshake on the counter. 'And twenty B&H, cheers, Paul.'

The newsagent reached behind, plucked a packet from the shelf and added it to the other items.

Flynn raised a hand to massage his temples. Bastard headache. His mind went back to the previous night. After the big guy had suddenly stumbled out, he'd slumped in his armchair, an uneasy feeling bringing him down. Something wasn't right, he knew that much. 'Got any headache pills, Paul?'

'Yup. Cheap ones or Anadin?'

'Cheap ones'll do.'

As the shop owner turned round to fetch them, Flynn glanced at the copies of the *Haverdale Herald* piled by the till. He felt the blood drain from his face and the pain in his head slowed, as if he was being pounded methodically by a hammer. Fuck.

Delving into his coat, he brought out his mobile phone and keyed in a number. Then he stepped outside, a copy of the paper in his shaking hand. 'It's me. Have you seen it?'

'What?'

'The *Herald*! Have you seen it?'

'Yes.'

'So they've found out who he is.'

'Problem?'

Flynn bowed his head, reading the caption below the first photo. 'David Spicer, aged thirty-three, of no fixed address.'

'I can read.'

Flynn's eyes went to the other photo alongside. 'He was in my house.'

'Yeah, I know.'

'Not David, the other bloke!' He stared at the image of Jon Spicer coming down the steps of Haverdale's police station. It had been snapped from across the road, but there was no mistaking the giant bastard. He read the caption once again. 'The fucking brother. DI Spicer, Greater Manchester Police. Oh fuck, he got me talking about doing a deal with him.'

'What do you mean, a deal?'

'Fucking drugs,' Flynn hissed. 'I said I could get him anything. Coke, E, ice. Oh no, man, oh no—'

'Shut up.'

'I'm fucked.'

'Shut up!'

Flynn gulped, the paper still held before him as he leaned against the wall, shaking his head in disbelief.

'What did you say about your source?'

'Nothing. We didn't get that far.'

'Did you sell him anything?'

'No. He got up – rushed off like he wanted to puke.'

'OK, listen to me. I want you to go straight home. Once you've calmed down, call me again. I need to know exactly what you said.'

Twenty One

Jon heard his mobile bleep. Bollocks, he thought, is Buchanon on my case again, already? He took it out and glanced at the screen. Two texts, coming in together. First from Carmel, senior crime reporter at the *Manchester Evening Chronicle*. He clicked on the envelope: 'My condolences, Jon. Call me. Please.'

Yeah, like fuck I will. He selected the next one. A text from Rick. Clicking on the envelope revealed eight words.

'I think Zoe has a kid – call me.'

Immediately, Jon's head turned to the framed photo on the desk. The hunch of the woman's shoulders: that's what he'd seen on the screen of Dave's mobile phone. She's holding a baby on her lap. Jesus Christ, he thought, as the implications began to sink in. He searched his mind. Who do I stand a chance of getting sympathy off in Mallin's team? He looked to the RSPB officer. 'Bill, do you have the number for Haverdale police station?'

'Yes. It's on the speed dial, in case of emergencies.' He pressed a button and handed the receiver to Jon.

'Hello, Haverdale police station.'

'DI Spicer for Constable Shazia Batyra, please.'

She came on the line a few moments later, her voice an urgent whisper. 'You got my message?'

Jon glanced at his mobile. 'No, what was it?'

'I called you late last night. I left a message on your answerphone.'

'Sorry, I've been avoiding it.' He selected missed calls. Of the six numbers the screen could display, five were from Buchanon and one had a 01297 prefix. Haverdale's area code. 'I can see it. What did you say?'

'I checked the maps and the walking book.'

'Dave's?'

'Yes. He'd marked out all the spots where digs have taken place – Rebellion Hill, Sharston Edge, Toot Hill, Round Knoll, they're all there.'

Hope began to flicker in Jon's chest and he made an effort to damp it back down. 'Really?'

'Really. So then I checked his train tickets, too. He travelled out here on two dates we're pretty certain coincide with nights when digs took place.'

Now his knees went weak and he had to sit on the edge of the desk, taking a long breath in. 'So, there's a good chance he really was out here looking for treasure.'

'Sorry? I didn't hear that.'

Jon realised he'd spoken out loud. He lifted his eyes to the ceiling, unable to hold the sense of relief in check. 'I said, there's a good chance he really was out here looking for treasure.'

'I don't know for certain, but it seems likely.'

Which means, Jon thought, someone else is supplying Flynn. 'Have you taken this to Mallin?'

'He's out, still focusing resources on finding the driver who fled that RTA. We're all meant to be on it at the moment.'

That figures, thought Jon. 'So no one is actually looking into my brother's death?'

'No,' she mumbled with embarrassment. 'I think Sheffield are due to send a team soon.'

'Can you do me a little favour, then?'

'Well ... what is it?'

'I just want you to check the screen of Dave's mobile phone. The lower half is obscured by blood. Through the plastic, can you use your nail to scrape it off, then turn the phone on and tell me what you see?'

'OK, I'm putting the receiver down. Give me a second.'

Jon turned to Riley. 'You got an internet connection here, Bill?'

'Yup.'

175

'Can you find me the details for the falconry centre Stuart Budd works at, please?'

'OK.'

Shazia's voice came back on the line. 'There's a baby on her lap. Little thing, it is. Perhaps a year old?'

If it's Dave's, Jon thought, that makes me an uncle. Jesus Christ. 'What does he look like?'

'I'm sorry?'

'The little one, is he ... does he look happy, healthy and that?'

'Yeah, he's a cute-looking thing.'

Cute-looking. Jon felt a lump in his throat. He doesn't know his Daddy's dead.

'Cheers, Shazia. I've got to go.'

'Where are you?'

'Not that far away, as it happens.'

'Have you seen today's paper?'

'No.'

'I'm sorry, Jon – Mallin released your brother's identity yesterday evening. And someone tipped them off about you. Your photo's on the front page, too.'

'The front page? I'm on the front page of the *Haverdale Herald*?'

'Next to a shot of your brother.'

'Does it say I'm a policeman?'

'Yes, and brother of the murder victim.'

Jon pinched the bridge of his nose. That lets the cat well and truly out of the bag. 'What does it say about my brother?'

'You know, conjecture about a gangland killing.'

'As in drugs?'

'I'm sorry.'

'OK, thanks for letting me know.'

He hung up and immediately called Rick's number. 'Morning, mate. I just got your text.'

'Jon! God, I thought you were never going to ring back. Buchanon's going ape shit, here. He's leaning on me now, saying it's my responsibility as your partner that you report in.'

'Well, fuck him. You can't get hold of me, right?'

Rick sighed. 'Right.'

'Did you see Alice last night?'

'Yeah.'

'And how was she?'

'Not too bad. Worried about you, though. You are heading home—'

Jon cut in. 'I'm calling her straight after this. I think you're bang on about Zoe having a kid. How did you find out?'

'Finally tracked down Jock. He remembers her, but the bloke's brain is mush. Could be a year since he last saw her. His mate, though, says she was near the cathedral the other day, bumming change to make a phone call.'

'You mean from a public call box?'

'That's right.'

'Probably the message she left on Dave's mobile.'

'Could have been. The bloke also said she had a nipper with her.'

'Yeah, there's a photo of her with one on Dave's mobile as well. You realise that could well be my nephew?'

'God, you're right. Oh – my contact in the Drug Squad got back to me. No Redino on the system, as an alias of Ian Flynn or otherwise.'

'Has Flynn got a record?'

'Nope.'

'Bollocks.' Jon thought for a second. 'Can you check the housing options out? If Zoe had a kid, she'd have been given accommodation – a one or two bed flat. In a tower block, probably.'

'I'll try, Jon. But as I said, Buchanon's breathing down my neck. If he sees me making strange phone calls, he'll twig.'

'Rick, I don't care how you do it. Get the numbers and ring from your car if needs be. My brother went back to the place of this bloke called Ian Flynn one time. They got wasted together and Dave ended up selling him a bit of weed. When Flynn said he had a load of other stuff, I just assumed it had come from Dave, too. Now I'm not so sure.'

'But you reckon this Flynn character killed your brother?'

'If he didn't, he can definitely point me to who did. The guy's got his fingers in all sorts of pies. What I need you to do is find this Zoe, and ask her if Redino's real name is Ian Flynn. Got that?'

'OK.'

He cut the connection and immediately called his mum and dad. It rang five times, then Mary's recorded voice came on the line. You're there, Jon thought. I know you are. 'Mum, it's me, Jon. Listen, do not believe the newspaper reports. They'll imply things that aren't true. Dave was not dealing drugs in Haverdale. I don't know what the hell he was up to out here, but it wasn't that. I'm going to find out, OK? I'll find the truth, I promise.' He waited for her to pick up, but the line remained silent.

He hit red and then selected his home number. Just as he was about to press the call button, Riley leaned back from the computer screen. 'If you want to see Stuart Budd, you'd best hurry. The Falconry Centre closes at lunchtime today.'

'How long will it take me to drive there from here?'

'The Lakes? A fair few hours.'

Jon selected answerphone mode once again and shoved his phone in his pocket.

Alice paused in the hallway. Handbag. Car keys. Drink and snacks for Holly. She looked at her daughter. 'OK, sweetie? We're going to the hospital. They're going to look at the baby in Mummy's tummy.'

'Tummy,' Holly mouthed the word back. 'Baby in Mummy's tummy.'

'That's right.' Her eyes touched on the phone on the windowsill yet again. There's still a chance he's going straight to the hospital to meet us there. There's still a chance that he hasn't just completely forgotten. One more time, she decided. I'll try his phone one more time. It can't be on answerphone for ever.

She was about to lift the receiver when it started to ring. 'Hello?'

'Alice?'

'Yes.'

'Alice, it's DCI Buchanon here. I'm sorry to call your home like this, but is Jon there?'

'Jon?' A hot flush surged across her face. 'How could my husband be here when you've sent him to Haverdale to assist in the investigation into his own brother's death?'

'I beg your pardon?'

'Sorry, DCI Buchanon, but I think it's despicable that you've put him in that position.' She waited for a response, but the man wasn't saying a thing. Suddenly, her shoulders sagged. 'You haven't sent him, have you?'

'No, I haven't, Alice.'

She held the receiver away from her face, feeling tears spring into her eyes. The fucking bastard. The lying fucking bastard. And Rick. Did he know about this as he sat here last night, eating his dinner? 'I have to go.'

'Alice? If you speak to him, please insist that he calls me.'

'Goodbye.' She had to take several deep breaths before she could look down at her daughter. 'Come on, princess, let's go.'

Twenty Two

Jon held the phone against his ear, hearing it click on to a recording of Alice yet again. Probably taken Holly to Mum's, he thought. She said she was going to try and help out. He strode past the sign that read 'Flying Area. Last display: 2.00 pm.' Suddenly he was glad to have driven over here so fast; he'd only just made it in time.

He rounded the corner of a barn-like building and the muffled words of the amplified voice abruptly became clearer.

'Now falcons will only perform like this when they're hungry. Once Felix here has gulped down a few more scraps of chicken, he won't be interested. Plus, the weight of the meat in his stomach makes him sluggish.'

No more than eight people were gathered at the wooden railings that marked out a rectangle of grass some fifty metres long by thirty metres wide. At each end of the paddock was a metal pole with a loudspeaker mounted on its top. A man was standing in the middle of the grass, swinging a line around his head like it was a lasso. High in the air above him a light-grey bird of prey cut across the sombre sky, suddenly swooping downwards, wings tucked in close to its body.

The man straightened his arm and lengthened the sweep of the lure, keeping it just in front of the bird's hooked beak. Then, with a jerk of his forearm, the bulbous object jinked to the side and the bird banked up, talons empty.

'Whoah! He nearly had it that time!'

It alighted on the speaker at the far end of the paddock, claws scrabbling for purchase on the smooth plastic.

'Oh, no. He's sulking,' the man laughed. 'He does this sometimes.'

Jon examined the falconer. He was in his late thirties, a hint of red in short curly hair that was retreating back up a freckled forehead. His build was heavy and swinging the lure was obviously taking some effort, as the laboured sound of his breathing over the speakers revealed.

The waiting room was crowded with people: women in varying stages of pregnancy, their mothers, husbands or partners hovering at their sides. Alice searched the long room, spotting a children's play area in the far corner.

'Come on, sweetie.' She took Holly's hand and led her between the rows of soft seats, pausing before a woman with what appeared to be a large cannon ball stuffed under her top. She was sitting low in the seat, legs stretched out before her. Seeing Alice, she made an effort to draw her feet in so they could get past.

'Not much longer for you, then?' Alice asked with a smile.

Cupping her distended stomach, the woman rolled her eyes. 'Thank God. You?'

'Just my first dating scan.' She looked down at Holly. 'A while before you have a little brother or sister, isn't it?'

'Baby.' Alice pointed to the other woman's midriff. 'Baby, in there.'

'Baby,' Holly repeated, eyes wide.

The two women shared a smile and Alice squeezed past towards the toys. 'Look, Holly, a cooker. Can you bake Mummy a cake?'

Seeing the plastic cooker with its brightly coloured dials, Holly dropped Alice's hand and ran over. 'Cake! Cake! Cake!'

'That's right. You make me one.' Alice sat down, glancing around the room once again. Though there was a lot of movement, she realised it was being created by the people who accompanied the mums-to-be. Men delving around in bags, offering their partners drinks or titbits to eat. Mothers, half-turned in their seats, fingers brushing stray strands of hair from their daughters' shoulders. Alice sat back and listened to the chorus of gentle voices that filled the room.

She became aware of the empty seat beside her and thought of Jon. How he'd lied. How she had no idea, absolutely no idea, where he was or what he was doing. Glancing up, her eyes connected with those of an elderly woman. She caught the hint of pity on the lady's face as her stare moved to Holly.

Alice knew what she was thinking. One child and another on the way and you're all on your own, you poor thing. Despite the fact that, at that moment, she couldn't think of Jon without feeling furious, Alice arranged her hands on her lap so her wedding ring was clearly on display.

From a doorway halfway down the room, a middle-aged woman in a green tunic called out her name.

'Come on, Felix, let's be having you again. Come on, boy!' Budd called, swinging the lure in lazy circles.

The bird sank down on its haunches, spread its wings and launched itself from the speaker. A few graceful beats of its wings took it up into the sky and it started prowling the air once again. Its head angled slightly to the side as the trajectory of the bait was weighed up. Then it dipped, sweeping in low, the path of its flight set to merge with that of the lure. Just before they connected, time seemed to stand still. Then the man jerked his arm, cheating the bird once more.

'Fast! But not fast enough. Did you know that peregrine falcons are the fastest animal on earth? One was clocked recently diving at a speed of two hundred and forty miles an hour. They literally punch their prey out of the sky. Each of their toes has five joints and they curl their feet into bony little balls before smashing into the other bird.'

Interesting as it was, Jon wished the bloke would shut up so he could appreciate the bird in silence. There was something inappropriate about his breathless commentary, like the prattle of a tour guide ruining the peace of a church.

'Which children here have seen *Kes* or read the book?' the man asked, glancing quickly at his audience. 'None? Oh, you must. It's a wonderful book about a kestrel and a boy, who's not much older than you lot. Barry Hines, that's the author.' He focused his attention back on the bird. 'OK, Felix, this time, this time.' He threw the lure upwards, encouraging the circling bird in once again. But this time he didn't alter his swing and the falcon embraced the lure with its curved claws, dropping to the earth with hardly a flutter. Pinning the oval lump of leather in the grass, it immediately began to rip the meat from the tassles.

The man let go of the other end of the lure and turned to his tiny audience. 'Thanks very much, ladies, gentlemen, boys and girls. That concludes today's show.'

The people stayed where they were, watching the falcon feed. Removing the leather gauntlet from his left hand, the man strode to the far end of the paddock. Dotting the grass of a side pen were six T-shaped pieces of wood, each about a foot tall. Perched on all but one was a bird of prey – other types of hawk, what looked like an eagle and two owls, one white and one brown with piercing orange eyes.

A woman with a dirty blonde ponytail that hung over the collar of a Barbour was walking among them, dipping a hand into a pouch and holding out strips of pale meat. As Jon reached them, the man was unhooking the microphone from his canvas waistcoat. He then removed the power pack clipped to his belt and, as he placed the device in a nylon case, glanced at the woman and said, 'Fancy eating at the Ring-o'-Bells, later?'

'Hello, there. Quite some show,' Jon announced.

The man glanced over his shoulder, a sheen of sweat making the broad bridge of his nose shine. 'Thanks.'

'The lady in reception said I could find you here. Stuart Budd, isn't it?'

He met Jon's eyes properly this time, and the woman's head turned, too. 'That's right. How can I help?'

Jon removed his warrant card. 'DI Spicer, Greater Manchester Police.'

No one spoke as he slipped his ID back into his jacket pocket. To their side, a flurry of movement broke out. One of the falcons had attempted to fly off, but the leather straps fastening its legs were only inches long.

Jon watched it flapping awkwardly, metal rings jingling as it regained the perch. It hunched its wings and smoothed a stray feather back into place as if nothing had happened.

'I'm investigating a murder.'

The man's head and shoulders dipped a fraction, as if in readiness for a blow. 'My brother?'

Jon's mouth was open, but the question had robbed him of his next comment.

'You've found Craig?' Stuart added.

Realisation dawned. 'Oh, no. Sorry – it's not your brother who's died.' It's mine. 'I think Craig is a witness. It's imperative we find him straight away.'

'You're asking me?' He turned to a bag that was balanced on a fold-out stool and began packing his things away. 'You do realise he's been on the run since last July? There's a warrant out for his arrest.'

'I do.'

'And you're familiar with our case? We're hardly on speaking terms.'

'I am. But you may not realise that, two nights ago, he cleaned out an osprey's nest in the Peak District.'

Stuart straightened up, though his gaze was still directed down at his bag. 'Overlooking Wimble reservoir?'

'Correct.'

'How do you know it was him?'

'A chicken egg was left in the nest, the word "Crag" written on it.'

He placed his hands on his hips, then let them fall so they hung limply at his sides. 'Oh, Jesus.'

The woman stepped closer to Stuart, searching out his eyes. 'You knew about the nest?'

'It's been mentioned in the press – and on the RSPB's website,' he replied guiltily.

'The night he took the eggs,' Jon continued, 'was the night a murder was committed on the adjacent hilltop, not three hundred metres away. I gather Craig uses night-vision goggles when conducting his nocturnal raids.'

'Yes, but that doesn't mean he saw anything.'

'He was hasty, or something made him clumsy. One of the osprey eggs was broken.'

'Oh.' Stuart removed his bag from the fold-up stool and sat down.

The woman moved to his side. 'He can't help you. He's not part of that scene any more. Stuart? Tell him. You're not part of it any more.'

Jon gave her a questioning look.

'I'm Nichola, his wife,' she stated defiantly. 'Do you realise what this – this damned business with birds' eggs has cost us?' She pointed to a static caravan at the edge of the barn. Curtains in the small windows and little wooden steps leading down to a modest area of decking. 'That's where we live now. We used to live in a four bedroom house near Preston. Stuart had his own business, manufacturing pipes. We lost everything when he was sentenced.'

She turned to her husband whose head was now bowed. 'You're not to get involved, do you bloody-well hear me?' She strode angrily into the paddock and began winding in the lure. With a look of disdain, the falcon stepped away from the bulbous weight as it began fleeing through the grass like a hairless rodent.

The room was small and windowless, the temperature verging on uncomfortably warm. Dominating it was a scanning machine and padded couch.

'My name's Wendy,' the sonographer said, glancing over Alice's notes. 'And this is your first dating scan. Thirteen weeks from the first day of your last period. Is that right, Alice?'

'It is,' she replied.

'Great.' The sonographer closed the file, then glanced momentarily to Holly before looking back to Alice. 'No other adult could accompany you today?'

'My husband should have, but he's got caught up with work at the last minute.'

'Oh dear.' She bent towards Holly, face thrust forward. 'And what's your name?'

Holly stared back in silence, an arm snaking round the back of Alice's knees.

'It's Holly, isn't it?' Alice prompted.

'Holly! What a pretty name. Would Holly like to sit on this grown-up chair while we look at mummy's tummy?'

Alice patted the seat. 'You sit here, sweetie.' She helped Holly up, then turned to the couch.

'Right.' The sonographer sat at the gently humming machine. 'I'm sure you remember how this goes. Just hop up on the couch and raise your top for me.'

Alice sat on the edge, swung her feet up and leaned back. Using both hands, she rolled up her sweatshirt to just below the line of her bra.

'Lovely.' The sonographer wheeled her chair over to Alice's side. Removing some tissue from a little trolley, she tucked it into the waistband of Alice's tracksuit bottoms, then pushed them down by a couple more inches. 'Now for the chilly bit.' She held a plastic bottle above Alice's stomach and squeezed out a large dollop of clear-blue gel.

'Ooh, I forgot how cold that is,' Alice said, turning to Holly. 'Chilly cold!'

'Killy cholled!' came the parroted reply.

'Let's spread it out so it warms up.' The sonographer began to circle the domed metal end of the transducer over Alice's skin, eyes on the small screen in the middle of the scanner's control panel.

Alice glanced over at Holly. 'She's looking inside mummy's tummy. Looking for the baby.'

But Holly's attention had wandered to the wall and the breast-feeding poster stuck to it. 'Baby,' she murmured distractedly.

Alice turned back to the sonographer, who was staring intently at the screen. 'It's funny, I was sure I could feel a few kicks the other day. But that's not possible this early, is it?'

The sonographer's eyes didn't move. 'It would be highly unusual. Could you just cough for me, Alice?'

She breathed in, and as she forced a cough, the sonographer

jiggled the transducer against the side of Alice's stomach. 'Just trying to get baby to turn a little.'

'You can see it?' Alice asked, now gazing up at the ceiling.

'Yes.' Her voice had steadied, as if a mechanism in her throat had been switched on that filtered it of emotion.

Alice found her gaze travelling down the wall to the side of the woman's face.

'Alice, have you been experiencing any bleeding or stomach cramps?'

Suddenly, the coldness of the gel sank through her skin and touched her spine. 'No, what's wrong?'

'What I'm seeing on the screen is giving me cause for concern.' She waited a second. 'I'm not able to find the baby's heartbeat.'

The circling of the transducer slowed to a stop.

Alice stared at the sonographer's profile. 'No heartbeat?'

Her bottom lip tensed a fraction as she swallowed. 'I'm sorry, Alice.'

'There's no heartbeat?'

She placed the transducer to the side and put a hand over Alice's.

'I've lost my baby?'

The sonographer lowered her eyes in agreement. 'I'm afraid so.'

Jon looked down at Stuart, directing his quiet words to the receding hair on the man's head. 'It's our only avenue, Stuart. We can't find out where he might be – only you can do that. Only you can get us that information.'

Stuart placed his head in his hands. 'If he's started again, he'll only be active for a few more days. Then you won't hear of him again until next spring.'

'Next spring?' Jon crouched so he could see the other man's face. 'What do you mean, next spring?'

Stuart met Jon's eyes through a lattice work of fingers. 'The eggs. Most large raptors are laying right now. You have to get them when they're freshly laid.'

'Why?'

'To blow them. The contents have to be liquid. Once the embryo starts to form you can never get it out without ruining the shell.'

Jon felt his eyes widen. Alice, in the kitchen, lips pressed against the top of the chicken's egg. Embryo. Oh Christ, it was the day of her scan. He stood and glanced at his watch. That's what Rick was trying to remind me about when I interrupted him this morning. Oh no.

Stuart's wife returned, the peregrine falcon now on her gloved hand. 'My husband cannot help you.'

She bent forward then shook her gloved hand, but the falcon was reluctant to return to its perch. 'Get on it, you bloody animal!' She shook her arm more vigorously. The bird started flapping its wings, stepping back up the glove.

Stuart was on the edge of his seat. 'Nichola, watch his feathers.'

Ignoring him, Nichola snarled, 'Get off!' She pushed at the bird's back with her free hand.

Jon had taken out his mobile, realising he'd had call divert on since yesterday. Stuart's wife raised a brass ring connected to the perch by a nylon cord and passed it through the slits at the ends of the bird's leg straps. 'Sort yourself out, then.' She shrugged her hand out of the glove, letting it and the falcon fall to the grass. Half-hanging upside down, the animal struggled to right itself, all poise and dignity lost.

Nichola glanced at Stuart. 'If you start up with this again, I'm leaving you. Do you understand?'

Stuart looked back down. 'She's right, officer. I've put all that behind me, now. I can't help.'

Jon was scrolling through his missed calls. There, a few down, was one from Alice. And another. And another. He looked to Stuart and saw his chance of locating Craig slipping away. 'Your younger brother is in danger. What I believe he witnessed was no ordinary murder. The victim was dismembered on that hill. Sawed into pieces and shoved in bin bags.'

Nichola forced Stuart to his feet and turned him in the

direction of the caravan. 'All the more reason not to get in-volved, then.'

Jon glimpsed the details of the most recent call. Today at 12.10. Oh no, she's gone there on her own. What will she have done with Holly? 'Stuart!' He fumbled for a card, following them across the grass. 'Call me. If you hear anything, call me.'

He reached back to take it from Jon's outstretched fingers, but Nichola's hand shot out. Claw-like fingers snatched it from Jon and she crumpled it up before shoving it in the side pocket of her Barbour.

Jon watched the pair go, then lifted the phone to his face. Alice's mobile started to ring.

'Hello?' Her voice sounded odd.

'Alice, I'm so, so sorry. I forgot my sodding answerphone was on. How did it go? Did they give you a photo of the little sprout? Alice? Hello? Can you hear me?'

A few pigeons were flying across the sky, every inch of their progress tracked by the tethered predators below. Jon looked at their keen eyes, full of such sharp yearning.

He heard a sniff and dread began to tickle at his scalp.

'Mum's here with me.' Alice's voice was flat.

'Your mum?' When did she start showing any interest? He saw an image of Amanda, strutting about in the clothes of a teenager, make-up habitually overdone. 'She went with you to the hospital?'

'I called her.'

'What? You mean from the hospital?'

'I lost the baby.'

'What?'

'It's gone.'

'What?'

'The baby's gone.'

He didn't move. Gone? My child is gone? 'What do you mean?'

'It ... the lady there, the sonographer, she said ... she said ...' The sentence collapsed into sobs.

Jon tipped his head back, eyelids sliding shut. Our baby's

gone, just like that. He dropped to his knees and let the phone fall from his fingers, trying to summon the strength to scream up at the clouds, the sky, the whole miserable fucking universe.

With teeth pinching her lower lip in concentration, Zoe raised the cigarette paper to her face and attempted to tuck the lower edge behind the sausage of tobacco caught in its fold. Slowly, she rocked the pads of her thumbs upwards.

'Mama?' His voice was now barely a whisper.

She thought about the day before: how she'd taken Salvio's little present and poured it down the toilet. He'd heard the flush and guessed what she'd done.

'Face it, sweetheart. That tosser's gone and left you. It's us now, just like the old days.'

Her anger had taken her by surprise. Salvio didn't dare touch her while she was with Dave. Not with the amount of people he knew. 'Just piss off, Salvio. You hear me? When Dave comes back, he's going to sort you out. Just fucking wait.'

His scornful laugh had slowly faded as he'd stalked off back down the stairwell.

Now look, she thought, glancing about the kitchen. Dave still isn't here. Should never have tipped the fucking H away.

A corner of paper popped out but she continued rolling, pressing hard with her fingers as she ran the tip of her tongue along the gummed edge.

The misshapen object had the look of a battered trumpet, and as she tried to light it, clumps of tobacco fell from the flared end. The paper caught fire, quickly burning back towards her fingers. 'Fuck it!'

She slammed the cigarette lighter on the table, hurling the rapidly disintegrating mess into the sink.

'Telly?' Coming from the next room, the word was barely audible.

'Shut up, will you? Just shut up! God!' She pressed her uppermost knuckles against her cheeks. 'Stop mithering me, OK?'

She looked at the window, eyes focused on the sky beyond. I never wanted this kid. You did, Dave. Not me. And now where the fuck are you? Another rasp from the front room, this one not even a word.

'For fuck's sake.' She stood up, and as she marched into the other room, the newsreader was talking about possible links to Sheffield. A body, found somewhere. Whatever, she thought, pointing the remote. CBeebies came on and Jake sank back against his cushions, breath going rapidly in and out, lungs sounding like crisp packets being repeatedly scrunched up.

She tried to count how fast he was breathing, but gave up after he'd taken almost thirty breaths in as many seconds.

She sighed, moving over to the window and looking out. Where the fuck was he? This was past a joke. What if the deal he'd been arranging with Redino in Haverdale had come off? Would he have just taken the money and disappeared without her? No, not Dave. She looked back over the wreckage of her life, doubts nagging away. After all, every other bastard had let her down, sooner or later.

The light was starting to fade, the distant hills a mere suggestion in the gloom. A memory fast losing strength. Tonight, she decided. If he doesn't come back tonight, that's it. Jake needs fucking medicine and I cannot stand it trapped in this flat any longer. Salvio can do what he likes.

Twenty Three

Come on, you cunt. Jon sped along the country road, eyes looking ahead but attention on the periphery of his vision. He imagined death was out there, somewhere in the dusky fields that bordered the road. Watching, waiting. Want to take me as well? He closed his eyes, and as he lifted his fingers from the steering wheel, he pressed the accelerator down. You've got my family in your sights, my brother, my unborn fucking child. Here's your chance with me.

The left-hand side of the car started to judder and he opened his eyes. The hedge was flying past far too close to his window and he saw that he'd drifted off the road and into a layby. Fifty metres in front, the rough tarmac ended and the yawning ditch began again. He stamped on the clutch and brake simultaneously, gripping the steering wheel as the tyres locked into a skid. The car came to a halt, metres from the drop. Oh, God. He leaned forward and started banging his forehead against the wheel. That was stupid. Oncoming traffic, a lorry parked up in the layby. I could have died.

He ran over the hurried conversation he'd had with Alice's mum. Foetal measurements indicated it had died several days ago. Signs of infection were present in Alice's womb and the consultant obstetrician was concerned enough to have taken Alice straight off for a D and C.

'What's that?' Jon had whispered.

'They've removed it, Jon. A minor operation under local anaesthetic.'

'It's gone? They took the baby?'

'She's on antibiotics and painkillers, Jon. They're sending us home.'

He thought about his wife and daughter. They would be back by now. Hopefully Holly would be asleep. And where am I? Racing through the countryside, flirting with the Grim Reaper. Jesus, get a bloody grip. He indicated right and pulled cautiously back onto the road, eyes lingering for a second on the edge. Searching for a cowled figure crouching behind it.

'Hello?' He paused in the hallway, head bowed as he listened for a response.

'Up here.'

Amanda's voice. They were upstairs in the bedroom. Punch appeared in the kitchen doorway, his stump of a tail hesitantly wagging. You know something's up, don't you? Jon crouched, slapping a palm against his thigh as he did so. His dog huffed in relief, quickly approaching to nuzzle his squashed nose into Jon's outstretched hands. He ran his fingers round behind the animal's ears, then lifted its chin so their eyes met. 'How is she?' he whispered, staring into its sad brown eyes. Bad, then.

He climbed the stairs with a mounting sense of fear. The door to Holly's room was slightly ajar, the interior softly lit by her night light. At least she's asleep, he thought, stepping into his and Alice's room.

His wife was under the covers, her back supported by several pillows. Amanda was next to her, sitting cross-legged on the covers, a book balanced in the V of her shins. His eyes caught on her white ankle socks. White with a pink band at the toes. At the end of the bed was a tray with two empty cups.

He looked at Alice's face. She was pale, drawn, exhausted-looking. Guilt burned inside him like bile. 'Hi there,' he coughed.

She glanced in his direction, but her eyes stayed at stomach level.

He walked round to her side of the bed and knelt down, hands searching out hers beneath the duvet. They were cupping her lower stomach and he had to worm his fingers between hers to lightly grasp them. 'I'm so sorry.'

Alice closed her eyes and he turned to Amanda for guidance,

support: just the faintest hint of how to proceed. He saw something flicker in her eyes and he knew exactly what she was thinking: my husband let me down and now you're doing the same to my daughter. Men.

Jon had to look away, certain of the hint of reproach in the arch of her pencilled eyebrows. Typical fucking Amanda. Never here for the good news, but wings straight in for the bad.

'I'll make some tea,' she stated, placing the book face down. She climbed off the bed and headed out of the room, tray in her hands.

Jon looked back at his wife. Her eyes were open again, but directed down at her stomach. He circled his thumbs, trying to coax a response, but her fingers were lifeless in his grasp. He felt like someone trying to spring open a lock with the wrong implement. I don't have the tools for this. 'Does it hurt?'

She moved her chin towards the bedside table and he spotted the bottles there. Christ, it didn't seem that long ago that she'd been weaned off her tablets for post-natal depression. 'Painkillers?'

She nodded. 'And antibiotics.'

'So what did they say at the hospital? Did the doctor give any reason ...' He stopped, knowing the urge to rake over the technicalities was for his satisfaction alone. 'How do you feel?'

Her head rocked a little as she let out breath through her nose. 'What do you think?'

'I don't know, Ali. Maybe numb?'

Her eyes swivelled to meet his. 'Dead. Inside, I feel dead.'

He swallowed. 'I'm so sorry, Ali.' He searched his mind for something positive. 'We've got a beautiful daughter right in the next room.'

Her eyes dropped, giving him nothing.

'We can try again. When you're ready, Ali, we can try for—'

'I don't want another! I want this one!' The tears came suddenly and she looked mournfully at the far wall. 'What did I do? Why didn't I protect you better? Oh, my little angel, I should have protected you better.'

Jon stared at his wife in shock. I'm not even here. She's talking to our dead baby. 'Ali.' He tried again to coax a response from her fingers. Ask me where I was. Demand to know. Just don't shut me out like this. He waited a second longer, but she wasn't going to speak. 'I'm so sorry, Ali. There was news about the night Dave died. A discovery.' He let the word hang, but it had no impact. 'A witness.' Still nothing. 'Someone who might have seen what happened. I got caught up trying to trace him – and my phone; I'd turned it off, stupidly. That's why I missed your calls. As soon as I realised . . .' Excuses. The ungainly scrabble of it all. Despair made him want to collapse on the bed next to her. She's not interested in what happened to my brother. I could carry on in the same whining tone, but just repeat the words 'blah, blah, blah' over and over again. It's what she's hearing, after all. He almost smiled. It's probably how I deserve to be heard.

Amanda walked back into the room, lowered the tray onto the bed and then sat on its edge. He turned to her. 'Have you spoken to Alan and Mary?'

'We've tried calling them,' she replied.

'But they're not answering their calls?' She gave him a look and Jon was suddenly aware of his mobile digging into his thigh. He glanced up at the ceiling, then back to Alice. She hadn't moved. Turning away, he saw Amanda's bag in the corner. 'You're staying the night?'

Amanda looked at Alice.

'That's cool,' he continued. 'I'll set up the sofa bed for you.'

'She's sleeping in here. I don't want to be on my own.'

Jon's eyes went to his wife.

'Perhaps I should take the sofa bed, Alice,' Amanda said. 'Now Jon's back.'

Alice slid her fingers out from under Jon's and a hand emerged from the covers. It sought out her mum's. 'No. I need you here. With me.'

Jon could see Amanda's eyes were starting to glisten. 'You stay in here,' he said. He pushed himself upright. 'I'll sleep downstairs, it's fine.' He looked at the top of his wife's head.

195

'I wish I could tell you more than just sorry, but I don't know what else to say. I really don't.'

Out on the landing he paused at his daughter's door, then eased it open and stepped inside. She was face down on the little bed, covers off, arms out at her sides, bottom in the air. He smiled through the tears that were causing his vision to swim. Draping the duvet back over her, he hoped that he could force closed the thing he felt opening up between him and his wife.

Ian Flynn yanked the handlebars towards him and his Kawasaki rocked back on its stand. There was light shining through the gap in the front room's curtains, but he knew he wouldn't be in there. Turning to the garage, he saw the crack of light at the base of the door. He gave his usual knock and waited.

'Who is it?'

'Me.'

The bolts were drawn back and the door half-opened. 'Have you got it together, yet?'

Flynn touched each temple with his fingertips, then rotated his hands towards the other man, keeping the space between his palms exact. 'Straight as an arrow.'

'You've been smoking.'

'I know,' he replied sheepishly. 'I had to chill myself out.'

'For fuck's sake.'

The person moved aside and Flynn stepped into the garage, taking in a breath. The table below the long strip light was lined with rows of pills. To the side was a pair of electronic scales, piles of plastic ziplock bags, semi-unwrapped blocks of compressed marijuana. Rolls of cling film and tinfoil. 'Did you read the newspaper?'

'Yes,' the man replied.

'It was going on about a link to Manchester or Sheffield.'

'Yes.'

'He wasn't known in Manchester, though. Was he? Your contact,' he nodded at the supplies covering the table, 'he'd never heard of him, right?'

'Doesn't mean he wasn't a player. There's more than one supplier in that city.'

Flynn picked at a tooth. 'What about the brother? Fucking Major Incident Team, whatever that is.'

The other man snapped open the lid of an airtight container and started spooning out white spiky shards onto the scales. 'What, exactly, did you say to him?'

Flynn plonked himself down in an old kitchen chair by the workbench that ran along one side of the garage. 'I dunno. Enough.'

'I need more than a "dunno", you halfwit. What the fuck did you say?'

Bending forwards, Flynn ran both palms over the stubble covering his scalp. 'That I could get him anything. Whizz, pills, ice. The works. Grass by the sackful.'

'What the hell were you even talking to him for?'

'We got chatting in the Spread, he said he was opening a club in Sheffield. Later, he hinted he might be interested in cutting a deal to supply it. It just sort of came out as we chatted. I thought we could clean up.'

'So you meet a stranger in the Spread and hours later he's in your house and you're offering to supply him with unlimited amounts of my drugs?'

'I know it sounds stupid now. But at the time, it didn't. Everything just flowed along, natural, like.'

'Imbecile. Did you say anything – I mean anything – about where you would get the drugs from?'

'No! Not a thing.'

'Talk me through what was said, word for word.'

Flynn's hands dropped to his lap and he looked up. 'We were in my front room. I was putting a number together. Using that little bit of grass I persuaded that Manc, Dave, to sell me. The really good shit. He asked me – the older brother – he asked me if that was the stuff I could supply him with. I said, no.' He pointed at the blocks of compressed leaves on the table. 'I said the stuff I could get hold of wouldn't be quite as good. He started acting strange – like he wasn't interested. So I said

I could get him all the other stuff, too. Even ice. Said the kids really loved the stuff. He turned white, man. I thought he was going to throw up. Then he just staggered out. Nothing more was said, I swear.'

The other man crossed his arms. 'That's not so bad.'

Flynn looked surprised. 'Really? But I told him, didn't I? Said I was his man.'

'True.' He looked at the ceiling, then said, almost reluctantly, 'Best you disappear until this blows over. Got anywhere you can go?'

'I've got some cousins. Down in Somerset.'

'Perfect.' The man walked over to a shelf and removed a folded-up sheet of plastic. 'Do you need cash?'

Flynn glanced over his shoulder. 'Could you? I'd appreciate it, man.'

Behind him, the other person unfolded the sheet, and it crackled as he lay it across the floor. 'Reach under that workbench. There's a block of twenties wrapped in cellophane, I taped them to the centre strut.'

'Oh, you're a star.' Flynn stretched a hand under and started groping around. 'You know the other bit in the paper. About the forensic stuff – footprints and a tyre track from a motorbike?'

'Yes.'

'I was thinking. I mean, I was pretty much out of it the whole weekend that Manc bloke got topped. Payday and all that. But didn't you come round mine to borrow my bike at some point?'

'Did I?'

'I've got this vague memory of you coming into my front room. Was that for real?'

'What, borrowing your bike?'

'Yeah, it seemed funny. I mean, that night in the Spread, when he was going on about finding some buried treasure, didn't you say there were a few places you could think of where it might be?'

'Did I? I can hardly remember, mate.'

'Yeah, you did. This cash – you said it's taped to the centre strut? I can't feel anything.'

'Reach further, it's right at the back.'

Flynn strained forward, the top of his chin now pressed against the wooden surface. Behind him, the other man lifted a large claw hammer from the row of tools hanging from the garage wall. He raised it to shoulder height and then, with a casual sweep, buried the long twin-points deep into the crown of Flynn's skull.

Twenty Four

'Thanks for getting back to me, I really appreciate your help,' Rick said, yet again. 'I know what a pain it is to be disturbed of an evening.'

He listened to the woman from the council claim it was no inconvenience at all, but her voice carried no conviction.

'Great, well, I won't take up any more of your time. Thanks again.' He hung up and turned to the piece of paper. He now had a list of eleven names. Zoe Price. Zoe Evans. Zoe Jackson. Zoe Croxton. No Zoe Spicer, though. There were addresses in Stretford, Longsight, Droylsden, Cheetham Hill, Openshaw. He imagined the terraces and tower blocks. Bloody grim. With a sigh, he ran a finger down the list; seven had phone numbers. He glanced at his watch: 10.10, at night. Not a reasonable hour to start phoning strangers to ask if they were seeing a petty criminal who had just been murdered. First thing in the morning, then.

He looked around the incident room, seeing he was now the only person there. Bloody hell, he thought. How come working with Jon Spicer is like holding down two jobs at once?

The springs in the sofa bed were digging into his back and the sleeping bag was too narrow. Jon raised himself onto one elbow. This was hopeless. With a downward sweep of his arm, he opened the zip and his bare legs slid out, like the stomach contents of a gutted crocodile. The look of utter desolation on Alice's face wouldn't go away. He rested his forehead against the heels of his hands. Christ, what's happening to us?

Punch raised himself from the carpet, placed his chin on Jon's knee and stared up at his master. Jon lowered a hand and looked into the animal's eyes, so sad and black in the gloom. 'I know, I know. Really fucked up this time, haven't I?'

His dog's gaze didn't waver.

Feeling numb and empty, Jon traced a forefinger down the velvety groove between the animal's eyes. Once again, the fragments of the case started circling in his head. He tried to blink them away, but they wouldn't disappear. Chances of Stuart Budd calling? He thought about the wife and how aggressive she'd become. Slim to non-existent, then. She'd made it plain what the bloke's choices were: help Jon and lose her.

His thoughts went back to Haverdale. Could he get Mallin to bring Ian Flynn in? There were issues about entrapment; after all, he'd posed as a security professional to get the guy to talk. But if he could persuade Mallin to press charges, they could go into Flynn's bungalow and turn it upside down. There had to be a saw somewhere with traces of Dave's blood. And shoes – the Norwegian army boots could still be lying around someplace.

He crossed his arms, the cool air starting to caress his torso. What else could he take to Mallin about Flynn? Think, Jon, think. It's all in the papers now; the bloke will be destroying any evidence of drug dealing. Probably doing it right now.

His mind went to the evening in the Spread Eagle, the crazy motorbike ride . . . fuck! The make of tyre. I forgot to ask Nikki to check the cast she'd taken against makes of Bridgestones.

He fumbled for his mobile, knocking a button and causing the screen to emit an ethereal glow: 5.16 in the morning. I can't ring her now. Give it until, when? Seven? Six thirty?

He lay back, hands behind his head and stared at the ceiling. Alice. He hadn't felt this powerless since being in hospital when Holly was born. Mopping his wife's forehead with a cool flannel, urging her to push through unimaginable pain when all he could feel was a mildly annoying hunger in his stomach. I haven't a clue what any of this really feels like for her. And without an understanding, I don't know what to say. He shut his eyes and pictured her lying there barely twelve feet above his head.

★

Now wearing his park ranger's uniform, Michael Lumm stepped back into his garage and regarded the corpse of Ian Flynn sitting upright in the chair. He could have been mistaken for someone sleeping if it wasn't for the rope looped around his torso. That and the head of the hammer embedded in his skull, its handle jutting out like a lever by which to crank the dead man back to life.

He stepped closer to the chair, each rear leg now standing in a plastic washing-up bowl. That hadn't been easy, Flynn twitching and gurgling as he'd lifted the back of the chair up to position a bowl beneath each leg, only the coils of rope preventing the dying man from sliding to the concrete floor.

Now, peering down, he could see it had been worth the effort. Both vessels were half full with viscous liquid. The whole garage reeked of its coppery tang. Bending down, he lifted the flap of material created by cutting across the seat of Flynn's trousers. The incisions he'd made into the man's buttocks gaped, blood jelly-like in the lower fold of flesh. He must have bled out hours ago.

Bracing his knees, Lumm hooked a hand under the backrest of the chair, and with his cheek pressed against Flynn's shoulder, raised the rear legs up. His other hand groped down, sliding one bowl clear, then the other. A grunt escaped him as he lowered the chair and straightened up. Inside the washing-up bowls, Flynn's blood gently shifted, its congealed surface thick as unwanted gravy.

Next, Lumm untied the knot and removed the rope coiled around Flynn's chest. Then, after placing a toe against the rear leg of the kitchen chair, he used both hands to tilt it backward, tipping Flynn onto the plastic sheeting. His head cracked against the hard floor and the hammer was dislodged from his skull. Immediately, watery blood trickled from the twin holes in the crown of his head.

Lumm looked down at the other man, surprised once again at how simple it was. He'd despatched so many animals in his capacity as a park ranger: foxes, mink, deer. So why did it seem strange that a human died just as easily? He thought back to that night on Highshaw Hill, how his hands had trembled as he'd slid the hammer out from his bag. But there'd been no need for nerves; he smiled at the memory of how the man from Manchester had dropped to the ground. Of course, the blood was a problem. He should have realised there'd be so much; after all, when they culled an adult stag, puddles of the stuff were left on the moor.

That's why, he thought smugly, I'm being more organised this time round. He turned to the array of tools and removed a medium-size hacksaw. Pointing the end of it at Flynn, he spoke. 'No one comes into this town and deals drugs, unless it's through me. No one, understand?'

Flynn's lifeless eyes gazed up, dried saliva like a fungus on his chin.

'Whatever bullshit he came out with about digging for treasure, he sold you drugs. That, my friend, is called a toehold. And I don't give those to anyone. You hear me?' He crouched, bending forward so his face was directly above Flynn's. 'You hear me?'

He glanced at his watch. Still an hour before he needed to be at the visitor centre, preparing for the day. Once there he could give Riley a call. See if the RSPB officer had worked out which other nests Craig Budd might try and target on his latest collecting spree.

A sudden surge of anxiety caused him to blink. If Riley had any ideas, the first person he would have passed them to was that bloody DI Spicer.

He looked back at the corpse laid out before him. 'Fucking idiot,' he cursed, lining up the serrated edge of the saw against the other man's neck.

Jon's eyes snapped open. Was that a beep? Did my mobile phone just beep? Weak light was now showing at the curtain's edges and he could hear a few birds' tentative twitters. Shit, I must have fallen asleep. The chorus of electronic notes sounded again. I didn't dream it! He reached to the side of his head and examined the number on the phone's screen. Buchanon using someone else's mobile? His eyes moved to the little clock . Surely not at 5.50 in the morning. He pressed green. 'DI Spicer.'

'It's Stuart Budd here.'

Christ, he must have retrieved my card from his wife's coat. 'Hello.'

'You said my brother was in danger because of what he saw near that reservoir.'

Jon sat up, knowing this would be his only shot at getting Stuart to help. He tried to clear his head. 'I believe your brother saw something – something serious enough to cause him to panic.'

Stuart kept his silence.

Getting to his feet, Jon paced towards the closed curtains. 'Perhaps the people who committed the murder realised Craig was there. Maybe that's what caused him to fumble the osprey's egg. He was in a rush to get away.'

Still no response.

Jon held up a hand, as if addressing an audience behind the hanging material. 'I've no idea who these people are, but if they find your brother, I've no doubt they'll kill him too.' He waited with his eyes shut. Please, please say you'll help me.

'I'm at Piccadilly station. Can you come and pick me up?'

As Jon started reaching for his trousers, he thought about Alice asleep upstairs. I can't just leave her. 'Now? You need to be picked up right now?'

'Yes.'

'Look, I could do with an hour or so, just to—'

'I know where he is. Craig. I know where my brother is. Anglesey. But we've got to get there – fast.'

Jon's head dipped and breath flowed from between his lips. 'OK.'

Even though most of the shops' shutters were still down, Piccadilly station was busier than Jon had imagined. Streams of men and women, hair neatly tied, ties neatly knotted. The clump of their footsteps filled the quiet hall as they flowed silently for city centre offices like a migrating herd.

Jon's eyes swept around, searching for a solitary figure that was standing still. Stuart Budd was over by the Virgin Trains' desk, shifting from foot to foot.

As he started towards the other man, Jon thought of the hastily scrawled note he'd left for Alice. Could she understand the urgency of the situation? Would she even want to? He imagined them staring at each other across a shapeless grey lake, separated by an inability to understand what the other felt. This, a voice in his ear announced, is how marriages end.

Another voice, this one for real. 'Jon, you're a bastard, you know that?'

He kept the phone against his ear as he drew closer to Budd. 'Sorry, Nikki – but I didn't want to miss you. Court or somewhere that doesn't allow mobiles.'

'At quarter past six on a Thursday morning? Which bloody courts do you know that are open then?'

'I'm sorry. Listen, I've got a make of motorbike tyre. That'll help narrow the search down, won't it?'

'Yes, by about ninety-nine point nine percent.' The line beeped. 'Go ahead, I'm recording this on voice notes.'

'OK, it's a Bridgestone. I didn't see the exact name. I think it was T and possibly an O. There were about five letters or numbers in all.'

'That's it?'

'That's it.'

The line beeped again. 'OK, got it. I don't need to ask how urgent this is; I read the report about your brother.'

'Which paper?'

'*Manchester Evening Chronicle.*'

'It was in that? When?'

'Yesterday. Page five.'

He thought of Carmel's text. My condolences. Yeah, right. Another thought hit: my parents have probably seen it, too.

'I'll get back to you, soon as.'

'Cheers, Nikki.' The line cut and he held up a hand to get Stuart Budd's attention. On seeing him, Budd picked up a small holdall. 'I'm parked out the back in the taxi rank,' Jon announced, turning round and leading the way back to the escalators.

They walked in silence, and as they went, the tannoy system announced a train departing somewhere. But there was a slight delay between the speakers dotted around the vast station and the announcement had a layered effect, like a dead person calling out in a horror film.

He drove up the Mancunian Way, leaving the short stretch of flyover motorway to join Princess Road, heading out of the city against a never-ending stream of cars coming the other way.

Soon they were on the M56, travelling west towards Wales. Jon turned his head and glanced at Stuart. The other man's reddish hair was all messed up and his hands were in his lap, nervously picking away at the cuticles of a nail. He looked like a schoolboy, sitting outside the headmaster's office.

'I'm guessing your wife doesn't know you're here,' Jon stated.

A little shake of his head. 'No, she doesn't.'

Join the gang, Jon thought. 'Will she take you back?'

He shrugged. 'Maybe. Probably not.'

'So why did you do it?'

'He's my brother. What else could I do?'

Jon nodded. 'How did you work out where he'd be?'

'I went online, to sites I swore to Nichola I'd never visit again.'

'Egg-collecting sites?'

'If you can call them that. Messages, coded names. Just lines of text, really. I told them I was starting again – I needed to find Craig. The Budd brothers, back together again.' He stared at his fingers in shame.

'Dyson and Crag.'

'Dyson and Crag.'

'And?'

'He's here for one more night, possibly two. Then he's gone.'

'What do you mean, gone?'

'He doesn't live in this country any more. Somewhere in

206

Amsterdam now – he collects on the continent where the laws against it are almost non-existent.'

'The RSPB officer said it was a peculiarly British crime.'

'He travels down to the Pyrenees, apparently. Climbing cliffs to steal from the nests of imperial eagles. He's even more of a legend now than he ever was.'

'Why take the risk of coming back? And why Anglesey?'

'The challenge. Ospreys haven't nested in the Peak District for over a hundred years. To have that clutch is a huge victory – except he lost one.'

'And Anglesey?'

Stuart glanced at Jon, and behind the look of embarrassment was just the faintest hint of awe. 'A pair of sea eagles, flown down from the west coast of Scotland.'

'Another big prize.'

'DI Spicer, sea eagles were driven to extinction in Britain back in the eighteen hundreds. They were only reintroduced to a few isolated spots in Scotland in 1975. There are now thirty-two territorial pairs in that country, thirty-one now these two have ventured south. In all that time only four clutches have ever been taken – and none since the year two thousand. I know this because my brother stole that fourth clutch.' He shook his head, digging away at the corner of his thumb. 'And now he's out to rob this pair of their eggs.'

'Surely there's some sort of protection in place?'

'Absolutely. The guard will be round the clock. There's barbed wire, CCTV, an exclusion zone stretching two hundred metres back from the edge of the cliff where the nest is located.'

Sounds like bloody Colditz, Jon thought. 'Why did you say one, maybe two nights before he vanishes?'

'The female laid two eggs, one the day before yesterday, the other a day before that. He has to get them in the next forty-eight hours—'

Jon closed his eyes. 'So they can be blown.'

'Precisely.'

They drove in silence, the massed metal chimneys and pipes

of the Stanlow Oil Refinery on their right. A burn-off flame wavered against the pale sky.

'The reason I called you,' Stuart suddenly said, 'is because not everyone thinks my brother is a legend. There are plenty of others who'd love to see him back inside. Maybe worse.'

'Who?'

'Other collectors.'

Jon remembered the RSPB officer describing how eggers sometimes sold each other out. 'You mean rivals?'

Stuart nodded. 'I rang you because I thought, what if anyone using the chatroom puts two and two together with the murder in Haverdale? I mean, he left his bloody calling card in the ospreys' nest. What if they figure Craig could have witnessed something and put it out there that he's on Anglesey? I'm sure the people you're after would love a piece of information like that.'

Jon straightened up. 'These eggers. What sort of people are we talking about, Stuart?'

'Type?' A dry laugh rattled in his throat. 'There are no types.'

'How do you mean?'

'Eggers are often from unskilled professions, but not exclusively. I know of businessmen, city types. There are two currently active who're in the police. A magistrate. They're everywhere.'

Keeping his thumbs hooked around the steering wheel, Jon straightened his fingers. The closest he could get to a placatory gesture. 'OK, let's not panic. There's a risk. But it just means we have to find him first.'

As they entered the tunnels of Conwy, Stuart reached into his bag and took something out. 'You didn't tell me it was your brother who was murdered.'

Jon glanced towards Stuart's lap and saw a copy of the *Manchester Evening Chronicle*. The paper was open on a page dominated by a grainy photo of Dave. Where the fuck did they dig that up from? 'Does it matter?'

'This isn't part of the official investigation, is it?'

Jon shot a look to his left, but Stuart was sparing him direct eye contact. 'No. No, it isn't.'

'So, what do you stand to lose by being here?'

'Pretty much the same as you.'

'Job?'

'Probably gone already.'

'Wife?'

The word sparked a series of images in Jon's head. The first time they'd met, just a small movement of her head transfixing him from across a crowded bar. He'd known then she was the one, even before they'd spoke. Their wedding day, everyone he cared about there to see his proudest moment. Alice giving birth to Holly, her focused calm while the delivery-room staff worked frantically around her. Their future together; becoming old and slow and doddery, but content in each other's company to do so. 'Not without a fight.'

Stuart glanced out of the side window at the towering peaks on their left. 'Families.'

Jon knew what he meant. The cause and cure of everything. 'How did it start with you and your brother?'

'Stealing eggs, you mean?'

'Yes.'

'It all began when I was nine, Craig was seven. We stole a tawny owl's egg from a nest in the woods at the bottom of our garden. Something about it completely captivated us. Maybe it's the potential – what it could be, there neatly encased, snug in the palm of your hand. Soon we were scouring local parks, hedgerows, thickets – robbing the nests of blackbirds, thrushes, robins, wrens. The thrill of finding a nest, reaching in and feeling those delicate oval shapes inside. Usually still warm from the mother's body heat. It's addictive. You start yearning for a larger collection, which means finding rarer species.'

Jon settled into his seat, the car in fifth gear as he cruised the long curving road leading them to Anglesey.

'Craig was always a climber,' Stuart continued. 'He got hooked on kestrels, sparrow-hawks, even herons. Tops of trees, swaying up there like a little monkey. Later, clambering up cliffs, fast as a lizard.'

'Hence the nickname, Crag? Or is it because of his good looks?'

'It came from climbing, originally. They seem to love nicknames in that sport. But it fits him in general, too.'

'The RSPB officer at Haverdale said he made a living from his climbing.'

'He did. All that went when we got sentenced. But yes, he had sponsorship from the likes of Red Chili, Berghaus and Petzl. He took part in all the UK competitions, won quite a few of them. I can't stand heights, so I kept to ground-nesting birds. Skylarks, curlew, red grouse, lapwings. Kingfishers, with a bit of digging. Then I discovered colonies. Birds that nest on islands. I've been everywhere with Craig. Mull, Orkney, Shetlands. Marsh harrier eggs from the Fens. For Craig, we've done the Cairngorms, Cuillins, Dyfed, Powys, the Lake District. All over.'

'Full-time hobby, then.'

Stuart examined the fringe of his thumbnail. Jon saw it was angry and red. 'We'd spend hours planning our raids. If it was a nest we knew birds would return to the next year, we'd have plotted it out months in advance. The rarer the bird, the bigger the challenge. You have the wardens to watch out for. When they toughened the law, you had to be really careful. I had my driving licence suspended to try and stop me reaching really remote places. That's when the business started to go wrong, but Craig would just drive me instead. We've paid thousands of pounds in fines, but nothing could stop us.'

Hearing the note of pride creeping into the other man's voice, Jon said, 'Until prison.'

'When they broke down my front door, you know what? I was glad. Thirty years it controlled my life. I actually cried with gratitude. Did Thurrock tell you that?'

'He said you handed in the collection.'

'Yes.'

'Without Craig's say-so.'

'No.' He went to pick at his cuticle again, and Jon had to look away. 'I thought it might break his habit, too. A complete ...' he bunched his fingertips and then spread them, 'letting go.

But it didn't. And now he hates me.' He sighed. 'You know my brother's escape from that prison down south?'

Jon nodded. 'The RSPB officer mentioned it. He over-powered a guard, right?'

'He broke the man's jaw. Then the gag he put on him almost caused the bloke to choke to death. According to the police, he would have died if another warden hadn't found him.'

Jon flexed his shoulders. 'He's in big shit then.'

'How long do you think he'd get, if they caught him again?'

'A lot, lot longer than first time round.'

'And you're going to arrest him?'

Jon ran a forefinger along the top of the steering wheel, removing dust that wasn't there. 'I'm after whoever killed my brother. So it's best you didn't actually tell me he'd nearly killed a prison guard, understand?'

Stuart nodded.

'The RSPB officer said you eggers get a tough time in prison.'

'Yes.'

'How tough?'

'I'd rather not talk about it.'

'Craig?'

'Worse. He cannot bear being cooped up, it really gets to him. Then he tried to stand up to the other prisoners, rather than just keep his head down.' He looked across Jon at the sea on the right-hand-side of the car. 'What happened between you and your brother? You're a police officer, he was a ... the paper suggested he was ...'

Jon shook his head. 'No. He may have been an addict. I don't know, he led a very different life to me. But did he deserve what happened? No, he didn't.'

Stuart adjusted the seat belt running across his chest, saying nothing. Jon was getting ready to recount facts when his phone started to ring. He looked at the screen. Another unrecognised number with an 01297 code. Shazia Batyra again? He flipped the phone open. 'DI Spicer.'

'Yes, hello. Is that Detective Inspector Spicer?'

A female voice, the cracks of old age creeping in. Jon frowned. 'That's correct. Who is this, please?'

'Mrs Morris, Head Librarian at Haverdale.'

The library! Jon remembered the note he'd slotted through the door.

'I'm terribly sorry to have not got back to you sooner. My assistant had put your note on my desk and I've been staying at my daughter's house in Bristol. I only discovered it when I opened up this morning.'

Jon hunched a shoulder, wedging the phone against his ear as he returned both hands to the wheel. 'That's fine – Stacey, isn't it?'

'Yes.'

'Did my letter make any sense?'

'Absolutely. I remember the young man most clearly. He spent a couple of afternoons in here conducting research of one sort or another.'

'Research of an archaeological nature?'

'Indeed. He asked for my help – I'm Chairperson of the Haverdale Archaeological Society, too.'

'Yes, I read your comments in the *Herald*. You thought someone was searching for ... what was it?'

'A barrow. It certainly is one possibility.'

'There might be another, you mean?'

'Your brother was interested specifically in Beaker burials. Are you familiar with the term?'

'Not really, no.'

'These types of burial date back to the early Bronze Age, around four and a half thousand years ago. It was a common practice to inhume the dead beneath an earthen mound with a form of pottery we have named beakers. These small urns would contain grave goods – beads, bone implements, flint tools and, of course, bronze items. Weapons, mainly.'

Jon was having to concentrate on the road. 'And finds like that would be worth money?'

'Considerable amounts. As the Bronze Age progressed, the

burials became richer. Gold items began to appear – buttons, hair decorations, even pendants.'

Gold, Jon thought. What had Zoe's phone message said? Struck gold, yet? 'So Dave was looking for a Beaker burial?'

'He was interested in knowing which hills on the outskirts of Haverdale might have met the criteria for a Bronze Age burial site.'

'And do any?'

'None have been discovered by archaeologists so far, and the area has been thoroughly searched down the years.'

'Did it not occur to you my brother might have been behind the spate of illegal digs?'

'Of course. But the sheer folly of it lent his efforts a kind of tragic air. That's why I stated so strongly to the *Herald* there are no undiscovered sites in the area. I told him as such too.'

'But the digs went on.'

'Hope, as they say, springs eternal.'

It does if you're desperate enough, Jon thought. 'Thank you for getting back to me.'

'My pleasure, Detective Inspector. And I'm very sorry for your loss. For what it's worth, your brother seemed to me a very nice young man.'

'Thank you. That means a lot to me, it really does.'

'Good bye, then.'

'Good bye.' The line went dead and Jon had to look out of his side window for a few moments, waiting for the tear in his eye to subside.

Half an hour later the squat towers of the Menai Bridge loomed into sight. They sped over the stretch of sea and on to Anglesey itself.

'Where are we headed?' asked Jon.

'Straight into Holyhead, then follow the RSPB signs for South Stack lighthouse.'

The stream of water tumbled down from the tap, hitting the narrow blade of the hacksaw and washing off the blood. Michael Lumm worked at the base of the blade with a brush, removing the clot that had built up there. At his feet the drain gurgled and spluttered as the pinkish liquid disappeared down it.

Straightening up, he examined the hacksaw, then his hands. Clean as a whistle. His gaze moved to Flynn's bike propped up on its stand. That would have to go. Where, he wasn't quite sure. The garage would do for the moment.

He stepped over to the bins by the back door and lifted one away from the wall. The shape of the rat filled the thick Perspex trap he'd laid there. The animal had eaten away the lever mechanism that had tripped the door behind it long ago. Now it lay motionless in the narrow, oblong container, nodules of gnawed plastic sticking to the matted fur on its underside.

Lumm squatted down and tapped the plastic. 'Still alive in there?' he asked. 'That's pretty impressive.' But he could see the animal was now close to death. He replaced the bin and stepped back inside the garage, hung the hacksaw in its place, then looked down at the padlock that secured the main door to the garage's concrete floor. Once he'd wheeled the Kawasaki in, he could remove the tyres, dispose of them and start dismantling the rest of the machine.

To the side of the table was a low stack of oddly shaped lumps, each one tightly wrapped in black bin liners. Glancing at them, Lumm paused, a look of puzzlement on his face. He ducked down and what he saw beneath the table caused him to shake his head in gentle admonishment. He reached under with his foot and nudged the football-shaped object back to the other body parts.

Keeping her eyes closed, Zoe stretched a hand out to Dave's side of the bed. Cold, flat sheets. She'd had a dream of him returning in the early hours and slipping into bed before wrapping his arms around her.

She looked round the bedroom. The clock sitting on the floor where a bedside table was meant to be read 8.40. How come Jake wasn't crying? He must be starving by now. But there was no milk. No bread either. No cigarettes, no Dave, no bloody anything. She threw the thin duvet back and sat on the edge of the bed. That was it, then. She was heading out of the flat and Salvio could do whatever he wanted.

She hugged herself, contemplating what that really meant. Memories of pacing the same short stretch of pavement, up and down, up and down. Smiling at the driver's side of any car that began to slow down. She turned to the window that gave a narrow view of those distant hills. What else can I do? You've left me on my own, what else can I bloody do?

With a sigh, she walked round to Jake's bedroom door. Silence. Jesus, she thought. Normally he'd be standing up, shaking the bars of his cot by now. Pushing his door open, she looked inside. He was motionless on the bed, blankets kicked into a clump at his feet. 'Jake? Jake?' A series of little steps took her to the cot's side. 'Jake?'

His eyes were open and his pale skin was covered in a light sheen. She reached out a hand, peering at the sweaty pyjama top, just able to see a flutter beneath the damp material. 'Oh, Christ, Jake.' His eyes still hadn't moved.

Reaching out her stick-thin arms, she easily lifted him from the cot and started patting his back. He was hot, really hot. After a few seconds, he managed a few coughs and his breathing slowed a fraction.

As she stepped out into the corridor, the letter box creaked open and a folded copy of the *Manchester Evening Chronicle* landed in the hall. 'Page five, sweetheart. Read the story on page five.'

Salvio, sounding strangely subdued. She pictured him on the other side of the door with his oily black hair and gold neck chains. Ignoring the request, she hurried down the corridor and through to the front room, where she laid Jake on his raft of cushions. 'Mummy's getting help, don't worry, kidder.' She walked back to the corridor and looked at the front door. The paper lay there.

'Zoe! Come on, have a look. It's all I'm asking, love.' He was using his soft voice, the one he reserved for those occasions when doubts used to take her. Only then would he put his arm around her, tell her that she was special, that he couldn't survive without her.

Slowly, she walked to the door and picked the paper up. 'I'm coming out, Salvio. Do what you want, but my baby needs the hospital, all right?' She unfolded the paper, seeing that it was already open at page five. The grainy photo of Dave was at the top of the page. She struggled over the headline and, as the words hit home, she felt the wall bump off her shoulder. She tried to regain her balance, but the bones in her legs felt like they'd melted. Gradually, her knees folded and she sank to the carpet.

'Me and you, babe. What do you say?' Salvio cooed. 'I've missed you, Zoe, missed you more than you can imagine.'

She heard the letter box creak and saw the tips of his fingers reaching through, trying to make contact. The old days again.

'Come on, Zoe. Open the door. I'm here. Let me help you, sweetheart.'

She stared at the paper, feeling the last part of her that had emerged with Dave wither and shrink.

'Zoe, just open the door. I've found it so hard without you. So hard. Please, babe, I need you.'

For a while she didn't move. Then, by stretching out an arm, she began to slide the bolts back.

Twenty Five

Holyhead had a sleepy feel to it, as if the town only came to life with the departure and arrival of the ferries criss-crossing the Irish Sea. Drab buildings from previous decades, pebble-dash bed and breakfasts and shops that weren't part of any national chain.

The brown RSPB signs directed them along the town's high street and then on to a single-lane road. They passed rough fields that were dotted with rock before another sign pointed them up a steeply rising side lane, made narrower by the parked cars lining its left-hand side.

Standing at the end of a driveway to a large white house was a person in a fluorescent orange bib, 'North Wales RSPB' emblazoned across its front. Jon noticed Stuart sink down in his seat as they came to a halt.

Jon lowered his window. 'Morning.'

'Hello there!' The man had bushy brown hair and a glow to his cheeks. 'Here for the flying barn doors?'

'Sorry?'

'The sea eagles?'

'Yes.'

'Then could I ask you to turn your car around on the guesthouse drive behind me and head back to Treaddur Bay? There's a park'n'ride service operating from that point every twenty minutes. Last bus back at seven thirty tonight. It's awfully crowded at the top.'

Jon produced his warrant card. 'We're actually here on police business.'

'Oh.' The man straightened up and Jon could tell he was dying to ask for more of an explanation. 'Nothing too serious, I hope?'

'No. Isn't there a corner I could squeeze into?'

'Follow the road until you see the cafe on your left. There are some spaces reserved for RSPB volunteers at the side.'

'Thanks very much.' He moved slowly up the hill, and as they got higher, the ground on their left opened up, allowing views across sloping heathland that abruptly ended about three hundred metres away. Beyond that was only ocean, stretching as far as Jon could see. 'Flying barn doors?'

'Their nickname, on account of how they're so bloody huge,' Stuart replied.

The grass verge was now two or three people deep, mostly with men. Many were using the top of a drystone wall as a platform for tripods. Bloody hell, Jon thought, I've never seen so many zoom cameras and telescopes.

Stuart reached into his bag, took out a canvas hat with a wide rim and pulled it low over his head.

'Nervous?' Jon asked.

Stuart's left hand was now against the side of his face, shielding it from the throng just beyond the glass. 'Some of these people will know my face. Quite a few would happily kick the crap out of me.'

Jon raised his eyebrows. 'Because of the egging?'

Stuart glanced at him. 'Because I've ruined so much of what they live for. These people will drive the length of the country just to glimpse a rare bird.'

'Just like you'd drive the length of the country to steal its eggs?'

'Exactly.'

Jon assessed the crowds, wondering if anyone else out there was also searching for Craig. 'What are these people known as, twitchers, isn't it?'

Stuart nodded.

'Never knew it was so popular. There's hundreds of them. How the hell will I ever spot your brother?'

'Look for someone similar to me.' He smiled briefly. 'Just younger, leaner and a lot better looking. Hang on, I've got a picture.' He took out his wallet and removed a small photo. 'He used to wear his hair in dreadlocks, but I'm not so sure now. Just look for someone who's a bit wrong, who doesn't quite fit in. He'll have poor quality optics, for a start.'

'Optics?'

'Binoculars, probably. He won't be spending loads on an expensive telescope. The binoculars will just be a prop; he's not here to birdwatch. And he'll probably have a big bag. Maybe one from his old climbing sponsors, Red Chili or Berghaus.'

The road levelled out slightly and Jon saw the cafe. Before it was a large car park, and on its far side was a caravan with 'RSPB Cymru' written on its side. Dozens of people were swarming around it.

Jon pulled in, and with a few toots of his horn, managed to force his way across to the side of the cafe. He parked next to a Volvo estate, its rear window peppered with stickers from various RSPB sanctuaries from across the country. 'OK, I'll have a scout round. You're staying in here, I presume?'

'Too right,' Stuart replied. He passed Jon a pair of green binoculars. 'Take these.' He propped his head on his hand as if settling down for a nap. 'I'll keep my eyes open.'

Jon climbed out of the car. Fresh sea air washed over his face and he breathed it in until his lungs could take no more. He examined the caravan again, realising most of the people beside it were actually in a long, snaking queue. Men of all ages, some in walking gear, some in camouflage cagoules, some in Aran-knit sweaters. All carried cameras, binoculars or telescopes. He noticed a large sign above the caravan door that read, 'Live CCTV images'.

Skirting round the end of the queue, he stepped onto an area that had been recently laid with wood chippings. A fence, its posts and handrail showing no sign of weathering, formed a perimeter to the edge of the heath. Just before the fence was a series of waist-high posts with telescopes mounted on them. More people were gathered round them, RSPB officers helping direct every lens to one particular point.

Jon stepped up to the handrail. Immediately beyond it a ribbon of police tape stretched from a series of metal poles that ran for hundreds of metres across the heath. Tracking it, Jon realised it formed an exclusion zone around a section of cliff perhaps five hundred metres long. Midway along the cordoned-off cliff edge was a smaller semicircle of fencing, and when Jon raised the binoculars for a closer look, he was shocked to see it was constructed from coils of razor wire. The loops curved round to disappear over the cliff itself. How the hell did Craig think he could get past all of that without being spotted? He pointed the binoculars towards the road and started examining the rows of faces above the drystone wall.

'You're looking in the wrong direction there.'

Jon glanced down to see an elderly woman wearing one of the fluorescent RSPB bibs.

'Go back to the bit of cliff protected by the wire and look for the witch's nose – a bobble of rock with a hook-like protrusion. The nest is tucked into its side.'

Jon swung the binoculars back and moved them slowly along the edge of the cliff, spotting the rock and then a straggly mass of branches and twigs at its base.

'She's on the nest right now. Can you see her head? Look for the yellow of her beak.'

Jon saw it. 'Yeah, got her. The nest is enormous.'

'Oh, that's a novice nest. First-time buyer stuff, that. If they keep returning each year, it will end up double that size.'

'Where's the male?'

'Fishing,' she snorted. 'Familiar story, hey? Wife at home, husband off somewhere else.'

Jon tried to smile as she moved off towards a nearby couple.

Rick drew a line through another of the names. Three down, four to go. And then there were the ones with no phone numbers. He glanced at his watch: 9.10. Shit, late again. Buchanon's going to be on my back. He folded the sheet of paper, wondering where the hell Jon might be now – knowing that, if finding his brother's killer meant travelling to the very end of the earth, that's exactly where he'd be.

He grabbed his jacket, doing a quick calculation. Buchanon

had him in the office all morning, and Rick knew his SIO would be watching him through the glass partitions of his office like a hawk. So the only opportunity to ring the next numbers would be from his car during what passed as a lunch break.

OK, try and get the other four done, then. And the remaining addresses with no number? I'll try knocking on those doors after work, whenever that might be.

He trotted down the stairs of the converted warehouse, Cathy and Isabelle snagging in the flow of his thoughts. They'd said forty-eight hours, but no messages had been left on his mobile or landline. That's it, he concluded with a sinking feeling. Some bloody George Clooney lookalike with a top job at the university or somewhere has got the nod. They could at least have had the courtesy to call me.

Clearing the last few steps into the foyer, he saw the building's elderly caretaker unlocking the metal container screwed to the inside of the front door, ready to start distributing the letters inside to each apartment's individual post box. 'Morning, Fred. Anything there for me?'

The other man glanced back. 'Morning, Rick. Let me see.'

He started leafing through the wedge of post. 'Here you go. Delivered by hand.' He held out a lilac-coloured envelope.

'Thanks.' His heart lurched a little as he took it and, once outside, he paused on the top step. What do I do? Open it now? He looked at the neat handwriting on its front, then slipped the envelope into his jacket and continued down the steps.

With an infinitesimal flicker, Jon's eyes made the leap from cliff edge to distant sea below. Small detail was lost looking down at it from that height and he suddenly saw the ocean for what it actually was: a solid mass of metallic grey that stretched for mile after countless mile. But for all its immeasurable weight, the thing wasn't actually still. Instead, its surface trembled and writhed, individual movements lost in the shifting whole. A skin, reptilian and disturbing in the manner of its movement.

Three white specks, moving swiftly above it. He lifted Stuart's binoculars and picked out a line of seagulls approaching the shore, wings beating in unison, bodies almost skimming the waves. Then the rearmost bird lost its slow and languid rhythm and their tight formation was broken. Its body tilted upwards and with a short flutter, it settled on the cold sea. Jon watched, curious as to what was happening. The other birds didn't react, instead continuing onward to disappear below the line of cliff.

Jon moved the binoculars back, eventually locating the solitary bird, observing as it bobbed contentedly about on the restless sea. After a few seconds it looked around then began to preen, happy to use the vast ocean as its perch.

On a finger of land down to Jon's right was a lighthouse, its tower painted a brilliant white. He chose one of the paths traversing the area of sloping scrub that hadn't been cordoned off, following a series of steps carved from enormous slabs of rust-coloured stone. The path curved down to run adjacent with the edge of the cliff itself, and as Jon drew closer, he could hear the dull roar of surf more clearly and riding on top of that, a higher pitched cacophony.

On the grass that bordered the path was a small wooden sign with exclamation marks at each end. Between the two symbols were the words, 'Dangerous Cliffs'.

Knowing how the pull of gravity seemed to increase the closer he got to any drop, Jon stepped gingerly onto the wiry grass. An upward rush of air hit him, carrying with it the sounds of the birds more clearly. Thousands and thousands of them packed the sheer rocky face that formed the other side of the cove. They lined every available ledge, dozens more wheeling about looking for a space, their chorus a collective shriek of cackles, caws, wails and clacks. At the base of the cliffs the sea – that seemed almost frozen further out – surged up, swamping boulders in thick foam before falling back and regrouping for its next assault.

Deciding to aim for the lighthouse, Jon doubled back and climbed another steep path to the single-lane track. It led to a small car park that was crammed with vehicles, the nearby benches occupied by rows of people chewing sandwiches, flasks and cups at their feet.

He headed over to an information board. The rust-coloured steps were made from Precambrian stone, five hundred million years old. The lighthouse was designed by Daniel Alexander, who was also the principal architect of Dartmoor Prison. The cliffs were colonised by guillemots, shearwaters, puffins, kittiwakes, razorbills and fulmars. The heathland was inhabited by stonechats, whitethroats and rock pipits. He searched the surrounding faces and cars for anyone resembling Craig Budd. Nothing.

As the kettle began to boil, Salvio peered into the fridge, tutting as he did so. 'Shit, Zoe, you're out of everything. No milk for a brew, even.'

She thought about his entrance. As soon as the Yale had clicked, he'd shoved the door open and rushed in so fast he'd practically fallen over where she lay on the floor. Sure enough, two of his little mates had been waiting outside, as well. The first thing they'd done was produce a crowbar and rip off all the bolts Dave had put up. Salvio had then crouched before her. 'No more locking me out, understand?'

'He needs medicine,' she stated now, staring blankly at the steam billowing from the kettle's spout. A click and the bubbling died to nothing.

Jake, draped limply across her lap, tried to raise a hand and touch the tears on her cheeks. She tilted her head away from his fingers. 'Not now, kidder.'

Salvio had started going through the cupboards. 'No way to treat a woman. No way, at all. What do you need, babe? Milk, bread, cereals, all that stuff?' He pulled some notes from his pocket, removed a couple of tens, paused, then peeled off a third. 'And I'll get something for you, Zoe. Ciggies, some chocolate. I'll treat you – we can't have you looking so sad.'

'He needs medicine. His lungs are fucked and he's got a fever. Can't you bloody see that? Just let me out, will you?'

Twenty Six

Jon climbed into his car and slammed the door behind him. The sound of surf and rumble of voices were instantly subdued. 'There are too many people. I could be searching this place for bloody hours and still never find him. Did that chat room say when he got here?'

Stuart straightened in his seat. 'Yesterday. By train.'

'The terminal in Holyhead? We passed it on the way.'

'I suppose so, I don't think there's another station on the island.'

'He's got no transport. He needs somewhere close to this spot. What about the big guesthouse at the end of this road?'

Stuart shook his head. 'That's where the RSPB volunteers are staying. He'd never risk it.'

'How do you ...' Realisation dawned. 'The chat room?'

'Yes. They warned me to steer well clear.'

'Holyhead, then. You could walk here in half an hour. Some anonymous B&B or that Travelodge near the ferry terminal.'

'So long as it's cheap.'

'Let's go.'

They'd lost a few hours checking all the B&Bs on the edge of town nearest to the lighthouse before driving towards the train station and parking up in one of the few spaces outside the Travelodge. Jon hurried up to the elderly woman in reception and placed his warrant card and Craig's photo on the counter. 'Hello, there. My name's DI Spicer. Any idea if this man is booked in here? His hair may well now be a lot shorter.'

She put her glasses on and looked down. 'I don't think so, but we've been really busy. The sea eagles, you know.'

'I do. Any single males booked in yesterday who arrived on foot?'

'Plenty. The majority of the rooms have been booked as single occupancy.'

That figures, thought Jon. Bunch of anoraks. 'OK, can I leave you my number in case you see him?'

'Well, I suppose so.'

Back out on the street, Jon looked towards the town centre. A couple of pub signs swayed in the breeze. Further along was a smaller notice that read, 'Hotel'. He walked quickly up to it, climbed the steps to the open door and found himself in the hallway of what was once a large house. A brass clock ticked away on the wall above an empty row of coat hooks. Jon looked at the time. Gone three o'clock, he thought, and I've only checked a handful of places out of bloody dozens. A living room was on his left, flowery sofas with ruffled trims. Fake coal in the fireplace. Beyond the closed doors to his right was a room with four small tables and a tiny bar. A notice said, 'Open at six'. Who, he thought, would choose to drink in there?

He pinged the bell on the small counter at the end of the hall and a man emerged from what Jon guessed was the kitchen. Wiping his hands on a white apron, he announced, 'Sorry, we're full.'

Jon placed his ID and the photo down. A card player who knew his hand was weak. 'He's not staying here, by any chance? Probably got a shorter haircut, now.'

The man picked the photo up for a closer look. Every button on his beige cardigan was done up and the knot of his tie was too small. 'No, can't say he is.' He tapped the photo against the nail of his thumb. 'In trouble, is he?'

'Cheers.' Jon plucked the photo from his fingers and walked out.

Stuart was standing on the pavement, speaking into his mobile. 'Call me, love. Please, just give me a ring.' He closed his phone and glanced at Jon, an awkward expression on his face. 'She's not answering.'

Jon took a long breath in. 'I'd better try Alice.' He fished his mobile out and walked away from Stuart. The phone buzzed once, twice, three times, four. Bollocks, it'll be the answerphone if she doesn't pick up right now. The machine clicked in. 'Alice, it's me. If you've read my note I hope you can understand the situation I'm in. If there was any way – any other way at all – I'd have taken it. But there isn't, Alice, there just isn't. I couldn't put this off. Can you see that?' He looked at the lamp posts on the other side of the street and saw the huge gulls perched there. Motionless, but watching. Albino vultures. 'I'm coming back, Ali. I just have to sort this out first.' He heard the faintest of ticks. 'This is making me feel so bad and I know it's nothing, not a thing, to what you're going through, I know that Alice, but I had no other choice.' But the faint hum in his ear had gone flat and he knew the machine was no longer recording.

He pressed red and immediately called his parents' number.

'Hello?'

'Dad, it's me, Jon. Is Mum there?'

'She's at church.'

Of course, should have known. 'How's it going between you two?'

'We've had a really good talk. A couple, in fact. It's helped. A lot.'

Jon felt some of the tension in his shoulders ease. 'Has she spoken to Alice or Ellie?'

'Your sister phoned earlier.'

'What did she say?'

'Come home, son.'

Jon turned from the birds' beady eyes, focusing on the bricks inches from his face. 'What did she say?'

'I think you're losing her, Jon. You should come back.'

'Who? Alice? Is she ill? What do you mean, I'm losing her?'

'She's not ill. I'm not talking about the thing that happened at the hospital. I mean you're losing her, Jon. You.'

He heard the sound of movement and could picture his father shifting in his seat.

'Listen to me, I wasn't thinking when we spoke out on the patio. I should never have asked you to go to Haverdale. I was angry. But I'm telling you now, son, give it up. Come home.'

Jon clenched a fist, uncurling it just in time so it was his palm, and not his knuckles, that slammed into the wall. 'Give it up?' He laughed incredulously. 'It's too fucking late for that now, Dad. You told me – no, you fucking ordered me – to do this. Now you're asking me to stop? Jesus fucking Christ!'

His father's voice had a hard edge. 'Jon, do as I say. I'm telling you to drop it.'

Even now, Jon thought, even now you know you're wrong, you still try to stay in control.

'Whatever Dave got himself into,' his Dad continued, 'is in the past. You've got to take care—'

'You think it was drugs, don't you?'

Silence.

Jon found himself walking along, finger stabbing the air in front of him. 'You do, don't you? You've read the papers and you think Dave is guilty.'

'I'm just saying—'

'Dad? Fuck off.' He snapped his phone shut and turned on Stuart. 'Think! I need to get home, so you need to fucking think.'

Stuart stepped back, whites of his eyes showing. 'Yeah, I know.'

Jon lowered his hand and breathed in and out. Calming his voice, he started again. 'You need to think where he'll be. We haven't got time to search this entire town. Is there anything that comes to mind? Places you stayed on your raids together. Something that links them.'

Stuart rubbed his forehead, lips twisted in a wince. 'Just convenience – for the nest. That's all.'

'Convenience. Right, he's got no car. So it'll be somewhere ...' His voice died away. We've already checked the B&Bs closest to the bastard nest. This was useless.

'There's that shuttle bus.'

Jon looked at the other man. 'What?'

'That shuttle bus. The RSPB volunteer mentioned it.'

Of course, Jon thought. 'Treaddur Bay.'

'Where is that?'

'Other side of the island, about three miles from here. I stayed there once.'

'What's there?'

'Not a lot. A big car park, a nice beach, the lifeboat house, a few shops. The Treaddur Bay Hotel is well known for its restaurant.'

'Too expensive. He'll be doing this on a shoestring. Anything else there?' asked Stuart.

'One of those permanent caravan parks and a youth hostel.'

'A youth hostel?'

'Yeah, why?'

'We stayed in those a couple of times. Up in Scotland and the Lake District.' He nodded. 'That'll be it. A bed in the hostel and the shuttle bus out to the sanctuary.'

Rick took a furtive look towards the police station, phone pressed close to his ear. 'So, you've been married seven years? And the name Dave Spicer means nothing to you? OK, thanks for your time, Mrs Evans.'

He hung up, reached across to the piece of paper on the passenger seat of his car and put a line through another name. That just left the ones with no phone numbers. He looked at the addresses. One in Longsight, five minutes away, maximum. Another in Openshaw, a bit closer to the city centre. Right, he decided. When I get out of work, I'll do those two first. Then it's across to the one in Cheetham Hill and, last, over the river to a Zoe Croxton in Salford.

He studied the Salford address. Collier tower on William Street. Flicking open his *A to Z*, he looked up the street name. Jesus, he thought. It must be that grim thing from the seventies that looms over Trinity Way. They should have demolished that eyesore years ago. Closing the booklet, he sat back in his seat, wondering how late in the evening it would be before Buchanon let him go.

His eyes crept to the lilac-coloured envelope lying next to his list. Let's get it over with, he thought. Slowly, he peeled the flap up, feeling just like he did when opening results from an exam. GCSEs. He smiled; this thing has brought back all the self-doubt and lack of confidence from my teenage years. A single piece of paper was inside, its colour matching that of the envelope. He slid it out, glanced momentarily out of the car's windows, then unfolded it.

Dear Rick,

Thanks again for talking to us the other day. What a beautiful apartment you have! As mentioned, we went to see the other man after our chat. Following careful consideration, we've decided that, if you're still happy to proceed, we would like you to be our donor.

Rick realised the skin beneath his thumbnails was white with pressure. It's me! They picked me! He swallowed. Jesus, I'm going to be a dad. A flash-frame from a documentary or news clip: a large, circular object, besieged on all sides by dots with frantically wriggling tails. Oh my God! He looked at his mobile, wondering whether to ring Alice with the good news. No, maybe later. Easing his grip on the paper, he read on.

Obviously there's still a lot to sort out, not least how we'll play the parental arrangements once the baby is born. However, it would be an honour if you'd agree to help us with this, our most heartfelt wish in the world.
    We're anxiously awaiting your response!
    Thanks again,
        Cathy and Isabelle.

Jon and Stuart followed the road as it hugged the curve of Treaddur Bay. It eventually led towards some pine trees and between them, Jon could see a lodge-type building, with a wooden balustrade running along its front.

He parked before the steps and they climbed up to the balcony. Further along, a couple of teenagers were crouched in front of a bench, adjusting the straps on a couple of rucksacks they'd propped there.

Jon pulled the front door open and stepped onto a vast door-mat. A notice on the wall requested that walking boots be cleaned before entering the building. Behind the reception desk was a man, late twenties or thereabouts. His long hair was tied back in a ponytail and on his T-shirt a silhouette of a snowboarder was airborne over the words, 'No one ever died wishing they'd spent more time in the office.'

'Can I help you, gents?'

Jon drew out his warrant card along with the shot of Craig. 'Hopefully. Could you tell me if this man is staying here?' As soon as the younger man looked back up, Jon knew they were in the right place. 'Which room is he in?'

The man tapped his chin with a forefinger. 'Do you need a warrant or something to do this?'

Jon looked off to the side. The telly was on in the empty lounge area, footage of a curving wall of water on the screen. A surfer plummeted down the slope, his wake shooting up behind him. Jon turned back to the receptionist. 'I asked which room is he in.'

'And I questioned whether you can just march in here like this.'

Jon felt the muscles in his jaw tighten. 'You want to fuck me around? I will haul you over this counter by your fucking hair. Which room?'

The man stared back, face now pale. 'He's paying for one of the doubles, insisted that he wouldn't share.'

'Is he in there now?'

He shook his head. 'He left mid-morning. He wanted to know if he could get back in if it was very late. We have a curfew, you see.'

'And can he?'

'No. I told him if it wasn't by midnight, he'd have to wait until we open up at dawn.'

'But he paid for the room anyway?'

'Yes. Said he needed somewhere for his stuff.'

Stuart stepped up to the counter. 'When he left, was he carrying any sort of bag?'

'Yes, a big thing. Like an army holdall.'

Stuart glanced at Jon. 'He's going for it tonight.'

'Keys.' Jon snapped his fingers at the younger man. 'Keys to his room, please.'

He turned round and unhooked a set from the board behind him. 'It's number three. Just down that corridor.'

Jon led the way, slotted the key in the lock and swung the door open. Two single beds, one slightly rumpled, the other covered with gear. An empty rucksack, folded T-shirts, jeans, socks, a couple of novels, a map, a bag of dried banana chips with foreign writing on the packet. Stuart peered into the wardrobe, then looked under the beds. 'His climbing stuff isn't here.'

Jon stood in the centre of the room, testing the air in his nostrils. He picked up the empty rucksack and shook it. Something was weighing the right-hand side down. He unzipped the side pocket, pulled out a canvas folder and opened it. 'Well, he isn't going anywhere now.' After flashing the Dutch passport at Stuart, he turned to the inside cover. 'Edmond Bosvelt. Your brother is organised.' He lifted out a plane ticket. 'Liverpool to Amsterdam. Tomorrow morning at eleven fifty. You know, we could just sit here and wait for him to return.'

'No.' Stuart shook his head. 'Not if there might be other people out there looking for him.'

'You're right. Come on, then. Let's head back to the lighthouse.'

'Hang on.' Stuart's eyes were roving the room. He tried the bedside cabinet, then looked up and started studying the ceiling tiles.

'Stuart, let's go. It'll be dark in another hour.'

Rather than reply, the other man climbed onto the bed that had been slept in and reached above his head. He pressed up with his fingertips and slid a tile into the roof cavity, then groped around with his hands. He stopped moving and looked down at Jon.

'What have you found?'

Stuart slid something to the edge of the opening then lowered it in his arms. He was holding a small square container that appeared to be made from brushed aluminium. Jon was reminded of a child's lunchbox. 'What is it?'

'Just take it.'

Jon did as he was asked and placed it on the other bed. He looked back at Stuart, who was still rooted in position. He gave a jerky nod of his head.

Slowly, Jon released the two catches and lifted the lid. The interior was lined with foam. On the left-hand side were two eggs, creamy tops stained with patches of chestnut at their base. A label had been stuck to the foam beneath them: 'Osprey. Wimble reservoir, Peak District. 16 April, 2006'. Next to the pair of eggs were another three spaces.

Jon heard Stuart speak in a whisper above him. 'One for the osprey egg he broke and two for the sea eagle's clutch.'

Carefully, Jon lifted out one of the eggs. It weighed next to nothing, and as he examined the tiny holes at each end, he was aware that Stuart had now climbed down.

'May I hold it?'

There was a note of reverence in his voice and Jon turned to look at him. Stuart's cupped palms were half raised and his lower lip glistened slightly. Jon held the egg out.

Abruptly, Stuart stepped back. 'No. No, I don't want to.' He dropped his hands and turned away. 'I can't.' Slowly, his head turned and his eyes went back to the egg. 'Birds that have never flown. That's what I say to myself whenever it grips me. All the eggs I stole; birds that have never flown.'

Christ, thought Jon, sensing the power of what came to control Stuart's very existence. 'So, he'll leave his plane ticket and passport lying around, but hide the eggs in the ceiling?'

Stuart nodded matter of factly. 'Those are his most important possessions. More precious to him than any diamond.'

Jon replaced the egg, closed the lid and lifted the case up.

'What are you doing with it?' Stuart asked, looking alarmed.

'Taking it with me. A bit of bargaining power.'

Twenty Seven

When they made it back to the observation point, the light was beginning to fail. A horn sounded, though no ship was visible. Climbing out of his car, Jon glanced about for the sun and saw a hazy veil of cloud had reduced it to no more than a pale orange disc: flat, weak and totally devoid of warmth. Shivering slightly, he searched below it for the horizon, but the slate-coloured sea now merged seamlessly with the sombre sky.

The lack of any reference point to anchor himself by caused a fleeting sense of discomfort. Similar, he guessed, to sailors of old as they pressed onward into the unknown. After all, if they ventured far enough, the edge of the world would surely be reached.

The long, sad bleat sounded again and Jon realised it was coming from the lighthouse down to his right. He waited for its light to revolve round, and when it did, he could see the bulb easily outshone the feeble sun. With visibility so poor, it had obviously been decided a further warning was needed. The fog horn sounded once more, forlorn, like some creature searching for a lost mate.

The car park was now almost deserted, just the vehicles belonging to the RSPB volunteers lining the side of the cafe. Jon could see a couple of them inside the caravan, no doubt settling down for a night spent guarding the sea eagles' nest.

The sound of an engine came from the road and the shuttle bus pulled up at the car park's entrance. The driver slid his window open. 'Last bus back, are you coming? It's a long walk to Treaddur Bay.'

Jon scanned the faces peering at him through the windows. No Craig in there. He pointed at his vehicle. 'No thanks, I'll make my own way.'

'Right you are.' The engine revved and the vehicle trundled off down the hill. Jon wandered back to his car and opened the door. Stuart looked up, his expression a mixture of fear and expectation.

'You coming?' Jon asked, lifting the case containing the eggs off the back seat.

Stuart got out, and as they crunched their way across the gravel, a voice rang out behind them. 'Can I help you?'

Jon turned to see the RSPB volunteers standing beside the caravan's open door.

'Just having a look around before it gets dark.'

Suspicion dropped like a veil over their faces. 'What are you hoping to see?'

Jon realised Stuart was keeping his head down. One of the volunteers, a thickly set man of around forty, took a couple of steps towards them and raised a finger. 'Stuart Budd.' He turned to his companion. 'That's bloody Stuart Budd!'

The other man joined him and they began to approach, shoulder to shoulder. Jon hastily produced his warrant card. 'He's with me. DI Spicer, Greater Manchester Police.'

The larger man walked right up to Jon. 'Oh yeah, and I'm Sherlock frigging Holmes. I've seen fake IDs before.' He dismissed the leather wallet with a wave and addressed Stuart directly. 'Dyson. What are you doing here, as if I need ask? You worthless piece of shit.'

'OK.' Jon raised an arm to form a barrier before the man. 'Call Greater Manchester Police, they'll verify who I am. You want the phone number?'

Warily, the man assessed Jon. 'What are you doing bringing that scummy bastard here?'

'We've got reason to believe his brother may be in the vicinity. I need to question him.'

The volunteers exchanged glances. 'Crag? He's here?' Both men looked back towards the cliff where the eagles' nest lay.

The larger man pointed back at the caravan. 'Call Richard. Tell him to get everyone up here. I'll fetch the torches from my boot.'

'Hang on!' Jon tried to interject. 'I'll handle this.'

'Will you, bollocks.' The shorter man jogged back towards the caravan.

Shit, Jon thought. He grabbed Stuart by the shoulder and pushed him towards the road. 'Where will he be?' he hissed. 'Where would you hide if you were Craig?'

Stuart licked his lips nervously. 'They're going to bloody lynch us.'

'No one's lynching anyone,' Jon growled. 'Now put yourself in Craig's shoes, we haven't got long.'

Stuart looked around. 'He'll need a spot that overlooks the nest site.' He gestured to a narrow track on the other side of the road, the mouth of which was barred by a metal pole running across it. Beyond it, the track curved up, passing between two outcrops of rock. 'There?'

Jon called over to the RSPB volunteer rummaging in the boot of his Volvo. 'Where does that track lead?'

'Top of the hill. There are telecommunications masts and satellite dishes up there. What are you going to do?'

'Come on.' Jon herded Stuart across the road and they ducked under the horizontal pole, then stepped onto a rippled concrete surface. Quickly, they marched up the slope and, within a few seconds, the road behind them was out of sight. Low heather laced with loops of thick bramble covered the ground on either side of the track. Clinging to the undergrowth were various lengths of withered toilet paper. Human faeces dotted the way, and further up, the occasional ragged condom.

Stuart spotted a sheep trail that branched off to a ledge over-looking the road below. 'It's a perfect view of the cliff. He's here somewhere, probably out of this wind.'

Jon studied the land in front. The tips of several radio masts were just visible above the brow of the hill. 'Let's try up here, then.'

Less than five minutes later they'd reached the top. The under-growth had given way to a bare, rocky surface and before them, the path split in two; one fork leading to what looked like a small military installation. Jon regarded the barbed-wire security fence surrounding the cluster of gigantic satellite dishes, three of which leaned out over the edge of the giant cliffs to look across the sea towards Ireland.

The other fork led towards a couple of low, windowless brick buildings. In each of the fenced-off pens to their sides was a large mast. Jon approached the nearest in order to read the triangular yellow sign attached to the chain links: 'Caution. Non-ionizing radiation!'

The wind whistled past his ears and the wires that anchored the masts to the rock clanked and rattled above the boom of surf carrying up from far below. Just audible above the low rumble was the unceasing clamour of nesting sea birds. Jon continued towards the first building. Realising its other side would offer protection from the relentless rush of air, he started circling it on a wide arc.

Gradually, the far side came into view, revealing a solitary man huddled in a military-style sleeping bag at the base of the wall. Jon had a sudden image of Dave, begging in Manchester's city centre. Sensing movement, the person raised his shaved head and Jon found himself fixed by a pair of piercing blue eyes. Craig Budd.

'Night, night.' Zoe kissed the tips of her fingers and touched them on Jake's brow. The Calpol that Salvio had brought back from the shops earlier on had made a difference, taking away Jake's fever and reducing the raggedness of his breathing. But it wasn't the stuff she'd asked him to get, and she knew from previous experience that when the Calpol wore off, his illness would kick in again worse than ever.

She thought he was about to punch her when she pointed out it was a Verasone inhaler and not bloody child-strength paracetamol that Jake needed. But his hands had stayed at his sides before he eventually smiled.

'OK, sweetheart. I'll go to the chemist, if that's what you really want.'

'I want you to let me out of this fucking flat.'

He shook his head.

'Then I want Verasone.'

'Cool. If you're happy, I'm happy.' And with that, he'd sauntered out the door.

She turned the bedroom light off and shut the door with a sigh of relief. Leaning against the wall for a moment, she let her eyes close. Like sediment stirred in a puddle, thoughts began to cloud her mind. She pictured the flat, seeing the empty hall and telly room beyond. A flimsy sofa obtained second hand through the housing people. Bare light bulbs. Crappy carpet. Dave was dead. She squeezed her eyes shut tighter. Dave was dead.

She needed something to blot it all out. In the kitchen, she opened a cupboard door. A few cans of food were now on the shelves. Baked beans, spaghetti hoops and tomato soup from Lidl. Weetabix and Sugar Puffs. On the lower shelf was the little plastic bag Salvio had left her with. She picked it up by its top edge and gazed at the brown sugar-like powder inside.

Her eyes went to the clock on the cooker: 7.40. Where's Salvio with the bloody medicine? At least he said he wouldn't send any punters up before ten. She flip-flopped the bag from side to side. Fuck it, what else am I supposed to do? She looked at the window. 'What else am I supposed to do?' she said out loud. In the black glass, her reflection stared at her in silence.

Blinking back tears, she opened the kitchen drawer, removed the roll of tin-foil and tore off a strip. After making a shallow crease down its middle, she took the straw from one of Jake's juice cartons and put it between her lips. She tipped some powder into the groove of the foil and lifted it. With her free hand, she picked the lighter from the table, clicked the button and raised the flame to the underside of the foil.

After a couple of seconds the brown powder began to liquefy, then bubble. As soon as a wisp of smoke appeared, it vanished up the plastic tube, into Zoe's mouth and down to her lungs. She tipped the foil from side to side, causing the lump of brown goo to slide about as its surface continued to blister. Above it, the straw chased after the trail of smoke it gave off. A few seconds later and the dirty globule had dried up. Her arms flopped onto the table and she sank forward to rest her head across them.

A series of sharp noises, a pause, then a few more. Knocking. Someone was knocking on the door. She raised her head and sought out the cooker's clock: 7.55. Salvio, you bastard, this is well early. She removed a cigarette from the packet, fascinated by how smooth the movements of her hands seemed. The lighter clicked and she dragged down smoke. That felt good. She sat back and let her eyelids droop. Really good.

The knocking sounded again and her eyes opened. Fuck. The cigarette was still between her fingers, a centimetre of ash now clinging to its end. Pushing on her knees, she rose unsteadily to her feet and shuffled out into the corridor. She willed back the old sense of detachment. It was just her body they would be licking, squeezing and thrusting into. Not her. They'd never really touch her. By keeping her eyes half-shut, she maintained the sense of serenity in her head. One of those women from Africa, she thought, gliding gracefully along. She passed the door to Jake's room, mind completely elsewhere.

The knocking sounded again. 'Give it a rest,' she mumbled, opening up and lifting the hand with the cigarette to her lips. A man was standing there and she vaguely clocked his smart clothes and trendily messed-up hair. 'Salvio sent you up, yeah? It's the second room on the left.'

Twenty Eight

Jon stared back at Craig Budd. His face really did match his nickname; strong, square jaw, angular nose and cheekbones, skin weathered by hours spent outside. But everything was ruined by the haunted look in his eyes. Suddenly, they widened and he jumped to his feet, trying to high-step out of the sleeping bag as he did so. Jon raised the little case, then held his other hand palm up. 'Easy, Craig. We need to talk: you're in serious danger.'

The other man glanced to the case, then back to Jon's face. His knees straightened and the tension in his body seemed to evaporate. 'Who are you?'

'DI Spicer, Greater Manchester Police. I'm not here to arrest you, understand?'

Craig remained motionless, then his eyes cut to the side. Jon heard a footstep behind him.

'Craig.' Stuart's voice was little more than a whisper.

The younger brother's face hardened. 'You fucking snake!'

Jon curled all but his index finger in, and pointed it at Craig. 'I gave him no choice. Now, listen. We're going to come over there, sit down out of this bloody wind and talk. You are not going to try anything – with me, or your brother. If you do, I'll take these osprey eggs and crush them in my hand. Do you understand?'

Craig's fingers flexed at his sides.

Jon raised the case up a few inches. 'Do you understand?'

Craig nodded.

'Good. Why don't you climb back into that sleeping bag and sit down where you were.'

Reluctantly, Craig obeyed.

Once he was leaning against the bricks, Jon spoke over his

shoulder. 'Stuart, keep to the other side of me.' They walked over to the small building and out of the buffeting air. Jon surveyed the coils of rope and line of carabiners neatly arranged on the ground. In the top of the holdall he could see a pair of night-vision goggles, the head straps unbuckled. Crazy bastard, Jon thought, you really were going to try for the nest.

'Craig.' Jon dropped to one knee, the case tucked behind his ankle. He realised the muscles in his legs were shaking slightly. This is it, he thought, taking a quick breath in. This person could well have seen who murdered my brother. 'You were in the Peak District a few nights ago. You were up the tree the ospreys' nest is in.'

Craig looked towards the satellite dishes, hands resting on the lump of his raised knees.

'Something happened on top of the next hill,' Jon continued. 'You saw it, didn't you?'

Craig blinked, and his eyes remained closed for the tiniest moment.

Jon had to resist grabbing the man by his throat and shaking the information out of him. 'Craig, I know you saw what happened.'

He flipped a hand over and studied his blackened nails. Jon waited.

Finally, Craig turned his head. 'What do you want?'

'I want to know what you saw.'

'And then what?'

'I'm out of here.'

'You're not going to arrest me?'

'No.'

'Why not?'

'You are the least of my concerns. I'm trying to solve a murder.'

'So, I'll be free to go?'

'You can do what the hell you want. Take that flight back to Amsterdam, whatever.'

'You've got my plane ticket?'

'No, it's still in your room at the hostel.'

'And the eggs?'

'They're of no use to me.'

'You'll let me have them?'

'They're of no use to me.'

'Is that a yes, or a no?'

'You can have them.'

Craig sat up straighter, eyes still on Jon. 'You're bullshitting me.'

Jon felt his fingers curling into a fist. Calm, keep calm. 'Want to run through the other choices you have here?'

Craig went to pick at the cuticle of a nail. Family bloody habit, Jon thought. 'And keep your hands where they were.'

Craig returned them to his knees.

Stuart's voice sounded over Jon's shoulder. 'How were you going to do it?'

Craig glanced down at the perfect coils of climbing rope. 'Low tide's in about ninety minutes. Down to the cliff base near the lighthouse, horizontal traverse of three hundred metres, ascending directly below the nest, cut the wire, grab the eggs, abseil back down. Two and a half, maybe three hours up, hour or so back.'

'My God.'

There was a note of admiration in Stuart's voice and Jon flicked him a quick look. The trace of a smile disappeared from his lips. Jon turned back to the younger brother. 'What happened, Craig?'

Craig leaned the back of his skull against the bricks. 'One guy at first. Appeared past midnight. I heard him before I saw him, tools clanking on his back, torch giving him away completely.'

'What did he look like? Age, height, build?'

'Thin, around thirty, I should think. Seemed quite tall.'

'Hair long or short?'

'Shaved.'

My brother, thought Jon, his eyes glued to Craig. You were the last person to see my brother alive. 'How did he seem?'

'You what?'

241

'His movements, the way he moved. Did he seem agitated, scared, what?'

Craig frowned. 'I don't know. He was ferreting around, testing the ground with his spade. Come to think of it, he was whistling at one point.'

Whistling, Jon thought, finding some solace in the fact Dave had seemed happy. 'Then what?'

'The bike appeared.'

'From which direction?'

'Haverdale. It came along the edge of the pine trees, then went up the far side of the hill. The guy parked it up just below the crest, then wandered over to the other man.'

'And?'

'They were discussing something, looking at a piece of paper the first man had.'

Oh, God. We're getting closer to when my brother died. 'Like a map?'

'Yeah. After a bit, they seemed to agree on a spot.' The words stopped as Craig took a moment, his lower lip pushing out in disbelief. 'He just whacked him over the head. No warning, nothing. Just whacked him with this hammer.'

Jon wanted to bow his head and close his eyes. 'Describe to me what happened.'

With a little shake of his head, Craig continued. 'The first guy to arrive had started digging. The bike rider took off his rucksack and produced this big hammer. He just stepped up behind the one who was digging and clocked him over the head with it. Like it was a job, some sort of chore. He treated the whole thing like it was a chore.'

'How do you mean?' Jon whispered.

As Craig cleared his throat, Jon caught the sound of voices on the wind.

'The guy went down like a sack of spuds.' He slapped a hand on his knee. 'Boof. Out of it. The other one then gets a saw – no kidding – he gets a fucking saw out of the bag.' Craig squeezed his eyes shut. 'I could hear the rasping noise when he

242

got to bone. I couldn't stand it. So I tried to grab the eggs and get away from there fast as I could.'

'You see a man murdered and you just continue on your egg-stealing mission like nothing happened?' Jon knew his lips were curled with disgust.

'No! Not like nothing happened. It's been doing my head in ever since. I just didn't know what to do.'

'You forgot that the number for the police in this country is nine, nine, nine?'

Craig licked his lips, trying to find an answer. His mouth closed. The voices were getting louder and Jon could now hear the sound of footsteps as well. Craig heard it too and his shoulders tensed. 'Who's that?'

'I don't know. I'll sort it out,' Jon replied, placing a hand on Craig's shoulder to stop him from jumping up. 'Tell me what he looked like.'

'Who?'

The voices were now really close. 'The man! The one with the hammer. What did he look like?'

Behind him, Jon heard Stuart get up and step to the corner of the building. 'Oh,' the older man said.

'There's one!' a voice shouted.

'They're by the shed!' someone else yelled.

Craig tried struggling to his feet and Jon, grabbing the case with one hand, placed his other against Craig's chest, pinning him to the wall. 'What did he look like!'

'I don't know!' Craig shouted back. 'He wore a crash helmet the whole time. Skull and crossbones on it. Let me up!'

The crunch of footsteps got louder and several figures came round the corner, Stuart backing away before them. Jon saw fluorescent RSPB bibs and a policeman's uniform before several torch beams blinded him. 'Get those things out of my face!' he snarled.

'Who are you?' a voice demanded, Welsh accent making it lift.

Taking his hand off Craig, Jon pulled his warrant card out and thrust it towards the light. 'DI Spicer, Greater Manchester

Police. Now stop shining those fucking things in my eyes.'

The torches were lowered and Jon stood. 'This is a witness in a murder investigation and he's coming with me.'

'On whose authority?' the police officer demanded.

Jon looked at the man's jacket. Sergeant. Shit, I could have done with a clueless constable, just started out in the job. 'The Major Incident Team, Greater Manchester Police.'

'I don't think so, not without the say-so of my boss. Nothing's been mentioned to me about any operation involving Manchester police on this island.'

Fuck, I don't have time for this, Jon thought. Flynn might just be stupid enough to have stayed in Haverdale, but he won't be there for much longer. 'Let's square this up later, shall we?'

The officer started reaching for his radio and Jon stepped closer. 'Hang on. Just listen to me a minute. It hasn't been cleared officially. Things were moving too fast.'

'Really, boyo?' The sergeant was grinning. 'That man is going nowhere, there's a warrant out for his arrest.'

'Craig!' Stuart suddenly stepped forward and Jon's head whipped round.

'I'm not going back inside, Stu. I'm not.' Craig was backing away, his head shaking violently from side to side.

Jon was about to open his mouth when a voice rang out.

'Grab him!'

Craig span on his heel and started sprinting along the path away from the group. A couple of RSPB volunteers started after him.

'Craig!' Stuart bellowed. 'Craig!'

Jon's eyes widened in horror as Craig raced towards the cliff. Oh no. Don't do it, Craig, don't ... He couldn't tear his eyes away as the other man reached the edge, then just carried on, legs taking a last stride in midair before he vanished.

Stuart sank to his knees and began to groan. The two volunteers reached the point where Craig had leapt, peered over the edge then turned round. Their faces were white in the dusk and one lifted a pale hand to waist height. Palm facing downwards, he swept it backwards and forwards across his body.

Feeling sick to the stomach, Jon turned to the sergeant. 'Nice work, boyo.' He crouched down and squeezed Stuart's shoulders. 'Stuart?' he whispered. 'Stuart?' No response. Jon rubbed his hand across the other man's shoulders. 'Stuart, do you want to come with me?'

The sergeant spoke out above him. 'Detective, there are issues—'

'Shut up! Stuart, I have to get back to Haverdale. Do you want to come with me? You don't have to stay here.'

Stuart shook his head. 'I'm not leaving Craig.'

'You're sure?'

A nod in reply. Jon stood up and addressed the sergeant directly. 'That was his brother. I want you to take care of this man, do you understand?'

The sergeant's face reddened and he started to fiddle with his radio.

'Do you hear me?' Jon demanded. 'If one of these idiots,' he gestured at the watching group, 'lays a finger on him, I'll come back here and break it.' He turned to the cluster of men. 'You lot got that?'

None of them would meet his eyes.

Jon started walking back the way he and Stuart had come. After ten metres, he realised he was still carrying the case in his hand. He stopped, regarded it for a second, then placed it on the ground and continued on his way.

Twenty Nine

Michael Lumm let himself in through the back door of their bungalow, took his shoes off while still standing on the door-mat, then paused to examine his hands. It had been a busy day at work, not helped by a flock of over eighty sheep escaping from their field onto the A6187. Grime emphasised the creases in his fingers and the edges of his nails. Knowing her eyesight was now too poor to notice such details, he stooped at the kitchen sink and took a nail brush to his hands, anyway. Mother did so dislike dirt.

A squirt of washing-up liquid soon created a thick lather, and as his slippery fingers writhed over each other, globules of foam dripped down like spawn from two amphibious creatures mating.

He dried his hands on a tea towel and walked through to a short corridor. Family photos lined the walls. Colour ones of him as a baby, and then a child. Black and white ones of his father, dead now almost thirty years. Lumm's eyes settled on the man's face. A person he had barely known, more alien to him than the hikers he gave directions to out on the moors.

As usual, he sought out the photo of his father seated on a rock, a stretch of Scottish shoreline behind him. Being beaten on that holiday by him was about the last memory Michael had of his father. He'd risen early, his father's penknife in his pocket, and headed down to the secluded beach where they'd spotted the dead seal the day before. He could still remember recoiling at the smell of putrefying fish. The sight of the sand fleas massed on the creature's underside. He'd just finished carving out his initials in the dead animal's blubber when his father's shadow had fallen across him.

Bending closer to the photo, Michael examined the man's bare chest, picturing the heart inside. Defective, weak, faulty. Ready to abruptly stop working just days after the photo had been taken, leaving his mum on her own with a young child. The years of struggle and hardship she had faced.

He walked in to the telly room where she sat, feet encased in thick sheepskin slippers, fan heater positioned inches from her ankles. She looked up from the large-print book on her lap, took off her glasses and smiled.

'Hi there, Mum. Everything OK? Would you like a drink?'

'No, I'm fine, thank you. Have you been tinkering in that garage again?'

He nodding. 'Putting the quad bike right. She's running smoothly, now.'

'You. So good with your hands. Maurice would be proud to see you now.'

He crouched at the side of her armchair. 'Did you look at the brochures? Any seem especially nice?'

She frowned, head turning to the glossy publications on the footstool. 'I still don't understand. How can I pick and choose like that?'

'Because they haven't been built, yet. You choose the type you want, and they put it up. How about the Greenwich? Two bedrooms, lovely kitchen with the latest features. A conservatory where you can sit and read.'

'But I like it here.'

'Mum, this place is on its last legs. The roof needs redoing, we've got damp coming in through the bathroom walls, rats running around in the kitchen.'

'I haven't spotted any rats for days.'

'Maybe not,' Michael replied. 'But this place will have a specially adapted bath. All the electricity points will be at waist height. Imagine that: no bending down to plug anything in.'

'But the price. How can you ever afford that for me?'

He patted the back of her hand. 'I've said. The investments I made.'

'You're not thinking of one of those loans, are you?'

247

'No, Mum. I have the money already; I don't need to borrow a thing.'

'Well.' She put her glasses back on. 'Pass them to me, would you?'

He placed the brochures on her lap. 'You have a good read through. Now, I've got to pop out. I'll be about an hour. Sure you don't want me to bring you a cup of tea?'

'No, I'm fine, thank you.'

'OK.'

Outside, he wheeled the quad bike round to the front of the garage, the pile of black packages now secured firmly to its rear platform by a tightly-stretched elastic mesh. After re-checking the garage was securely locked, he gunned the machine into life and set off for the south side of town.

Barely eight at night and most people were in their houses, brains on stand-by as they stared blankly at TV screens. Many, he knew, would have his pills and powders coursing through their systems. A little something to spice up their miserable existences. He joined the high street just before the level crossing, continued over the little bridge then turned into the deserted parking area for Sharston Edge. He drove on to the track, dropping the revs so he could negotiate the steep climb. Coming to a halt at the top, he killed the engine, climbed off the bike and unhooked the elastic mesh. Then he picked up a package in each hand, walked to the edge of the cliff, placed them to the side of one of the oddly shaped rock formations and returned to the bike for two more.

As he worked, he cursed himself for overlooking this option in the first place. What had he been thinking of when he'd come up with the poached deer plan? Mind you, it had so nearly worked. If it hadn't been for that bloody mobile phone going off, the sacks would have been incinerated, just like the dozens of others containing deer which they'd burned over the years. He threw two more packages to the ground. How he'd hoped against hope that Wood couldn't hear the little chorus of notes. He'd even tried patting his own pockets, as if it was his mobile making the noise. But the bloody thing had continued to ring and eventually his fellow ranger had pointed to the second bin liner.

Now with all the packages in a neat pile, he shone his heavy-duty torch over the edge. Forty feet below, the beam picked out the motionless cascade of boulders. Before them was the opening in the ground. A narrow passage discounted as impossible to negotiate by the local potholing club. Wood had been right in the visitor centre: these spots were a far, far better place for disposing of a body.

He picked out the patch of grass forming a triangle between two boulders and the cliff's base, then started dropping the packages down, keeping count as he did so. In the silence of the night they thudded against each other. Once all twenty had gone over the edge, he set off for the trail that would lead him down and then round to where they lay. After that, he thought, there was only Flynn's bike to dismantle. That posed no major problem – the parts could vanish below ground with the body.

As he negotiated the twisting path, he planned his reaction if anyone asked him about Flynn's disappearance. Yes, that's right. I saw him on the evening of Wednesday the twentieth. He was on his bike, a rucksack on his back. Where was he heading? North, towards the A57. Manchester or Sheffield. Maybe further. After all, once he got to the M6 I suppose he could have continued all the way up to Scotland, if he wanted.

If it was any of the town police, the story would do fine. But, he reflected, Flynn went and talked to that officer from Manchester. Lumm thought about the hulking great bastard, the way he'd perked up at the realisation there might have been a witness to his brother's death. He fiddled with the torch. Thank God I was wearing Flynn's crash helmet. Now that imbecile won't be saying another word, the trail can't lead back to me. Can it? He thought about Spicer and found himself picking nervously at the torch once again. There was something relentless about the bloke.

Thirty

Jon was twenty metres from his car when his phone began to ring. Please, he thought, immediately flipping it open, let that be Alice. 'Hey . . .'

'Hey, yourself.' Nikki Kingston's voice. 'I've got some news that'll give you such a hard-on.'

Jon felt his pace slow, disappointment and excitement mixing in his head. 'What is it?'

'The tyre for the motorbike. You were right! It's a Bridgestone TW301. I spoke to a specialist supplier and, I quote, it's good for smaller capacity trail bikes. And, get this: decent handling, despite a knobbly pattern.' She paused. 'Are you still there?'

'Yeah.'

'Well don't overdo it, Jon. I bust a bloody gut getting you this.'

'Sorry, I appreciate it, I really do. Did they say which makes of bike it goes with?'

'Yeah, though the names mean nothing to me. Mainly CRM 250s, DR 350s and KDX 250s, if that's any help.'

KDX 250. The make of Kawasaki that Flynn owned. 'Yup. It confirms what I thought.'

'What about the Timberlands?'

'Sorry?'

'The Timberland hiking boots I took a cast of. Does your suspect own a pair?'

'I'll find out soon.'

'Are you OK, Jon? You sound – I don't know – distracted?'

He placed a hand on the roof of his car and let the coldness seep into his palm. 'I'm OK. Just absolutely bloody exhausted. Thanks, Nikki. I owe you, as usual.'

'Where are you, by the way? I hear Buchanon's called the proverbial search party out on you.'

'Yeah. I'll be checking in soon.'

'Well, good luck. Don't leave it too long.'

'Cheers.'

He snapped his phone shut, got into his car, and after plugging his phone into the charger on the dashboard, swung the vehicle round. The road led him back down the hill and into Holyhead. He accelerated through the drab port, just able to keep his speed down until he reached the dual carriageway where he could really open the engine up.

As he raced along, lines of headlights slid smoothly towards him. Tightly clustered and silent at first, the space separating each pair from the ones behind slowly widened until, with a succession of whooshes, the convoys flashed past his car. Oblivious to the play of lights and sound, his mind was fixed on everything that had happened. And what was about to occur. Flynn, he thought. The vermin who'd so needlessly snuffed out his brother's life.

He reached Conwy and dropped his speed to swerve across the series of roundabouts lining the seafront. More cars approached. From a distance the windscreens reflected the street lights and it was only at the point of actually passing that he could see through the glass to the driver behind. Faces, glimpsed for an instant before his stare skipped to the next car. Expressions slack, eyes on the rear lights of the vehicle in front. He thought of their lives and imagined the families they were heading home to.

Prestatyn and memories of a childhood holiday at the top of his mind. Dave on the beach, high-kneeing it through the shallows, gasping with laughter as he tried to catch the falling Frisbee. The sun-lit water that had sprayed out with each step. The dim room to the side of the campsite cafe, monotonous beeps of the Space Invader machines growing steadily quicker. The pair of them waiting their turn, warm ten-pence pieces in their sweaty palms.

Flynn had destroyed all that, fractured those memories and

ensured no fresh ones could ever take their place. Flynn. He conjured the man's features from the dark and held them in his mind's eye. An orange flicker off to his left. The massed towers and chimneys of the oil refinery and a solitary burn-off flame, lighting the night like a beacon to the dead.

The man standing at Zoe's front door remained where he was.

'Come on,' she beckoned. 'You're letting in the fucking cold.'

He reached into his pocket and removed a thin leather wallet.

She shook her head. 'You pay Salvio, not me.'

He frowned, holding a badge up. 'My name's Rick Saville, Greater Manchester Police.'

Zoe leaned a shoulder against the door frame.

'Are you Zoe Croxton?'

She shrugged. 'Yes.'

'Do you know someone called Dave Spicer?'

She took another drag, eyes closing completely.

'You do?'

Keeping the cigarette against her lips, she cupped her elbow with her free hand and shivered. 'So what?'

'Zoe, can I come in? We need to talk.'

She moved back down the corridor without replying, walking past a closed door with the little plaque reading, 'Jake's Den'.

Trailing behind, Rick thought he heard something as he passed it. A faint moan or gasp. Zoe carried on into the front room and slumped on the sofa. Rick followed, taking in the TV, scattering of kids' toys and general lack of furniture. 'Mind if I sit?'

'Whatever you want. Just don't take all night about it.'

He eased himself onto the other end of the sofa and turned to face her. 'When did you last hear from David?'

'Dave.'

'Sorry?'

She leaned her head back, thinking of the newspaper she'd

dropped down the tower block's rubbish chute. Dave's face falling away into the blackness. Gone, for ever. 'He was called Dave.'

'You know what's happened?'

She closed her eyes again. 'Yes.'

'I'm so sorry for your loss, Zoe. We're trying to find who did it. I'm hoping you might be able to tell me what he was doing out in Haverdale.'

While he spoke, she'd settled lower and now her head was completely supported by the back of the sofa. 'Zoe?'

'Mmm?' She looked up. 'Pass us that ashtray, would you?' She waved her cigarette towards the television.

Rick got up and walked over. The dirty ashtray on top of it had a Stella Artois logo emblazoned across the bottom. Stolen from some pub. 'Here you go.'

She balanced it on her knee and tapped ash. 'It was our way out.'

'What was?'

'The pot.'

Oh no, Rick thought. So he was dealing. 'You mean marijuana?'

'No,' she sighed, dragging so deeply the cigarette crackled. 'Pot. With stuff in it. Gold and that – from caveman times.'

Rick perched on the sofa's edge. 'Dave was out there looking for a pot with gold in it. Like buried treasure?'

'The prof. It was him who sold Dave the map.'

Rick stared at the ill-looking woman. 'Who's the prof?'

'The prof. Brainy bastard who knows all about that stuff. He mentioned it to Dave one time, when he was off his head.'

Rick was looking down at his feet. 'Go on.'

She sounded like she was trying to stifle a yawn. 'Dave got him to draw a map, but he wanted money for it first. So Dave borrows cash from Salvio. Only it was wrong, surprise fucking surprise. He said it was buried on this one hill, but it wasn't.'

Rick waited for her to carry on. When nothing more was said, he looked to his side. Zoe's eyes were half closed. 'You were saying?'

Her chin lifted. 'What?'

'You were saying that it wasn't the hill marked on the map.'

'Yeah.' She took another drag. 'So Dave has to keep going back, digging around on all the other bloody hills. And Salvio wants his money back.'

'What did the prof have to say?'

'He fucked off, once Dave handed over the cash.'

'Where does he live?'

'Don't know.'

'How did Dave meet him?'

'Knocking around. He went to the Booth Centre and that.'

'So he's homeless, this prof?'

'Yes.' There was a bored note to her voice, like the answer should have been obvious.

'OK. So Dave bought a map that should have shown the location of some treasure buried out near Haverdale. But it wasn't accurate. And that's why he was digging around on the surrounding hills?'

No reply. He looked to his side and saw her head had now tipped forward. A trail of smoke was flattening out across her forehead before curling over her right ear and seeping up into her hair. He plucked the butt from her fingers and stubbed it out. 'Zoe!'

Her eyes flickered.

'Are you using, Zoe?'

'What do you think?' she sighed.

'Heroin?'

'Yes.'

'Was Dave using, too?'

'He was clean. A bit of weed, that's all.'

'Was he dealing?'

'No. Just the odd bit here and there, to mates. We don't have cash – that's why he borrowed off of Salvio.' She shook her head. 'Borrowed off of Salvio.'

'How much?'

'Hundreds.'

'Who is Salvio?'

'Salvio?' She looked for her cigarette, frowning when she realised it was no longer in her fingers. She raised her hand to nibble at a thumbnail instead. 'You don't want to meet Salvio.'

'Jesus, what a mess. Can I use your toilet?'

She waved a hand towards the door. 'Back there.'

Rick got to his feet and headed for the corridor. Zoe had indicated which room was hers, so he went past that door. That left two others, one with 'Jake's Den' on it.

He opened the one opposite. A bath, with a few plastic toys gathered at the plughole. He positioned himself before the toilet in the corner. The water seemed discoloured, but when he bent forward he saw it was the ceramic sides beneath the surface that were stained brown. When was that last cleaned? After washing his hands, he looked about for a towel. None. Once he'd dabbed his hands dry with toilet paper, he rotated his shoulders, readying himself to drive the questioning forward and find out who this Redino character was.

Back in the corridor, his eyes settled on the letter's spelling 'Jake's Den' once more. What a tragedy. He'd been looking forward to seeing Jon's jaw drop when he told him he was going to be a dad, but it wouldn't be right with all this going on. He stepped across to listen. Not a sound inside. Just as he was about to walk back to the front room, he thought he heard a rattling intake of breath. That, he thought, remembering a spell in hospital when he was younger, sounded like the old man in the next bed who had pneumonia. He angled his head to the side, and after another second, the noise came again. Someone fighting to drag in oxygen.

Slowly, he opened the door to peer inside. Light from the corridor spilled across the floor and onto the cot in the corner. Inside was a crumpled blanket and little more than a pale manikin, head too big for its body. The shuddering, sucking noise came again and Rick flicked on the light. Oh my God. The infant was on his back, lips blue and eyes rolled up. Pinpricks of sweat covered his face.

He whirled round and ran back to the front room. 'Zoe! Your son ...'

The room was empty. As he looked around, the click of a lighter came from the kitchen. She was sitting at the table, foil below her face, straw above the bubbling brown lump. 'For fuck's sake! Zoe!'

She continued sucking at the smoke.

'Zoe! What's wrong with your son? He's hardly breathing!'

Pupils swollen, her eyes drifted up, straw still in her mouth. 'Jake?' she slurred. 'Is he OK?'

'No! Does he need medicine, an inhaler or something?'

'Salvio,' she mumbled, tears now filling her eyes. The straw fell from her mouth and she prodded a forefinger weakly at the door. 'He's gone to get it ... he's ...' The words died away. 'Salvio.'

'What's wrong with Jake? What do I tell them in A & E?'

She half curled her fingers and banged them lightly against her chest. 'Lungs are clogged up. RS Virus or something.'

Rick ran back down the corridor, wrapped Jake in his blanket and raced from the flat.

Jon's phone rang again and his chin lifted from his chest. Jesus, he thought. I was almost asleep there. This time he checked the screen before answering. When he saw the name, he wedged the phone between his shoulder and ear, heart suddenly racing. 'Alice?'

'Yes.'

'Thank God you rang. Did you get my note?'

'Yes.'

'And my message on the phone? I was gabbing on, I'm not sure if it recorded everything I said.'

'Are you coming home?'

He looked at the motorway lights stretching away before him. 'Soon as I can, Ali.'

'Not now?'

'I know who did it. I've got the identity of who killed Dave.'

Nothing.

'He'll know I'm on to him by now. I've got to find him, before he disappears.'

'You won't come home?'

'Yes, I will. I'll be there.'

'But not now. Not when I ask you.'

He shut his eyes for a second. Shit, please don't do this. 'I can't come home this minute, Ali, I owe it to Dave. Can't you see that? This whole fucking disaster, what's happening to Mum and Dad, it's my chance to sort it all out. Just a few hours, Ali, and I'll be there.'

Her sigh reminded him of the wind about his ears on the hilltop where Dave had died.

'Are you in the car at the moment?'

'Yeah, on my way back from Anglesey. I have to get to Haverdale.'

'You're on the motorway?'

'Yes.'

'Whereabouts?'

He looked at the approaching gantry. A sign on it said junction two was up ahead. He could be home in fifteen minutes. 'Near Manchester.'

'You're on the M60 right now? You're passing me by, aren't you?'

Now it was his turn to say nothing.

'Jon.' Her voice was now barely more than a whisper. 'I don't think I can do this any more.'

He winced. 'Ali, you know how it is with an investigation. I can't break off just like that.'

'You're not on any investigation. Buchanon called me. You're doing this all on your own.'

Oh God, he thought. 'Buchanon called you?'

'If things weren't bad enough, you lied to me. And you got Rick to lie to me, too. Didn't you?'

He thought about the conversation on the patio with his Dad. 'It wasn't a—'

'You're lying again! Can you not hear yourself? Christ, I am so sick of this.'

'I was stuck, Ali. Stuck.'

'You lied.'

'Yes, I'm sorry.'

'There's just no change of direction with you. You're like a freight train, hurtling along the rails. Nothing can alter your course.'

He glanced at the dashboard. Ninety-seven miles an hour. The exit for junction two was floating past.

'I'm not sure if I can live with it any more.'

'Ali, please. Just give me until daybreak, can you do that? I'll be back before morning, I promise.'

'I don't know.'

'What do you mean?'

'I'm so tired, Jon. Tired of everything. I'm hanging up now.'

'No! Don't. Alice? Alice! Are you there?' He removed the handset from his shoulder and saw the 'Call ended' message filling the screen. His foot lifted from the accelerator and his speed ebbed a fraction. Junction one wasn't far off. He could still exit there and take the A6 back round to his house. But the image of Flynn rose up in front of him. The man's weasel eyes and bobbing head. His dirty, grasping hands. Hands that had killed his brother. He saw Dave's head in the bag, the ragged skin where his neck had been sawn through. Jon's jaw tightened and he roared with frustration through clenched teeth. I can't turn back, he thought. Not now.

Thirty One

Rick rapped on the door to Zoe's flat, his hand falling to his side as he thought about his headlong rush into A & E. The woman at the reception desk had hardly glanced at his warrant card; as soon as she saw Jake, she ran out from behind the counter, yelling at people crowding the reception area to get out of the way.

As they burst into the treatment area, she shouted out, 'We need some help here!'

A doctor dropped the files he was studying, hurried over and looked down at Jake's floppy, pale form. 'Pre-terminal. Into the resuscitation room, now!'

'Where's that?' Rick yelled back.

'Here.' As the doctor marched towards a pair of swing doors, he waved to a watching colleague. 'Send a crash call to the paediatric team!'

Once in the side room, the doctor ordered Rick to lay Jake on a trolley. In seconds, an oxygen mask was over the infant's face and little pads had been stuck to his chest. 'Get a sats probe on his finger,' the doctor ordered the nurse hovering at his side. He then turned to Rick and barked, 'History?'

'I don't know,' Rick had gasped in reply. 'Just pulled him out of his cot. He was in the flat of a heroin user. The mum said something about RS Virus.'

Another doctor had placed a wide tape measure alongside Jake. Numerous dosages of drugs were listed out next to the calibration in centimetres. 'How old is this child?'

Rick turned to her. 'I think a year, or so.'

Sliding a stethoscope round the back of Jake's chest, she shook her head. 'Twelve months? He should be far bigger than this.'

'Is he going to die?'

The female doctor looked at her colleague. 'I'd say bron-chiolitis. Possible bacterial pneumonia, too?'

He nodded. 'Let's hope not. Where the fuck is the paeds team?'

'I don't know,' the nurse replied, attaching a thimble-like clip to one of Jake's fingers, then glancing despairingly towards the door.

'OK. Let's get a bolus shot of ceftriaxone in,' he continued. 'And I want an X-ray of his chest.'

'Will he die?' Rick repeated.

The doctor glanced at him. 'Depends.'

This, Rick had thought, is what being a parent really boils down to: being responsible for someone else's very life. Am I ready for that?

He rapped on the door again then tentatively tried the handle. It swung open. Closing it behind him, he walked past Jake's empty bedroom and into the front room. Empty. With a sigh, he stepped through to the kitchen.

Her arms were rigid, jaw set tight and he knew it would be easier to take a bone off a hungry rottweiler than deprive her of the hit. Instead, he watched as she made circles with the lighter flame, sucking all the time. Finally the heroin burnt out and she looked at him with red-rimmed eyes. Her lips pushed out slightly as a breath escaped her.

'Finished?'

'Is he all right?' Each word seeped into the next.

'He'll live. They're keeping him in for observation.'

'Salvio promised. He was meant to be getting the medicine.'

'Don't,' Rick said. 'Don't try and excuse yourself.'

She continued staring at the spot where he'd just been stand-ing as he filled the kettle at the sink. Inside a cupboard, he found a half-empty bag of sugar and a box of economy tea bags. From the fridge he took a plastic carton of milk. As he waited for the kettle to boil, he regarded her. Both hands had now slipped off the table into her lap. He reached down and slid the dirty foil and cigarette lighter from her slack fingers. The action stirred her and she slapped a protective palm over the little bag of powder.

After placing the square of foil with the others on the table, he splashed plenty of milk into a cup, added two sugars, poured in water, mashed the bag against the side of the cup, flipped the tea bag in the sink and banged the mug of tea down in front of her. 'Drink some, will you?'

Her head lolled forward.

'Zoe?' He thought about lifting her head and placing it against the cup. Shit. 'Zoe?' he tried again, sitting opposite her. 'I need to ask you some questions. Zoe!'

Nothing. Just a lump, slouched on the chair.

Rick tapped his fingers on the table. How the hell am I going to get anything about who Redino is out of her? He sat back, wondering whether it would come to slapping her about the face.

The sharp banging made them both jump. 'Zoe! Open up, Zoe!'

Suddenly, her eyes were wide, pupils unfocused.

As Rick looked over his shoulder towards the corridor, the hammering began again.

'Zoe! It's me, Salvio! Don't you make me bust the lock off this door!'

She started breathing more quickly. 'Don't say you're police.'

'What?'

'Have you got money?' Her eyes were on his jacket. 'Cash?'

'Who's Salvio?'

'Just pay him. Say it's for the night.' She got unsteadily to her feet and raked a hand through her hair. 'Tell him you're a punter and I'll tell you everything you need to know.'

The shouting started again. 'Zoe! Come on!'

'How much will he want?' Rick asked.

'Eighty? I don't know.'

Rick set off down the corridor, reaching for his wallet. He got to the front door, noticing jagged holes in the metal panels where several bolts had once been. Opening up, he looked out. A greasy-looking scrote in designer gear was standing beside an unshaven, overweight man in his late fifties.

The scrote peered over Rick's shoulder. 'What's this?'

'I want to pay for the night.'

He looked Rick up and down, smoothing long strands of black hair behind both ears as he did so. 'The little minx.' He smiled, before directing his next comment into the flat. 'You been busy already? Good girl, Zoe, good girl.' His eyes slid back to Rick. 'The night?'

'Here.' Rick held out several twenties. 'Eighty do it?'

The man looked at the wallet. 'One hundred.' He winked and lowered his voice to a whisper. 'One twenty and she's yours any way you want her. Just make sure she can still work tomorrow.'

Rick added another two notes and handed them over.

They vanished inside the man's shirt. 'Come on,' he said to his companion, nodding towards the stairwell. 'I've got someone else you'll like.'

Rick took a step forward. 'Oh . . .'

The man glanced back. 'Yeah?'

Rick made a half-hearted wave into the flat, feigning indifference. 'She mentioned something about medicine you were bringing. Make any sense?'

Salvio rolled his eyes. 'Tell her tomorrow.'

'OK,' Rick replied. Her son, he thought, could be dead in that room and you wouldn't give a shit. 'Tomorrow.'

Back in the kitchen she had sat down again. Gradually, she lowered her hands from her face. 'Is he gone?'

'He's gone.'

Her shoulders relaxed and her hands fell to the table with a thump. Rick moved round to the sink, took a glass off the window sill, held it up to check it was clean, then filled it from the tap. Right, he thought. Redino. I've got to find out who the hell he is. He gulped back the water, then turned round. Her chin had sagged back to her chest and she appeared to be fast asleep.

He stood behind her, hooked his hands under her armpits and started trying to lift her up.

'Get off!' She twisted from his grip. 'I'm not a fucking cripple.'

'Let's sit through there.'

'Let's sit through there,' she parroted, shuffling through into the front room and collapsing on the sofa.

He sat at the other end. 'Zoe, you called Dave when he was out in Haverdale, left a message on his phone.'

'Left loads of messages on his fucking phone,' she murmured.

'In one message you mentioned a name,' Rick continued. 'It was the last message you left. You rang from a public payphone near the cathedral. Do you remember?'

Her eyelids had started to droop. 'Cathedral?'

Seeing she was drifting off again, he stood. 'Zoe! I'm leaving this flat and sending Salvio back in.'

'No.' She struggled upright and began rubbing her face. 'What did you want?'

Rick stayed standing. 'You asked Dave how things were going. You mentioned if he'd struck gold yet.'

'That treasure. I told you.'

'I know. You also mentioned a name. You asked if someone called Redino had been any help. Who is Redino?'

She snorted.

'Zoe, we think this Redino is vital to finding out what happened to Dave. Is it a name used for someone called Ian Flynn?'

She shook her head. 'Redino's right here.'

Rick glanced about. 'Here? Redino is here in this flat?'

'Yeah.' She nodded at the Power Ranger next to her on the sofa. 'Meet Red Dino.'

Thirty Two

The car's suspension jolted as Jon drove across Haverdale's level crossing at almost forty miles an hour. He took the second left, slowing to a halt outside the Spread Eagle. Lights were still on inside, but there was no sign of Flynn's bike out the back. He drove on, retracing the route Flynn had taken the night they went back to his bungalow.

A few minutes later, he pulled up and surveyed the dark property. He's gone, a voice in his head announced. Left town already. Jon checked the dashboard clock: 11.25. Maybe he's in bed, catching up on some sleep. Quietly, he opened his car door, climbed out and closed it. He walked up the steep drive, checking the side of the garage and the rear garden. No bike. Shit! You're too late, Jon. This has all been for nothing. He flexed his fingers, then reached for the porch door. It opened and he stepped inside. He closed his eyes. OK. Living room on the left. Kitchen straight ahead. That leaves a bathroom and probably two bedrooms. The glass was frosted on the bungalow's corner window. So, that's the bathroom. Bedrooms will be after that.

He turned the handle of the front door, puzzled to find it open, and stepped into the hall. No sound, no lights on. Placing his heels down first, he transferred his weight slowly onto the front part of his foot and made his way forward, creeping past the deserted living room towards the door on his right. It was half open and he could see the bath inside. The next door was also ajar. He peered in, just able to make out furniture and boxes piled up. The spare room.

The last door was closed. He listened for over a minute. Nothing. Quickly he turned the handle, pushed the door open and scrabbled for the light switch. It clicked on, bathing the room in a harsh glow. The bed was empty. He pushed the door right back on its hinges so he could be sure no one was behind it. Then he stepped fully inside.

Dirty clothes were piled in one corner. He examined the bedside table, seeing about ten quid in scattered change. A wallet with sixty-five pounds in notes, a Halifax cashpoint card and a Debenham's store card. The chest of drawers was littered with more stuff: membership card for a video shop and another for topping up his mobile phone. He pulled open drawers. T-shirts and tops, badly folded. A few pairs of combat trousers and jeans. He checked the wardrobe for a pair of Timberland boots, but found none. In the front room, he closed the curtains and turned on the light.

The *Haverdale Herald* was open on the coffee table and Jon looked down at the photo of himself. He walked over to the desk in the corner. Bills for electricity, gas and water. Another for the man's mobile phone. Jon pocketed the piece of paper.

He rummaged round in the top drawer, finding a driving licence. Below it was a passport and he checked it was Flynn's. The guy hasn't done a runner, I'm sure. He looked round the room. So where could you be, gone eleven at night? Not that nightclub, Kelly's. You're barred from there, you told me. You're somewhere you needed your bike to get to.

The evening they'd spent together in the Spread Eagle came back to him. William Beaumont pulling up in his Aston Martin and the exchange that had taken place. Could Beaumont be supplying Flynn with his drugs? If so, there was a chance Flynn was at Beaumont's place. What had Shazia said? Grinstay House, that was it. Huge place to the west of town.

After five minutes of driving, Jon's headlights lit up a pair of imposing gates at the mouth of a sweeping turn-off. To the side of the left-hand gate was an octagonal-shaped building, lattice-work windows set in narrow, arched frames. Jon continued past, parked a hundred metres further along at the base of the huge wall bordering the road, then jogged back to the gatehouse.

It was plunged in darkness and Jon could tell no one was in. He stooped to examine the chain looped through the wrought-iron gates. Padlocked. The sinking feeling inside him rapidly growing, he paced about, searching for Flynn's motorbike. A door was built into the wall a few metres to the side of the building. He grasped the handle and tried to shake it. The thing felt solid enough to withstand a battering ram.

He turned and leaned against the wood. Where the hell could he be? Probably hiding in some village in the middle of nowhere. Jon thrust his hands into his pockets and set off back along the deserted country lane, wondering how many hours could be spent scouring CCTV footage of the nearby motorways in the hope of glimpsing Flynn as he raced by.

Face it, he thought. It's all been for nothing. The thought of Alice brought a lump to his throat. I should be with you, he thought. Not here, poking around in the bloody countryside. He glanced about, and as he pictured the miles of empty hills separating him from his wife, a thought occurred. Could Flynn be out poaching? He felt the familiar surge of his pulse. Is that what you're up to? Out looking for deer? There was just a chance the bloke was stupid enough.

The roads were deserted as Jon drove back to the high street. He crossed straight over and pulled up in front of the National Park visitor centre so his headlights were trained on the front of the building. At the front doors, he stooped forward to read the notice he'd spotted on his initial visit: 'Visitor Centre Opening Hours: 8.00 a.m. to 5.00 p.m., Monday to Saturday. 11 a.m. to 5 p.m., Sundays and Bank Holidays. In the event of an emergency that requires a park ranger, please call the mobile number below.'

Jon keyed the digits into his phone and pressed green. Come on, come on, he jiggled from foot to foot. Someone fucking answer. His call was picked up on the fourth ring.

'Michael Lumm, Peak District Park Rangers.'

Lumm, Jon thought. The younger ranger who'd been with the RSPB officer the other morning. God, how long ago did that seem? 'Michael, it's DI Jon Spicer here.'

'Detective Spicer?'

The man couldn't have sounded more taken aback. 'I know,

sorry to ring you on your mobile so late. I didn't wake you, I hope.'

'No, it's fine. What's up, Jon?'

You need a drink of water, Jon thought. Your voice sounds painfully hoarse. 'I need to locate Ian Flynn. I've been to his bungalow and there's no sign of him or his bike. It occurred to me that he might be out poaching. If anyone knows where that might be, I thought it would be a park ranger.'

'You need to find Ian Flynn?'

'Yes.'

'Is this to do with the murder?'

'Correct. It's absolutely vital I find him.'

'You mean right now?'

For Christ's sake. 'Yes.'

'Have you not spoken to Sergeant Brooks – or whoever's on duty at the police station?'

Jon raised his eyes to the night sky, barely registering the immense spray of stars. 'I haven't. I thought the ranger service would be a better bet. Any ideas?'

'Sorry if I'm being a bit slow, but how did you get this number, then?'

'It's on the front doors of the visitor centre.'

'You're here? In Haverdale?' Surprise lifted his voice.

'Yes. Michael, any idea where he might be?'

'Who's with you?'

His arms tingled with irritation. 'Is that relevant?'

'To help with the search, I mean.'

'It's just me.'

'You're on your own?'

'Yes.'

'Detective, I saw the local paper. Is this part of Superintendent Mallin's investigation?'

Bollocks, Jon thought. He's not going to help me. Not without the say-so of that twat. 'He hasn't sanctioned it, no.'

'So, you're here alone. Do any of your colleagues even know your whereabouts?'

'No, it's just me. Listen, Michael, I have to find Flynn. Can you help me, or not?' There was a long silence. 'Michael?'

'Do you know where Sharston Edge is?'

'Yes – the A6187 just out of town.'

'Deer often shelter at the base of the cliff. Can you meet me in the car park there?'

'How soon?'

'I'm here right now. Just been checking on a badgers' sett nearby. And Detective, I saw Ian Flynn heading up to the top earlier on.'

His headlights swept across the trees lining the car park's perimeter, picking out Michael Lumm in the far corner. Nervously, the man beckoned Jon across, directing him to park behind a squat hedge. As Jon scrabbled in the glove compartment for a pair of cuffs, he thought his car would be invisible from the road. He got out and raised a hand in greeting. 'I really appreciate this, Michael.'

They shook hands, Lumm's grip loose and slightly shaky. 'No problem. Why the urgency to find Flynn?'

Jon looked around. 'I thought you'd be on your quad bike.'

'I am. It's parked further up, closer to the location of the badgers' sett.'

'Oh. I'll explain everything as we walk. It's up this path, isn't it?'

'Yes.' Lumm led the way up the gravel track. 'So, Flynn's of some importance?'

'Prime suspect. I just need to find the bastard.'

'You think he killed your brother?'

'I found that egg thief. He's given me some information. And we have more on the crime-scene forensics.'

'Well, I'm pretty certain we'll find him up here.'

'Good. I'll make the arrest, OK? You just point out where he is.' He paused. 'How will you spot him?'

Lumm half turned, raising a baton-like torch. 'This has plenty of range. But he's probably made a kill by now, in which case his own light will give his position away.'

'He'll be armed with a crossbow, won't he?'

'Yes, but I thought about that. If he's started butchering the deer, he'll have packed that away by now. Though he'll have a knife.'

Jon examined the other man. He sounded nervous as hell. 'Michael, you don't need to worry. I'll deal with him, knife or no knife – especially if you lend me that dirty great club of a night light.'

'No problem.'

They continued upward, Jon running the situation over in his head. 'So, he uses Sharston Edge as a vantage point?' he whispered.

'Yes. It's got great views across a huge swathe of the country. But the beauty from a poacher's point of view is the deer come to you. Just position yourself on the cliff then take one out once they've settled for the night directly below you.'

Jon nodded. 'Looks like I've got myself the perfect guide.'

Lumm continued his plodding pace, slowing a few minutes later. 'The top is just up there.' Crouching down, he picked his way forward.

Jon followed, coming to a halt as Lumm waved a hand. The other man slowly straightened. 'No sign of him. That means he's probably made his kill.'

'Can we take a look?'

'Yes.'

Jon stopped out onto the summit, just able to make out the sentinel-like formations of rock standing guard on the precipice itself. The night seemed unnaturally quiet. 'You reckon he'll be at the bottom?' Jon murmured.

Lumm nodded.

Not caring how comical he looked, Jon tiptoed towards the edge.

Rick stared at the plastic toy. 'I'm confused.'

'Red Dino. That's what Dave called him.'

'Flynn? He named Flynn after a Power Ranger?'

269

Zoe slumped back. 'I need a cigarette. Get us one from the kitchen, will you?'

'In a second,' Rick replied. 'Why did he name Flynn after a Power Ranger?'

'Who's Flynn?'

'He lives in Haverdale. The one who ...' Rick stopped, suddenly realising Zoe wouldn't realise Flynn could well have murdered Dave. 'The one Dave was involved with.'

'He never mentioned any Flynn to me.'

Rick was trying to link the scraps of information together. 'Dave sold a bit of weed to him. He went back to the guy's place one time.'

'Him? He's just some loser Dave got stoned with. He's not Red Dino.' Sluggishly, she started to get up.

'Zoe, if Flynn's not Red Dino, who is?'

She raised herself to her feet and, swaying slightly, looked at him. 'The ranger, of course.'

'The who?'

She waved a hand as she started for the kitchen. 'The ranger! He knows all about the area. Dave spoke to him about the map – wanted to show it to him.'

He followed her into the kitchen and watched as she bent over the table, took a cigarette from the packet there and lit up. 'I told him don't be so fucking stupid. So he described it to the ranger. Said he'd split the money with him if this guy knew which hill the prof meant.'

'You mean a park ranger? Red Dino is a park ranger?'

'Yes! Young guy. He was meeting Dave out on the hill.'

Oh my God, Rick thought. Jon's been after the wrong man. He turned into the front room, yanked his mobile out and called Jon's number.

Thirty Three

Against Jon's palm, the millstone grit felt like sandpaper made for a giant. He pictured the boulders in the darkness far below and shuddered to think what hitting them from this height would do to a man's body.

Keeping one hand pressed against the pillar, he leaned out and looked down. Blackness, unbroken by the glow of any torch. Somewhere far beneath, a sheep bleated, anguished and alone. Warm air was flowing up over the cliff edge, washing against Jon's face like the sigh from a weak oven. Stepping back, he was surprised to see Lumm hovering directly behind him.

There was a light sheen of sweat covering his forehead. He licked his lips. The bloke is shitting himself, Jon thought. He looked at the other man for a brief second longer, wondering why he was so strung-out. 'Can't see a thing,' he breathed. 'It's a bloody long way down, though.'

Lumm retreated a step. 'I know, I can't stand heights. I'll let you do the looking.'

'OK. Maybe further along?'

He glanced uncertainly off to his right. 'Could be. There's a big outcrop over there. The deer sometimes huddle behind it.'

Jon walked along for about thirty metres, Lumm like a shadow behind him. 'About here?'

The park ranger nodded.

As Jon started inching towards the drop, his phone went off, the succession of notes muffled in his pocket. Jesus! He stepped back, grappling for the handset. The fastest way to shut the noise off in the dark was to flip the lid and take the call. His eyes caught on the screen. Fucking Rick. 'I'll call you back,' Jon hissed.

'It wasn't Flynn! Redino is a park ranger!'

Jon cupped his hand over the phone. 'You what?'

'Redino isn't Flynn. He's a park ranger! A young guy – that's who Dave was meeting!'

The hairs on Jon's neck suddenly bristled and he lowered his chin to his chest. By looking slightly to the side, he saw Lumm's hiking boots as the other man crept silently up behind him.

'Can you hear me, Jon!'

He registered the make: Timberland. The make of shoe Nikki had identified. One gave the tiniest of creaks and Jon knew Lumm's knees were flexing as he steadied himself for the shove. The cliff was less than four feet in front of him and beyond that only darkness yawned. He let his own legs buckle, hunching forward and trying to drop his weight to the ground as fast as possible. As he collapsed, he felt one of Lumm's palms glance off his back and the other man gave a grunt of surprise as he stumbled forward.

Jon felt the welcome sensation of solid rock against his hips and side. He twisted, reached up with both arms, closed his fingers on the belt around Lumm's trousers and pulled. A foot came down on his stomach and another on his face as, gasping, the ranger tried to regain his balance.

Keeping his grip, Jon yanked the other man over him and he heard a cry of terror as Lumm landed on the cliff edge. A clatter as the torch hit stone, beam coming on and sweeping across the scene before it rolled over the edge. Jon saw they were now lying side by side, Lumm's waist level with his head. He felt the tug on his arms suddenly increase and immediately he knew it was only his grip preventing the other man from plunging to the boulders below.

Lumm's breath was coming out in a series of whimpers and a hand flailed about, scrabbling for a moment at Jon's head, trying to grasp a handful of non-existent hair before moving onto the stone surface. Jon angled his torso back, forearms now straining as he thought about uncurling his fingers. But the sensation of his fist slamming into the man's head all those months ago suddenly returned. He'd watched as the burning figure had then crumpled into the turf, and he knew the memory of what he'd done would haunt him to the grave.

'Do not move.' He gave a quick yank, letting Lumm know his life depended on doing what he was told. 'I said, do not move.'

Lumm's hand stopped thrashing about.

Next to his head, Jon could hear a tinny shouting. 'Jon! Jon! Are you there? For fuck's sake, answer me!'

He tipped his head to the side, saw the bluish glow of his mobile's screen and smiled. 'Got him.' He began to laugh. 'I've got him!'

Thirty Four

Jon took the concrete stairs three at a time, bounding up flight after flight, images of Alice's face and snatches of their last conversation swirling in his head. He turned back on himself and climbed ever upward, the need to make sure his nephew was OK the only thing driving his tired legs on. Then he could finally go home to Alice.

He reached the eleventh floor and emerged onto the walkway which linked the flats on that level. Five doors covered by metal grilles separated him from Rick, who was standing with a broad grin on his face.

Jon felt his own features light up as he walked breathlessly towards his partner. Rick's hand was half raised, ready to slap palms but Jon's sense of gratitude was far too strong for such a gesture. He marched up to Rick, clamped both arms around him and squeezed.

Rick's hand began slapping him on the back. 'You did it, mate. God knows how, but you did it.'

Jon stepped back as a wave of sadness washed through him. You got Dave's killer, he told himself. At least give yourself that. 'He's confessed to the lot.'

'How do you mean?'

'Everything. Dealing drugs, killing Dave, he blurted the lot – and on tape.'

'Was he really right behind you when I rang?'

Raising a thumb and forefinger, Jon gave a nod. 'This far. This far from shoving me off that cliff.' He glanced over the side of the balcony to the courtyard far below. 'The drop was nearly as nasty as this one.'

Rick blew air through his lips. 'We were lucky.'

Jon immediately waved a finger. 'No, I was lucky – because you pulled out all the stops. I will never forget what I owe you, understand? Never.'

His partner's hands went up. 'Easy, it was only a phone call.'

'Only a phone call, my arse,' Jon muttered. 'It was a fuck of a lot more than that.' He glanced at the flat's half-open front door.

'Where is he now?'

He looked back at Rick. 'Who?'

'The park ranger.'

'Lumm? I took him to Haverdale nick. Got the duty sergeant to drag Mallin out of bed. Him and the rest of them were eating shit pie when I left. The only one who deserved to hold her head up was the Asian lass, Shazia. I told her so when we got the chance for a quiet word.' He looked at Zoe's flat once again, and as he took a step towards it, felt Rick's hand on his upper arm.

'Hang on. She's in a bad way.'

'So would I be. She's had a heck of a lot to cope with these last few days.'

'No, Jon. It's worse than that. She's had a lot to cope with all her life.'

Jon turned to him, eyebrows raised.

Rick sighed. 'If what she's told me is true, she's been in care homes since turning fifteen. Pimped out by a string of older so-called boyfriends ever since. Drugs, the lot.'

'You mean Dave was ...'

'Christ, no. Your brother lifted her out of it. Got her off drugs somehow, kept the pimps away from her. But she's slipped back.'

'But there's the kid. She's got a kid, now.' He stepped forward again.

Rick's hand held him back. 'She's on heroin again, Jon. This fucking scumbag called Salvio gave her some, along with the copy of the *Chronicle* covering Dave's death.'

Jon raised his eyes, past the last few floors of the tower block to the square of night sky above him. 'And the boy?'

Rick's nostrils flared. 'Ah, shit. I took him to hospital earlier on. He's got a severe case of bronchiolitis. They want to keep him in for a while.'

'Is he going to be OK?'

'Yes, but he's a little thing, mate. Frail. He'll always be prone to health problems, according to the paediatrician who checked him over.'

'Always? How can they tell?'

Rick looked briefly toward the flat. 'Zoe uses smack—'

'He's a heroin baby?'

His partner met his eyes. 'Yes. He has immature lungs, probably was born prematurely. Like I said, he's just a little mite. Half the size of Holly.'

Holly. Jon wiped his fingers across his brow and felt the grazes on his skin. He looked down at himself. Dirty trousers, ripped at the knee. Badly scuffed shoes, buttons missing from his shirt. The smell of sweat. Fine fucking dad, you are. He wiped his hands down the front of his shirt, as if his daughter was there in front of him, asking to be picked up. Christ, Holly, I miss you. He looked at the flat once again. 'And you were the one to get him to hospital. Because she was too off her head?'

Rick held up a hand. 'She was trying to get help. But finding out about Dave ...' He shook his head. 'She's a right mess.'

'What's his name?'

'Who?'

'The kid. My nephew.'

'Jake.'

'Jake?' A faint smile played on his lips. 'I like it. What's she doing now?'

'She's in bed, but I doubt she's asleep. She's been smoking that stuff most of the night.'

Jon closed his eyes, the elation of having caught Lumm rapidly fading. 'I need a brew.'

'Come on, I'll make you one.'

They walked into the flat, Rick leading him down the bare corridor to the front room. Jon took in the shabby sofa, naked walls and meagre amounts of kids' toys. Oh no, he thought, social services will have to get involved here. And that probably means the kid going straight from hospital into care, and whatever slim chance he has in life disappearing.

He went over to the window and looked out. The shade of sky was altering, taller buildings just visible against the horizon. A trickle of traffic was moving along Trinity Way directly below. Night-shift workers returning home, the first commuters heading into deserted offices. Jon flexed his neck from side to side. Another night of no sleep.

'Sugar?' Rick's voice had come from the kitchen.

'Yeah, one. No, make it two. Cheers.' He stepped through and looked at the blackened squares of foil next to the ashtray.

Rick placed the mugs on the table and sat down. 'I don't understand why the ranger did it.'

Jon slid out a chair, feeling his mood darken. He took a cigarette from the open pack on the table and lit up. 'You mean, kill Dave?'

Rick nodded.

Jon blew smoke at the ripple-effect plaster above him. 'Some poxy misunderstanding. Lumm was supplying Haverdale with all its drugs – letting Flynn do the actual dealing.'

'Where was Lumm getting it from?'

'An old school mate. They were in the same class at Haverdale High. Only the other kids' parents moved to Manchester when he was sixteen, so he ended up at a new school near Failsworth.'

'OK. But Dave wasn't a threat, surely? He was only there on that ridiculous scheme to find buried treasure.'

'Correct. I told you how he got trashed with Flynn one time, and the poacher persuaded Dave to sell him a bit of grass?'

Rick nodded.

'Lumm got wind of it and saw it as the thin end of the wedge. Competition on his patch and all that shit.'

'That's what it all boiled down to? Christ.' Rick looked away. 'You know, there were times during all this that I doubted what Dave was up to out there. I'm sorry.'

Jon stared at him for a second, then shrugged. 'Don't worry. I had the odd wobble myself, to be honest.'

Rick's features relaxed, before a frown appeared. 'So Lumm just kills him in cold blood?'

'And Flynn. His remains are at the bottom of some pothole, apparently. All to protect his precious mother, he claims. You should have heard him in the interview room. As if that justified killing people and fucking up an entire town: just providing for little old mum.'

'How sweet.'

'Sad thing is, the old dear will end up in a council home, now. Proceeds of Crime Act. All Flynn's assets will be seized, ruining his plans to build her a flat. He wailed like a child when I told him.'

'And was there ever any map?'

Jon tapped ash from his cigarette. Craig Budd's description of seeing the two men studying a piece of paper on the adjacent hilltop coming back to him. God, I hope Stuart's OK. 'If there was, I reckon it went up in the incinerator.'

'We could try and locate the guy who sold it to your brother.'

'I suppose. My bet is it was just a rip-off.' He ground out the cigarette. 'Tell me about Zoe.'

'The whole scheme about the treasure was Dave's attempt to get them out of all this. He borrowed money from this Salvio character to buy the map.'

Jon almost crashed a fist down on the table. Why didn't he come to me? He had my bloody number. 'Salvio being a pimp?'

'Yes. You know how I said Zoe was trying to get help? She gave Jake's prescription to Salvio, who promised to get the medication Jake needed. The lowlife showed up earlier on. He had a punter with him, but no medicine. He couldn't have given a shit.'

'And he's the one who's got her back on this?' Jon shoved the pieces of foil away from him, revulsion and anger rising in his chest. 'And he's bringing punters here, knowing there's a little kid in the flat? You saw him, right? We can find this bastard?'

'What? You don't mean right now?'

'No, not now. Jesus, if I got my hands on him now, I'd probably regret it.'

Rick sat back. 'Thank God for that.'

Jon watched as something occurred to make his partner's face tense up again. Rick crooked a finger and brushed a knuckle across the tip of his nose. 'I tried calling Alice earlier today. She said she couldn't speak; practically put the phone down on me. Is everything OK?'

Jon's eyes dropped to the table. Is everything OK? He picked up his tea and took a sip. 'I'm praying she isn't kicking me out.'

'Kicking you out?' Incredulity filled Rick's voice. 'She was worried about you, not annoyed.'

'No. Buchanon called her. She found out the truth.'

'Oh, bollocks.' His eyes cut to the side. 'And me?'

Jon waved a hand. 'I'll take the blame for that.' He rubbed at his temples with the heels of his hands. 'There's more. We had some bad news.'

'Meaning?'

He tried to blink away the sensation prickling at his lower eyelids. 'We lost the baby. A miscarriage.'

'Oh, no. When?'

'Yesterday.'

Rick slumped forward in his seat. 'How is she?'

'Pretty bad.' He lowered his hands. 'I wasn't even there, Rick. That's the worst thing.'

Rick flipped a palm to show he didn't understand.

'You tried to remind me about the scan, didn't you? I was up in the Lake District. Totally fucking forgot.'

'You weren't with her at the hospital when she lost the baby?'

'I know, I know – I'm a useless twat.'

'Jon, I cannot believe—'

'You won't make me feel any worse.'

'I'm not talking about the scan! Fuck's sake, Jon. What are you doing here!'

'I just wanted to find out …' He stammered, looking towards the corridor. 'I wanted to make sure the little fellow …'

'For Christ's sake, Jon.' Anger filled Rick's voice. 'This all could have waited. Get home, you bloody idiot!'

'It's all right,' he replied, getting to his feet. 'I promised her I'd be home by dawn.'

'Dawn? It practically is fucking—'

'Zoe!'

Rick's eyes locked on Jon's.

'You in here, Zoe? The door was open, babe.'

Jon saw the blood drain from his partner's face and realisation dawned. 'That's Salvio?'

Rick tried to get up, reaching across the table as he did so. 'Wait.'

The veins in Jon's temples snapped tight. All the shit – Dave's death, my mum and dad's grief, my lost baby and Alice's pain – all the shit and now here is this scum, within my reach. The fury surged through him, searching for a release.

Brushing Rick's hand away, he strode through the front room to the corridor. A man was halfway down, shiny leather coat hanging to his knees, black hair tied back in a ponytail.

'Who the fuck are you? Where's the other guy?'

Jon heard Rick's footsteps behind him.

Salvio spread his palms. 'Hey, hey, hey! I never said two of you. That, my friend, is extra.'

Jon kept walking.

'Get out of here!' Rick shouted.

Jon saw a look of alarm appearing on Salvio's face and the man took a step back, one hand reaching into his leather coat. Without breaking his step, Jon swung a fist, connecting hard with the side of Salvio's head. He crashed against the wall and a snub-nosed handgun thudded to the floor. As he bent forward to try and pick it up, Jon grabbed the man's collar and pulled the leather coat half-over his head, tangling the other man's arms up in its sleeves. He let fly with a knee and Salvio's head snapped back, two teeth spinning off to the side, the bloody stump of one clicking off the wall.

Before Salvio could fall over, Jon gripped him by the shoulders and reversed him out of the flat, marched him across the walkway and bent him over the balcony. Railing digging into the base of his spine, his arms started windmilling about.

'Jon! Jon, for fuck's sake, stop!' Rick grabbed at him from behind.

Jon held the other man over the edge. Somewhere he could hear birdsong trilling out and the sky was now tinted with orange above him. He yanked Salvio back onto the landing and threw him against the metal grille of the nearest door. Cowering there with his arms raised, Salvio tried to look up. Shrugging Rick's hands off, Jon cuffed the pimp across the head, the slap of his palm echoing off the far wall.

'Please . . . !' Salvio gasped.

Jon cuffed him again and then again, forcing the man back, droplets of blood peppering the wall with each blow. They reached the stairwell and Jon changed hands, slapping him even harder. Salvio swayed for a moment at the top then crashed down the flight of stone steps. He came to a stop at the bottom, one wrist bent at an unnatural angle.

Jon jumped down the steps, grasped him by the hair and lifted his head up. 'You see who I am? You see?' His voice boomed around the empty stairwell.

Salvio tried to focus. 'I know who you are,' he gasped. 'Dave's brother, you're Dave's brother.'

'That's right, you piece of shit. Which makes me that kid's and that girl's family. Go near them again and I will snap your arms and your legs, one after the other.' He clamped his fingers on Salvio's lower jaw, holding his head steady so he could look into the other man's eyes and whisper almost affectionately. 'Then I'll stamp on your face until even that rank whore who shat you out will have no idea who the fuck you are. Understand?'

Salvio tried to say something, blood bubbling from his mouth.

He let the other man go. 'Understand?'

Salvio wiped at his lips and chin, nodding as he did so.

'Understand?'

'Yes! Yes, I understand.'

'Get up.'

'What?'

'Get up!'

Salvio struggled to his feet, cradling his broken wrist. Jon advanced on him once again, forcing him round the corner to the top of the next flight. Salvio glanced fearfully over his shoulder.

'Now fuck off out my sight.'

Salvio immediately turned round, and without a word, started hobbling down the steps.

Before Jon got back to Zoe's front door he could hear voices raised inside. Rick's, then a female's. He walked slowly down the corridor and looked in the last room on the left. A holdall was on the double bed and Zoe was stuffing clothes into it, eyes wild.

'I can't. I cannot do this.'

Jon spoke. 'Salvio's not coming back. Not ever.'

She looked at him for a second before ramming more clothes in. 'I can't be here. I can't do it, not without Dave.'

'Zoe,' Rick implored. 'Calm down. Try and think – Jake needs you.'

'No!' she yelled. 'He doesn't need me. I'm the last fucking thing he needs. He needs Dave, but Dave's dead.' She started pushing the last of her clothes into the bag, weeping as she did so.

Rick held both hands towards her. 'Zoe, what will happen to Jake if you walk out on him?'

She paused for a moment, then looked up at Jon. He felt a jolt go through him as her eyes bored into his. 'You're Dave's brother, right? He talked about you. You're Jake's uncle and you've got kids.' She leaned forward, dragged a file out from under the bed and thrust it at Jon. 'Dave put that together. It's got all Jake's records from hospital and that. Dr Griffiths' number, everything. Here.'

Jon looked at the file in her shaking hands.

'You'll look after him, right? I can't. Not now, not on my own.'

'Zoe,' Rick pleaded. 'Don't leave, for God's sake.'

Her eyes were still on Jon. 'Here.'

He took the file without a word.

'Zoe, let's just sit down,' Rick whispered.

She grabbed her holdall, squeezed past Jon and out into the corridor. With tears streaming down her face, she touched her fingertips against Jake's door, turned to the right and vanished from Jon's view.

'Christ,' Rick hissed, stepping round Jon and into the corridor. 'Zoe, stop!'

'Let her go.'

'What?'

Jon looked at his partner, who was staring back at him, mouth half-open. 'Let her go.' He turned his head, eyes sweeping across the bedroom. Cracks of sunlight were now forcing their way round the gaps in the curtains, bathing the room in a warm glow.

Epilogue

Jon watched as his mum placed a crumpled plastic bag on the grass, then lowered one knee on to it. Tesco. Not for the first time the make of bag struck him as completely out of place. Maybe he should get her something more in keeping with their surroundings. Did any shop have black bags?

She took the bunch of withered flowers from the vase, lay them to one side and inserted fresh ones. Daffodils, bright and somehow alert as a light breeze played over the grave.

Jon regarded the headstone, hardly able to believe it had now stood there for several months.

'David Paul Spicer. Born 23 February, 1973, died 17 April, 2006. Aged 33 years. Sleep peacefully, our darling boy.'

His dad stepped forward, helping Mary back to her feet. Before standing fully, she swung an arm to scrape the plastic bag up, carefully folding the faded flowers into it. He watched his parents in silence. Their arms were now around each other and he thought they hadn't seemed this close in a long time.

'Lay-bir!'

His head moved to his right where Jake was crouched, finger pointing at the grass.

'That's right, ladybird,' Ellie replied, bending forward with her hands between her knees. She gazed down at the top of the boy's head, a dreamy look on her face.

'O!' Jake's chin lifted and Jon could make out the insect's blurred wings as it rose into the air. The creature vanished into the longer grass beneath a nearby bush and Jon's gaze returned to Jake, still amazed at how closely he resembled Dave.

'Fly away, ladybird,' Ellie sang quietly. 'Your house is on fire and your children are gone.' She reached out a hand to stroke Jake's hair.

'Fly 'way lay-bir,' he replied. Taking Ellie's hand, he struggled to his feet. Slowly, she led him towards the gravel path. Jon realised that, as usual, his father had skirted round him without a word. The old man took his grandson's other hand and the three of them set off for the cemetery gates, Jake tottering happily along in the middle as autumn sunlight threw their shadows far in front.

Fingers slid round the inside of his elbow and he looked down to see a hand, then an arm, being linked through his. 'Bet it takes you back,' he said. 'Having a little one in the house all over again.'

There was a hint of sadness in his mother's smile. 'It does,' she replied. 'So much life makes me feel younger, too.'

Jon looked at Jake, and reflected on how his nephew now slept in the very same bedroom he'd occupied as a child. He thought of Ellie and her little flat, his own bed just a single mattress on the floor in her box room, his work shirts hanging from coat hooks along the picture rail.

A low honking sound and he looked up to see a V of Canada geese departing for their winter feeding grounds, slipstream of the older birds helping the younger ones along. Mary took a step forward. 'Let's find a bin for these.'

'OK.' And though he knew no one else was behind him, he couldn't help look over his shoulder for Alice and Holly.

Author's Note

While many issues are touched upon in this novel, that of the sad and obsessive characters who steal rare birds' eggs is perhaps the most interesting.

However, I wouldn't want anyone to overestimate the threat these people pose to Britain's birds of prey. True, egg collectors do a lot of damage, but it is nothing compared to the slaughter committed by gamekeepers and others working for private shooting estates across Britain.

The Peak District National Park is one area that, due to large swathes of it being privately owned, has far fewer breeding birds of prey than it could support. In fact, it's easier to see nesting peregrine falcons in the centre of Manchester than it is in the Peak District.

Tragically, the region could viably support numerous pairs of our most charismatic raptors – including hen harriers, goshawks, buzzards, red kites and peregrines. But, to protect populations of grouse, these birds of prey are illegally trapped, poisoned or shot – and their nests destroyed – whenever they try to colonise certain areas within the National Park.

To read more about the issue, visit the RSPB's website: www. rspb.org.uk. Along with details of their campaign to protect our birds of prey, you'll find a fascinating report on criminal activity in the National Park, entitled 'Peak Malpractice'.

On the subject of national parks, the idea for Dave's murder is based on a real-life case that occurred in Exmoor's National Park in March, 2002. The body was that of a dark-haired man in his twenties. His identity, and that of his murderer, remain unknown.

Acknowledgements

For expertly guiding this novel through its stumbling first drafts, my gratitude to Stephanie and Jane at Gregory & Company and then Jon at Orion – ably backed, as ever, by Jade and the rest of the team.

It always surprises me how people are so willing to give up time to some weirdo who contacts them out of the blue with strange and disturbing research requests. For this book, thanks go to:

Guy Shorrock – Chief Investigations Officer, the RSPB.

Janet Fiddler – midwife, Stepping Hill hospital.

Darren Kilroy – A & E Consultant, Stepping Hill hospital.

Andy Timmis – the Cheshire Falconry Centre.

The staff at the National Park visitor centre, Edale.

Juanita Bullough from the Eagle Eye Inc.

Nessy, for your Morse-like knowledge.

Any inaccuracies were either made for dramatic purposes, or are mistakes on my part.